SUPREME IN SUSPENSE . . .

In the words of Anthony Boucher, in the *New York Times:*

"Twenty years ago, the American detective story meant nothing to the general reader. Today, American short stories of crime and detection not only lead in the international suspense market but often demand attention as literature. This happy change has been effected solely through the existence of *Ellery Queen's Mystery Magazine*.

"*EQMM* has published every important crime writer who ever wrote a short story. It also has published an unbelievable number of Big Names . . . including 27 Pulitzer and eight Nobel Prize winners."

It follows then that the annual *EQMM* collection is the best of the best. Here, therefore, is the year's best possible collection, *Ellery Queen's Mystery Mix* . . .

MYSTERY MASTERS FREDERIC DANNAY and MANFRED B. LEE

who, as everyone knows, are Ellery Queen—have written 51 books, and edited 45 more. A conservative estimate has placed their total sales in various editions at more than 50,000,000 copies.

Ellery Queen is internationally known as an editor—*Ellery Queen's Mystery Magazine* celebrated its 22nd anniversary in 1963—and his library of first editions contains the finest collection of detective literature in existence.

These facts about Queen bear out the judgment of Anthony Boucher, in his profile of Manfred B. Lee and Frederic Dannay: "Ellery Queen *is* the American detective story."

ELLERY QUEEN'S MYSTERY MIX

20 STORIES FROM
ELLERY QUEEN'S
MYSTERY MAGAZINE

Edited by
ELLERY QUEEN

POPULAR LIBRARY • NEW YORK
Ned L. Pines • President
Frank P. Lualdi • Publisher

POPULAR LIBRARY EDITION

Library of Congress Catalog Card Number: 46-8129

Published by arrangement with Random House, Inc.
Random House edition published in October, 1963
First printing: July, 1963

Published simultaneously in Toronto, Canada, by Random House of Canada, Limited

ACKNOWLEDGMENTS
The Editors hereby make grateful acknowledgment to the following authors and authors' representatives for giving permission to reprint the material in this volume:

Margaret Austin for *Introducing Ellery's Mom.*

Brandt & Brandt for *The Other Shoe,* by Charlotte Armstrong; and *A Kind of Murder,* by Hugh Pentecost.

Curtis Brown, Ltd. for *What Happened in Act One,* by William Bankier; and *The Question My Son Asked,* by Stanley Ellin.

John Dickson Carr for *The Grandest Game in the World.*

Jacques Chambrun for *Stop Me—If You've Heard This One,* by Ring Lardner, copyright 1929 by Ring Lardner, renewed.

Harold R. Daniels for *Inquest on a Dead Tiger.*

Samuel French, Inc. for *In The Confessional,* by Alice Scanlan Reach.

Joe Gores for *Darl I Luv U.*

Patricia Highsmith for *The Terrapin.*

The Sterling Lord Agency for *By the Scruff of the Soul,* by Dorothy Salisbury Davis.
Pat McGerr for *Justice Has a High Price.*
Robert P. Mills for *Revolver,* by Avram Davidson.
H. C. Neal for *The Pegasus Pilfer.*
Harold Ober Associates, Inc. for *Monday Is a Quiet Place,* by Marjorie Carleton; and *The People Across the Canyon,* by Margaret Millar.
Paul R. Reynolds & Son for *Murder Under the Mistletoe,* by Margery Allingham; and *The Most Wanted Man in the World,* by Youngman Carter.
James M. Ullman for *The Stock Market Detective.*
Cornell Woolrich for *One Drop of Blood.*

PRINTED IN THE UNITED STATES OF AMERICA

CONTENTS

CONTENTS

Discovery

Detection, Crime . . . and Suspense

CORNELL WOOLRICH

One Drop of Blood

WINNER OF FIRST PRIZE

The First Prize Winner this year is Cornell Woolrich's "One Drop of Blood," a memorable example of the contemporary inverted-detective story . . . The first two-thirds of the story deals with the crime—and the events leading up to it; the last one-third of the story deals wih the detection—and how the detective proved it. Mr. Woolrich poses this question: Can a man commit murder without premeditation, and be clever enough, thorough enough, to get away with it?

Mr. Woolrich poses other questions. As in some Woolrich short stories, the detective is anonymous, and in this story even the criminal has no name. Is the murderer Everyman? Is the detective, the murderer's nemesis, Everyman?

"One Drop of Blood" is surely one of Cornell Woolrich's most absorbing stories—with a startling, satisfying, and original solution—and with remarkable "suspension of disbelief."

I: The Crime—and the Events Leading Up to It

He didn't premeditate it, and yet, he told himself afterward, it all turned out better than if he had. Much better. He might have done all the wrong things, he told himself. Picked the wrong place, the wrong time, the wrong weapon. Too much careful planning ahead might have made him nervous, as it had many another. In the effort to remember *not* to forget something, he might have forgotten *something else*. How often that had happened!

This way, there was nothing to forget—because there had been nothing to remember in the first place. He just walked through the whole thing "cold," for the first time, without having had any rehearsal. And everything just seemed to fall into place—the right place, by itself. These hair-split timetables are very hard to stick to. Impromptu, the way he did it, the time element doesn't become important. You can't trip over a loose thirty seconds and fall flat on your face when there aren't a loose thirty seconds to trip over.

The situation itself was old and trite. One of the oldest, one of the tritest. Not to him, of course, and not to her—it never is to those involved. It's always new, first-time-new.

To begin with, he was single, and had no troubles whatsoever to deal with. He had a car, he had a job, he had health, and he had good looks. But mainly, he had freedom. If he came home at ten o'clock or if he came at two, if he had one drink or if he had a few, there was no one but himself to keep score.

He was the personification of the male spirit, that restless roving spirit that can only get into trouble because it didn't have any trouble to start with, that had no other way to go but —from lack of trouble into a mess of trouble.

And so we find him one star-spiked May evening, in a $95 suit, with $75 in his wallet, with a new convertible waiting outside to take him in any direction he wanted to go, and with a girl named Corinne in his arms—a very pretty Corinne too, dexterously dancing and spinning around together, breaking apart, coming together again, and above all (a favorite step of theirs) making an overhead loop of their two hands so that she could walk through it, turn, then go back through it again. All in excellent time and in excellent rhythm to the tune of *The Night They Invented Champagne,* played by an excellent band.

Beautiful to watch, but what a fatal dance that was, because—it was their first together. They should have turned and fled from each other in opposite directions.

Instead they went out to the car. She patted it admiringly as he beamed, proudly possessive as only a young male car-owner can be. Then they drove to where she lived, sat a while and watched the stars, and kissed and kissed and watched the stars . . . and that was it.

Another night, another dance, same car, same stars, same kisses—or same lips, anyway. She got out to go in. He got out to keep her from going in. Then they both got in the car again and went to a motel . . . And that was it again.

After some time had gone by, she asked him about marriage. But she didn't get much of an answer. He liked it the way it was. She hadn't asked him soon enough, or in the right order of things. So, afraid that she would lose him altogether, and preferring to have him this way rather than no way at all, she didn't ask him again.

It was a peaceful, comfortable existence. It was definitely not sordid—she was not a sordid girl. She was no different, in effect, from any other girl on her street who had stepped out and married. Only she had stepped out and not married. He was the first man she had ever loved, and it stopped there. The only thing was, she had left freedom of action, freedom of choice, entirely in his hands—which was a tactical error of the worst sort in the never-ending war between the sexes. She was a very poor soldier, for a woman. They were not actually living together. They were keeping company, one might say, on a permanent basis.

At any rate, one night when he called to take her out, she complained of not feeling well. In fact, it was easy to see she wasn't shamming, and noticing that she was alternately shivering and burning up, he sent for a doctor and remained there while the doctor examined her. (She spoke of him as her fiancé whenever it became necessary in front of a third person.) It was nothing serious—merely an attack of the flu, but she had to go to bed.

He would not—to give him some credit—have walked out on her then and there; but she was feeling so miserable that for her part she wished he would leave her alone. So, noticing this, he kissed her—a mere peck—and left.

His original intention—at least, from the door to the car—was to go to his own apartment and make the best of an unexpected solitary evening. But the stars were at their dirty work again, and his wrist watch didn't help either (9:48); he was twenty-eight and *didn't* have the flu, so—

Her name was Allie.

And she wasn't going to be like Corinne—he found that out right from the start. She could enjoy the stars, sure, and she could kiss, sure, but she'd take up both those occupations on his time, as his officially credited fiancée or his lawfully wedded wife—not on her own time, as a free-lance, if you get the distinction.

And her sense of timing was much better, too. He came

out three or four kisses short the first meeting. So he wanted to see her again, to try to make up the shortage. But she always knew just when to stop. He was still a couple short the second meeting, so that made him want to see her a third time. By then he was so hopelessly in hock to her that his only chance of clearing up the debt was to marry her, and try to work it out on a lifetime payment plan.

She was a five-star general in the battle of the sexes. And it must have been inborn, because she'd never heard a shot fired until she met him.

At first he managed to sandwich the two of them in together. He saw Allie a couple of nights in the week, saw Corinne a couple of others. In fact, he would have liked to continue this three-way-stretch arrangement indefinitely; the difficulty, however, lay not with them but with himself. Soon more and more nights with Corinne reminded him of the night she'd had the flu: the stars above and the wrist watch were there, but not Corinne's stars any more and not Corinne's time. A waste of Allie's time, instead.

Finally there were no more nights with Corinne—just one last station-break and the program went off the air.

"You've lost interest in me. I'm not blind. I've noticed it for some time now."

"That's the chance you have to take," he told her, "when you're in love."

"But why did it happen to you," she wanted to know, "and not to me? Shouldn't we both come out even?"

"You don't come out even in love," he told her. "Someone always has to come out behind." And then he added, "I'll call you up some night." Which is the way some men say goodbye to a woman when they're finished with the campaign.

She'll find somebody else, he thought; she was easy for me, she'll be easy for the next one. And he shrugged her off.

But there are three things in this world you can't shrug off: death, taxes—and a girl who loves you.

Now they were in the homestretch, Allie and he. Now when they looped their hands above their heads on the dance floor, her engagement-diamond blazed toward the lights, proclaiming, "This is mine. Hands off." Not to jewel thieves, but to stealers of men.

Now all the tribal customs were brought to bear—

everything the world insists shall surround the lawful mating of a man and a woman. The meetings with the relatives from far-off places; the luncheons, dinners, parties, showers; the choosing of a trousseau; the finding of their first home; even the purchase of the furniture that was to go into it.

Now the date was set, the license applied for, the church reserved, the flowers and the caterers and the champagne arranged for. Now even the blood tests were taken, and they were both declared pure. All that remained was the marrying and the honeymoon.

Now the boys got together and gave him his bachelor party, his last night to howl. And the howls were something to hear. Three separate times around town they were arrested *en masse,* and twice the arresting officers not only released them but even accompanied them for a short part of the way, and the third time wished them well and urged them only to "keep it down, boys." Then finally the last two survivors, the diehards whose pledge had been to see him safely home, had him at his door, and after much fumbling with keys, and draping of arms across shoulders, and swaying and tottering, they thrust him inside, closed the door, and left him.

And suddenly he was sober, stone-cold, ice-cold sober, and the whole party had been a waste of liquor—at least, for him.

Corinne was sitting there. Waiting for him.

"You took so long to get back," she complained mildly. "I knew you still lived here, but I thought you'd never get back."

"Had a little party," he said. He was starkly sober, but his tongue hadn't yet quite caught up with the rest of him. A warning bell started ringing: I wonder if she knows, I wonder if she knows.

"I'm not criticizing," she went on. "You're free to go out with your pals—free every night in the week. It's only natural, so what's the harm?"

The warning bell stopped suddenly. There was silence. She doesn't know, he told himself, *and she's not going to know from me.*

Business of fooling around with a cigarette, so he'd use up time and wouldn't have to say too much to her. Maybe she'd go away.

"I know it's late," she said.

He looked at the wrist watch that had played such a double-crossing part in their little story. Meaning, it is late.

She doesn't want to start over again, does she? For Pete's sake, not that! Love is a one-way street.

"Aren't you working?" he asked. "Don't you have to get up early in the morning?"

"I haven't been working since last week," she said. Then, understandingly, "You're tired; I know."

"Aren't you?"

"Yes, but I do have to talk to you about something. I've got to. It's very important."

Now he knew, more or less. There were only two things a girl could possibly want from a man, in all the world, in all this life: love or money. And since love was out, that left only money. Another thing told him: she was much too tractable, noticeably taking pains not to antagonize or ruffle him in any way.

"Won't it keep till tomorrow?" he said by way of acquiescence. "I'm beat. Completely beat. I'll come over to see you tomorrow."

"But will you?" she asked, frowning, but still with that air of not wanting to push him, not wanting to crowd him.

"Aw, for the love of Mike, Cor," he said impatiently, "when did you ever know me to break my word to you?"

It was true. He never had—not in the little things.

She had to accept that—it was the best she could get.

"I've moved since the last time I saw you," she said, and gave him the new address.

"All right, I'll be there, Allie," he promised. He was almost nudging the door inch by inch right in her face, anxious to get rid of her.

For a moment he lost an inch or two. "Allie?" she said. "Who's Allie?"

"That's Al," he said quickly. "Fellow I go around with—with him tonight. I'm so used to saying his name every five minutes or so."

He finally got the door shut and went "Whew!"—from the shoelaces up. Money, he said, that's all it is—she wants money. That hint about not working. All right, I'll give her some. Wind the thing up that way. She was entitled to something after all, he supposed.

He took five hundred out of his savings account the next day, during his lunch hour. The nick it made wasn't too bad. There was still plenty to cover the honeymoon expenses and the first few months of married life. And he was making a good salary.

Then right in front of the bank, coming out, he met Dunc, Allie's brother. Dunc glanced up at the bank façade, then at him, and said, "Look, if you could use a little extra—I know how it is at a time like this, I went through the mill myself three years ago."

Bing! another two hundred and fifty from Dunc, smack in his palm. His face didn't even change color. After all, they were both going to be in the same family, weren't they?

First, he thought, I'll put two fifty on my own back. Then he thought, why be a rat—let her have it all, it's only money. So she was coming out pretty good for a last year's leftover crush; she had no kick coming. She'll fall all over my neck, he thought complacently. But no fooling around tonight; I'm going to unwind her arms and give them back to her.

The bungalow was 'way out at the end of nowhere—dim in the growing darkness. Even the road in front of it wasn't paved yet, just surfaced with some kind of black stuff. But there were going to be other bungalows—he could just make out the skeleton frames of some of them already starting up in a straight line past hers, getting thinner as they went along, until there were only foundations, then just a bulldozer.

She had it fixed up real pretty, the way women like to do, even women with broken hearts. Chintz curtains fluttering out the windows, like vermilion lips coaxing to be kissed.

She didn't even give him a chance to get onto the porch and ring the bell. She was waiting there for him. She had on a little apron to match the curtains. Last year's love, playing house all by herself.

"I wasn't sure you were really coming."

He raised his brows. "Did I ever break my word to you?"

"No," she said. "Not your word. Only—"

She had cocktails frosting in a shaker.

"You used to like martinis best," she said.

He looked at her. "I don't like martinis any more," he said, and let that sink in.

She traced a finger on the frosting of the shaker and made a little track, shiny as a mirror. "I've got to talk to you."

"We don't have to," he said. "This talks better than anything. This talks best." He'd taken the money out and laid it down.

"What's that for?" she said, her face suddenly white with shock and insult and hurt.

"Well, if you don't know why, don't ask me."

She sat in a chair for a few moments getting over it—or, it would be more correct to say, getting familiar with it. She had a slow temper. Until this moment, as a matter of fact, he hadn't known she had any temper at all.

Then she got up, and her face was unlike any face he'd ever seen her wear before. She flung the words point-blank at him.

"You don't have to do *this* to me! You don't have to do *this* to me!"

"Then what else is there?" In all honesty he couldn't understand her outrage. He'd lost her train of thought, and the situation was becoming an irritant.

"What *else* is there? You have to stand by me, that's what else there is! I can't go it alone!"

Now his voice went up, almost into a wail of incomprehension. "Stand by you! What does that mean?"

She took her open hand and slammed it down on the table, so hard that the ice in the shaker went *tlink!* "I'm going to have your baby, that's what that means!"

The shock was dizzying. He had to reach out and hold on to something for a moment.

"How do I—?"

"There never was another man in my life, that's how you know."

And he did know.

"All right," he said.

"All right what?"

"I'll take care of everything. Hospital and—"

Now finally she screamed piercingly at him in her passion and torment, and she wasn't the kind to scream. "Hospital? I don't want a hospital, I want a husband!"

The second shock, on top of the first, completely unbalanced him. The rest was just physical reflex, not mental reaction at all.

She said only one thing more in her life. In her entire life.

"You're going to marry me, do you understand? You're going to *marry* me!"

The object was suddenly in his hand, as though it had

jumped into his hand of its own accord. He hadn't seen it before, hadn't even known it was in the room.

She died at almost the very first blow. But he kept striking on and on and on, to the point of frenzy, to the point of mania, to the point of sheer hallucination. And then she was gone, and it was over. And the thing that a hundred other men, a thousand other men, had done, and that he'd thought he'd never do—now he'd done it too. And the thing he'd read about a hundred times, a thousand times, now he wasn't reading about it, he was living it. And he liked it much better the other way.

He looked at the object he was still holding, and he realized he actually didn't know what it was even now. What could have been more unpremeditated than that? Some sort of long curving blade, razor-keen. Then at last he identified it—more by hearsay than by actual recognition. A Samurai sword, souvenir of the long-ago war with Japan. He remembered now she had once mentioned she had a brother who had served in the Pacific theater—only to come back and die in a car crash not long after. Many men had brought these back with them at the time.

He let go, and it dropped with a muffled thud.

After a while he located the bracket she had driven into the wall. It must have been hanging up there. When he went over to it he found, on the floor underneath, the severed cord it had hung by and the empty scabbard. His subconscious mind must have recognized it for a weapon, for he had no recollection whatever of snatching it down, and yet he must have, in the blinding red explosion that had burst in his brain and ended in murder.

In the beginning he was very mechanical, as the glaze of shock that coated him all over slowly thawed and loosened. He tipped the cocktail shaker into one of the two glasses and drank. He even ate one of the two olives she'd had ready at the bottoms of the two glasses. Not calloused. His instinct told him he needed it, if he wanted to try to live. And he wanted to try to live very badly. Even more so now that he'd looked at death this close with his own eyes. Then he poured a second one, but let it stand. Then he emptied what remained in the shaker down the sink.

It seemed hopeless. There seemed no place to begin. The room was daubed with her, as though a house painter had taken a bucket of her blood, dipped his paint brush in it, then splashed it this way and that way and every which way all over the walls. He was splattered himself, but fortunately he was wearing a dark suit and it didn't show up much; and that part of the job could wait until later.

The first thing to do was to get her out of here. All the little hers . . . He went to her closet and found a number of opaque plastic garment bags—even more than he needed, in fact . . . and finally he zippered them up securely and let them lean there a moment.

Then he went out to his car, opened the trunk compartment, and made room. He went around to the front seat, got the evening newspaper that he remembered having left there, and papered the entire trunk with it, to prevent any errant stains or smears. It was so incredibly unpeopled out here that he didn't even have to be furtive about it. Just an occasional precautionary look around him.

Then he went in again, brought out the garment bags, put them in the trunk, and locked it. He stepped back into the bungalow to put out the lights, took her key with him so he'd be able to get back in again, got in his car, and drove off.

And as far as that part went, that was all. There was nothing more to it.

He drove steadily for some hours. And strangely enough, at a rather slow pace, almost a desultory glide. He could do that because, again strangely enough, he felt no panic whatever. Even his fear was not acute or urgent. It would be untrue to say that he felt no fear at all; but it was distant and objective, rather than imminent and personal—more on the level of ordinary prudence and caution. And this must have been because it had all come up so suddenly, and blown over so suddenly, that his nerves hadn't had time to be subjected to a long, fraying strain. They were the nerves of an almost normal person, not of a man who had just taken another person's life.

He even stopped once, left the car, and bought a fresh pack of cigarettes at a place he saw was still open. He even stayed there for a few moments, parked in front of it, smoking, then finally slithered on again.

At last his driving stopped being directionless, took on purpose, as he finally made up his mind about a destination. There was very little noticeable change in it, and he still didn't hurry. He simply made fewer haphazard turns and roundabouts, and perhaps stepped it up another five miles per hour.

Even with a target, he still continued driving for several more hours. The metropolitan section was now left far behind. On the final lap he was purring steadily along a road that paralleled a railroad right-of-way. An occasional pair of lights would blink past him going the other way. There was nothing for anyone else to see or recall—just a relaxed silhouette behind the wheel, with a red coal near its lips, and tooling by. Although a good, wide road, it was not a main artery of traffic.

More than half the night had now gone by, but he still drove on. This had to be done, and when a thing has to be done, it should be done right, no matter how much time it takes.

At last, as he neared the outskirts of a large-sized town, the railroad tracks broadened into numerous sidings, and these blossomed finally into strings of stagnant freight cars of assorted lengths, some only two or three coupled together, others almost endless chains.

He came to a halt finally by the side of the road, took out a flashlight, and left the car. He disappeared into one of the dark lanes between the freight cars, an occasional soft crunch of gravel the only indication of his movements. He was gone for some time, taking his time in this as in everything else. Almost like a shopper shopping for something that exactly suits him, and refusing to be satisfied with anything less.

When he came back to his car there was very little more to it. He went out to the middle of the road, stood there first looking up one way, then down the other. When he was sure there were no lights approaching even in the remotest distance, he stepped over to his car, moving deftly and quickly but still by no means frightenedly, opened the trunk, and took out the garment bags. He propped them for a moment against the car while he took the precaution of closing the trunk, so that it might not attract attention in case anyone should drive by while he was gone.

Then, half supporting and half trailing the garment bags, he disappeared into the lane of his choice between the parallels of freight cars—the one that led to the freight car he had found with its door left unfastened. There was the sound of the slide grating open, then in a few moments the sound of it grating closed again. And that was all.

When he came back to the car he was alone, unburdened.

The drive back was as uneventful as the drive out. If he had been of a cynical nature, he might have been tempted to ask: What's there to a murder? What's there to worry about?

In due course he came back to the point where the route that led out to her bungalow diverged from the route that would eventually bring him to his own apartment. He didn't even hesitate. He took the road home. He was taking a gamble of a sort, and yet it wasn't as great a gamble as it appeared; he felt now that the longer odds were in his favor, and besides, there was nothing more he could do in her bungalow at this time. She had told him she had stopped working. There was a good chance no one would go there to seek her out during the course of the next day or two. And if someone should, there was an even better chance they would not force entry into the bungalow.

So he decided to go home, leave the bloodstained room the way it was for the time being, and not return until after he'd had a chance to make the necessary preparations for cleaning it up.

He set his alarm for nine, and slept the three hours remaining until then. Which is three hours more sleep than the average murderer can usually get on the first night following his crime.

When he awoke it was Saturday morning, and without even breakfasting he went to a paint store completely across town from where he lived and explained to the clerk that his so-and-so of a landlord wouldn't paint for him; so he was going to do the job himself and be damned to him.

The man in the paint store was sympathetic. "What color you want?" he asked.

"What color would you advise?"

"What color is it now?"

He picked it out with positive accuracy on a color chart the man showed him.

"Well, your best bet to cover that would be either a medium green or a medium brown," the clerk said. "Otherwise the color on now is going to show through and you'd have to give it two coats."

He thought of the color of dried blood and promptly selected the brown—a sort of light cinnamon with a reddish overtone. Then he bought a like shade of glossy paint for the woodwork, a ladder, and the requisite brushes and mixing fluids. Then he went to a clothing store—not a haberdashery but the sort of outlet that sells work clothes—and purchased a pair of overalls, and added a pair of gauntlets so that he wouldn't get any paint under his fingernails. Such a thing could be the devil to pay.

Then he went back to where he'd killed her.

It was only just past mid-morning when he got there. This time he drove off the unpaved roadway, detoured around to the back of the bungalow, and parked directly behind it in such a way that the house itself hid his car.

There was really no need for this precaution. Being Saturday, the neighborhood was empty—no workmen, no residents; but he felt better taking every possible safeguard, even against an unlikely prowler.

Then on foot he circled around to the front and examined the porch before unloading anything from his car. It was just as he had left it. There was every evidence that his gamble had paid off, that no one had come near the bungalow since it had happened. From a remark she had dropped at his place when they were setting up what had turned out to be the murder appointment, he knew she had no telephone. She was on the waiting list but they hadn't got to her yet. From their old days together he remembered she had never been much of a newspaper reader, so it was extremely improbable she would have regular delivery service, especially in this deserted section. As for milk, there were no signs of that either; she must have brought home a carton from the grocery store whenever she needed it. Finally, the mail slot opened directly into the house itself, so there was no way of telling from the outside whether the mail had been picked up by its recipient or not.

There wasn't a single thing that wasn't in his favor. He almost marveled at it himself.

He gave another precautionary look around, then opened up the front door with her key, and went in.

For a moment—and for the first time—his heart almost failed him. It looked even worse than he'd remembered from the night before. Maybe he'd been too taken up with removing her to give it due notice. There was only one wall that was completely sterile. Two more were in bad-to-middling shape. But the fourth was practically marbleized, it had such veins and skeins twining all over it. It resembled nothing so much as a great upright slab of white-and-brown marble.

He could see what had caused the marbleized effect. It wasn't that the blood had spurted of its own accord: it was the strokes of the Samurai sword that had splashed it like that—all over everything.

It was too big a job; he felt he could never swing it.

And then he reminded himself: you got rid of her body, didn't you? If you did that, you can do this too.

He then did another of those incongruous things that he kept doing all the way through. He picked up the shaker from the night before, got out the gin and the vermouth, and made himself two more martinis. He left out the olives though.

Feeling more confident now, he changed to his work clothes. He even took off his shoes and remained in his socks. Paint spots on shoes could be just as hard to remove and just as incriminating as paint underneath fingernails.

When he began the new paint job, he realized that he didn't have to be too finicky about it—they couldn't arrest you just because your painting wasn't up to major league standards. The daubing went as fast as a speed-cop's motorcycle on the way with a ticket. Almost before he knew it, he had all four sides done, including the one that hadn't needed it. This latter he threw in by way of artistic flourish. The room would have looked queer with three walls one color and the fourth another.

The ladder folded, the buckets out of the way, the overalls and gauntlets stripped off, he stood in the center of the room and took a comprehensive look at his handiwork—and drew a deep sigh. Not only of relief, but somewhat of cocksure pride.

It might not have been the best paint job that had ever been done, but it guaranteed one thing: the walls were bloodless; the damning stains were completely covered up.

The furniture, of course, was going to be a different matter. Fortunately, the cushions on the settee and chair were removable. But the rug was an impossibility—nothing could be done with it. Again, fortunately, it wasn't outsized, the room itself being fairly small. He rolled up the rug and stood it in a corner, just inside the front door.

This part of the program, he knew, would be less arduous than the walls, but it was also going to be a good deal more risky. It necessitated arson.

He slipped out and made a tour of inspection of the

skeleton bungalows that sprouted past hers, giving the interior of each one a quick glance.

The first three were too close to hers for his purpose—the inference might be a little too easy to draw. The one at the opposite end was nothing but a gouged-out foundation and poured concrete. The next-to-the-last already had its two-by-fours up, but no flooring or roofing. The next one in had enough wooden construction—plus a lot of shavings—to be ideal: it was like starting a fire in an empty lathe-basket.

Three trips were necessary. He carried the rolled rug, the removable cushions from settee and chair, a small end-table, a parchment lampshade, and whatever else had been stained beyond hope of cover-up, to the unfinished bungalow. He didn't forget to include the suit he had worn the night before. He made a pyre of these, topped it off with the paint-impregnated overalls, gauntlets, and brushes, and poured on the highly inflammable residue from the paint cans themselves.

Then he drained gas from his car, using a receptacle he'd brought from the bungalow, leaving just enough in the tank to get him home, and liberally doused it not only on the mound itself but on the wood around it.

He turned his car around, facing in the direction he was to go, killed the engine, and sat waiting, looking all around him. Finally he started the engine again, very softly, like a new-born kitten purring, picked up a furled newspaper, took a lighter out of his pocket, clicked it twice to make sure it was in working order, got out of the car leaving the door open in readiness, and went inside the unfinished house.

He came out again at a run—this was the first time since he'd killed her that he moved fast—jumped in the car and started off with a surge. He only closed the door after he was careening along, foot tight to the floor. This part of the operation, if no other, was split-second schedule, and not a stray moment could be spared.

For as long as the place remained in sight behind him, he could see no sign of flickering flame, or incipient fire. After that—who was around to care?

He got out in front of his own door, locked the car, tossed his keys jauntily up into the air and caught them deftly in the same hand.

Upstairs, he sprawled out in a chair, legs wide apart, and let out a great sigh of completion, of finality.

"Now let them say I've killed her." Then, sensibly, he amended it to: "Now let them *prove* I killed her."

II: The Detection—and How They Proved It

They did neither the one nor the other. They started very circumspectly, very offhandedly, in a very minor key—as those things often happen.

A ring at the doorbell.

Two men were standing there.

"Are you—?"

"Yes, I'm—"

"Like to ask you a few questions. Mind if we come in?"

"Come in if you want. I have no objections. Why should I?"

"Do you know a Corinne Matthews?"

"I did at one time."

"When was the last time you saw her?"

"What is this—June, isn't it? Either late February or early March. I'm not sure which."

"Not since then?"

"You asked me a minute ago and I told you. If I'd seen her since then, I'd say so."

"Not since then. That's your statement?"

"My statement, right."

"Any objection to coming downtown with us? We'd like to question you in further detail."

"You're the police. When you ask people to come downtown with you, they come downtown with you. No objection."

They came back again that evening. He went down again the next day. Then back again, down again. Then—

Down again for good.

Held on suspicion of murder.

A back room. Many different rooms, but a back room in particular.

"I suppose now you're going to beat the hell out of me."

"No, we're not going to beat the hell out of you—never do. Besides, we're too sure of you; we don't want anything to backfire. Juries are funny sometimes. No, we're going to treat you with kid gloves. In fact, you're even going to wear kid shorts when you squat down in the old Easy Chair."

"Is that what I'm going to do," he asked wryly, "for something I didn't do?"

"Save it," he was advised. "Save it for when you need it and you're going to need it plenty."

All through the long weary day identification followed identification.

"Is this the man who bought a pack of cigarettes from you, and handed you in payment a dollar bill with the print of a bloody thumb on one side and the print of a bloody forefinger on the other?"

"That's him. I thought it was an advertising gag at first, the prints were both so clear. Like for one of them horror movies, where they stencil bloody footprints on the sidewalk in front of the theater, to pull the customers inside. I couldn't help looking at him while he was pocketing his change. I didn't call him on it because I could tell the bill wasn't queer, and he acted so natural, so nonchalant. I even saw him sitting out there smoking for a while afterwards. Yes sir, that's him all right!"

"I don't deny it."

"Is this the man who bought a can of Number Two russet-brown paint from you? *And* gloss. *And* brushes. *And* a folding stepladder."

"That's him."

"I don't deny it."

"Is this the man who bought a pair of overalls from you? And a pair of work gloves?"

"That's him."

"I don't deny it."

Room cleared of identifying witnesses.

"Then you took the materials you've just confessed you bought and went to work on the living room at One Eighty-two."

"That I don't admit."

"You deny you repainted that room? Why, it's the identical shade and grade of paint you bought from this paint store!"

"I didn't say I denied it. What I said was, I don't admit it."

"What does that mean?"

"Prove I painted there. Prove I didn't paint somewhere else."

They knew they couldn't. So did he.

"Show us where you painted somewhere else, then."

"No, sir. No, *sir*. That's up to you, not up to me. I didn't say I painted somewhere else. I didn't say I didn't pour it down a sewer. I didn't say I didn't give it away as a present to a friend of mine. I didn't say I didn't leave it standing around some place for a minute and someone stole it from me."

The two detectives turned their backs on him for a minute. One smote himself on the top of the head and murmured to his companion, "Oh, this man! He's got a pretzel for a tongue."

The plastic garment bags and their hideous contents were finally located. Perhaps all the way across the country in some siding or railroad yard in Duluth or Kansas City or Abilene. They didn't tell him that outright, in so many words, or exactly where, but he could sense it by the subtle turn their questioning took.

They had their *corpus delicti* now, but they still couldn't pin it on him. What was holding them up, what was blocking them, he realized with grim satisfaction, was that they couldn't unearth a single witness who could place him at or near the freight yard he'd driven to that night—or at any other freight yard anywhere else on any other night. The car itself, after exhaustive tests and examinations, must have turned out pasteurizedly pure, antibiotically bloodless. He'd seen to that. And the garment bags had been her own to begin with.

There was nothing to trace him by.

Even the Samurai sword—which he had had the audacity to send right along with her, encased in a pair of her nylon stockings—was worthless to them. It had belonged to her, and even if it hadn't, there was no way of checking on such a thing—as there would have been in the case of a firearm. Being a war souvenir, it was nonregisterable.

Finally, there was the total lack of an alibi. Instead of counting against him, it seemed to have intensified the deadlock. From the very beginning he had offered none, laid claim to none, therefore gave them none to break down. He'd simply said he'd gone home and stayed there, and admitted from the start he couldn't prove it. But then they couldn't prove he'd been out to the bungalow either. Result: each cancelled the other out. Stand-off. Stalemate.

As if to show that they had reached a point of desperation, they finally had recourse, during several of the periods of interrogation, to stronger measures. Not violence: no blows were struck, nothing was done that might leave a mark on him afterward. Nor were any threats or promises made. It was a sort of tacit coercion, one might say. He understood it, they understood it, he understood they did, and they understood he did.

Unsuspectingly he accepted some punishingly salty food they sent out for and gave to him. Pickled or smoked herring. But no water.

A fire was made in the boiler room and the radiator in one of the basement detention rooms was turned on full blast, even though it was an oppressively hot turn-of-spring-into-summer day. Still no water.

As though this weren't enough, an electric heater was plugged into an outlet and aimed at his straight-backed chair. He was seated in it and compelled to keep two or three heavy blankets bundled around him. In no time, the floor around his feet had darkened with the slow seep of his perspiration. But still no water.

Then a tantalizingly frosted glass pitcher, brimming with crystal-clear water and studded with alluring ice cubes, was brought in and set down on a table just within arm's reach.

But each time he reached for it, he was asked a question. And while waiting for the answer, the nearest detective would, absently, draw the pitcher away—just beyond his reach—as if not being aware of what he was doing, the way a man doodles with a pencil or fiddles with a paperweight while talking to someone. When he asked openly for a drink, he was told (for the record): "Help yourself. It's right there in front of you. That's what it's here for." They were very meticulous about it. Nothing could be proved afterward.

He didn't get a drink of water. But they didn't get the answers they wanted either. Another stalemate.

They rang in a couple of ingenious variations after that, once with cigarettes, another time by a refusal of the comfort facilities of the building. With even less result, since neither impulse was as strong as thirst.

"All we need is one drop of blood," the detective kept warning him. "One drop of blood."

"You won't get it out of me."

"We have identified the remains, to show there *was* a

crime—somewhere. We've found traces of blood on articles handled by you—like the dollar bill you gave the storekeeper —to show, presumably, that you were involved in some crime —somewhere. We've placed *you* in the vicinity of the bungalow: metal bits from the overalls and remains of the paint cans and brush handles in the ashes of the fire. Now all we've got to do is place the *crime itself* there. And that will close the circuit.

"One drop of blood will do it. One single drop of blood."

"It seems a shame that such a modest requirement can't be met," was his ironic comment.

And then suddenly, when least expected, he was released.

Whether there was some legal technicality involved and they were afraid of losing him altogether in the long run if they charged him too quickly; whether it was just a temporary expedient so that they could watch him all the closer—anyway, release.

One of the detectives came in, stood looking at him.

"Good morning," he said finally to the detective, sardonically, to break the optical deadlock.

"I suppose you'd like to get out of here."

"There are places I've liked better."

The detective jerked his head. "You can go. That's all for now. Sign a receipt and the property clerk will return your valuables."

He didn't stir. "Not if there are any strings attached to it."

"What do you want, an apology or something?"

"No, I just want to know where I stand. Am I in or am I out—or what?"

"You were never actually under arrest, so what're you beefing about?"

"Well, if I wasn't, there sure has been something hampering my freedom. Maybe my shoelaces were tied together."

"Just hold yourself available in case you're needed. Don't leave town."

He finally walked out behind the detective, throwing an empty cigarette pack on the floor. "Was any of this in the newspapers?"

"I don't keep a scrapbook. I wouldn't know," said the detective.

He picked one up, and it was, had been, and was going to be.

The first thing he did was to phone Allie. She wouldn't come to the phone—or they wouldn't let her. She was ill in bed, they said. That much he didn't disbelieve, nor wonder at. There was also a coldness, an iciness: he'd hurt these people badly.

He hung up. He tried again later. And then again. And still again. He wouldn't give up. His whole happiness was at stake now.

Finally he went back to his own apartment. There was nothing left for him to do. It was already well after midnight by this time. The phone was ringing as he keyed the door open. It sounded as if it had been ringing for some time and was about to die out. He grabbed at it.

"Darling," Allie said in a pathetically weak voice, "I'm calling you from the phone next to my bed. They don't know I'm doing it, or they—"

"You don't believe what you've been reading about me?"

"Not if you tell me not to."

"It was just a routine questioning. I used to know the girl a long time ago, and they grabbed at every straw that came their way."

"We'll have to change everything—go off quietly by ourselves. But I don't care."

"I've got to see you. Shall I come up there?"

"No," she said fearfully. "Not yet. You'd better wait a while first. Give them a little more time."

"But then how am I going to—?"

"I'll dress and come out and meet you somewhere."

"Can you make it?"

"I'm getting better every minute. Just hearing your voice, hearing you say that it was not true—that's better than all their tranquilizers."

"There's a quiet little cocktail lounge called 'For Lovers Only.' Not noisy, not jammed. The end booth."

Her voice was getting stronger. "We were there once, remember?"

"Wear the same dress you did that night."

It was on all over again. "Hurry. I'm waiting for your hello-kiss."

He pulled his shirt off so exuberantly that he split the sleeve halfway down. He didn't care. He shook the shave-cream bomb until it nearly exploded in his hand. He went back to the phone and called a florist.

"I want an orchid sent somewhere—end booth—she'll be wearing pale yellow. I didn't ask you that, but what does come after the fifteen-dollar one? Then make it two fifteen-dollar ones. And on the card you just say this—'From a fellow to his girl.' "

And because he was young and in love—completely, sincerely in love, even though he'd killed someone who had once loved him the same way—he started, in his high spirits, in his release from long-sustained tension, to do a mimic Indian war dance, prancing around the room, now reared up high, now bent down low, drumming his hand against his mouth. "O-wah-o-wah!"

I beat it! he told himself, I've got it made. Just take it easy from here in, just talk with a small mouth—and I'm the one in a thousand who beat it!

Then someone knocked quietly on his door.

Less than an hour after going to bed, one of the detectives stirred and finally sat up again.

His wife heard him groping for his shoes to put them back on. "What's the matter?" she asked sleepily. "You want a drink of water?"

"No," he said. "I want a drop of blood."

"If you couldn't find a drop of blood in the daytime, how are you going to find it at night?"

He didn't answer; he just went ahead pulling his pants on.

"Oh, God," the poor woman moaned, "why did I ever marry a detective?"

"Oh, God," he groaned back from the direction of the door, "what makes you think you have?"

"O-wah-o-wah!"

Someone knocked quietly on his door.

He went over to it, and it was one of them again.

He looked at the intruder ruefully—confidently but ruefully. "What, again?" he sighed.

"This time it's for real."

"What was it all the other times, a rehearsal without costumes?"

"Hard to convince, aren't you? All right, I'll make it official," the detective said obligingly. "You're under arrest for the murder of Corinne Matthews. Anything-you-say-may-be-held-against-you-kindly-come-with-me."

"You did that like a professional," he smirked, still confident.

The detective had brought a car with him. They got in it.

"This is going to blow right up in your face. You know that, don't you? I'll sue for false arrest—I'll sue the city for a million."

"All right, I'll show you."

They drove to the bungalow that had been Corinne Matthews', and parked. They got out and went in together. They had to go through the doorway on the bias. The detective had him on handcuffs now—he wasn't taking any chances.

The detective left it dark. He took out his pocket-flash, and made a big dazzling cartwheel of light by holding it nozzle-close against one section of the wall.

"Take a good look," he said.

"Why don't you put the lights on?"

"Take a good look this way first."

Just a newly painted, spotless wall, and at one side the light switch, tripped to OFF.

"Now look at it this way."

He killed the pocket-light, snapped up the wall switch, and the room lit up. Still just a newly painted, spotless wall, and at one side the light switch, reversed now to ON.

And on it a small blob of blood.

"That's what I needed. And look, that's what I got."

The accused sat down, the accuser at the other end of the handcuffs, standing, his arm at elbow height.

"How can a guy win?" the murderer whispered.

"You killed her at night, when the lights were on, when the switch was up like this, showing ON. You came back and painted in the daylight hours, when the lights were not on, when the switch was down, showing OFF. We cased this room a hundred times, for a hundred hours—*but always in the daytime too,* when the lights were not on, when the switch was down, showing OFF. And on the part of the switch *that never showed in the daytime,* the part marked ON, the way it is now, there was one drop of blood that we never found—until tonight."

The murderer was quiet for a minute, then he said the final words—no good to hold them back any more. "Sure," he said, "it was like that. That's what it was like."

His head went over, and a great huff of hot breath came surging out of him, rippling down his necktie, like the vital force, the will to resist, emptying itself.

The end of another story.

The end of another life.

STANLEY ELLIN

The Question My Son Asked

WINNER OF A SECOND PRIZE

Surely one of Stanley Ellin's most curious stories, and surely one of his most disturbing . . . and it would be editorially wiser if we did not say another word about this newest scalpel-incision by the one and only Mr. Ellin. Read the tale and judge for yourself . . .

I am an electrocutioner . . . I prefer this word to executioner; I think words make a difference. When I was a boy, people who buried the dead were undertakers, and then somewhere along the way they became morticians and are better off for it.

Take the one who used to be the undertaker in my town. He was a decent, respectable man; very friendly if you'd let him be, but hardly anybody would let him be. Today, his son —who now runs the business—is not an undertaker but a mortician, and is welcome everywhere. As a matter of fact, he's an officer in my Lodge and is one of the most popular members we have. And all it took to do that was changing one word to another. The job's the same but the word is different, and people somehow will always go by words rather than meanings.

So, as I said, I am an electrocutioner—which is the proper professional word for it in my state where the electric chair is the means of execution.

Not that this is my profession. Actually, it's a sideline, as it is for most of us who perform executions. My real business is running an electrical supply and repair shop just as my father did before me. When he died I inherited not only the business from him, but also the position of state's electrocutioner.

We established a tradition, my father and I. He was

running the shop profitably even before the turn of the century when electricity was a comparatively new thing, and he was the first man to perform a successful electrocution for the state. It was not the state's first electrocution, however. That one was an experiment and was badly bungled by the engineer who installed the chair in the state prison. My father, who had helped install the chair, was the assistant at the electrocution, and he told me that everything that could go wrong that day did go wrong. The current was eccentric, his boss froze on the switch, and the man in the chair was alive and kicking at the same time he was being burned to a crisp. The next time, my father offered to do the job himself, rewired the chair, and handled the switch so well that he was offered the job of official electrocutioner.

I followed in his footsteps, which is how a tradition is made, but I am afraid this one ends with me. I have a son, and what I said to him and what he said to me is the crux of the matter. He asked me a question—well, in my opinion, it was the kind of question that's at the bottom of most of the world's troubles today. There are some sleeping dogs that should be left to lie; there are some questions that should not be asked.

To understand all this, I think you have to understand me, and nothing could be easier. I'm sixty, just beginning to look my age, a little overweight, suffer sometimes from arthritis when the weather is damp. I'm a good citizen, complain about my taxes but pay them on schedule, vote for the right party, and run my business well enough to make a comfortable living from it.

I've been married thirty-five years and never looked at another woman in all that time. Well, looked maybe, but no more than that. I have a married daughter and a granddaughter almost a year old, and the prettiest, smilingest baby in town. I spoil her and don't apologize for it, because in my opinion that is what grandfathers were made for—to spoil their grandchildren. Let mama and papa attend to the business; grandpa is there for the fun.

And beyond all that I have a son who asks questions. The kind that shouldn't be asked.

Put the picture together, and what you get is someone like yourself. I might be your next-door neighbor, I might be your old friend, I might be the uncle you meet whenever the family gets together at a wedding or a funeral. I'm like you.

Naturally, we all look different on the outside but we can still recognize each other on sight as the same kind of people. Deep down inside where it matters we have the same feelings, and we know that without any questions being asked about them.

"But," you might say, "there is a difference between us. You're the one who performs the executions, and I'm the one who reads about them in the papers, and that's a big difference, no matter how you look at it."

Is it? Well, look at it without prejudice, look at it with absolute honesty, and you'll have to admit that you're being unfair.

Let's face the facts, we're all in this together. If an old friend of yours happens to serve on a jury that finds a murderer guilty, you don't lock the door against him, do you? More than that: if you could get an introduction to the judge who sentences that murderer to the electric chair, you'd be proud of it, wouldn't you? You'd be honored to have him sit at your table, and you'd be quick enough to let the world know about it.

And since you're so willing to be friendly with the jury that convicts and the judge that sentences, what about the man who has to pull the switch? He's finished the job you wanted done, he's made the world a better place for it. Why must he go hide away in a dark corner until the next time he's needed?

There's no use denying that nearly everybody feels he should, and there's less use denying that it's a cruel thing for anyone in my position to face. If you don't mind some strong language, it's a damned outrage to hire a man for an unpleasant job, and then despise him for it. Sometimes it's hard to abide such righteousness.

How do I get along in the face of it? The only way possible—by keeping my secret locked up tight and never being tempted to give it away. I don't like it that way, but I'm no fool about it.

The trouble is that I'm naturally easygoing and friendly. I'm the sociable kind. I like people, and I want them to like me. At Lodge meetings or in the clubhouse down at the golf course I'm always the center of the crowd. And I know what would happen if at any such time I ever opened my mouth and let that secret out. A five minute sensation, and after that the slow chill setting in. It would mean the end of my whole life then and there, the kind of life I want to live, and no man in his right mind throws away sixty years of his life for a five minute sensation.

You can see I've given the matter a lot of thought. More than that, it hasn't been idle thought. I don't pretend to be an educated man, but I'm willing to read books on any subject that interests me, and execution has been one of my main interests ever since I got into the line. I have the books sent to the shop where nobody takes notice of another piece of mail, and I keep them locked in a bin in my office so that I can read them in private.

There's a nasty smell about having to do it this way—at my age you hate to feel like a kid hiding himself away to read a dirty magazine—but I have no choice. There isn't a soul on earth outside of the warden at state's prison and a couple of picked guards there who knows I'm the one pulling the switch at an execution, and I intend it to remain that way.

Oh, yes, my son knows now. Well, he's difficult in some ways, but he's no fool. If I wasn't sure he would keep his mouth shut about what I told him, I wouldn't have told it to him in the first place.

Have I learned anything from those books? At least enough to take a pride in what I'm doing for the state and the way I do it. As far back in history as you want to go there have always been executioners. The day that men first made laws to help keep peace among themselves was the day the first executioner was born. There have always been lawbreakers; there must always be a way of punishing them. It's as simple as that.

The trouble is that nowadays there are too many people who don't want it to be as simple as that. I'm no hypocrite, I'm not one of those narrow-minded fools who thinks that every time a man comes up with a generous impulse he's some kind of crackpot. But he can be mistaken. I'd put most of the people who are against capital punishment in that class. They are fine, high-minded citizens who've never in their lives been close enough to a murderer or rapist to smell the evil in him. In fact, they're so fine and high-minded that they can't imagine anyone in the world not being like themselves. In that case, they say anybody who commits murder or rape is just a plain, ordinary human being who's had a bad spell. He's no criminal, they say, he's just sick. He doesn't need the electric chair; all he needs is a kindly old doctor to examine his head and straighten out the kinks in his brain.

In fact, they say there is no such thing as a criminal at all. There are only well people and sick people, and the ones who deserve all your worry and consideration are the sick ones. If they happen to murder or rape a few of the well ones now and then, why, just run for the doctor.

This is the argument from beginning to end, and I'd be the last one to deny that it's built on honest charity and good intentions. But it's a mistaken argument. It omits the one fact that matters. When anyone commits murder or rape he is no longer in the human race. A man has a human brain and a God-given soul to control his animal nature. When the animal in him takes control he's not a human being any more. Then he has to be exterminated the way any animal must be if it goes wild in the middle of helpless people. And my duty is to be the exterminator.

It could be that people just don't understand the meaning of the word *duty* any more. I don't want to sound old-fashioned, God forbid, but when I was a boy things were more straightforward and clear-cut. You learned to tell right from wrong, you learned to do what had to be done, and you didn't ask questions every step of the way. Or if you had to ask any questions, the ones that mattered were *how* and *when.*

Then along came psychology, along came the professors, and the main question was always *why*. Ask yourself *why, why, why* about everything you do, and you'll end up doing nothing. Let a couple of generations go along that way, and you'll finally have a breed of people who sit around in trees like monkeys, scratching their heads.

Does this sound far-fetched? Well, it isn't. Life is a complicated thing to live. All his life a man finds himself facing one situation after another, and the way to handle them is to live by the rules. Ask yourself *why* once too often, and you can find yourself so tangled up that you go under. The show must go on. Why? Women and children first. Why? My country, right or wrong. Why? Never mind your duty. Just keep asking *why* until it's too late to do anything about it.

Around the time I first started going to school my father gave me a dog, a collie pup named Rex. A few years after Rex suddenly became unfriendly, the way a dog will sometimes, and then vicious, and then one day he bit my mother when she reached down to pat him.

The day after that I saw my father leaving the house with his hunting rifle under his arm and with Rex on a leash. It wasn't the hunting season, so I knew what was going to happen to Rex and I knew why. But it's forgivable in a boy to ask things that a man should be smart enough not to ask.

"Where are you taking Rex?" I asked my father. "What are you going to do with him?"

"I'm taking him out back of town," my father said. "I'm going to shoot him."

"But why?" I said, and that was when my father let me see that there is only one answer to such a question.

"Because it has to be done," he said.

I never forgot that lesson. It came hard; for a while I hated my father for it, but as I grew up I came to see how right he was. We both knew why the dog had to be killed. Beyond that, all questions would lead nowhere. Why the dog had become vicious, why God had put a dog on earth to be killed this way—these are the questions that you can talk out to the end of time, and while you're talking about them you still have a vicious dog on your hands.

It is strange to look back and realize now that when the business of the dog happened, and long before it and long after it, my father was an electrocutioner, and I never knew it. Nobody knew it, not even my mother. A few times a year my father would pack his bag and a few tools and go away for a couple of days, but that was all any of us knew. If you asked him where he was going he would simply say he had a job to do out of town. He was not a man you'd ever suspect of philandering or going off on a solitary drunk, so nobody gave it a second thought.

It worked the same way in my case. I found out how well it worked when I finally told my son what I had been doing on those jobs out of town, and that I had gotten the warden's permission to take him on as an assistant and train him to handle the chair himself when I retired. I could tell from the way he took it that he was as thunderstruck at this as I had been thirty years before when my father had taken me into his confidence.

"Electrocutioner?" said my son. "An *electrocutioner*?"

"Well, there's no disgrace to it," I said. "And since it's got to be done, and somebody has to do it, why not keep it in the family? If you knew anything about it, you'd know it's a profession that's often passed down in a family from generation to generation. What's wrong with a good, sound tradition? If more people believed in tradition you wouldn't have so many troubles in the world today."

It was the kind of argument that would have been more than enough to convince me when I was his age. What I hadn't taken into account was that my son wasn't like me, much as I wanted him to be. He was a grown man in his own right, but a grown man who had never settled down to his responsibilities. I had always kept closing my eyes to that, I had always seen him the way I wanted to and not the way he was.

When he left college after a year, I said, all right, there are some people who aren't made for college, I never went there, so what difference does it make. When he went out with one girl after another and could never make up his mind to marrying any of them, I said, well, he's young, he's sowing his wild oats, the time will come soon enough when he's ready to take care of a home and family. When he sat daydreaming in the shop instead of tending to business I never made a fuss about it. I knew when he put his mind to it he was as good an electrician as you could ask for, and in these soft times people are allowed to do a lot more dreaming and a lot less working than they used to.

The truth was that the only thing that mattered to me was being his friend. For all his faults he was a fine-looking boy with a good mind. He wasn't much for mixing with people, but if he wanted to he could win anyone over. And in the back of my mind all the while he was growing up was the thought that he was the only one who would learn my secret some day, and would share it with me, and make it easier to bear. I'm not secretive by nature. A man like me needs a thought like that to sustain him.

So when the time came to tell him he shook his head and said no. I felt that my legs had been kicked out from under me. I argued with him and he still said no, and I lost my temper.

"Are you against capital punishment?" I asked him. "You don't have to apologize if you are. I'd think all the more of you, if that's your only reason."

"I don't know if it is," he said.

"Well, you ought to make up your mind one way or the

other," I told him. "I'd hate to think you were like every other hypocrite around who says it's all right to condemn a man to the electric chair and all wrong to pull the switch."

"Do I have to be the one to pull it?" he said. "Do you?"

"Somebody has to do it. Somebody always has to do the dirty work for the rest of us. It's not like the Old Testament days when everybody did it for himself. Do you know how they executed a man in those days? They laid him on the ground tied hand and foot, and everybody around had to heave rocks on him until he was crushed to death. They didn't invite anybody to stand around and watch. You wouldn't have had much choice then, would you?"

"I don't know," he said. And then because he was as smart as they come and knew how to turn your words against you, he said, "After all, I'm not without sin."

"Don't talk like a child," I said. "You're without the sin of murder on you or any kind of sin that calls for execution. And if you're so sure the Bible has all the answers, you might remember that you're supposed to render unto Caesar the things that are Caesar's."

"Well," he said, "in this case I'll let you do the rendering."

I knew then and there from the way he said it and the way he looked at me that it was no use trying to argue with him. The worst of it was knowing that we had somehow moved far apart from each other and would never really be close again. I should have had sense enough to let it go at that. I should have just told him to forget the whole thing and keep his mouth shut about it.

Maybe if I had ever considered the possibility of his saying no, I would have done it. But because I hadn't considered any such possibility I was caught off balance, I was too much upset to think straight. I will admit it now. It was my own fault that I made an issue of things and led him to ask the one question he should never have asked.

"I see," I told him. "It's the same old story, isn't it? Let somebody else do it. But if they pull your number out of a hat and you have to serve on a jury and send a man to the chair, that's all right with you. At least, it's all right as long as there's somebody else to do the job that you and the judge and every decent citizen wants done. Let's face the facts, boy, you don't have the guts. I'd hate to think of you even walking by the death house. The shop is where you belong. You can be nice and cozy there, wiring up fixtures and ringing the cash register. I can handle my duties without your help."

It hurt me to say it. I had never talked like that to him before, and it hurt. The strange thing was that he didn't seem angry about it; he only looked at me puzzled.

"Is that all it is to you?" he said. "A duty?"

"Yes."

"But you get paid for it, don't you?"

"I get paid little enough for it."

He kept looking at me that way. "Only a duty?" he said, and never took his eyes off me. "But you enjoy it, don't you?"

That was the question he asked.

You enjoy it, don't you? You stand there looking through a peephole in the wall at the chair. In thirty years I have stood there more than a hundred times looking at that chair. The guards bring somebody in. Usually he is in a daze; sometimes he screams, throws himself around and fights. Sometimes it is a woman, and a woman can be as hard to handle as a man when she is led to the chair. Sooner or later, whoever it is is strapped down and the black hood is dropped over his head. Now your hand is on the switch.

The warden signals, and you pull the switch. The current hits the body like a tremendous rush of air suddenly filling it. The body leaps out of the chair with only the straps holding it back. The head jerks, and a curl of smoke comes from it. You release the switch and the body falls back again.

You do it once more, do it a third time to make sure. And whenever your hand presses the switch you can see in your mind what the current is doing to that body and what the face under the hood must look like.

Enjoy it?

That was the question my son asked me. That was what he said to me, as if I didn't have the same feeling deep down in me that we all have.

Enjoy it?

But, my God, how could anyone *not* enjoy it!

HAROLD R. DANIELS

Inquest on a Dead Tiger

WINNER OF A SECOND PRIZE

When Deputy Inspector Kerwin was called "Javert," the residents of the Cabbage Patch did not understand; but being Javert was only Kerwin's way of doing his job . . . A first-rate procedural story, with the honest smack of realism—and, yes, of romance—and with an Irish glow that will warm the cockles of your heart, and brighten the cockles of your mind . . .

A literate plainclothesman from Traffic Division once referred to Deputy Inspector Pete Kerwin as Javert. The allusion was completely wasted on the hard-bitten Traffic Squad. If the policeman had said that Kerwin was a dedicated policeman who hung in there like a bulldog—and that's what he meant—he would have been better understood.

One overcast, muggy day Kerwin walked up the steps of Third Precinct Headquarters. He wore a dark-blue suit with a vest and a plain dark tie at a time when the Commissioner himself wore a sports jacket and a tieless shirt to his office. He turned left inside the door and walked through a dank and smelly hallway to the booking room.

A uniformed sergeant and a civilian were working behind a wooden railing. The uniformed sergeant recognized Kerwin at once and stood up. "Something I can do for you, Inspector?" he asked.

Kerwin said, "No, thanks. I want to see Lieutenant Shaw. He's expecting me." He walked through a door leading off the far end of the room.

The civilian watched him go with a look of malicious anticipation on his face. He drew his finger across his throat and made a strangling noise. "Kerwin," he said. "The gestapo."

The sergeant said in a bored voice, "Why don't you close your big mouth and file those summonses like you're supposed to."

The clerk, not at all disconcerted, said, "The Commissioner's hatchet man. He's here to bust Shaw down for lousing up the Gallagher thing. Bet you a buck."

"Save your money."

"What I say, it's about time. Shaw lost his grip a long time ago. Thinks he owns this precinct."

The sergeant turned to stare at the clerk. "You're a poisonous little louse. The Lieutenant saved your job twice that I know of. Now close your mouth like I told you."

Lieutenant Shaw had his head bent over some paper work when Kerwin walked into the office. Kerwin had time to study him briefly before he looked up. Shaw was in his early fifties. His hair was iron-gray over a florid face with a bold nose and a strong jaw. Kerwin had known Shaw for twenty years. They were friends, of sorts. Yet Kerwin knew that Shaw would greet him with the blend of contempt and amused tolerance that he reserved for all City Hall Precinct cops.

He did. He said, "Hello, Pete. Haven't seen you since you got promoted out of Safe and Loft." The way he said "promoted" made a slur out of the remark.

Kerwin had promised himself that he would not let Shaw needle him. The assignment he had this day was miserable enough without needling. He said, "That so? I guess it has been a long time. How are things, Ed?"

"Not so good or you wouldn't be here." Shaw stood up. "You phoned and said you'd be down. You didn't come to audit the property book. What's on your mind—the Gallagher homicide?"

Kerwin said, "Don't get thick with me. I just do what they tell me."

"I know." Shaw sat down again. "Sit down, Pete. I'm not sore at you. How much muscle did they give you?"

"Enough." Kerwin took a typed piece of paper from his pocket and passed it across the desk.

Shaw read a couple of sentences out loud, remaining slouched in his chair with a sardonic expression on his face.

"—to make inquiry into the homicide of Daniel Gallagher on July 16th and to determine if any laxity existed in the investigation by the police official having jurisdiction."

Shaw passed the paper back to Kerwin. "Like you said, muscle enough. At least they didn't take the Patch away from me yet."

"The Patch?"

"That's what they call the Third Precinct around here—the Cabbage Patch. It goes back to the days when it was all Irish." Shaw suddenly stood up and banged his big fist on the desk. "All this for a no-good hoodlum like Dinny Gallagher. I never had to stand an investigation in all the years I've had the Precinct."

Kerwin said, "Gallagher had lots of friends. He was a character in his own way. The papers have been making a thing of it."

Shaw said disgustedly, "You can call him a character if you want to. The papers—I read them. How he used to be a prizefighter and how game he was. How he called the Mayor by his first name. I say he was a liar and a thief and a hoodlum. You know what they called him in the Patch? The Tiger. Tiger Gallagher. I booked him a half a dozen times right in this station."

"You never stuck him with a felony, Ed."

"Because he was an ex-pug and a harp in an Irish ward. Because he had a way about him."

"I'm not down here to pass judgment on him," Kerwin said. "I'm supposed to find out who killed him."

"And if I tried to find out the way the book says."

"That's what it says on my orders. You know the score, Ed. There's more to it than whether or not you tried to solve it. There's been some loose talk that you had reasons for not pushing the investigation. I've got to say it—I don't try to judge Gallagher and I won't try to judge you. I'm going to find out what I can. What I find out I'm going to report to the Commissioner."

Shaw said coldly, "That's your job." He pushed a button on the intercom and said, "Lou, bring me the Gallagher file."

Both men waited in silence until the sergeant came in with a manila folder. He handed it to Shaw and left the room again. Shaw passed the folder to Kerwin. "It's all in there," he said. "Autopsy report. Record of arrests. A summary of my investigation. I had two men assigned to me from Homicide. Their reports are in there too."

Kerwin said drily, "I've seen their reports. Both of them complained that you interfered with them."

"I told them what to do. It's my Precinct."

"They're competent men, Ed. They only wanted to do their jobs."

"Ah, sure."

Kerwin stood up, holding the folder. "I'll look the rest of this stuff over later. This place where Gallagher was killed—the Dublin Social Club?"

Shaw said, "Six blocks South on Green Avenue."

Kerwin said, "I'll see you later, Ed."

Shaw nodded. "Sure. Say hello to Augie Schwartz for me." He watched Kerwin go. He smiled faintly, but a wary and tired expression swiftly eroded the smile.

The Dublin Social Club was a nondescript bar with a decor that leaned strongly toward shamrocks. There were two customers at the bar. Kerwin ignored them and spoke directly to the bartender, a small neat man in his fifties. He asked, "Are you Mr. Schwartz?"

The bartender said, "I am. Can I get you something?"

"Not when I'm on duty." Kerwin held his badge out for Schwartz to see. "I'm looking into the Gallagher business."

One of the customers, an old man with an Irish lantern-jaw and the pink skin of a baby said, "Ah, now, poor Dinny." He pointed toward the floor. "Right there is where he was lying in his own blood, poor, poor lad."

The second customer said proudly, "He was a friend of mine, Dinny was. Used to call me his old buddy. The place isn't the same with him gone. Yes, sir. Called me his old buddy. He was a prizefighter once, you know."

Schwartz said gently, "The gentleman knows all that." He drew two beers. "Now you boys go on over to a booth and play a hand of crib. Take these with you." After they had drifted away he said to Kerwin, "I thought Lieutenant Shaw was all the police we needed in the Patch."

Kerwin said awkwardly, "This is something a little out of the ordinary."

Schwartz asked shrewdly, "Is Shaw in some kind of trouble?"

"What made you ask that?"

Schwartz bent down to polish the shining bar. "I don't know, exactly. There's been a lot of noise made over Gallagher." He nodded toward the two men in the booth. "The two old-timers there. Ready to cry about poor Dinny. You know what they used to hope when he walked into my bar? They hoped he wouldn't notice them. He was a mean and vicious man and the only decent thing he ever did was to get himself killed. I'm just sorry he picked my bar to do it in."

Kerwin asked, "Were you working here that night?"

"You're from the police. You know I was. You don't have to beat around the bush."

Kerwin said, "Sorry," and meant it. Schwartz had a quiet dignity that demanded respect. "Would you tell me about it?"

Schwartz leaned on the bar. "It was a slow night," he said reflectively. "Most of my trade are longshoremen and cargo handlers and there was a ship loading. The *Newark Merchant*. And Tiger Gallagher came in. He was a weak man, Inspector. He had the strength of a bull elephant yet he was a weak man. He never walked in my bar. He always made an entrance. Being weak he had to have attention. Do you understand what I mean?"

Kerwin nodded.

"He had to let everyone know that Gallagher was here. There were only a couple of men at the bar. Gallagher said in his loud voice, 'Who's buying? Who's the live one?' And you'd have thought him a jovial man, Inspector." Kerwin nodded, and Schwartz went on. "One of the men at the bar bought him a shot and a beer. Al Murphy, that was, and him out of work and nursing his three beers for a whole evening."

Kerwin asked, "Why would he do that?"

"Because Gallagher put his arm around his shoulder and pinched his cheek. As if he was being playful but enough to hurt. And saying, 'Murphy is my old buddy. Murph' will buy the Tiger a shot and a beer.' And Murphy bought. With tears of pain running down his cheeks he bought. What else could he do?"

There wasn't much you could do, Kerwin thought, in the face of raw brutality.

Schwartz drew a small beer for himself and nodded politely at Kerwin. "Change your mind? It's a hot day and it would be my pleasure."

"All right. Make mine a short one."

Schwartz drew the cool beer and set it in front of Kerwin. "Right after that," he continued, "George Fath come in. George is a little man with glasses. He walked up to Tiger Gallagher and said, 'I want to talk to you, Gallagher.' His voice was high and scared but brave too. You know?"

Kerwin sipped at his beer. "I know."

"And Gallagher turned around and said, 'What do you know. Another one of my buddies. Come on over, Georgie. We ain't got any secrets here. You got another fifty bucks for me, George? George is my real buddy. Pays me not to come around to his place, don't you, George?' "

Schwartz finished his own glass of beer. "Fath got really mad then. He shook his little fist at Gallagher and shouted, 'You were up there this afternoon, trying to get her to see you. She told me about it. You let her alone, Gallagher. You just keep away and let her alone!' "

"What did Gallagher do?" Kerwin asked.

"He grinned in his dirty fashion and asked, 'What makes you think she didn't let me in, Georgie?' And Georgie lunged at him, trying to hit him. Gallagher just pushed him away at first, laughing all the time. Then he got mad and twisted George's arm until the little man went down to his knees. Gallagher said, 'Knock it off, Georgie, or I'll break your arm.' So George just sort of wilted in on himself and went out the door."

Schwartz drew two glasses of beer and brought them over to the two old-timers at the cribbage table. When he came back he said, "After Fath left, Gallagher started to tell Al Murphy how he had gone up to Fath's tenement and what he had done there. Al didn't want to listen. He said he had to go home. So did the other customer. That left me alone with Gallagher. I didn't want to hear him talk with his dirty mouth, so I went down to the basement to tap a keg of ale. I've got a trap door here behind the bar. It's awkward getting up and down. I heard the shot from down below but it took me a few seconds to scramble up. When I did, I saw Dinny Gallagher sitting on the floor, his hands stretched out as if he was trying to pull himself to his feet. But he was dead. I took a dime out of the cash register and tried to call Lieutenant Shaw."

"Tried to call him?"

"He was out getting coffee. I told the desk sergeant what

had happened. Before I finished telling him, Shaw himself got back and I told him what had happened."

"What did he say?"

"He told me to hold on and not touch anything, that he'd be right over. Right after I hung up, young Joe Harrison came in—he's one of my regulars. I told him to run down the block and find the regular beat patrolman. Moore his name was. He was about due to come by. Then I waited."

"How long?"

"Just a few minutes. Until Lieutenant Shaw came in."

While Schwartz was talking, a painfully thin man in his early thirties had come into the bar. Schwartz drew a beer and handed it to the man with a nod, saying, "Hello, Conn."

Conn bobbed his head but did not speak.

Kerwin said, "I think I'll have another beer. Have one with me." He put money on the bar. Schwartz drew two beers and came back to lean against the bar opposite the Deputy Inspector.

"What time did the patrolman—Moore—get here?"

"A few minutes after Lieutenant Shaw."

The man named Conn said bitterly, "Shaw."

Schwartz started to speak and Kerwin shushed him with a wave of his hand. "What about Shaw?" he asked Conn.

"What about him? They ought to investigate him, that's what about him. He pushed poor Dinny Gallagher around for twenty years. Now poor Dinny is dead, God rest him, and Shaw and the rest of the cops are just forgetting the whole thing." Conn sipped at his beer and said sourly, "Don't kid yourself. They know who killed Dinny."

"What do you mean, he pushed Gallagher around?"

"Every time there was even a street fight around here he had poor Dinny pinched."

"Conn, you're like all the Irish. You were scared stiff of Tiger Gallagher like everyone else in the Patch. Now that he's dead he's suddenly become a saint, according to you," Schwartz said.

"He wasn't any saint. But he had a lot of good points. Even you have to admit that." Conn turned to Kerwin. "He was a fighter, you know—used to fight as a middleweight. Never was knocked out."

Schwartz answered disgustedly, "That's a lie. He was suspended by the Boxing Commission for going into the tank.

And I saw the third mate from the *Newark Merchant* half kill him in this very club a couple of months ago. You were here yourself, Conn. The sailor was twenty pounds lighter, too."

Kerwin frowned. "You made a statement," he said to Conn. "You said that Lieutenant Shaw knew who killed Gallagher."

Conn said importantly, "Sure he knows. All the big-shot cops down at City Hall know. Gallagher was cutting in on the bookies. They're the ones that had him killed. Augie Schwartz will tell you that Shaw left here that same night that Gallagher was shot dead and was gone for over an hour. The other cops and the reporters were looking for him."

"Where do you think he went?" Kerwin asked.

"Right over to O'Garry's place to get his orders. That's what I think."

"O'Garry?"

"O'Garry the bookie. Not only that, Shaw was seen with O'Garry the next day. A lot of guys saw him."

Kerwin stood up to go. Before he did he said to Conn, softly, "You know, it's a funny thing. I'm a cop and I'm from City Hall. But I'm damned if *I* knew who killed Gallagher." As he left he heard Schwartz chuckling.

Lieuenant Shaw was in his office when Kerwin got back to the Third Precinct. He grinned and asked, "How did it go, Fearless Fosdick?"

Kerwin flared up briefly. "I told you once, Ed. I'm just doing a job. If you'd done yours better I wouldn't have to be here. I'll put it on the line—I don't know how you usually handle homicides in your precinct, but you butchered this one."

"I did, eh? Tell me about it."

Kerwin said disgustedly, "Oh, knock it off. You've had this precinct what—ten years?"

"So?"

"Maybe you've grown too personal about it. You're not out on an island by yourself. I talked to a couple of people and I got a picture. Lieutenant Shaw, the master of the precinct, the captain of the ship. Maybe we're busy with big crime and small politics down at City Hall but we get the same picture."

"It's nice they know I'm here. I thought they forgot the Third outside of election years."

"That's a stupid remark, Ed. You know who cries about

City Hall politics? The old has-beens who can't handle their jobs any more. Bill Pickerel in Traffic. Or Jake Eno out in the Fifth Precinct. Is that the way it is with you? If it is, you ought to get out."

Shaw said slowly, "The day I can't handle this Precinct they won't have to ask me to get out. Is there anything else you want to point out?"

"Just this. I think you're covering up for somebody. If you are, I hope you didn't take a dime for it. I hope to God you didn't."

Shaw stood up and leaned on his desk. His voice was thick as he said slowly, "You shut your mouth."

Kerwin stared at Shaw until he looked away again. Shaw passed his hand over his face. "I never took a nickel in my life, Pete."

Kerwin tapped the Gallagher file. "I have to go by this. It needs explaining. On the night of the sixteenth, a few minutes after the murder, you called Homicide and had two men assigned to you. These are the two men who claimed that you hampered them."

"I told you once—it's my Precinct. I could have put them out on the street tagging parking violators if I'd wanted to."

"That's not the point. They both stated that you weren't at the Dublin Club when they got there. They checked in at Precinct and you weren't there either. You have a murder on your hands and you disappear. Does that make sense?"

Surprisingly Shaw grinned. "Did you ask Schwartz?"

"No."

"He could have told you."

"Told me what—that you went to see O'Garry the bookie?"

"Who said that?"

"Does it make a difference who said it? Somebody said it. Somebody believes it. You know how that makes you look."

Shaw said thoughtfully, "I suppose so. It's funny the way things turn out sometimes. I never tried to hide where I went. It didn't strike me that it was anybody's business. There wasn't anything I could do for Dinny Gallagher. I'd sent for the Homicide men and put in a call for the Medical Examiner. I had Moore there, keeping people out of the place . . ."

"Moore? He's the beat patrolman?"

"Was. And Schwartz had told me about the argument

between Gallagher and George Fath. I had a pickup out on Fath."

"Let's get back to Moore," Kerwin said. "Schwartz sent a man out to find him, yet he didn't get there until after you arrived. Don't tell me he got lost on his own beat."

"He found a door on Koppelman's meat market unlocked. He stopped to check the building and to tell Koppelman to come down and lock up."

Shaw fumbled in the drawer of his desk and brought out a tin of tobacco. He lit his pipe and went on. "Annie Gallagher came in right after Moore got there. I've known Annie for thirty years—her and old Dan Gallagher. Schwartz had put a tablecloth over the body. She walked over and lifted a corner of it before I could get to her." Shaw's pipe had gone out. He looked at it and frowned. "Pure Irish. She crossed herself and said, 'I had to see him with my own eyes. Thirty-five years old and dead now.' So I took her home."

"If you felt that someone should take her home, why didn't you send Moore? It strikes me that you had things to do."

Shaw said in a faintly surprised voice, "I told you. I've known her for thirty years, her and old Dan. Old Dan has been in and out of veteran's hospitals since the First World War. Think of that, Pete. That's more than forty years."

Kerwin, annoyed that the conversation was drifting away from the main subject, asked dutifully, "What happened to him?"

"Gassed. They sent him home to die a dozen times, but he's one of those tough wiry little guys and he just hung in there. Annie ran a little bakery to help but the old man didn't know that. He was sick, a wreck of a man, and he saw in his son Dinny what he could have been. Dinny couldn't do anything wrong in his eyes and Annie let him go right on feeling that way. There aren't many like her."

"Sure." Kerwin made an attempt to steer Shaw back to the subject but Shaw refused to be diverted.

"Mornings, when I walked a beat in the Patch, she'd call me in for a cup of coffee. Four o'clock in the morning, and she'd be baking—humping hundred-pound sacks of flour, and Dinny up in bed. That's your Tiger that the papers call a character."

Kerwin said in small desperation, "Let's get back to

Fath." He glanced at the Gallagher folder. "He made an assault complaint against Gallagher two months ago, according to this. Then he dropped it. On the sixteenth—the day Gallagher was shot—he had trouble with Gallagher in the Dublin Club, less than an hour before the shooting."

"We picked Fath up two hours after the shooting."

"I read that in here," Kerwin said. "He claimed he was sore at Gallagher and that he stopped in at a couple of bars after he left the Dublin Club. There's damned little substantiation in here."

"He wasn't carrying a gun when we picked him up."

"He could have ditched it somewhere. What was between him and Gallagher?"

"Fath's wife used to be Gallagher's common-law wife. Name is Edith. Gallagher beat her up one too many times and she walked out on him. She wasn't much—but neither was Fath. Left alone they would have made out. Gallagher wouldn't let them alone."

"What about this assault complaint?"

"I handled that myself. If I had my way, Fath wouldn't have dropped it. Gallagher got drunk one afternoon and went up to see Edith Fath. George was there and he tried to stop Gallagher from coming in. Someone called the beat cop—it was Moore—and he went there to try and break it up. He got a little shook—Gallagher was tough if you didn't know him inside—and Moore pulled a gun on Gallagher. A neighbor called the Precinct and said an officer was in trouble. I took the call myself. You know how it is. You get a call like that and you don't wait for anything."

"What happened then?"

"I came up the stairs to Fath's tenement and there they were. I told Moore, 'Don't ever pull a gun on a slob like this,' and started to cuff Gallagher around. A pig like that, you don't need a gun. And I took him in. But Fath withdrew his complaint."

"Why?"

"The way I see it, Gallagher still had something for Edith Fath. She was afraid to be alone when he came around and I guess she made Fath understand. Fath started paying Gallagher to stay away from her."

"It figures that if Gallagher still kept bothering Fath's wife, he had good reason to kill him."

"I never said he didn't. So did a lot of other people. I picked several of them up the same night I had Fath picked up."

"All right. He had a reason. He didn't have a solid alibi. Why did you let him go two days later?"

"I was satisfied he didn't do it," Shaw said.

Kerwin said angrily, "I'm not. Didn't you even put a tail on him?"

Shaw shook his head.

Kerwin flared out at the Lieutenant. "You can't judge these things for yourself. Who are you to sit there and say you're satisfied he didn't do it? You're not the Commissioner. You're not a Felony Court judge. You're a police lieutenant in command of a precinct! Now either you know who did kill Gallagher or you think you're big enough to condemn him all by yourself and let it die in your Record Room. You're not that big, Ed. I'm going to pull Fath and his wife in but I won't do you the courtesy of booking them in your precinct. I'll take them downtown."

Shaw smiled. "Go ahead. You'll have to extradite them."

"Extradite them?"

"They've left town. By bus. I think they were headed for Des Moines."

"And you let it happen." Kerwin stood up. "All right. We can trace them. We can extradite them. I'll have a fugitive warrant out for them in half an hour."

"Go ahead. But I wouldn't sign it if I were you. Get the Commissioner to do it. He can stand a suit for false arrest easier than you can."

Kerwin said bitterly, "I'll risk it." He picked up the desk phone and started to dial a number. He dialed three digits and hung up the phone. Shaw had risen and was staring out the window. Kerwin, still furious, said, "Ed, I don't want to burn you down, but you don't give me any choice. I can't cover for you."

"I didn't ask you," Shaw said without turning around.

Kerwin slammed the Gallagher folder down. "That's the hell of it. If you had asked me I could burn you without thinking twice about it. All right. We'll forget Fath for a while. What about O'Garry?"

"The bookie?"

"The bookie. I've got it that you went to see him the day after the murder. Why?"

"Well now, why don't you ask O'Garry?"

"I will."

"You'll find him in the Avalon Travel Agency—that's his cover. It's three blocks south of the Dublin Club."

Kerwin said sardonically, "Thanks."

"I'll call and tell him you're coming," Shaw promised. "Otherwise you won't get anything out of him except travel folders." He hesitated. "Pete?"

"Yeah."

"You think it's pretty rotten, don't you? Me being buddy-buddy with a bookie."

Kerwin said stiffly, "I'm not assigned to the Vice Squad."

"It's not the way you think it is. I don't take anything from O'Garry. He's not with the mob. He's a little guy, an independent."

"He's still a bookie."

Shaw said disgustedly, "Ah, knock it off. You've got big bookies downtown. I've got O'Garry. He doesn't let anyone get in over his head. No loan sharks. No rough stuff. If anyone starts betting big, I get to hear about it. You think these people in the Patch wouldn't go downtown if I closed up O'Garry?"

Shaw wheeled around to see that Kerwin had already left. He sat down at his desk and put his head in his hands wearily. Then he remembered that he had promised to call O'Garry and he picked up the telephone and dialed a number . . .

O'Garry, a pudgy little man in his sixties, said to Deputy Inspector Kerwin a few minutes later, "Why did Lieutenant Shaw come to see me? Because he wanted to know if I knew anything about who killed Tiger Gallagher."

"Why would he think that?" Kerwin asked. "Did you have any trouble with Gallagher?"

O'Garry shrugged. "Who didn't?" The telephone rang and he picked it up and said, "Call me later," before he turned back to Kerwin. "A year ago he came in here just before the seventh race at Hialeah." O'Garry gestured toward a radio on the shelf behind him. "They broadcast it. There were a dozen three-year-olds in the race. Black Simon was the favorite but there was a six-to-one shot in there by the name of Colony Bid that looked good. There were half a dozen horse players around. Pretty good action on the races they broadcast, you know. Black Simon got out in front by six or seven lengths but Colony Bid wore him down in the stretch and won. And Gallagher said, 'Hot damn. I had ten bucks on him to win.' I told him, 'Not with me, you didn't.' "

The telephone rang again. O'Garry picked it up and said again, "Call me later."

Kerwin asked, "Did he have a bet?"

"Of course not. He was pulling the old past-post trick. He came over and grabbed me by the arm and asked the horse players, 'You guys heard me bet Colony Bid, didn't you?' And there wasn't one of them that had the nerve to call him a liar." O'Garry shrugged. "Neither did I. I paid him. After that he pulled the same trick once, maybe twice a week. And there wasn't a thing I could do about it. If I didn't pay him he would have wrecked the place, maybe put me in the hospital with a broken face."

"Did Lieutenant Shaw know all this?" Kerwin asked.

"I never told him about it but he knew. Not much went on in the Patch that he didn't know. That's why he came to see me. He thought Gallagher might have tried the same strong-arm stuff on the big books downtown."

"Did he?"

"Not that I know of. If he did, he'd have been dead a lot sooner."

Kerwin thanked O'Garry and started to leave. O'Garry held him.

"Inspector?"

"Yes?"

"About Shaw. He's a good officer. People like me know the good ones. If I ever offered him money he would have broken my back."

"Sure."

After leaving O'Garry's, Kerwin started to walk back toward the Third Precinct. He passed the Dublin Social Club and, on an impulse, stopped in.

Schwartz was alone behind the bar, tinkering with a clock. He looked up as Kerwin walked in. "Inspector," he said. "A cold glass of beer with me?"

Kerwin said wearily, "I guess so."

Schwartz put the beer in front of Kerwin and picked up the broken clock. Absently he said, "That Conn that was talking so much. Don't pay attention to him. He's a liar."

"I know the type," Kerwin said. "Listen, Schwartz. You were talking about a fight Gallagher had with the third mate of some ship. What was his name?"

"Wendell. Olaf Wendell."

"And he gave Gallagher a beating?"

Schwartz smiled. "He did. Gallagher was a great one for picking fights with smaller men and drunks. Wendell was small —but he was chunky. Gallagher came in here while Wendell was quietly drinking his beer. He winked at the boys at the bar and jostled Wendell so that he spilled his beer. Wendell didn't say anything. He just ordered another beer. Gallagher, thinking Wendell was scared of him, jostled him again. The sailor ordered another beer. When he got it he poured it down Gallagher's front and said, 'Now move away, you swine.' "

"So Gallagher started a fight?"

"He started it and that's about all. Wendell gave him a terrible beating. After he knocked Gallagher down the fifth or sixth time, Gallagher begged, 'Enough.' So Wendell stepped back and dropped his hands. And Gallagher drove his two thumbs into Wendell's eyes. We had to take him to the hospital. He still wears a patch over his left eye. The retina is detached and he'll be half blind the rest of his days."

"And Gallagher got away with that? That's mayhem!"

"Lieutenant Shaw practically got down on his knees and begged Wendell to make a charge against Gallagher. He wouldn't do it. Said he'd take care of Gallagher in his own way when the time came."

"Shaw knew about the fight, then?"

"Of course."

"What ship was Wendell with?"

"The *Newark Merchant.*"

Kerwin rubbed his forehead. "Just a minute, now. You say Wendell was with the *Newark Merchant.* Was he back at work at the time Gallagher was murdered?"

"You mean, out of the hospital? Back with his ship? Yes."

"Listen now, Schwartz. Didn't you tell me that the night of the sixteenth, the night Gallagher was murdered, business was slow because the dock workers were loading the *Newark Merchant?* Sure you did. So Wendell was in port."

Schwartz finished assembling the clock and held it to his ear. He nodded in satisfaction. "Good as new. You're thinking

Wendell may have shot Gallagher to get even for the loss of his eye? I suppose it's possible. Lieutenant Shaw thought of the same thing. He sent a patrol car down to the docks to pick up Wendell the same night Gallagher was killed. But he didn't hold him. The *Newark Merchant* sailed for Antwerp on the eighteenth. Olaf Wendell was aboard."

"How would you know that?"

"My trade are dock workers. They talk ships when they aren't talking women or gambling."

Kerwin finished his beer and left the Dublin Club. He went on home without stopping in at the Third Precinct.

The next morning the Deputy Inspector ate an early breakfast in the Patch before he again visited the Third. The same civilian was behind the desk when he did get there and he fawned at Kerwin. "Good morning, Inspector."

Kerwin mumbled something unintelligible and moved past him. The clerk glanced down the hall to see if the sergeant was in sight. He wasn't and the clerk said, "Inspector?"

Kerwin paused. "What is it?"

"Lieutenant Shaw isn't in yet."

"All right. He isn't in yet. Anything else on your mind?"

"I was just wondering how you were making out on the Gallagher deal."

Kerwin asked angrily, "Who told you what I was working on? What business is it of yours?"

"I'm not stupid, Inspector. I've got a pretty good idea of what goes on around here."

"You have, have you. What's your name?"

"Harrison."

"It's like this, Harrison. You talk too much."

Harrison said bitterly, "You cops are all alike. Once you get a little rank you scratch each other's backs. You'll whitewash Shaw just like he covered up for Moore. I was trying to help you out and you act like I was dirt."

Kerwin said ominously, "I guess you better talk a little more at that."

"I don't have to tell you anything—and you don't have to make any cracks about getting my job. You'll have to go to the Civil Service Commission and I don't think you guys want to do that."

"You think wrong, Harrison. I'm not whitewashing Shaw

or anyone else. I'm investigating a homicide and I'd just as soon book you as a material witness as try to con information out of you."

Aware that he had pushed too far, Harrison said nervously, "Oh, I'll tell you anything you want to know. I didn't mean anything personal. I just get tired of being treated like an orphan just because I don't wear a uniform. The record sergeant is always on me."

"I can believe it. What about Moore? Is that the same Moore that had the beat where Gallagher was shot?"

"That's him."

"What about him?"

"All I know is he asked for a transfer half a dozen times in the last couple of months. Shaw wouldn't give it to him."

"That was Shaw's business."

"Yeah. But two days after Tiger Gallagher was shot dead, Shaw gave him a transfer to the Traffic Division and had him take his annual leave effective at once."

"And what do you read into that?" Kerwin growled.

"Moore was scared of Gallagher. That's why he wanted the transfer. He had trouble with Gallagher a couple of times."

There was a stir at the door and Lieutenant Shaw walked in followed by a rawboned woman in her sixties. He said, "Hello, Pete. Annie, this is Inspector Kerwin. Pete, this is Annie Gallagher. I've got a few things of Dinny's that I told her I'd release to her. Come on in my office."

Kerwin said awkwardly, "Pleasure, Mrs. Gallagher."

She said, "I'm pleased to meet you, Inspector."

Shaw took a key from his desk. "I've got to go down to the property room. Dinny had some personal stuff. A few bucks." He left.

Kerwin, trying to make conversation, said, "Won't you sit down, Mrs. Gallagher?"

She said, "Thank you," and sat primly in a chair, clutching her handbag to her.

"I'm sorry about your son."

"About Dinny? Why? No—wait. I don't mean it that way. I'm not bitter about what happened. I just can't understand why you should be sorry, Dinny being what he was. He was nothing, Inspector. Nothing. I guess you think it's a terrible thing to hear a mother talk about her son that way?"

Kerwin said nervously, "Well, I—"

"I don't see why I should lie about it. I didn't feel sorry about Dinny myself. I didn't even cry. The time for crying about Dinny was years ago when he was a little boy."

Kerwin tried to change the subject. "How is Mr. Gallagher? Lieutenant Shaw says he's home from the hospital."

She said calmly, "Dan is dying. The doctor is with him now. That's how I could get away to get Dinny's things. It's no more than a matter of days."

"I'm sorry. I mean, I'm really sorry."

She nodded. "I thank you for it. Dan is a good man. He's been a good man all his life. Do you know, for all the years in the hospitals and all the pain and all he missed out on, he never complained. Oh, I'll cry for Dan, I will. But he lives with pain and they can do nothing for him, so it's better, perhaps."

Shaw came back into the room with a manila envelope which he handed to Annie Gallagher. "Here it is, Annie," he said. "He had thirty dollars in his billfold. It's in here with his knife and watch and a few other things."

She stood up. "Thank you, Eddie Shaw," she said and started for the door. When she reached it she turned. "Eddie, Dinny didn't have more than a dollar or two on him when he left the house that night. You put thirty dollars in the envelope, didn't you?"

Shaw reddened. "No. Why, no, I didn't. Dinny must have met someone who owed him some money. I can show you the receipt book if you want me to."

"Never mind. Goodbye, Eddie. Goodbye, Inspector."

Kerwin stood up. "Goodbye, Mrs. Gallagher."

Both men stared at the door after she left. Then Kerwin asked, "Did you?"

"Did I what?"

"Put money in the envelope."

"Do you want to see the receipt?"

"No." Kerwin reached for his billfold and took out a ten-dollar bill. He put it on the desk. "Get that to Mrs. Gallagher some way if you can. She makes me feel the same way you do." He stood up. "All right, Ed. That was something else, something personal. It was a privilege to meet a woman like her. Now I've got to lay it on the line officially. Did you pick up a seaman by the name of Olaf Wendell on the night Gallagher was murdered?"

"I did. I released him the next night."

"And he got on a boat for Antwerp. Didn't you even give him the routine about staying available for questioning?"

"No. He had an alibi. He was working cargo aboard his ship."

"I've seen ships being loaded. They're like a madhouse. Nobody could keep track of anybody else at a time like that. It's a lousy alibi and I don't see how you could have let him go, not in your right mind."

Shaw said stubbornly, "I was satisfied he didn't kill Gallagher."

Kerwin shouted angrily, "You were satisfied he didn't do it! You were satisfied that George Fath didn't do it! You can't just satisfy yourself, Ed. You've got to satisfy the Commissioner. And, yes, by God, you've got to satisfy me. I'll tell you again. You don't have the authority to sit in judgment on Gallagher or anyone else." He leaned forward and lowered his voice. "Damn it, Ed, are you covering up for one of your own officers?"

"Like who?"

"Like Moore. The beat cop who had trouble with Gallagher. I've got it that you turned him down a couple of times when he wanted a transfer—and then let it go through right after Gallagher was killed."

Shaw shook his head. "I didn't transfer him because he killed Gallagher."

"In the spot you're in, you'll have to prove that. He had trouble with Gallagher, didn't he?"

"Sure he did. I told you he pulled a gun on Gallagher once. I made a mistake then. I cuffed Gallagher around, shamed him in front of Moore. Gallagher was too yellow to try and get even with me. So a few nights later he had some of his cronies give Moore a going-over. They took his gun away and gave him a shellacking."

"Why didn't Moore turn him in?"

"Gallagher was too smart to lay a hand on him himself. He stood by and watched it."

"What about the others? Didn't Moore recognize them?"

"Sure he did, but it was his word against theirs. I told him to forget it and next time use the gun. Then I took a sergeant and a couple of men and went down in the Patch and worked a few of them over. That's all I could do."

"You could have been broken for it."

"I doubt it, Pete. This time I had the witnesses. If I didn't do it, they'd have crippled the next man I put on the beat. It's my Precinct, Pete. I know how to handle it."

"Was that why Moore asked for a transfer?"

"I suppose so. But I couldn't let him have it then." Shaw fumbled for his pipe. "Moore isn't a real cop, Pete. He's not yellow, but he has too much imagination. He'll do fine in Traffic on an administrative job. If I'd let him transfer then, Gallagher would have bragged how he ran him off the beat. That would make it tough for the other patrolmen. And Moore would wonder, all the rest of his days, if he had dogged it in the clutch."

"But Moore was sore at Gallagher and he was late making his rounds the night he was killed."

"That occurred to me."

Kerwin reached for the telephone and Shaw asked, "What are you going to do?"

Kerwin said angrily, "I'm going to locate Moore and have him sent down here."

Shaw shrugged. "Be my guest. He's up in the Gaspé Peninsula on vacation. Fishing."

"Damn you, Ed, you sent him up there."

"He likes to fish. Can't help that."

Kerwin said in a level voice, "Fath out of the state. Wendell out of the country. Moore in Canada. Three people who could have killed Gallagher and you let them all get away. And you never checked the bookie angle downtown. You've bungled this thing from start to finish, Ed. I've got to recommend that you be relieved and suspended and that the investigation be opened wide."

Shaw looked away. "It's your party."

Kerwin, in frustration, said, "I don't get it, Ed. You picked up Fath and Wendell. You started out in a competent manner. What happened?"

Before Shaw could answer, the telephone rang. Shaw picked it up. "Yes," he said. "Yes. I know. What? When did it happen? Yeah. Maybe it is at that. No, that's all right. There won't be any trouble. I'm sorry, Annie. I'll drop over sometime today." He hung up the telephone and turned to Kerwin. "That was Annie Gallagher. Old Dan is dead."

"That's too bad, Ed."

"But you don't care about that. You want some answers

about Dinny Gallagher." Shaw walked over to look out the window. "What will you tell the Commissioner? That I have delusions and think I'm King of the Patch? Or that somebody bought me off?"

"He'll make up his own mind," Kerwin said.

"I guess he will at that." Shaw came back from the window. "Are you in a hurry?"

"We might as well get it over with. I'm supposed to call the Commissioner whenever I'm ready to make a recommendation."

Shaw sprawled in his chair. "You know," he said reflectively, "I thought Wendell did it. Fath is a lightweight. I couldn't see him using a gun."

"What made you stop thinking Wendell did it?"

"I went to Gallagher's wake."

Kerwin said impatiently, "All right. You went to Gallagher's wake."

"Remember I told you about Annie Gallagher coming into the Dublin Club to see Dinny's body. She said, 'I had to see him with my own eyes.' She didn't say, 'Who did it?' I thought about that and it came to me that she had to know or she would have asked. At the wake I asked her about it. I think she would have told me anyway when she heard that I was questioning Fath and Wendell. She's a decent woman, Annie."

Kerwin exhaled. "Lord. Her own son."

Shaw glanced at the Inspector. "You've a habit of jumping the gun," he said. "Shall I tell you what she told me?"

"By all means," Kerwin said sardonically.

"In her own words then. This is how it happened . . . Dinny, early in the evening, came into the kitchen and took a bottle of milk from the icebox. Annie followed him out and said, 'Dinny, I've got something to say to you.'

"And Dinny said, 'Ah, look. I've got my own problems. Don't give me that routine about getting a job and turning in some money to keep the joint going.'

" 'I haven't asked you about a job in five years.'

" 'Then get off my back.'

" 'You're going to listen to me, Dinny,' she said.

" 'I said get off my back.' He was shouting at her by this time.

"Annie said, 'Keep your voice down. Your father is sleeping.'

" 'So what? All he ever did in his life was sleep and make like a wounded hero. Why don't he stay in the Vet's hospital where people don't have to look at him?' "

Shaw relit his pipe. "What Annie didn't know then is that old Dan had got out of bed and was standing in the kitchen door listening to all this. And don't forget, until right then he thought the sun rose and set on Dinny."

Kerwin asked, "You got another pipe? Lend it to me. But don't stop."

Shaw passed pipe and tobacco over. "So then Annie said, 'Your father belongs here. This is his home. If you don't want to look at him, why don't you get out? I don't want you. How does it feel, Dinny, to hear that? I don't want you. I wish I never had to see you again.'

"And Dinny said, 'That doesn't bother me.'

" 'Nothing bothers you,' she told him.

" 'You know something?' he asked her. 'You bother me. You think I don't get tired of looking at you too? Moping around making like it was such a big deal keeping a roof over the old man's head. Putting on an act for people to see how hard you work and what a bum I am for not helping out.'

"Annie asked him—and she meant it—'Where did you come from, Dinny? From Hell? Dan and I couldn't have a son like you.'

" 'You should know,' he told her.

" 'I'd have slapped you for that once,' she said.

"And he told her—don't forget, old Dan was hearing all this— 'Yeah, and you know what happened when you tried belting me. So don't try it again.'

" 'I won't,' she told him. 'Dinny, that girl you went with once came up to see me today. She wanted me to make you leave her alone.'

"Dinny laughed. 'Edith Fath?'

" 'Edith Fath. She's married and she's trying to make something of it. You leave her alone, Dinny, or you'll be sorry.'

" 'What can you do about it?' he asked her.

" 'I've got friends in the Patch, Dinny. Men who work on the docks. Truck drivers. Produce men. Big men. If you go near that woman again, I'm going to get some of them to beat you half to death.'

" 'You'd do it. I believe you'd do it.'

"She moved over and stood in front of him and asked him again, 'Are you going to leave that woman alone?'

" 'Get out of my way,' he told her.

" 'Are you?'

"He said, 'Ah, shut up and leave me alone.' And then he pushed her away. She grabbed at his arm and he half pushed, half hit her. 'I said get out of my way,' he shouted. And right then old Dan came into the kitchen. Annie had slumped into a kitchen chair with her head in her arms. Old Dan bent over her and asked, 'Are you all right, darlin'?' "

Kerwin realized that he was holding his breath. "Go on," he urged.

"Annie got right up and tried to cover up what had happened. 'You shouldn't be out of bed, Dan,' she told him.

"Old Dan didn't pay any attention. He started moving toward Dinny. 'Now, then, by God,' he said. And Dinny backed away, scared of the look in the old man's eye. He said, 'Get away from me, old man,' but Dan kept coming toward him. All this time Annie is saying, 'Go on back to bed, Dan. Let me help you back to bed.'

" 'I'll kill you with my two hands,' the old man said. And Dinny, backing around the table, pleading with him. 'I don't want to hit you. You're making me do it. Make him stop, Ma!' "

Kerwin heard a clicking noise and felt a sharp twinge on his lower lip. Only when the pipe refused to draw did he realize that he had bitten through the stem. Shaw passed him another one.

"Right then old Dan lunged and grabbed Dinny. Dinny tried to push him away and Annie was on Dinny like a tigress, scratching at his face and neck with her nails, all the time screaming at Dinny to let the old man alone. She hurt him. He drew back his fist and knocked her to the floor. She was almost unconscious. When she knew what was happening again, Dinny was gone and the old man was bending over her. There were tears in his eyes. 'He hurt you, Annie?' he said. 'Nor was it the first time.'

" 'I'm all right,' she told him. 'Let me help you back to bed.'

" 'All this time,' old Dan said, 'you telling me what a help he was and how good things were going with me flat on my back.'

"He left her then and went to the bedroom. When he came back he said, 'He'll be at the Dublin, I suppose.'

" 'What are you going to do, Dan?'

" 'That would be my business, Annie.'

" 'What have you got in your pocket?' she asked him.

"He showed her. An Army .45. Annie tried to stop him but he would have none of it.

" 'You stay here,' he told her. 'I'm not the man you deserved, Annie. I've done little in all the years to be a husband to you. But no man can hurt you and live. Not while I live.'

" 'Ah, Dan—' she pleaded.

" 'I'm his father. I'm responsible for his life. And I'll be responsible for taking it away from him.' "

Shaw tamped out his pipe and stretched. "And that's the way it was."

Kerwin sighed. "Good God!"

"That's how I felt."

"But why didn't you make a report on it? Why did you stick your neck out?"

Shaw smiled. "It would have made me look good downtown, wouldn't it? A first-degree homicide closed out in forty-eight hours. The catch was that I'd have had to arrest that old man. He spent forty years in hospitals, Pete—he was only the shadow of the man he could have been. I made a ruling. The Patch owed him and Annie whatever time he had left. Not the department. Not the Commissioner. The Patch. Me. So I gave them that time. Are you going to tell me that I didn't have the authority and that I'm just a lousy Precinct Lieutenant? Because, if you are, I've got all morning to listen."

Kerwin said thoughtfully, "Why, no. No. I'd say that this was strictly a Precinct matter and that you handled it very efficiently. I'll work something out with the Commissioner." He stood up. "Ed, I haven't had a drink before lunch in twenty years. But I'm going down and see Schwartz at the Dublin Club and have one now. I'd be proud, Ed, if you'd join me."

HUGH PENTECOST

A Kind of Murder

WINNER OF A SECOND PRIZE

An unusual and moving story, told by someone who has lived for many years with a burden on his conscience—the burden of having been responsible for the existence of a walking dead man . . .

You might say this is the story of a murder—although nobody was killed. I don't know what has become of Mr. Silas Warren, but I have lived for many years with the burden on my conscience of having been responsible for the existence of a walking dead man.

I was fifteen years old during the brief span of days that I knew Mr. Silas Warren. It was toward the end of the winter term at Morgan Military Academy. Mr. Etsweiler, the chemistry and physics teacher at Morgan, had died of a heart attack one afternoon while he was helping to coach the hockey team on the lake. Mr. Henry Huntingdon Hadley, the headmaster, had gone to New York to find a replacement. That replacement was Mr. Silas Warren.

I may have been one of the first people to see Mr. Warren at the Academy. I had been excused from the afternoon study period because of a heavy cold, and allowed to take my books to my room to work there. I saw Mr. Warren come walking across the quadrangle toward Mr. Hadley's office, which was located on the ground floor under the hall where my room was.

Mr. Warren didn't look like a man who was coming to stay long. He carried one small, flimsy suitcase spattered with travel labels. Although it was a bitter March day he wore a thin, summer-weight topcoat. He stopped beside a kind of brown lump in the snow. That brown lump was Teddy, the school dog.

Teddy was an ancient collie. They said that in the old days you could throw a stick for Teddy to retrieve until you, not he, dropped from exhaustion. Now the old, gray-muzzled dog was pretty much ignored by everyone except the chef, who fed him scraps from the dining room after the noon meal. Teddy would be at the kitchen door, promptly on time, and then find a comfortable spot to lie down. He'd stay there until someone forced him to move.

Mr. Warren stopped by Teddy, bent down, and scratched the dog's head. The old, burr-clotted tail thumped wearily in the snow. Mr. Warren straightened up and looked around. He had narrow, stooped shoulders. His eyes were pale blue, and they had a kind of frightened look in them. *He's scared,* I thought; *coming to a new place in the middle of a term, he's scared.*

I guess most of the other fellows didn't see Mr. Warren until he turned up at supper time at the head of one of the tables in the dining room. We marched into the dining room and stood behind our chairs waiting for the cadet major to give the order to be seated. The order was delayed. Mr. Henry Huntingdon Hadley, known as Old Beaver because of his snowy white beard, made an announcement.

"Mr. Warren has joined our teaching staff to fill the vacancy created by the unfortunate demise of Mr. Etsweiler." Old Beaver had false teeth and his s's whistled musically. "I trust you will give him a cordial welcome."

"Be seated," the cadet major snapped.

We sat. Old Beaver said grace. Then we all began to talk. I was at Mr. Warren's right. He had a genial, want-to-be-liked smile.

"And your name is?" he asked me, in a pleasant but flat voice.

"Pentecost, sir."

He leaned toward me. "How's that?" he asked.

"Pentecost, sir."

Sammy Callahan sat across from me on Mr. Warren's left. Sammy was a fine athlete and a terrible practical joker. I saw a gleam of interest in his eyes. As Mr. Warren turned toward him Sammy spoke in an ordinary conversational tone. "Why don't you go take a jump in the lake, sir?"

Mr. Warren smiled. "Yes, I guess you're right," he said.

Sammy grinned at me. There was no doubt about it—Mr. Warren was quite deaf!

It was a strange kind of secret Sammy and I had. We didn't really know what to do with it, but we found out that night. Old Beaver was not a man to start anyone in gradually. It would have been Mr. Etsweiler's turn to take the night study hour, so that hour was passed on to Mr. Warren.

He sat on the little platform at the head of the study hall—smiling and smiling. I think there must have been terror in his heart then. I think he may even have been praying.

Everyone seemed unusually busy studying, but we were all waiting for the test. The test always came for a new master the first time he had night study hour. There would be a minor disturbance and we'd find out promptly whether this man could maintain discipline or not. It came after about five minutes—a loud, artificial belch.

Mr. Warren smiled and smiled. He hadn't heard it.

Belches sprang up all over the room. Then somebody threw a handful of torn paper in the air. Mr. Warren's smile froze.

"Now, now, boys," he said.

More belches. More torn paper.

"Boys!" Mr. Warren cried out, like someone in pain.

Then Old Beaver appeared, his eyes glittering behind rimless spectacles. There was something I never understood about Old Beaver. Ordinarily his shoes squeaked. You could hear him coming from quite a distance away—squeak-squeak, squeak-squeak. But somehow, when he chose, he could approach as noiseless as a cat, without any squeak at all. And there he was.

The study hall was quiet as a tomb. But the silence was frighteningly loud, and the place was littered with paper.

"There will be ten demerit marks against every student in this room," Old Beaver said in his icy voice. "I want every scrap of paper picked up instantly."

Several of us scrambled down on our hands and knees. Mr. Warren smiled at the headmaster.

"Consider the lilies of the field," Mr. Warren said. "They toil not, neither do they spin. Yet I tell you that Solomon in all his glory—"

There was an uncontrollable outburst of laughter.

"Silence!" Old Beaver hissed, with all the menace of a

poised cobra. He turned to Mr. Warren. "I'll take the balance of this period, Mr. Warren. I suggest you go to your room and prepare yourself for tomorrow's curriculum."

I didn't have any classes with Mr. Warren the next day, but all you heard as you passed in the corridors from one class period to the next were tales of the jokes and disorders in the physics and chemistry courses. Somehow nobody thought it was wrong to take advantage of Mr. Warren.

The climax came very quickly. In the winter, if you weren't out for the hockey or winter sports teams, you had to exercise in the gym. There were the parallel bars, and the rings, and the tumbling mats. And there was boxing.

The boxing teacher was Major Durand, the military commandant. I know now that he was a sadist. Major Durand was filled with contempt for everyone but Major Durand. I saw the look on his face when Mr. Warren appeared.

Mr. Warren had been assigned to help in the gym. He was something to see—just skin and bones. He had on a pair of ordinary black socks and, I suspect, the only pair of shoes he owned—black oxfords. He'd borrowed a pair of shorts that could have been wrapped twice around his skinny waist. Above that was a much mended short-sleeved undershirt. He looked around, hopeless, amiable.

"Mr. Warren!" Major Durand said. "I'd like you to help me demonstrate. Put on these gloves if you will." He tossed a pair of boxing gloves at Mr. Warren who stared at them stupidly. One of the boys helped him tie the laces.

"Now, Mr. Warren," Durand said. The Major danced and bobbed and weaved, and shot out his gloves in short vicious jabs at the air. "You will hold your gloves up to your face, sir. When you're ready you'll say 'Hit'—and I shall hit you."

I'd seen Major Durand do this with a boy he didn't like. You held up the gloves and you covered your face and then, with your throat dry and aching, you said "Hit!"—and Major Durand's left or right would smash through your guard and pulverize your nose or mouth. It was sheer strength, I know now, not skill.

Mr. Warren held up his gloves, and he looked like an actor in an old Mack Sennett comedy—the absurd clothes, the sickly smile.

Durand danced in front of him. "Whenever you say, Mr. Warren. Now watch this, boys. The feint—and the jab."

"Hit!" said Mr. Warren, his voice suddenly falsetto.

Pow! Major Durand's left jab smashed through the guard of Mr. Warren's nose. There was a sudden geyser of blood.

"Again, Mr. Warren!" the Major commanded, his eyes glittering.

"I think I'd better retire to repair the damage," Mr. Warren said. His undershirt was spattered with blood and he had produced a soiled handkerchief which he held to his nose. He hurried out of the gym at a sort of shambling gallop.

That night the payoff came in study hall. Mr. Warren was called on this time to substitute for Old Beaver, who had taken over for him the night before. Sammy Callahan staged it. Suddenly handkerchiefs were waved from all parts of the room —handkerchiefs stained red. Red ink, of course.

"Hit!" somebody shouted. "Hit, hit!" Nearly all the boys were bobbing, weaving, jabbing.

Mr. Warren, pale as a ghost, cotton visibly stuffed in one nostril, stared at us like a dead man.

Then there was Old Beaver again.

Somehow the word was out at breakfast the next morning. Mr. Warren was leaving. He didn't show at the breakfast table. I felt a little squeamish about it. He hadn't been given a chance. Maybe he wasn't such a bad guy.

It was during the morning classroom period that we heard it. It was a warm day for March and the ice was breaking up on the lake. The scream was piercing and terrified. Somebody went to the window. The scream came again.

"Somebody's fallen through the ice!"

The whole school—a hundred and fifty boys and masters —hurried down to the shore of the lake. The sun was so bright that all we could see was a dark shape flopping out there, pulling itself up on the ice and then disappearing under water as the ice broke. Each time the figure rose there was a wailing scream.

Then the identification. "It's Teddy!" someone shouted.

The school dog. He'd walked out there and the ice had caved in on him. The screams were growing weaker. A couple of us made for the edge of the ice. Old Beaver and Major Durand confronted us.

"I'm sorry, boys," Old Beaver said. "It's a tragic thing to

have to stand here and watch the old dog drown. But no one—no one connected with the school—is to try to get to him. I'm responsible for your safety. That's an order."

We stood there, sick with it. Old Teddy must have seen us because for a moment there seemed to be new hope in his strangled wailing.

Then I saw Mr. Warren. He was by the boathouse, his old suitcase in his hand. He looked out at the dog, and so help me there were tears in Mr. Warren's eyes. Then, very calmly, he put down his bag, took off his thin topcoat and suit jacket. He righted one of the overturned boats on the shore and pulled it to the edge of the lake.

"Mr. Warren! You heard my order!" Old Beaver shouted at him.

Mr. Warren turned to the headmaster, smiling. "You seem to forget, sir, I am no longer connected with Morgan Military Academy, and therefore not subject to your orders."

"Stop him!" Major Durand ordered.

But before anyone could reach him, Mr. Warren had slid the flat-bottomed rowboat out onto the ice. He crept along on the ice himself, clinging to the boat, pushing it across the shiny surface toward Teddy. I heard Mr. Warren's thin, flat voice.

"Hold on, old man! I'm coming."

The ice gave way under him, but he clung to the boat and scrambled up—and on.

"Hold on, old man!"

It seemed to take forever. Just before what must have been the last, despairing shriek from the half-frozen dog, Mr. Warren reached him. How he found the strength to lift the water-soaked collie into the boat I don't know; but he managed, and then he came back toward us, creeping along the cracking ice, pushing the boat to shore.

The chef wrapped Teddy in blankets, put him behind the stove in the kitchen, and gave him a dose of warm milk and cooking brandy. Mr. Warren was hustled to the infirmary. Did I say that when he reached the shore with Teddy the whole school cheered him?

Old Beaver, for all his tyranny, must have been a pretty decent guy. He announced that night that Mr. Warren was not leaving after all. He trusted that, after Mr. Warren's display of valor, the boys would show him the respect he deserved.

I went to see Mr. Warren in the infirmary that first evening. He looked pretty done in, but he also looked happier than I'd ever seen him.

"What you did took an awful lot of courage," I told him. "Everybody thinks it was a swell thing to do."

Mr. Warren smiled at me—a thoughtful kind of a smile. "Courage is a matter of definition," he said. "It doesn't take courage to stand up and let yourself get punched in the nose, boy. It takes courage to walk away. As for Teddy—somebody had to go after him. There wasn't anyone who could but me, so courage or not, I went. You'd have gone if Mr. Hadley hadn't issued orders." He sighed. "I'm glad to get a second chance here. Very glad."

Somehow I got the notion it was a last chance—the very last chance he'd ever have.

It was a week before Mr. Warren had the night study hall again. It was a kind of test. For perhaps fifteen minutes nothing happened, and then I heard Sammy give his fine, artificial belch. I looked up at Mr. Warren. He was smiling happily. He hadn't heard. A delighted giggle ran around the room.

I was on my feet. "If there's one more sound in this room I'm going after Old Beaver," I said. "And after that I'll personally take on every guy in this school, if necessary, to knock sense into him!"

The room quieted. I was on the student council and I was also captain of the boxing team. The rest of the study period was continued in an orderly fashion. When it was over and we were headed for our rooms, Mr. Warren flagged me down.

"I don't know quite what was going on, Pentecost," he said, "but I gather you saved the day for me. Thank you. Thank you very much. Perhaps when the boys get to know me a little better they'll come to realize—" He made a helpless little gesture with his bony hands.

"I'm sure they will, sir," I said. "I'm sure of it."

"They're not cruel," Mr. Warren said. "It's just high spirits, I know."

Sammy Callahan was waiting for me in my room. "What are you, some kind of a do-gooder?" he said.

"Give the guy a chance," I said. "He proved he has guts when it's needed. But he's helpless there in the study hall."

Sammy gave me a sour grin. "You and he should get

along fine," he said. "And you'll need to. The guys aren't going to be chummy with a do-gooder like you."

It was a week before Mr. Warren's turn to run the study hour came around again. In that time I'd found that Sammy was right. I was being given the cold shoulder. Major Durand, who must have hated Mr. Warren for stealing the heroic spotlight from him, was giving me a hard time. One of the guys I knew well came to me.

"You're making a mistake," he told me. "He's a grown man and you're just a kid. If he can't take care of himself it's not your headache."

I don't like telling the next part of it, but it happened.

When Mr. Warren's night came again, the study hall was quiet enough for a while. Then came a belch. I looked up at Mr. Warren. He was smiling. Then someone waved one of those fake bloody handkerchiefs. Then, so help me, somebody let out a baying howl—like Teddy in the lake.

Mr. Warren knew what was happening now. He looked down at me, and there was an agonizing, wordless plea for help in his eyes. I—well, I looked away. I was fifteen. I didn't want to be called a do-gooder. I didn't want to be snubbed. Mr. Warren *was* a grown man and he should have been able to take care of himself. The boys weren't cruel: they were just high spirited—hadn't Mr. Warren himself said so?

I looked up from behind a book. Mr. Warren was standing, looking out over the room. His stooped, skinny shoulders were squared away. Two great tears ran down his pale cheeks. His last chance was played out.

Then he turned and walked out of the study hall.

No one ever saw him again. He must have gone straight to his room, thrown his meager belongings into the battered old suitcase, and taken off on foot into the night.

You see what I mean when I say it was a kind of murder?

And I was the murderer.

DOROTHY SALISBURY DAVIS

By the Scruff of the Soul

WINNER OF A SECOND PRIZE

"That's how it happens up here in the hills: one generation and there'll be aunts and uncles galore, and the next, you got two maiden ladies"—and one of them a wild one from the start . . .

Most people, when they go down from the Ragapoo Hills, never come back; or if they do, for a funeral maybe—weddings don't count for so much around here any more either—you can see them fidgeting to get away again. As for me, I'm one of those rare birds they didn't have any trouble keeping down on the farm after he'd seen Paree.

It's forty years since I've seen the bright lights, but I don't figure I've missed an awful lot. Hell, I can remember the Ku Klux Klan marching right out in the open. My first case had to do with a revenue agent—I won it, too, and we haven't had a government man up here since. And take the League of Nations—I felt awful sorry in those days for Mr. Wilson though I didn't hold with his ideas.

Maybe things have changed, but sometimes I wonder just how much. This bomb I don't understand, fallout and all, but I've seen what a plague of locusts can do to a wheat field and I don't think man's ever going to beat nature when it comes to pure, ornery destruction. I could be wrong about that. Our new parson says I am and he's a mighty knowing man. Too knowing, maybe. I figure that's why the Synod shipped him up to us in Webbtown.

As I said, I don't figure I'm missing much. There's a couple of television sets in town and sometimes of an evening I'll sit for an hour or so in front of whichever one of them's working best. One of them gets the shimmies every time the wind blows and the other don't bring in anything except by way of Canada. Same shows but different commercials. That kind of tickles me, all them companies advertising stuff you couldn't buy if you wanted to instead of stuff you wouldn't want if you could buy it.

But, as you've probably guessed by now, I'd rather talk than most anything, and since you asked about The Red Lantern, I'll tell you about the McCracken sisters who used to run it—and poor old Matt Sawyer.

I'm a lawyer, by the way. I don't get much practice up here. I'm also Justice of the Peace. I don't get much practice out of that either, but between the two I make a living. For pleasure I fish for trout and play the violin, and at this point in my life I think I can say from experience that practice ain't everything.

I did the fiddling at Clara McCracken's christening party, I remember, just after coming home from the first World War. Maudie was about my age then, so's that'd make a difference of maybe twenty years between the sisters, and neither chit nor chizzler in between, and after them, the whole family suddenly dies out. That's how it happens up here in the hills: one generation and there'll be aunts and uncles galore, and the next, you get two maiden ladies and a bobtailed cat.

The Red Lantern Inn's boarded up now, as you saw, but it was in the McCracken family since just after the American Revolution. It was burned down once—in a reprisal raid during the War of 1812, and two of the McCrackens were taken hostage. Did you know Washington, D.C. was also burned in reprisal? It was. At least that's how they tell it over in Canada—for the way our boys tore up the town they call Toronto now. You know, history's like a story in a way: it depends on who's telling it.

Anyway, Maudie ran the inn after the old folks died, and she raised Clara the best she could, but Clara was a wild one from the start. We used to call her a changling: one minute she'd be sitting at the stove and the next she'd be off somewhere in the hills. She wasn't a pretty girl—the jutting McCracken jaw spoiled that—but there were times she was mighty feminine, and many a lad got thorny feet chasing after the will-o'-the-wisp.

As Clara was coming to age, Maudie used to keep a birch stick behind the bar, and now and then I dare say she'd use it, though I never saw it happen but once myself. But that birch stick and Old Faithful, her father's shotgun, stood in the corner side by side, and I guess we made some pretty rude jokes about them in those days. Anyways, Maudie swore to tame the girl and marry her to what she called a "settled" man.

By the time Clara was of a marrying age, The Red Lantern was getting pretty well rundown. And so was Maudie. She wasn't an easy woman by any calculation. She had a tongue you'd think was sharpened on the grindstone and a store of sayings that'd shock you if you didn't know your Bible. The inn was peeling paint and wanting shutters to the northeast, which is where they're needed most. But inside, Maudie kept the rooms as clean and plain as a glass egg. And most times they were about as empty.

It was the taproom kept the sisters going. They drew the best beer this side of Cornwall, England. If they knew you, that is. If they didn't know you, they served you a labeled bottle, stuff you'd recognize by the signboard pictures. About once a month, Maudie had to buy a case of that—which gives you an idea how many strangers stopped over in Webbtown. We had more stores then and the flour mill was working, so the farmers'd come in regular. But none of them were strangers. You see, even to go to Ragapoo City, the county seat, you've got to go twenty miles around—unless you're like Clara was, skipping over the mountain.

Matt Sawyer came through every week or two in those days and he always stopped at Prouty's Hardware Store. Matt was a paint salesman. I suppose he sold Prouty a few gallons over the years. Who bought it from Prouty, I couldn't say. But Prouty liked Matt. I did myself when I got to know him. Or maybe I just felt sorry for him.

It was during the spring storms, this particular day. The rain was popping blisters on Main Street. Most everyone in Webbtown seems to have been inside looking out that day. Half the town claimed afterwards to have seen Matt come out of Prouty's raising his black umbrella over Maudie's head and walking her home. I saw them myself, Maudie pulling herself in and Matt half in and half out. I know for a fact she'd never been under an umbrella before in her life.

Prouty told me afterwards he'd forgot she was in the store when he was talking to Matt: Maudie took a mighty long time making up her mind before buying anything. Like he always did, Prouty was joshing Matt about having enough money to find himself a nice little woman and give up the road. Maudie wasn't backward. She took a direct line: she just up and asked Matt since he had an umbrella, would he mind walking her home. Matt was more of a gentleman than anybody I ever knew. He said it would be a pleasure. Maybe it was, but that was the beginning of the doggonedest three-cornered courtship in the county history. And it's all documented today in the county court records over in Ragapoo City. But I'm getting ahead of myself.

I've got my office in my hat, you might say, and I hang that in rooms over Kincaid's Drug Store. I was standing at the window when Matt and Maudie came out of Prouty's. I remember I was trying to tune my violin. You can't keep a fiddle in tune weather like that. I played kind of ex tempore for a while, drifting from one thing to another—sad songs mostly, like "The Vacant Chair." *We shall meet but we shall miss him . . . there will be one vacant chair*. I got myself so depressed I hung up the fiddle and went down to The Red Lantern for a glass of Maudie's Own.

Well, sure enough, there was Matt Sawyer sitting at the bar advising Maudie on the costs of paint and trimming and how to estimate the amount of paint a place the size of The Red Lantern would need. Now I knew Maudie couldn't afford whitewash much less the highclass line of stuff Matt represented. But there she was, leaning on the bar, chin in hand and her rump in the air like a swaybacked mule. She drew me a beer and put a head on Matt's. Then she went back to listening to him.

I don't know how long it took me to notice what was really going on: I'm slow sometimes, but all this while Clara was standing on a stool polishing a row of fancy mugs Maudie kept on a ledge over the back mirror. The whole row of lights was on under the ledge and shining double in the mirror. Hell, Matt Sawyer wasn't actually making sense at all, what he was saying in facts and figures. He was just making up words to keep old Maudie distracted—he thought—and all the while him gazing up at Clara every chance he'd get. I might as well be honest with you: it was looking at Clara myself I realized what was going on in that room. The way she was reaching up and down in front of that mirror and with a silk petticoat kind of dress on, you'd have sworn she was stark naked.

Well, sir, just think about that. Matt, being a gentleman, was blushing and yearning—I guess you'd call it that—but making conversation all the time; and Maudie was conniving a match for Clara with a man who could talk a thousand dollars' worth of paint without jumping his Adam's apple. I'll say this about Maudie: for an unmarried lady she was mighty knowing in the fundamentals. Clara was the only innocent one in the room, I got to thinking.

All of a sudden Maudie says to me, "Hank, how's your fiddle these days?"

"It's got four strings," I said.

"You bring it up after supper, hear?" It was Maudie's way never to ask for something. She told you what you were going to do and most often you did it. Clara looked round at me from that perch of hers and clapped her hands.

Maudie laid a bony finger on Matt's hand. "You'll stay to supper with us, Mr. Sawyer. Our Clara's got a leg of lamb in the oven like you never tasted. It's home hung and roasted with garden herbs."

Now I knew for a fact the only thing Clara ever put in the oven was maybe a pair of shoes to warm them of a winter's morning. And it was just about then Clara caught on, too, to what Maudie was maneuvering. Her eyes got a real wild look in them, like a fox cornered in a chicken coop. She bounded down and across that room . . .

I've often wondered what would've happened if I hadn't spoken then. It gives me a cold chill thinking about it—words said with the best intentions in the world. I called out just as she got to the door: "Clara, I'll be bringing up my fiddle."

I don't suppose there ever was a party in Webbtown like Maudie put on that night. Word got around. Even the young folks came that mightn't have if it was spooning weather. Maudie wore her best dress—the one she was saving, we used to say, for Clara's wedding and her own funeral. It was black, but on happier occasions she'd liven it up with a piece of red silk at the collar. I remember Prouty saying once that patch of red turned Maudie from a Holstein into a Guernsey. Prouty, by the way, runs the undertaking parlor as well as the hardware store.

I near split my fingers that night fiddling. Maudie tapped a special keg. Everybody paid for his first glass, but after that she put the cash box away and you might say she drew by heart.

Matt was having a grand time just watching mostly. Matt was one of those creamy-looking fellows, with cheeks as pink as winter apples. He must've been fifty but there wasn't a line or wrinkle in his face. And I never seen him without his collar and tie on. Like I said, a gentleman.

Clara took to music like a bird to wing. I always got the feeling no matter who was taking her in or out she was actually dancing alone; she could do two steps to everybody else's one. Matt never took his eyes off her, and once he danced with her when Maudie pushed him into it.

That was trouble's start—although we didn't know it at the time. Prouty said afterwards he did, but Prouty's a man who knows everything after the fact. That's being an undertaker, I dare say. Anyway, Matt was hesitating after Clara—and it was like that, her sort of skipping ahead and leading him on, when all of a sudden, young Reuben White leaped in between them and danced with Clara the way she needed to be danced with.

Now Reuben didn't have much to recommend him, especially to Maudie. He did an odd job now and then—in fact, he hauled water for Maudie from the well she had up by the brewhouse back of Maple Tree Ridge. And this you ought to know about Maudie if you don't by now—anybody she could boss around, she had no use for.

Anyways, watching that boy dance with Clara that night should've set us all to thinking, him whirling her and tossing her up in the air, them spinning round together like an August twister. My fiddle's got a devil in it at a time like that. Faster and faster I was bowing, till plunk I broke a string, but I went right on playing.

Matt fell back with the other folks, clapping and cheering, but Maudie I could see going after her stick. I bowed even faster, seeing her. It was like a race we were all in together. Then all of a sudden, like something dying high up in the sky and falling mute, my E string broke and I wasn't playing any more. In the center of the tavern floor Clara and Reuben just folded up together and slumped down into a heap.

Everybody was real still for about a half a minute. Then Maudie came charging out, slashing the air with that switch of hers. She grabbed Clara by the hair—I swear she lifted the girl to her feet that way and flung her towards the bar. Then she turned on Reuben. That boy slithered clear across the barroom floor, every time just getting out of the way of a slash from Maudie's stick. People by then were cheering in a kind of rhythm—for him or Maudie, you couldn't just be sure, and maybe they weren't for either. "Now!" they'd shout at every whistle of the switch. "Now! Now! *Now!*"

Prouty opened the door just when Reuben got there, and when the boy was out Prouty closed it against Maudie. I thought for a minute she was going to turn on him. But she just stood looking and then burst out laughing. Everybody started clouting her on the back and having a hell of a time.

I was at the bar by then and so was Matt. I heard him, leaning close to Clara, say, "Miss Clara, I never saw anything as beautiful as you in all my life."

Clara's eyes snapped back at him but she didn't say a word.

Well, it was noon the next day before Matt pulled out of town, and sure enough, he forgot his umbrella and came back that night. I went up to The Red Lantern for my five o'clock usual, and him and Maudie were tête à tête, as they say, across the bar. Maudie was spouting the praises of her Clara—how she could sew and cook and bake a cherry pie, Billy Boy. The only attention she paid me was as a collaborating witness.

I'll say this for Clara: when she did appear, she looked almost civilized, her hair in a ribbon, and her wearing a new striped skirt and a grandmother blouse clear up to her chin. That night, by glory, she went to the movie with Matt. We had movies every night except Sundays in those days. A year or so ago, they closed up the Bellevue altogether. Why did she go with him? My guess is she wanted to get away from Maudie, or maybe for Reuben to see her dressed up that way.

The next time I saw all of them together was Decoration Day. Matt was back in town, arranging his route so's he'd have to stop over the holiday in Webbtown. One of them carnival outfits had set up on the grounds back of the schoolhouse. Like I said before, we don't have any population to speak of in Webbtown, but we're central for the whole valley, and in the old days traveling entertainers could do all right if they didn't come too often.

There was all sorts of raffle booths—Indian blankets and

kewpie dolls, a shooting gallery and one of those things where you throw baseballs at wooden bottles and get a cane if you knock 'em off. And there was an apparatus for testing a man's muscle: you know, you hit the target on the stand with a sledgehammer and then a little ball runs up a track that looks like a big thermometer and registers your strength in pounds.

I knew there was a trick to it no matter what the barker said about it being fair and square. Besides, nobody cares how strong a lawyer is as long as he can whisper in the judge's ear. I could see old Maudie itching herself to have a swing at it, but she wasn't taking any chance of giving Matt the wrong impression about either of the McCracken girls.

Matt took off his coat, folded it, and gave it to Clara to hold. It was a warm day for that time of year and you could see where Matt had been sweating under the coat, but like I said, he was all gentleman. He even turned his back to the ladies before spitting on his hands. It took Matt three swings—twenty-five cents worth—but on the last one that little ball crawled the last few inches up the track and just sort of tinkled the bell at the top. The womenfolk clapped, and Matt put on his coat again, blushing and pleased with himself.

I suppose you've guessed that Reuben showed up then. He did, wearing a cotton shirt open halfway down to his belly.

"Now, my boy," the barker says, "show the ladies, show the world that you're a man! How many?"

Reuben sniggled a coin out of his watch pocket, and mighty cocky for him, he said, "Keep the change."

Well, you've guessed the next part, too: Reuben took one swing and you could hear that gong ring out clear across the valley. It brought a lot of people running and the carnival man was so pleased he took out a big cigar and gave it to Reuben. "That, young fellow, wins you a fifty-cent Havana. But I'll send you the bill if you broke the ma-chine, ha! ha!"

Reuben grinned and took the cigar, and strutting across to Clara, he made her a present of it. Now in Matt's book, you didn't give a lady a cigar, no, sir. Not saying a word, Matt brought his fist up with everything he had dead to center under Reuben's chin. We were all of us plain stunned, but nobody more than Reuben. He lay on the ground with his eyes rolling round in his head like marbles.

You'd say that was the blow struck for romance, wouldn't you? Not if you knew our Clara. She plopped down beside

Reuben like he was the dying gladiator, or maybe just something she'd come on helpless in the woods. It was Maudie who clucked and crowed over Matt. All of a sudden Clara leaped up—Reuben was coming round by then—and she gave a whisk of that fancy skirt and took off for the hills, Maudie bawling after her like a hogcaller. And at that point, Reuben scrambled to his feet and galloped after Clara. It wasn't long till all you could see of where they'd gone was a little whiff of dust at the edge of the dogwood grove. I picked up the cigar and tried to smoke it afterwards. I'd have been better off on a mixture of oak leaf and poison ivy.

Everything changed for the worse at The Red Lantern after that. Clara found her tongue and sassed her sister, giving Maudie back word for word, like a common scold. One was getting mean and the other meaner. And short of chaining her, Maudie couldn't keep Clara at home any more, not when Clara wanted to go.

Matt kept calling at The Red Lantern regularly, and Maudie kept making excuses for Clara's not being there. The only times I'd go to the inn in those days was when I'd see Matt's car outside. The place would brighten up then, Maudie putting on a show for him. Otherwise, I'd have as soon sat in Prouty's cool room. It was about as cheerful. Even Maudie's beer was turning sour.

Matt was a patient man if anything, and I guess being smitten for the first time at his age he got it worse than most of us would: he'd sit all evening just waiting for a sight of that girl. When we saw he wasn't going to get over it, Prouty and I undertook one day in late summer to give him some advice. What made us think we were authorities, I don't know. I've been living with my fiddle for years and I've already told you what Prouty'd been living with. Anyways, we advised Matt to get himself some hunting clothes—the season was coming round—and to put away that doggone collar and tie of his and get out in the open country where the game was.

Matt tried. Next time he came to Webbtown, as soon as he put in at The Red Lantern, he changed into a plaid wool shirt, brand-new khaki britches, and boots laced up to his knees, and with Prouty and me cheering him on, he headed for the hills. But like Cox's army, or whoever it was, he marched up the hill and marched down again.

But he kept at it. Every week-end he'd show up, change,

and set out, going farther and farther every time. One day, when the wind was coming sharp from the northeast, I heard him calling out up there: "Clara . . . Clara . . ."

I'll tell you, that gave me a cold chill, and I wished to the Almighty that Prouty and I had minded our own business. Maudie would stand at the tavern door and watch him off, and I wondered how long it was going to take for her to go with him. By then, I'd lost whatever feeling I ever had for Maudie and I didn't have much left for Clara either. But what made me plain sick one day was Maudie confiding in me that she was thinking of locking Clara in her room and giving Matt the key. I said something mighty close to obscene such as I'd never said to a woman before in my life and walked out of the tavern.

It was one of those October days, you know, when the clouds keep building up like suds and then just seem to wash away. You could hear the school bell echo, and way off the hawking of the wild geese, and you'd know the only sound of birds till spring would be the lonesome cawing of the crows. I was working on a couple of things I had coming up in Quarter Sessions Court when Prouty pounded up my stairs. Prouty's a pretty dignified man who seldom runs.

"Hank," he said, "I just seen Matt Sawyer going up the hill. He's carrying old man McCracken's shotgun."

I laughed kind of, seeing the picture in my mind. "What do you think he aims to do with it?"

"If he was to fire it, Hank, he'd be likely to blow himself to eternity."

"Maybe the poor buzzard'd be as well off," I said.

"And something else, Hank—Maudie just closed up the tavern. She's stalking him into the hills."

"That's something else," I said, and reached for my pipe.

"What are we going to do?" Prouty fumbled through his pockets for some matches for me. He couldn't keep his hands still.

"Nothing," I said. "The less people in them hills right now the better."

Prouty came to see it my way, but neither one of us could do much work that afternoon. I'd go to the window every few minutes and see Prouty standing in the doorway. He'd look down toward The Red Lantern and shake his head, and I'd know Maudie hadn't come back yet.

Funny, how things go on just the same in a town at a time like that. Tom Kincaid, the druggist, came out and swept the sidewalk clean, passed the time of day with Prouty, and went inside again. The kids were coming home from school. Pretty soon they were all indoors doing their homework before chore time. Doc Sissler stopped at Kincaid's—he liked to supervise the making up of his prescriptions. It was Miss Dorman, the schoolteacher, who gave the first alarm. She always did her next day's lessons before going home, so it was maybe an hour after school let out. I heard her scream and ran to the window.

There was Matt coming down the street on Prouty's side, trailing the gun behind him. You could see he was saying something to himself or just out loud. I opened my window and shouted down to him. He came on then across the street. His step on the stair was like the drum in a death march. When he got to my doorway he just stood there, saying, "I killed her, Hank. I killed her dead."

I got him into a chair and splashed some whiskey out for him. He dropped the gun on the floor beside him and I let it lie there, stepping over it. By then Prouty had come upstairs, and by the time we got the whiskey inside Matt, Luke Weber, the constable, was there.

"He says he killed somebody," I told Weber. "I don't know who."

Matt rolled his eyes towards me like I'd betrayed him just saying what he told me. His face was hanging limp and white as a strung goose. "I know Matt Sawyer," I added then, "and if there was any killing, I'd swear before Jehovah it must've been an accident."

That put a little life back in him. "It was," he said, "it was truly." And bit by piece we got the story out of him.

"I got to say in fairness to myself, taking the gun up there wasn't my own idea," he started. "Look at me, duded up like this—I had no business from the start pretending I was something I wasn't."

"That was me and Hank's fault," Prouty said, mostly to the constable, "advising him on how to court Miss Clara."

He didn't have to explain that to Weber. Everybody in town knew it.

"I'm not blaming either one of you," Matt said. "It should've been enough for me, chasing an echo every time I thought I'd found her. And both of them once sitting up in a tree laughing at me fit to bust and pelting me with acorns . . ."

We knew he was talking about Reuben and Clara. It was pathetic listening to a man tell that kind of story on himself, and I couldn't help but think what kind of an impression it was going to make on a jury. I had to be realistic about it: there's some people up here would hang a man for making a fool of himself where they'd let him go for murder. I put the jury business straight out of my mind and kept hoping it was clear-cut accident. He hadn't said yet who was dead, but I thought I knew by then.

"Well, I found them for myself today," he made himself go on, "Clara and Reuben, that is. They were cosied in together in the sheepcote back of Maudie's well. It made me feel ashamed just being there and I was set to sneak away and give the whole thing up for good. But Maudie came up on me and took me by surprise. She held me there—by the scruff of the soul, you might say—and made me listen with her to them giggling and carrying on. I was plain sick with jealousy, I'll admit that.

"Then Maudie gave a shout: 'Come out, you two! Or else we'll blow you out!' Something like that.

"It was a minute or two: nothing happened. Then we saw Reuben going full speed the other way, off towards the woods.

" 'Shoot, Matt, now!' That's what Maudie shouted at me. 'You got him clear to sight.' But just then Clara sauntered out of the shelter towards us—just as innocent and sweet, like the first time I ever laid eyes on her."

I'm going to tell you, Prouty and me looked at each other when he said that.

The constable interrupted him and asked his question straight: "Did she have her clothes on?"

"All but her shoes. She was barefoot and I don't consider that unbecoming in a country girl."

"Go on," Weber told him.

Matt took a long drag of air and then plunged ahead. "Maudie kept hollering at the boy—insults, I guess—I know I'd have been insulted. Then he stopped running and turned around and started coming back. I forget what it was she said to me then—something about my manhood. But she kept saying, 'Shoot, Matt! Shoot, shoot!' I was getting desperate, her hounding me that way. I slammed the gun down between us, butt-end on the ground. The muzzle of it, I guess, was looking her way. And it went off.

"It was like the ground exploding underneath us. Hell smoke and brimstone—that's what went through my mind. I don't know whether it was in my imagination—my ears weren't hearing proper after all that noise—but like ringing in my head I could hear Clara laughing, just laughing like hysterics . . . And then when I could see, there was Maudie lying on the ground. I couldn't even find her face for all that was left of her head."

We stood all of us for a while after that. Listening to the tick of my alarm clock on the shelf over the washstand, I was. Weber picked up the gun then and took it over to the window where he examined the breech.

Then he said, "What did you think you were going to do with this when you took it from the tavern?"

Matt shook his head. "I don't know. When Maudie gave it to me, I thought it looked pretty good on me in the mirror."

I couldn't wait to hear the prosecutor try that one on the jury.

Weber said, "We better get on up there before dark and you show us how it happened."

We stopped by at Prouty's on the way and picked up his wicker basket. There wasn't any way of driving beyond the dogwood grove. People were following us by then. Weber sent them back to town and deputized two or three among them to be sure they kept the peace.

We hadn't got very far beyond the grove, the four of us, just walking, climbing up, and saying nothing. Hearing the crows a-screaming not far ahead gave me a crawling stomach. They're scavengers, you know.

Well, sir, down the hill fair-to-flying, her hair streaming out in the wind, came Clara to meet us. She never hesitated, throwing herself straight at Matt. It was instinct made him put his arms out to catch her and she dove into them and flung her own arms around his neck, hugging him and holding him, and saying things like, "Darling Matt . . . wonderful Matt. I love Matt." I heard her say that.

You'd have thought to see Matt, he'd turned to stone. Weber was staring at them, a mighty puzzled look on his face.

"Miss Clara," I said, "behave yourself."

She looked at me—I swear she was smiling—and said, "You hush, old Hank, or we won't let you play the fiddle at our wedding."

It was Prouty said, hoisting his basket up on his shoulders, "Let's take one thing at a time."

That got us started on our way again, Clara skipping along at Matt's side, trying to catch his hand. Luke Weber didn't say a word.

I'm not going into the details now of what we saw. It was just about like Matt had told it in my office. I was sick a couple of times. I don't think Matt had anything left in him to be sick with. When it came to telling what had happened first, Clara was called on to corroborate. And Weber asked her, "Where's Reuben now, Miss Clara?"

"Gone," she said, "and I don't care."

"Didn't care much about your sister either, did you?" Weber drawled, and I began to see how really bad a spot old Matt was in. There was no accounting Clara's change of heart about him—except he'd killed her sister. The corroborating witness we needed right then was Reuben White.

Prouty got Weber's go-ahead on the job he had to do. I couldn't help him though I tried. What I did when he asked it, was go up to Maudie's well to draw him a pail of water so's he could wash his hands when he was done. Well, sir, I'd have been better off helping him direct. I couldn't get the bucket down to where it would draw the water.

After trying a couple of times, I called out to Weber asking if he had a flashlight. He brought it and threw the beam of light down into the well. Just above the water level a pair of size-twelve shoes were staring up at us—the soles of them like Orphan Annie's eyes.

There wasn't any doubt in our minds that what was holding them up like that was Reuben White, headfirst in the well.

The constable called Clara to him and took a short-cut in his questioning.

"How'd it happen, girl?"

"I guess I pushed him," Clara said, almost casual.

"It took a heap of pushing," Weber said.

"No, it didn't. I just got him to look down and then I tumbled him in."

"Why?"

"Matt," she said, and smiled like a Christmas cherub.

Matt groaned, and I did too inside.

"Leastways, it come to that," Clara explained. Then in that quick-changing way of hers, she turned deep serious. "Weber, you wouldn't believe me if I told you what Reuben White wanted me to do with him—in the sheepcote this afternoon."

"I might," Luke Weber said.

I looked at Prouty and drew my first half-easy breath. I could see he felt the same. We're both old-fashioned enough to take warmly to a girl's defending her virtue.

But Weber didn't bat an eye. "And where does Matt here come in on it?" he said.

"I figure he won't ever want me to do a thing like that," Clara said, and gazed up at old stoneface with a look of pure adoration.

"Where was Matt when you . . . tumbled Reuben in?" Weber asked, and I could tell he was well on his way to believing her.

"He'd gone down the hill to tell you what'd happened to Sister Maudie."

"And when was it Reuben made this—this proposal to you?" Weber said. I could see he was getting at the question of premeditation. Luke Weber's a pretty fair policeman.

"It was Matt proposed to me," Clara said. "That's why I'm going to marry him. Reuben just wanted . . ."

Weber interrupted. "Why, if he wasn't molesting you just then, and if you'd decided to marry Matt Sawyer, why did you have to kill him? You must've known a well's no place for diving."

Clara shrugged her pretty shoulders. "By then I was feeling kind of sorry for him. He'd have been mighty lonesome after I went to live with Matt."

Well, there isn't much more to tell. We sort of disengaged Matt, you might say. His story of how Maudie died stood up with the coroner, Prouty and I vouching for the kind of man he was. I haven't seen him since.

Clara—she'll be getting out soon, coming home to the hills, and maybe opening up The Red Lantern again. I defended her at the trial, pleading temporary insanity. Nobody was willing to say she was insane exactly. We don't like saying such things about one another up here. But the jury agreed she was a temporary sort of woman. Twenty years to life, she got, with time off for good behavior.

You come around some time next spring. I'll introduce you.

PAT McGERR

Justice Has a High Price

WINNER OF A SECOND PRIZE

The case against Charles Selden was one bad break after another—a case in which everything went wrong. Was there any power on earth that could save him?

Charles Selden was dreaming—one of those oppressive, frustrating nightmares that had lately become so frequent for him—and the scream at first seemed part of the pattern. Then he was awake and realized it was his wife's voice, high-pitched and ear-shattering.

He opened his eyes to see her sitting upright in the adjoining bed, one arm pointing toward the bureau. In the same instant there was an explosion and a flash of fire, and the scream was cut off and she slumped down in the bed.

Moving by instinct, without time for thought or fear, he threw aside the covers and leaped toward the shadowy figure across the room. The gun spoke again. He didn't count the shots, hardly felt the bullet that seared his left shoulder. In seconds he was on the intruder with an impact that knocked the gun from his hand and made it skim across the slick bedroom floor.

There was no contest. The stranger, slightly built and now weaponless, wanted only to escape. Twisting from Selden's grasp, he hurled himself through the ground-floor window by which he had entered. Racing after him, Selden's bare foot collided with the dropped pistol. He picked it up and carried it to the window, but the intruder had vanished into the trees behind the cabin. Clearly visible in the moonlight, the man's footprints marked the light coating of fresh snow.

Snow, Charles noted with a rush of familiar irritation. I

told Helen we were due for bad weather. It was sheer stubborn nonsense to stay on in a summer cottage until snow falls. Then the thought struck him that they would not argue about this, or anything else, again. Helen's been killed and I— His hand went to his shoulder, felt the blood sticky on his pajama collar, and he knew a sudden faintness. Must get help. A doctor. Police. He started for the telephone between the two beds . . .

"Then I must have blacked out." Again and again he was to tell his story—first to the police, later to his lawyer, finally at the trial. "The next thing I remember, I was lying on the floor with my head feeling very fuzzy. I pulled myself up, got to Helen, and she—she wasn't breathing. There was no pulse, and I knew she was dead. I dialed the operator—I guess I couldn't have been very coherent, but she got word to the right people —and then there was nothing to do but wait."

The first policeman listened with a sort of stolid sympathy, asking few questions, making many notes. The only hint of skepticism came when Selden, striving for a description of the man he had grappled with so briefly, suggested, "There are footprints in the snow outside. Won't they give you some idea of his size and help in identification?"

"Not now, there aren't," the officer answered. "It started snowing again about the time your call came through. That's what slowed us getting here. So if there were any prints, they're all filled in."

"Bad luck." Following another thought, Charles missed the significance of the policeman's *if*. "That road up the mountain's hard going when it's wet and slippery."

"And even worse when it's icy, like tonight. We don't usually have summer people here after the end of September. Yours is the only cabin still open."

"I know," Charles said. "The Davises, next door, went home ten days ago. I suppose that prowler, whoever he was, thought the whole area was deserted. A good time to pick up anything valuable that might have been left behind."

"Yeah, I guess that's what he thought," the officer said absently. He looked up as the medical examiner came out of the bedroom. "You finished in there, Doc?"

"All finished. No use trying to get an ambulance up here till daylight."

"I'll leave Murph on duty," the police captain said. "You

be all right here, Mr. Selden? Or would you like to ride into town with us?"

"I'll stay here," Charles answered. "Unless there's some way I can help find the man who did it."

"Leave that to us. If he's still in the woods, we'll have him before morning. If he's gotten farther away—well, it'll take a little longer. Ready to go, Doc?"

"Ready. Don't worry about that shoulder, Mr. Selden." He glanced with professional satisfaction at the dressing he'd applied. "The bullet just grazed the flesh. Lucky for you it wasn't a couple of inches to the right."

Lucky. The word rang strangely in Charles's ears as he watched their car head down the narrow road. Very lucky. Deliberately he kept his thoughts away from the bedroom where a young police sergeant kept watch over Helen's body.

When the captain returned the next day, his inquiry veered quickly away from the subject of the prowler and went on to other matters.

"This is the fourth year you've come here, right, Mr. Selden? Do you always stay on into October?"

"No, we usually leave much earlier. But my wife loves—loved the outdoors. She never got tired of tramping over the hills or fishing the streams. So she was set on staying as long as the good weather lasted." More set on it, he added mentally, because she knew I was dying to get back to the city. Knew that and probably guessed why.

"And you didn't have to hurry back to a job?"

"My job can always wait." Bitterness edged Charles's voice. "It's with the family firm."

"Your family's?"

"No, my wife's."

The questions then grew more pressing, more personal—till Selden finally exploded.

"What the devil are you driving at? My wife's been killed, her murderer's on the loose, and you sit here prying into our private life! Sure, we had arguments. Show me any couple married five years who doesn't. But that's not going to help you find the man who shot her."

"We'll find him," the captain said, "if you'll just be patient. I know this is a bad time for you, Mr. Selden, but we have to cover all the angles."

So Charles went on answering questions whose relevance he didn't understand until the interview was interrupted by the arrival of Helen's brother. They exchanged awkward condolences, discussed the necessary funeral arrangements. Charles had never been at ease with Arthur and if there was now an additional restraint, it seemed sufficiently explained by the circumstances.

But Charles still had no sense of his own jeopardy. Awareness began only when he read the evening paper. His story of the prowler with a gun was hedged throughout with doubting phrases—"Selden said," "Selden claimed," "according to Selden."

"My God!" He spoke aloud to the empty room. "They make it sound as if I'd invented the whole thing, as if there were no burglar, as if—oh, my God!"

But his panic quickly faded, snuffed out by his knowledge that there had indeed been a burglar. They'll find him, he thought, and that will be the end of it. Or even if the search fails, there must be plenty of evidence that the man was here. They have his gun—it can surely be traced. He probably left fingerprints. One way or another, there will be a dozen proofs of his existence.

Charles's confidence held through more interrogations and up to the time, right after Helen's burial, when he was arrested. He sat, stunned with disbelief, in a sparsely furnished jail cell, charged with the murder of his wife.

It was impossible, incredible, a new nightmare from which he must soon awaken. But it did not take on full reality until he sat across a table from the lawyer sent by his brother-in-law. From him came a crushing bit of news. The gun dropped by the intruder had been checked: it belonged to the owner of the cabin next door.

"Len Davis?" Charles asked, puzzled. "That doesn't make sense."

"The lock on the Davis' back door was broken. The rooms were disordered. Mr. Davis says he kept the gun in a desk drawer."

"Then the fellow must have gone in there before he came to our place." Charles's spirits lifted. "That adds up, doesn't it? Proves there was a stranger in the area, even if the police haven't been able to round him up. So why are they holding me?"

"They have a different theory," the lawyer answered. "Davis told them you knew about the gun."

"Sure I knew about it. Most of the summer he was only able to get out of town on week-ends and his wife was a little nervous about being up there alone. He got the gun for her protection. He even set up a target on one of the trees where she could practice. But what's that got to do with— No! Are they saying I broke into the Davis place and stole his gun and tried to make it look like— But that's crazy!"

"We have to face facts," the lawyer said. "The Davises left two weeks ago. That left you alone on the hilltop, free to plan and do whatever you chose in complete privacy. That's how it looks to the police."

"Facts, hell! I'll tell you how it looks to the police. They've a killing to solve and the killer's disappeared. What they want is a sitting duck—a nice neat solution worked out without leaving their armchairs. They've called off the hunt now, haven't they? They can save themselves a lot of trouble by simply pinning it on me."

"I'm sure the search is still on. But the chances of finding the man get less with each day that passes."

"No fingerprints, I suppose?"

"No. Presumably he wore gloves."

"One bad break after another! No prints—a gun from next door—snow covering his tracks. What else have they got against me?"

"The police have your pajama top with powder burns around the bullet hole. That's a clear indication of a self-inflicted wound. At least, it proves the gun was fired at close range."

"Of course it was fired at close range," Charles snapped. "I was damn near on top of the fellow when the bullet hit me. Everything they have is negative. There's no evidence at all pointing my way."

The case in the newspapers, though, began to appear more positive. Without taking a stand on Charles's guilt or innocence, the stories made it clear that there was only his unsupported word to indicate the existence of a prowler. Even the simple biographical details about him, it seemed to Charles, were slanted toward the worst possible interpretation.

"The jury's obliged to come to court without an opinion." He slammed the paper down in front of the lawyer. "But there won't be an unbiased juror in the state if they keep printing stuff like that."

"We can't stop them," the other returned, "unless they publish something that's not true."

"There are ways of twisting the truth, of making it seem worse than it is." Charles crumpled the sheet into a ball, flung it across the room. "I don't deny that Helen was rich and I was poor. I was a salesman for the Kent Company when I started taking her out and after the wedding I was vice-president. But that isn't why I married her. And even if it had been, it's a long jump from marrying for money to killing for it."

"A very long jump," the lawyer agreed.

"There was something between us in the beginning," Charles went on. "But it didn't last. How could it in that setup? I wasn't cut out to be a gigolo. I had ideas about the company, ways of improving distribution, reorganizing the sales force—but everything I suggested ran into Arthur's veto. He was willing to give me a fancy title, an upholstered office, and a generous drawing account. All he asked in return was that I keep my nose out of the business and make his sister happy. I scored high on the first requirement, but struck out on the second. Helen started drinking too much, and so did I. And sometimes we shouted at each other in public. But I'm sure you've heard all this from Arthur."

"He filled in some of the background, yes."

"There are plenty of witnesses to the failure of our marriage. They won't help my case, will they?"

"No," the lawyer said, "they won't. But none of that will matter if the real killer is found. And I've some good news for you there. Mr. Kent has engaged a private investigator to supplement the police search."

"That's decent of Arthur—and a little surprising. The way we've gotten along the last few years, I'd have expected him to dance at my hanging. I don't like taking favors from him either, but as things stand I don't have much choice. Justice has a high price tag. And I don't suppose there's much chance of my using any of Helen's money till I get out of here."

"No chance at all," the lawyer said. "So long as you're charged with her murder, you can't be her heir."

"Funny thing, once I'm acquitted, everything Helen owned will belong to me, including her half of the Kent Company. But if I should be convicted, it would all go to

Arthur. Under the circumstances, I wonder if I'm being smart to let him pick my lawyer."

"Our firm has represented the Kent family for many years, Mr. Selden," the other said stiffly. "But of course if you feel that someone else could—"

"No offense," Charles said. "The thought just struck me. Arthur isn't going to like having me for a partner. But I don't really believe he'd try to frame me for murder. Not unless he thinks I did it. That's a possibility too."

"Mr. Kent is convinced of your innocence," the lawyer said. "We discussed the matter thoroughly before I accepted the case. As you say, he does not have a very high regard for you. But he has known you for a long time and he doesn't believe you capable of premeditated murder."

"Lack of brains?" Charles asked. "Or lack of guts?"

"I don't pretend—" The lawyer then ignored the question. "He is chiefly motivated by concern for your welfare. Most of all, he wants his sister's murderer captured and brought to justice. He would also like to avoid the scandal that would inevitably result from your trial and conviction."

"That's a typically Arthurian motive," Charles said. "It's no disgrace to be shot by a stranger, but a murder within the family is a permanent blot. I'll concede that hard as it must be for him, Arthur's on my side. But what if the picture changes? If the evidence gets blacker against me, he may change his mind."

"Do you know of such evidence, Mr. Selden?"

"There's no evidence," Charles said firmly, "to support this charge of murder. Anything the police turn up has to confirm my story, help prove there was a robber in the house that night and that he shot Helen. But there are other facts—facts unrelated to the shooting—that might tip the scales for Arthur. Then what becomes of my defense?"

"Mr. Kent is paying my fee, Mr. Selden, but you are my client. My obligation to defend you is not subject to outside influences. I hope I may have your full confidence."

"I'm sure you'll do your best," Charles answered with perfunctory politeness.

He did not, even then, believe that the quality of his defense was of real importance. To cooperate with the attorney, to answer his questions, to go through the motions of preparing for the trial—this was a routine that must be followed until the burglar was found. If Charles's hopes had temporarily sagged in the bleak atmosphere of the jail, they were freshly buoyed by the knowledge that a private investigator had entered the case. Today, tomorrow—it was only a matter of time till the criminal was taken. Then Charles would be free.

But the private search was no more fruitful than the official.

Time ran out and suddenly it was the day of the trial. Charles was swept by a near numbness as he sat in court, his attorney by his side, the prosecution staff across the aisle. He looked up at the judge, over to the jury box, back to the crowded spectators' section.

It was like an old movie into which he had suddenly been thrust as the leading actor. It can't be happening, his mind throbbed the refrain. It can't be happening to me. Memory swerved back to the beginning, to that moment of sudden awakening, to the sight of the stranger in the bedroom, to the roar and flash of the intruder's gun.

It will be all right, Charles told himself as he fought his mounting tension. I'll tell my story to the jury and they'll believe me—they'll *have* to believe me. Yet he had told that story to the police and they had arrested him for murder; he'd told it to the press and their reports had insinuated his guilt.

"That man!" His control failed and he reached out to clutch his lawyer's arm. "Why can't they find him? They've got to find the man!"

They didn't find the man, but they found the woman.

On the third day after the jury was chosen, Diane took the stand as the prosecution's star witness and Charles watched his hopes dwindle to near zero.

She testified reluctantly, but the reluctance sprang from concern for her own reputation, not for his life. Once he caught her eye and she turned quickly away, but not before her glance had told him that she, like everyone else, believed he had killed his wife, believed he had done it for her—and feared and despised him for it. Yet looking at her in this courtroom he felt again the obsessive desire that had for so many months ruled his life.

Question by question, the prosecutor dragged from her the damning facts about their relationship. Her admission that she had been his mistress came in a voice that was barely audible, but Charles knew how loudly it must have sounded in the ears of the jurors.

"Did you have reason to believe," the questioning continued, "that the defendant intended to marry you?"

"Oh, yes." To this she could speak more firmly. "From the first he promised to get a divorce so that we could be married. He said it would take a little time to arrange, that I'd have to be patient. If I hadn't believed that, I would never have had anything to do with him."

"And when you found out that he wasn't going ahead with the divorce?"

"Then I told him that it had to be all over between us, that I wouldn't see him again, not ever."

The truth, Charles thought, but not the whole truth. That version left her with some shreds of respectability and he wouldn't strip them from her—wouldn't and couldn't, since to do so would establish even more strongly his reason for wishing his wife dead. He had a vivid recollection of that scene in Diane's apartment when she had at last forced a showdown.

"I'm not going on like this any longer, Charles." Her petulant little-girl voice had had an undertone of steel. "You still haven't said one word to your wife about a divorce and I don't believe you're ever going to. Are you, Charles?"

"It's not something to rush into, Diane." He had moved across the room to run his fingers through the soft fur of the scarf she had tossed on a chair. "Give me time."

"Time!" she had snapped. "For weeks and weeks you've made promises and done nothing. Does it take so much time to sit down with your wife and tell her you're through?"

"That could be done very quickly," he'd admitted. "What takes time is the financial settlement."

"Financial? You mean she'll hold you up for a lot of alimony?"

"Alimony?" He'd stared at her, startled. "Are you serious, Diane? Don't you understand how things are with me?"

"What is there to understand? You have plenty of money—haven't you?"

"I don't have a dime. All I have is a high-sounding job that I got by marrying the boss' sister." He'd found a grim satisfaction in pressing it home. "You were my secretary for three weeks. I thought my situation was the talk of the company."

"Nobody said a word. Somebody should have warned me. *You* should have told me."

"I'm telling you now." He'd picked up the fur, waved it at her. "My wife's money paid for this. My wife's money pays for everything. And the day she agrees to a divorce, I'll be out on the street."

"You lied to me," she had said furiously. "You let me think you were rich and that we could be married. And all the time you were making a fool of me."

"That isn't what I had in mind." He'd gone back to the couch, put his hands on her shoulders, tried to pull her toward him. "Is that all it ever was, Diane? Just money? Haven't you any—"

"Don't touch me." She had given him a hard push. "Liar! Fourflusher!"

"Diane, please—"

"Get out!" She had sprung up, run to open the door to the hall. "Get out and don't come back. I never want to see you again, not ever."

It was that evening, in the finality of Diane's anger, that he agreed to go with Helen to the mountain cabin. But as the weeks passed he persuaded himself that the girl's decision was less than final, and he began to make allowances for her. Her rage, her disappointment were understandable. He had broken the news to her too abruptly. Naturally she felt herself deceived, ill-used. It wasn't true that she cared only for his money, and nothing for him. She had struck out only to hurt him.

He wrote her then and received no answer, and knew a growing anxiety to return to the city. He was sure that Helen sensed this and that it lay behind her insistence that they extend their stay in the cabin. Now in the courtroom he watched with horror as his letter to Diane was introduced as evidence.

What had he said? Desperately he tried to recall the phrases. I love you, I miss you, I need you. Certainly he had said that. But what more? "I promise you, my darling, that I will very soon make arrangements so that we can be together.

Nothing else matters." He had written that and had meant simply the firm resolution to find a job, any job outside the Kent Company, so that he could divorce Helen and marry Diane. But read aloud here, with the prosecutor's special emphasis, the "arrangements" translated to coldly calculated murder.

Watching Diane leave the stand, he felt for the first time a sense of total hopelessness. To anyone who saw her as he did, she must supply a full and compelling motive. To the others—to the virtuous, to the women on the jury—he was branded an adulterer. What matter if they found "reasonable doubt" of his guilt of the lesser crime? There could be no doubt that this girl was both desirable and expensive. To keep her he had to rid himself of his wife and retain his wife's money. What else could the jury believe?

This blanket of despair covered him through the rest of the trial. When it was his turn on the stand, he told his story with a robot-like precision which he knew, without being able to do anything about it, must rob it of all conviction. The cross-examination was heavy with sarcasm. Taking him through the whole tale again, the prosecutor began almost every question with the phrase, "You ask us to believe," in a way that drove a wide gap between each detail and human credibility.

"You ask us to believe, Mr. Selden—" the fortieth repetition grated on all his nerve ends "—that this unknown man who was an expert marksman when he was aiming at your wife turned into a rank amateur when you were the target."

"I don't know what kind of a marksman he was."

"Then let me refresh your memory. There were three bullets fired. One killed your wife. One was found by the police in the wall between the beds. One scraped your shoulder. So you ask us to believe that this alleged prowler was able to send a bullet directly through your wife's heart and then missed you entirely at the same distance."

"I was moving when he shot at me."

"Ah, yes, you were moving. So his first shot went wild and he shot again. And you ask us to believe that this mysterious stranger, firing at a moving target, placed his next bullet in a spot where it could draw a little blood, leave a small wound for the police to see, but do you no lasting damage. Do you really expect anyone to *believe* that?"

"It's the truth," Charles said doggedly. "It's the way it happened."

"The truth is what we're seeking," the prosecutor assured him. "But I think we can come a little closer to it than you have so far. I suggest that after you killed your wife, you fired another bullet into the wall and then shot yourself in the shoulder to support your story of a prowler in the night."

"I didn't shoot myself," Charles said. "There was a prowler. That is the exact truth . . ."

By the time his testimony ended he felt a deadly certainty that, in the minds of judge, jury, and spectators, the prowler was a phantom, a man who never existed and could never be found. Almost with impatience he sat through his counsel's closing argument, seeing the weakness of his defense, its total dependence on his own word—in which no one now believed.

The prosecution's closing argument was circumstantial and convincing. If he was talking about someone else, Charles thought, I'd believe him—believe that this man, driven by desire, must have plotted the murder of his wife, broken into his neighbor's empty cabin to steal the gun he knew was there, and then, at his own convenience in the middle of the night, used it to kill his wife.

"But what a fool that makes me," he protested to his lawyer while they waited for the verdict. "I might have done all the things he said, but I'd know I couldn't get away with it, that I was putting my neck in a noose. To invent a robber who didn't exist would be too transparent, too stupid. But he did exist, he does exist, and somebody's got to find him."

"We're trying," the lawyer said. "We'll keep on trying."

The verdict was swift in coming and held no surprises. Guilty of murder in the first degree.

"We'll appeal, of course," the lawyer said. "And I've persuaded Mr. Kent to offer a substantial reward for information leading to the real murderer. We're not finished."

Oh, yes, I'm finished, Charles thought. I'm through clinging to slim hopes. It's easier to face the worst and just drift toward the end. He took for granted the denial of his appeal, listened stoically to the pronouncement of the death sentence, and expected no more from Arthur's offer of a reward than the usual lineup of crackpots.

So complete was his resignation that when his lawyer, ten

days before the date set for the execution, brought him a fresh strand of hope, Charles almost refused to accept it.

"I know we've had a string of cranks who were only after the money or the publicity," the lawyer admitted. "It's the reward that brought this man forward, too, and he's not a very savory character, but his story checks out. He was driving on the main highway that links with the road to your cabin about 3:00 A.M. on the night of the murder. The police got your call at 3:10. Assuming it took the killer half an hour to get down the mountain, that would allow less than an hour from the time he was in your house till you put in the call. That time fits pretty well, doesn't it?"

"I guess so. I wasn't watching the clock."

"This man's story is that a young chap hailed him and he stopped to pick him up. Said he looked about twenty or twenty-one, not tall, skinny, wearing jeans and a leather jacket. That matches your description, as much as you could give us."

"He was smaller than I," Charles agreed. "I remember at the time thinking that was good luck."

"Our witness says the young man was very nervous, talked about having to get out of town in a hurry. He also told us there was a long scratch down the left side of his face that looked as if it might have been made by a fingernail."

"A scratch? Yes, of course!" For the first time Charles felt a renewal of life. Remember carefully now, he told himself. Remember how it was. He had dived at the stranger, his fingers had clutched at his face. "I could have scratched him. I must have scratched him. And it was with my right hand, the side where I hadn't been shot, so it would be his left cheek. Your man's telling the truth. He saw the prowler, gave him a ride, he can prove my story. Oh, my God, it's going to be all right!"

"I think so," the lawyer said more temperately. "I think this is the link we need."

Charles had a week of soaring spirits. Their thudding drop on the seventh day was almost unendurable. The judge had appraised the new evidence, and decided it did not justify a new trial; the governor had also been unmoved by it.

"But that's impossible," Charles cried. "We've an eyewitness who backs up my story. They've *got* to believe him! Why would he lie to help me?"

"For the reward," the lawyer answered. "Unfortunately, our witness has a very bad record. He's served two terms for receiving stolen property, and been convicted once of perjury. The way the judge and governor see it, he'd swear to anything for a thousand dollars. Even if he had come forward before the trial, I don't think he'd have been much help to your case."

"But he *saw* the man," Charles insisted. "At least, he can furnish a lead on where he went."

"He dropped him at the railroad station. Nobody there remembers seeing him, which isn't surprising. He could have taken a train in either direction. Or he could have walked a few blocks to the bus depot and left town that way. There just aren't any more leads—not a single one."

"No," Charles said dully, "I guess I shouldn't have expected anything. But wouldn't you have thought that when a witness did turn up, he'd be a man whose word was worth something? Everything has gone wrong. I haven't had one good break, not one."

From then on it was a matter of marking time, of waiting for it to be over.

Constantly his mind went back to the beginning when it had all appeared so simple and so safe. He'd been standing at the window looking at the footprints in the snow, getting used to the idea of his wife's death. He'd turned back into the room and taken a few steps toward the phone.

"Is he gone?" Helen's voice had cut sharply through the dark. "Did you let him get away?"

"Yes, he's gone. I thought he'd killed you."

"I must have ducked just as he fired. It was close—but not close enough." She reached out to click on the bedside lamp. In its glow her smile taunted him. "Disappointed? Were you already counting your chickens, the ones you and that little tart could hatch? If only he'd been a better marksman, it would have made it so easy for you."

"Yes," he'd agreed quietly, "it would have made it so easy."

Somewhere out there, he'd thought, is a man who brought this gun here and fired it at Helen. When they find him and tell him she's dead, he won't be able to deny he killed her.

Slowly Charles had raised the gun and taken careful aim. He had watched her expression change from mockery to unbelief to fear. Then, as a scream formed on her lips, he had pulled the trigger.

MARGARET AUSTIN

Introducing Ellery's Mom

Mom's First Two Cases

WINNER OF A SECOND PRIZE

Well, we've had other "Mom" stories in the pages of EQMM (notably James Yaffe's). But here is a new "Mom"—and what a welcome addition she is to our gallery of family portraits! The first part of Mrs. Austin's story is charming, and the second part, you will discover, grows firmer and more substantial as it goes along—altogether an auspicious beginning for a new series.

Mom is a good sort, short and kind of pudgy—what Dad calls "a comfortable armful"—and looks like she might belong to the Garden Club, which she does. I guess it's 'cause we've known her all our lives that we don't think of her as Katherine Sanders MacKay, with her name on as many mystery book jackets as Agatha Christie's.

To Dad she's just "Kate," and to us five kids, "Mom." To the town busybodies for a good many years she was "that woman who neglects those poor kids, my, I don't know how the doctor stands it!" Only Mom didn't look at it that way. She said making our own peanut butter sandwiches taught us self-reliance and independence and that after being around disinfected neatness all day, it relaxed Dad to come home to a place that was lived-in.

As for Dad, I think he liked Mom being a writer. When he was called out at night, she'd get up and beat out a few hundred words, then when he got home they'd drink coffee and discuss their respective cases.

Anyway, we grew up with Father Brown, Arsène Lupin, and Hercule Poirot the way most kids grow up with Joe Di

Maggio, Yogi Berra, and Mickey Mantle. We knew about aconite, the poison, long before we saw aconite, the flower. And not one of us would have eaten a castor bean more willingly than we swallowed castor oil.

'Course, sometimes I think Mom carried this murder business too far. It's convenient for a mystery writer to have a doctor on tap but it kind of rocked Dad to have her ask, right in the middle of serving scrambled eggs, "Where would you knife a person to have instantaneous death and very little blood?" or have her suddenly come out of a reverie with "I think I'll freeze him to death." What I mean is, it isn't normal conversation.

Then, too, there were the names. She was still getting printed rejection slips when Nicholas (Nick) Charles was born, followed a year later by Hildegarde, both now in college. I was next, then came Ngaio, then Perry, the baby, though he's in second grade now. He got named that by default; Dad tromped on Mom's first suggestions—said the kid would have enough burdens in this vale of tears without bearing "Sherlock," "Philo," or "Nero," which were Mom's first choices.

Me, I'm Ellery, though mostly everyone says "Ray," me not being the Ellery type.

By the time Perry came along, Mom was well known to the lending libraries. MURDER IN THE MATERNITY WARD came out soon after and the TV sale and reprint checks started piling up, so she hired a housekeeper and Perry never got to learn self-reliance and independence.

Anyway, by the day James Griggs, the chemistry teacher, died, Mom was something of a celebrity around Maplecrest, where we live.

Once I asked Mom if she couldn't get more inspiration living in a city where more exciting things happened than in Maplecrest, which took a sleeping pill sometime in the 1880s.

"My goodness, no!" she replied. "What you need for inspiration is not excitement—it's character. City dwellers don't know five people as well as I know most of the population here. I just ask myself what Ross Hammond would do if his wife started chasing around, and pretty soon I have a story."

We were close enough to New York so she could go in three or four times a year for research and editorial conferences, yet far enough to keep the would-be commuters from moving out to Maplecrest. Most of the houses in town were old and big and comfortable and most of them had a History, which is why they built the new High School of colonial brick, even though it's low and sprawling and completely modern inside.

Which brings me back to the day Mr. Griggs, the chemistry teacher, died and why I needed to talk to Mom.

Since I'd been at baseball tryouts after school, the halls were deserted when I went to my locker. First, there's the West entrance, which goes out to the parking lot, then the chemistry lab, chemistry classroom, and another classroom, then the bank of lockers where I was assigned—so that I had a position in the dugout, so to say, for what happened.

It started when Miss Dean came out of the chem lab. She turned at the door and trilled, "I'll see you tomorrow night at eight, then?" She listened briefly to someone inside the lab and continued, "No, I'm sure he doesn't suspect anything—it would be terrible if he did!"

She clicked briskly down the hall, stuffing a bright card into an envelope as she came. I wished I could have shrunk into the locker or gone into orbit or something, but I just stood there and said, "Hello, Miss Dean," real original-like.

Sure, it startled her, but she recovered quickly, threw me a brief wave, and clicked on. I was shook up enough to dump everything off the locker shelf trying to dig out the U. S. History book, so I said a few short pithy words—not from one of Mom's books—and scooped up a year's accumulation of junk. What with that and getting on the jacket and cap Mom always insisted on my wearing, even if the weather was spring-balmy, it must have been five minutes before I heard Mr. Griggs scream. Men usually yell but this was a scream, like in agony, along with a great thumping and crashing of glass—then silence.

Well, naturally, I raced down the hall but even so, I wasn't the first one there. The principal, Mr. Wilson, pelted through the West door and beat me to the lab by a good thirty feet.

"Stay back, stay back, boy!" he yelled, so I parked in the doorway.

Mr. Wilson was kneeling on the floor in a mess of broken test tubes and crucibles, some of them still leaking unfinished experiments. The principal blocked the view but those were unmistakably Mr. Griggs' long skinny legs. His feet flopped out with one toe pointing to me and the other to the open window across the room. Just looking at those feet, you knew he was dead.

I stood there, peering at the mess until old Smitty, the janitor who's been with the schools for the last century, tapped my shoulder. Then, of course, I moved into the room to let him through.

The principal stood up, pulled a handkerchief from his pocket, and wiped it across his forehead. Now all of Mr. Griggs was exposed. You'd think, with Dad being a doctor and Mom writing about death all the time, that I'd be hardened. But it doesn't look the same in real life as it does in books.

Nobody ever called Mr. Griggs handsome. His eyes kind of bulged, maybe from looking at too many Bunsen burners, his nose hooked under at the end, and his chin slipped toward his Adam's apple. A couple of weeks ago, when Miss Dean started pussyfooting around in quiet corners with him, I sure wondered why.

Sprawled there on the lab floor he was even less appealing. His skin was gray, like rain-soaked paper . . . Well, let's skip the details.

One thing really fascinated me, though. His shirt sleeves were rolled up and on his left forearm, which had fallen across his chest, there was a small red spot. As I watched, the spot grew bigger and redder. Seemed mighty indecent for a spot to do that on a dead man.

"Smitty," Mr. Wilson said, "Clean up this broken stuff before someone is cut. He's dead"—nodding toward Mr. Griggs "—probably his heart, but I'll call Doc Morton." Noticing me, he added like an apology, "His office is right across the street."

"Ray," he went on, almost kindly, "there's nothing we can do. Go on home and try not to think about this."

Well, I can tell when I'm dismissed, so I went outside—but not home. Nossirreebob! I went out to the parking lot, then circled back through the evergreens until I was outside the chem lab window. And was I glad I did! There in the soft earth under the window was a mess of footprints—blurred, like whoever stood there had shuffled around some—but maybe the police could find one clear enough for a cast.

It wasn't long till voices came through the lab window. Coronary attack, all right, Dr. Morton pronounced, and it didn't surprise him one bit, the way Jim Griggs wouldn't listen when he was told to take it easy. More talk, medical stuff, then a discussion of which funeral home to call since the deceased didn't have any relatives in Maplecrest. Dr. Morton said they'd better notify Police Chief Higgins—no business for him but he likes to know what's going on around town.

I got careless and Mr. Wilson spied my red cap above the window sill. A principal has lots of practice reading the riot act to boys—so I blasted off for home and Mom.

The housekeeper said Mom was on the sun porch. 'Course, it's been soundproofed and winterized now for Mom's office, but we still call it the sun porch. Snitching a couple of fresh cookies, I headed that way.

Mom was whittling away at a sheaf of yellow paper, her fat black pencil moving fast and furiously. The editor must of gotten tough about the deadline on MAKE MINE MURDER, the current epic.

"Hello, dear—have a nice day?" The pencil didn't break its flying rhythm.

"Mom, something strange happened this afternoon."

"Don't talk with your mouth full, Ray."

I gulped down the rest of the cookie. "Mr. Griggs died."

"Hmm. That's nice, dear." The pencil still flew.

"Mom," I said loudly, "it might be M-U-R-D-E-R."

That stopped the pencil in mid-flight.

"Ray, there hasn't been a murder in Maplecrest since 1858, when a slave dealer found half the town in the Underground Railroad—and that was more a lynching than murder! Poor dear, you've inherited my imagination, but sit down and tell me all about it."

I told her everything, just the way it had happened.

"But Bob Wilson is engaged to that pretty Clara Dean, isn't he?"

"That's it, Mom! He gave her the ring at Christmas. They're supposed to be married this summer. But for the last couple of weeks she's been sneaking around with Mr. Griggs, and then he dies and Mr. Wilson is right there on the scene!"

"Bob Wilson has always been most cooperative with the

P T A. Hmm. What do you think of him, Ellery?" She's getting serious when she starts calling me Ellery.

"For a principal, he's always seemed like a right guy. He was even pretty decent about it when he lifted my peashooter —" Too late. There I stood with a mouth full of size-ten brogan.

"What's this, young man?"

"Aw, Mom, all the gang has them, like everybody had hula hoops a couple of years ago. There's nothing wrong with 'em—we use paper and it doesn't even sting."

"In the future you will tend to your studies and not to shooting paper wads." She kind of snorted. "At girls, no doubt." With that taken care of, she got back to the case.

"Wish they'd called your father. Old Dr. Morton should have retired years ago—he couldn't tell a heart attack from . . ." Her voice trailed off and she got that spark in her eye, like when she's finally worked out the solution to a locked-room mystery. "Ellery, get your father's MODERN DRUG ENCYCLOPEDIA."

She whipped through the pages until she found what she wanted, then she scribbled a few lines on a sheet of yellow paper and jammed it in her pocket.

"I still don't see . . ." she murmured to herself. "If he came in the West door, the footprints . . ." Then to me, "Were there screens on that window? No—that's it, of course!"

"Got it solved, Mom?" I asked hopefully.

"Absolutely! Identical to THE CASE OF THE ERRANT ANTHROPOLOGIST—stupid of me not to see it immediately. Oh, he was clever and he would have got clean away with it if you hadn't been there. Come on, we're going to talk to Chief Higgins—you can be sure he won't see it!" She added generously, "Of course, he doesn't have all the facts, as I do."

It wasn't as plain to me as it was to her, but rather than be classified with the Chief, I pretended to be with it.

She refused a ride on my bike—this wasn't the time, she said, to arrive at the Town Hall on the crossbar of a bicycle. So we walked—it's only four blocks.

Mom bounced along full of purpose and I trailed her.

Chief Higgins greeted us cheerfully. He and Mom have gotten to know each other pretty well through the years, what with her having to check on police procedure and such.

"Well, Kate MacKay! This is a pleasant surprise! How's the doctor and the rest of the family?"

With the small talk out of the way, Mom brought the business meeting to order: "Chief, I've heard about Jim Griggs' death at the High School this afternoon. Ray was there when it happened and I think between us we might be helpful to you. I don't mean to be poking my nose into your department, but some facts may have been concealed."

"There isn't a police chief in this country who wouldn't be honored to have the assistance of the most skillful mystery authoress writing today."

Wow!—didn't know the old guy had it in him!

Mom sat there, glowing and smoothing her dress over her knees. Then, armed with his compliment, she told what I'd heard and seen.

The Chief pulled out the bottom desk drawer, leaned 'way back in his leather swivel chair, and stuck his big boots on top of the drawer. You could see by the scratches that this was routine.

When Mom finished my part in the case, the Chief looked puzzled and said slowly, "Yes, that's the way it happened, but I don't see what you're drivin' at."

So Mom gave him the rest.

"Well, I didn't see it either, at first. But did you know Clara Dean is engaged to Bob Wilson? And that she's been two-timing him with Jim Griggs recently—Ellery has seen them together several times. That certainly gives Bob Wilson a motive and he was right at the scene. From the footprints outside the window, I believe he was standing there when Griggs started screaming. He could have run from there to the chemistry laboratory much quicker than Ellery could from his locker.

"All that tied together very neatly but it left the question of how he actually committed the murder—the *modus operandi*, Chief. That baffled me until Ellery let slip about the principal's taking a peashooter away from him. There you have it! The natives of Borneo use blowguns with poisoned darts most effectively and at far greater distances than Wilson was from Griggs. Then, when Wilson reached the body he ordered Ellery to stay back *while he removed the dart*—you'll find a puncture on Griggs' left arm, I'm sure—and pocketed it under the pretense of removing his handkerchief.

"Oh, yes," she finished, "an autopsy will probably show that Quinidine was the poison used." She took the slip of yellow paper from her pocket and put it on his desk. "As principal, he could easily unlock the nurse's office at night and take all he needed. If the theft were noticed, it would be reported to him and that would be the end of it—he'd simply 'forget' it. Quinidine gives the reaction and appearance of a heart attack. Another doctor might have been suspicious but, confidentially, you and I both know that Dr. Morton is fighting senility. That is probably why Bob Wilson called him."

No doubt about it, Chief Higgins was jolted. He sat there for a few moments, then carefully took his feet off the drawer, came back to vertical, kicked in the drawer, and put his arms on top of the desk.

"Kate, for a long time now I've been a great admirer of yours. I've read all your books and, frankly, the hero usually figures out the murderer before I do. But this beats anything you ever wrote. It's as logical and tidy, with no loose ends, as any bit of deduction ever was. My hat's off to you."

Mom sat there, flushed and beaming—even more than she did the night the Mystery Writers of America gave her an "Edgar."

"In fact," the Chief continued, "it makes me downright ashamed to tell you that it didn't happen that way at all." Then he added generously, "Of course, you don't have all the facts, like I do.

"First, there wasn't anything between Jim Griggs and Clara Dean—except plans for Bob Wilson's surprise birthday party tomorrow night. The whole faculty were in on it, but those two were getting the present and handling all the details.

"Second, it was Smitty the janitor who made those tracks in the dirt outside the window—while he was washing it. Bob Wilson had forgotten some Merit Scholarship forms and returned for them—Smitty saw him come straight from the parking lot."

Well, Mom was deflating like a busted balloon.

"Third," the Chief went on, "Jim Griggs did have a heart condition—has had it for several years—but he's kept quiet about it because he didn't want the school board to find out. You're right about the puncture on his arm. Made by an early wasp, though—there's your murderer. Griggs crashed around in the lab trying to kill it. The exertion, plus excitement, plus shock from the wasp's sting, set off the heart attack."

Man! Maybe you think we didn't have a funeral march all the way home! Mom really took it hard, and I forgot my own goof, worrying about her.

When we reached the front porch, Mom plunked into the swing. Like our house, it's old-fashioned, hanging by chains from the porch ceiling, and it squeaked and rattled when she sat down.

I dropped on the steps and made like "The Thinker," of which Dad has a pair of bookends in his office.

Dad came home soon, and seeing me sitting there he asked, "Why the gloom?"

"There is no joy in Mudville tonight," I replied.

"What?"

I told him the whole humiliating story and when I got to the poison he started grinning. "She should have called me," he said. "It would take a harpoon to carry a lethal load of Quinidine."

I threw him a look of pain and said how it was going to ruin Mom as a writer—maybe even give her all sorts of complexes—and just about wreck our family life. So he wiped off the grin.

We both looked down to the end of the porch where Mom still sat in the swing.

Her eyes had that over-the-hills-and-far-away glaze they always get when she's plotting a new novel.

"Who do you suppose," she asked dreamily, "knew about Jim Griggs' heart condition and wanted him out of the way badly enough to leave a wasp in the chemistry laboratory?"

Mom's Second Case

Chief of Police Higgins must of called Mom as a peace offering, like a fellow sends candy to his steady when they've had a blow-up. Not, of course, that there was anything like that between the Chief and Mom—they're both married to someone else with kids and homes and all, but they've been friends practically forever.

Anyway, after Mom's big goof, thinking Jim Griggs was murdered when all the time a wasp caused a heart attack, why, I guess the Chief felt bad—like maybe it should of been murder 'cause Mom figured it out so clever. So that's why he phoned Mom when the double deaths happened at Rockwood.

I got home early that afternoon—no baseball practice. Mom was just hanging up, real excited and thoughtful. "Ray, there's been a murder at Rockwood and Chief Higgins has kindly asked if I'd care to ride out there with him. You may come, too, if you'd like."

"A murder! What are they doing—playing ten little Indians?"

"Ray! That will be enough! It's one thing to be facetious about death and violence in my books, but this is not a book and you'll speak with respect. Besides," she continued, simmering down to normal, "Marcia Bancroft's death this morning was an accident, a fall from her horse. This new one is quite different. That nice little Japanese gardener has been strangled. Well, do you want to come?"

Man, did I! Ever since Ambassador Bancroft—they call him that although he's retired—reopened the family home, I'd been working on a reason to see the place. It sure set our town of Maplecrest buzzing, what with the estate closed so many years while he served in one of those Oriental countries with lots of mystery and glamor. Marcia was sent to England to learn ladylike manners and when to say "Tallyho!" Then after he retired, they lived in Japan until some ten months ago when they returned to cultivate his two big interests, horticulture and horses.

Town gossip had it he'd paid a half million for Battle Song, the retired Derby winner—and that was just one of the horses he bought. Seemed nearly every week the lovely Marcia's face beamed out of the local paper, with a horse peeking over her shoulder and her cuddling a silver cup like other girls do a baby. The Bancrofts didn't get into town often but their big red horse-van sailed through frequently. They must of covered the whole Eastern show circuit.

To manage the flower part of his hobbies, the Ambassador brought with him from Japan a gardener named Iso Nakata, and his grandson. Iso, we heard, once worked for the Emperor himself.

Rockwood was about six hundred acres of fancy real estate—Dad said with the taxes it paid, we didn't need a big industrial plant in the county. I wanted to see it like Roger Maris wanted that sixty-first home run!

So Mom told the housekeeper not to hold dinner if we were delayed and when the Chief honked, we piled into the car, Mom up front with him, me in back where I could hang over the seat to listen.

"Who would kill that nice little Mr. Nakata?" Mom asked without even greeting the Chief—not like her at all 'cause she's usually very polite and makes us kids mind our manners, too. "Do you have any clues?"

"Strictly speaking, Kate, it isn't even my case since it's outside the town corporation limits. It's the county sheriff's, but we work together, so he asked me to back him up. He thinks one of the other gardeners might be guilty. They were free of real authority for so long that having a boss again was like a cutworm in the tomato patch—'specially an imported boss who doesn't speak English."

Mom protested. "You couldn't hate such a gentle person as Iso Nakata any more than you could hate flowers. He gave a demonstration of floral arrangements at the garden club last month—he was an Ikebana master, you know—and a sweeter, more polite individual I've never met."

"Thought he couldn't speak English?"

"Oh, he can't, just the crudest pidgin. He did the demonstrations while his grandson, Joe, translated. Joe grew up during the occupation and speaks as well as Ray." She considered. "Better than Ray, in fact."

She quizzed Chief Higgins again. "Do you suppose there's any connection between Marcia's accident this morning and Mr. Nakata's murder this afternoon?"

"Can't see it offhand. I was out there after they found her and it looked authentic. Horse spooked and threw her down a ravine. Banged her head in the fall. That's all there was to it but we'll double-check . . . Downright shame, that accident. Everybody seems to have been fond of her—why, the Ambassador's secretary even needed a sedative. He—"

"He?" Mom interrupted.

"Yes, young chap—Richard Gillespie. I got the impression he might have been sweet on the Bancroft girl. Anyway, this will sure hit the Ambassador hard when he hears about it."

The Chief filled us in on how Joe Nakata had driven into New York early that morning to meet the Ambassador's one p.m. flight from Ireland, where he'd been buying more horses.

They weren't expected back for a couple more hours, longer if the flight was delayed.

Then he quit talking to concentrate on the road. For the past few miles it had been swinging in wide curves and gradually climbing a mountain. 'Course, visitors from the west snort and say they aren't even decent foothills, but they still can be tricky to negotiate. I sure wouldn't of wanted to drive a horse-van down this one.

For a while we paralleled a high stone wall; then, where it humped into stone gates, we turned into Rockwood. The concrete road twisted through open woods with an occasional trail leading off to the side, usually marked *Caution, Bridle Path.*

About a half mile in, the road forked. A rustic sign saying *Rockwood* pointed to the right, and a smaller sign to the left read *Service.*

"Want to see where the accident happened?" the Chief asked, swinging the car down the Service road.

We circled the mountain top and descended to a bridge spanning a deep ravine, where the Chief pulled over. "It's up that trail about a hundred yards."

Well, Mom tumbled out and charged the trail like the hundred yard dash, me and the Chief tagging behind. "Whoa! You're going too far," he called as we rounded a curve and saw Mom still bouncing off in the distance.

It was a good place for an accident, all right. The trail was about six feet wide and must of been blasted right out of the mountain. A straight rocky cliff shot above it on the mountain side, maybe fifteen feet high, then leveled off before climbing gradually up into trees again. The ravine side was a rock-studded drop to a little river about thirty feet below. The low rail guarding the drop wouldn't help a person thrown from a horse.

I mean the goosebumps were making base hits up my spine, just thinking about it, but Mom asked calmly, "How'd they find her, hidden so far from the road?"

"The river bed below is in plain view. Her horse ran back to the stables—they're just beyond that last clump of woods across the ravine—and the stable boys came out looking for her."

"What would frighten the horse?"

"Several things could have—a rabbit, a falling leaf, one of these stones breaking from the cliff."

He indicated the stones lying at the trail's edge. "Who knows what spooks a horse? Often it's only something they think they see."

Right then I got real ashamed of Mom. Here they were talking seriously about death, the Chief even holding his cap, when Mom lets out a delighted "OOoouuuu!"—just like she's received a huge royalty check.

She was looking across the ravine. "Isn't that the most marvelous cherry tree ever! I simply must see it closer. Chief, would you mind terribly if I went ahead to look at it while you're getting the car?"

Well, I could see the Chief wishing he'd drowned his kindly impulse to ask her along, but we didn't talk about it as we got the car and drove to where Mom was Ooouuuuing and Ahhhhing over the tree. It was pretty all right—covered all over with big rosy-pink blossoms—but this was no garden club tour.

Mom returned to the car bearing a branch of the blooms. "Do you think anyone will mind? I'm sure it's a Sekiyama cherry but I'd like to verify it at home." She added, like an afterthought, "That means Gateway to the Mountains. Most appropriate—really, most appropriate."

Beyond the last clump of woods the whole layout spread before us. The manor house—you've got to call a pile of bricks that big a manor house—was on the last slope, with hedges and gardens all around. Our road twined around service buildings and training rings to the far left of the manor, then joined the main road to the house. White rail fences chopped through rolling pastures below the buildings—I mean, like something out of old Virginy, which probably was what the Ambassador's grandfather planned when he sold the plantation and moved North before the Civil War.

"Let's stop at the stables first." The Chief braked hard before a brick building that sprawled off in a long T. Horses are better to look at than a dead man any day, so that was okay by me.

The crossbar of the T, where we entered, held the tack and trophy rooms on one side and the office and manager's quarters on the other. Beyond these stretched a tanbark aisle between box stalls the size of Mom's writing office. Man, there are people—millions of 'em—not living half as good as those horses! Their stalls were solid mahogany oiled like a catcher's mitt, each with its own mahogany feed box, copper pail for water, and brass nameplate on the stall door.

A tall black-haired man, maybe in his early forties, slapped together some record books and whipped out of the office. He moved in his tan breeches, plaid shirt, and worn black boots like he'd been born in them. Even the leather gloves poked out of his hip pocket with the right casual air. I'd of traded my baseball uniform any minute to look like that!

The Chief introduced him as Charlie Mason, the stable manager, and they yakked about Mr. Nakata before the Chief asked to see Marcia Bancroft's horse.

"Witchcraft? Sure, she's down here."

Only she wasn't. Her stall was empty and she was dancing between crossties on a tile-floored washrack. One man in blue jeans held a stick-gadget, ending with a rope, twisted around her upper lip. Another guy in jeans had hold of her tail with one hand and was trying to smear some gooky white salve on her hip with the other. He'd touch her, she'd lash out with a hind foot, he'd swear, and the first guy would take a half turn on the stick. Then she'd snort and roll her eyes and they'd start all over again.

Mason sprang forward with a yell. "Sam, you trying to ruin that mare? Get away from her!" He stroked her head and talked to her until she quieted down, then he stepped around her, running his hand along her neck, across her back, and down the rear leg. Cupping a hand around her foot, he lifted it and doubled it back.

"Now, Sam, come here and hold his foot up. Gus, get a good grip on that twitch," he commanded softly.

Mason circled the mare again, talking all the time, picked up the jar of salve from a shelf, and spread it gently. When he finished, a white patch about the size and shape of a football stood out against the sleek chestnut hip and the mare was led back to her stall without further fuss.

"Mare get that scrape this morning?" the Chief asked.

"Yeah, must have reared and fallen. That would be when Miss Bancroft went off," he replied. "Shame, too. She's a top show horse but if this doesn't heal right she may never be inside a ring again."

Seemed kind of heartless to me, fussing about the horse

when the girl was the one killed. But I guess he and the Chief had covered that in the morning.

"Mason," the Chief asked, "did Marcia Bancroft always follow the same trail on her rides?"

"No, sometimes she'd take one, sometimes another."

"Hmm," the Chief mused. "But she'd always have to cross that bridge to come back, wouldn't she?"

"Suppose she could have taken the other bridge on the main road, but this one leads directly to the stable."

Mom was standing in front of the next stall, examining one of those copper water pails. Smiling brightly, she waved the pail and said, "Wouldn't this be absolutely perfect for chrysanthemums, Ray?"

When I wouldn't answer, she huffed off toward the trophy room. Soon, I got to feeling guilty—after all, she is my mother, so I followed.

In addition to a stone fireplace, bookshelves, and a lot of deep leather chairs, the room had a glass trophy case stretching clear across one wall. In the center were shelves for cups. Cork squares were framed off on each side, with different horses' names on them.

Witchcraft's square held a blue marked *Working Hunter, National Horse Show,* a couple of big purple rosettes marked *Hunter Championship* with other show names below, some more blues for other hunter classes, and maybe ten reds. Guess they don't display anything lower than second, or maybe she never won anything less.

There wasn't much to look at in there, so we wandered back to the Chief and Mason. When they were through, Mom asked, "Isn't Battle Song here? His name isn't on a stall."

Mason smiled at her. "He's over in the stud barn with the other two stallions. We don't keep them in with these horses."

"I didn't know the Ambassador had so many stallions. Do you charge as much for the others as for Battle Song?"

Mason scuffed his foot in the tanbark, like he wanted to change the subject, but with five kids and maybe ten times that many murders to her credit, Mom doesn't embarrass easy. She waited bright-eyed.

"We charge $5,000 for Battle Song and it's a bargain. Some of his foals are worth three, four times that the minute they drop. We charge $1,000 for each of the other studs."

"Why do you have the others?" I asked, getting curious, too.

"It's a matter of bloodlines. You can't breed every mare to the same stud and you can't keep breeding successive generations to the same stud. Some bloodlines nick and some don't. Now, the Ambassador aims to breed the best hunters and the best steeplechasers this country has ever seen. Battle Song has the speed but . . ."

He hadn't reached the home stretch when the Chief said we'd better get over to the greenhouse or the Sheriff would wrap up the case and head home before we arrived.

In the car we realized that Mom wasn't with us. A honk on the horn brought her trotting, a copper pail in hand.

"Wasn't it nice of Mr. Mason to give me a pail for the chrysanthemums!" she exclaimed.

The Chief and I exchanged glances—guess we felt the same way about it.

"Chief," I asked, "doesn't a hunter have to be pretty steady?"

"Sure does, Ray. By the time he's trained, a good one won't twitch his ears at snapping whips, hounds, tin cans, or most anything else. Why?"

"I was just wondering. That Witchcraft has a whole mess of ribbons."

"Hmm. See what you mean. While you're being so observant, what did you think of the sore on her rump?"

I hadn't thought about it but obviously he expected me to say something bright, so I said it seemed tidy. Must of been the right thing 'cause the Chief beamed.

Mom was still polishing that fool pail with a handkerchief when we parked by the greenhouse.

Well, Mom nearly flipped when the Chief escorted us into a big flower-arranging room. It could of been a Fifth Avenue florist shop, what with a sink and long wooden counter along one wall, with cabinets below, and shelves of vases above, and more shelves with wires and wraps and spikes—it could handle anything from a single pansy to a Derby wreath. Across from the vases was a big glass-doored refrigerator loaded with cut flowers and some finished arrangements.

Not that we had much time to look. The Chief herded us through to another room set up as an office, with files and desks and such. It also held the Sheriff and Mr. Nakata—I deduced the sheet-covered hump on the floor was the murdered gardener. There wasn't much doubt that the big hump on the chair, looking like a football player thirty years after training, was the Sheriff.

When we were introduced, the Sheriff said he was honored to meet Mom, that he'd read some of her books, and offered to show them the body, kind of pointedly excluding me. He raised the sheet so that it blocked my view. Mom let out a gaspy "Oooofffff"—just like when my kid brother Perry crashed smack into her middle one day.

"No, a victim of strangulation isn't very attractive," the Sheriff said, like he regretted having shown the body.

Mom said she didn't think she could ever arrange any more flowers after seeing that floral wire around his neck and the Chief eased her into a chair. He picked a desk chair for himself, hooked the bottom drawer out with his toe, stuck his feet on top of the drawer, and leaned back, like he was in his own office. Then he asked if they'd found the killer.

The Sheriff put on a glum face and told us he'd run out of ideas. The medical examiner fixed the time of death as somewhere between 10:00 a.m. and noon, which cleared all the other gardeners. They were working in the rose garden on the far side of the house.

"The whole business is senseless," the Sheriff concluded. "Why would anyone else want to kill the old guy? There's no reason—not a single motive."

"Ralph," Chief Higgins said, "we just may have stirred up a motive for you. Now suppose—just suppose, you understand—that Marcia Bancroft's death wasn't an accident. Suppose Nakata knew it wasn't. Would that be motive enough?"

"You have any proof?" The Sheriff sat up as straight and stiff as his paunch would let him.

"Heck, no—that's what you've got to find. All I have to go on is that she was riding a horse that wouldn't spook easy and that probably hadn't reared since it finished basic training. Also that the horse is wearing one compact sore high on the rump, where if it fell it should be skinned more on the haunch and leg.

"Remember where the accident happened? Now suppose someone hid on top of that cliff above the trail. When she rode along there, which she had to do to reach the bridge—few horsemen will ride on a concrete road—she'd be a perfect target. Maybe one rock on the horse's rump to make it act up, then maybe another on Marcia's head if she didn't go down the ravine on the first try."

Mom's fictional detectives couldn't have tied it up neater. The Chief really had his little gray cells working. The Sheriff said that when his deputies returned from interviewing the household staff he'd send them out to look for horsehair or blood on the loose rocks and signs of someone's being on the cliff. He eased his glasses up on his forehead and rubbed the bridge of his nose, kind of perplexed like.

"But if Nakata did see her killed—that is, if she was murdered—why didn't he come to us when we were here this morning?" Scarcely pausing, he answered himself. "Of course, he could have been dead by the time we got here. We didn't go into the greenhouse."

"Why would anyone kill Marcia, though—and who?" Mom inquired quietly.

The Sheriff snapped his fingers. "Gillespie, that's who! He was nuts about her but he wasn't a type she would go for. Scorned love—that's the cause of more than one killing."

He phoned the house and asked the secretary to come over. While we waited, an ambulance came for Mr. Nakata, which was a big relief. That hump on the floor kind of kept me from concentrating on who might of put it there. I think it affected Mom the same way—she's usually bubbling with deductions, like when Mr. Griggs had his heart attack.

Two deputies reported that the household staff seemed in the clear and the Sheriff sent them off to the ravine. Finally, Gillespie slipped through the door. When Mom puts such an oddball in a book, she usually writes "esthetic." I mean, he was sorry-looking—real shook up, with eyes fixed in a dopey glaze and fingers plucking like at harp strings.

Well, the Sheriff started pitching questions and Gillespie couldn't field them. He just kept protesting. No, he hadn't killed either of them—he loved Marcia too much but she was unaware of it; no, he'd never harm her, and Iso Nakata was a splendid old man. He even claimed he hadn't known Marcia was home; he thought she'd planned to drive into New York to meet her father—she must have changed her mind this morning, but, no, he hadn't seen her.

Mom sneaked off to the flower-arranging room, which I guess is where she wanted to be all along. We heard her poking around, shifting vases and opening drawers, and soon I heard what must have been the big refrigerator door open, then close again.

Fairly soon she came back in and tapped Chief Higgins' shoulder. Reluctantly he followed her and I followed him. Mom had one of the flower arrangements on the wooden counter.

"There," she said triumphantly, pointing to it. The Chief eyed her, cool-like.

"Don't you see?" she asked impatiently. "It's the Sekiyama cherry—identical with the branch I took from the tree across the ravine! That places Nakata definitely where he could have seen Marcia killed. Of course, we can't prove what time . . ." She trailed off as the Chief rushed back to tell the Sheriff.

Well, I know when I'm on the losing team, so I apologized to Mom for thinking she was only interested in flowers. While I was doing the honesty bit, I had to add that it wasn't much of a flower arrangement—the one the cherry branch was used in—and if that was Japanese art, please include me out.

It was really a mess—the arrangement, I mean. Little black rocks were scattered on the bottom of a flat dish and heaped around the flower stems. The cherry branch dipped way down to the left so that one end touched water and the other touched rock. A pine branch was angled above it at about 45°. Sticking up from the center was one tall white chrysanthemum. The only other flower was a single narcissus stuck over by itself to the right, its stem bent, almost broken.

Frowning, Mom reached out to adjust it into better balance. Then her hand jerked back so fast I expected a bee to buzz out. "Ray, get Chief Higgins!" she ordered.

As I opened the door, the Chief's big voice was booming, "All right, so maybe you didn't kill her because she didn't know you were alive. Maybe you've been juggling the Ambassador's accounts and she found out." The secretary, white as that narcissus, was still protesting.

"Pssst, Chief, Mom wants to see you," I interrupted. "It's something important." He turned Gillespie back to the Sheriff.

"That poor little man," Mom said to us sadly. "He sat in this room arranging flowers when he knew that Marcia had been murdered and that he would be next—and couldn't tell anyone about it. The only ones he could talk with, his grandson and the Ambassador, were away."

"Kate MacKay, did you get me out here to sympathize with the dead man?" the Chief demanded.

"Yes," Mom said calmly. "We all should sympathize with him—and thank him, too, for leaving this dying message." She indicated the awkward arrangement. "In Ikebana art, flowers are arranged according to rule and symbolism, with three main elements—Heaven, Man, and Earth. Others may be added but Nakata used only these three—and the narcissus. In Ikebana symbolism the narcissus means a farewell to the past—or himself, nearly broken, awaiting death.

"For the Heaven line he chose a white chrysanthemum. That symbolizes dignity—so we can interpret it as directed to the Ambassador, certainly a dignified man and one who was in the heavens in an airplane."

I'd started off thinking she'd sprung a leak in the cranium—but now it was getting interesting.

"This line," she continued, tracing the cherry branch, "is the Earth line. Cherry blossoms symbolize purity—so it's fair to interpret this as Marcia Bancroft, crushed to the rocks. Above it is the Man line, and here Nakata chose to use a pine branch. That symbolizes energy and manhood—certainly not that frightened secretary! Now, who would you say is the most energetic and manliest person around here?"

"Charlie Mason," the Chief and I replied in unison.

The Chief called the Sheriff and Mom explained it again—all about the Heaven, Earth, and Man lines. You'd think it would have cheered him up, but it only made him gloomier. "So I have a good suspect and two possible motives. Now you try to sell me another suspect—and on what kind of evidence? A few flowers that would wilt before we could get them into court. No *proof,* no *motive*—just a bunch of guesses hung on a pine branch. Huh!"

It was true. Mom knew it. She sat on a stool by the counter and put her chin on her hands.

"Maybe he was in love with her, too," I offered feebly.

"He was nearly old enough to be her father," the Chief replied.

"Well, Charlie Chaplin . . ."

"Shush, Ray!" Mom commanded.

The secretary poked his head through the door and peeped, "And what is more, you may have access to my accounts at any time."

"Accounts!" the Chief exclaimed.

Mom chimed in, "That's it! A stable manager also handles accounts—and big ones. Why, those stud fees alone . . ."

She and the Chief were back in harmony. "Do you think he would dare?"

"Who'd find out if he was careful about it?"

"And then Marcia came to the stables this morning when she was supposed to be driving to New York to meet her father's plane . . ."

"Embezzlement, that's it! And even if the Bancrofts didn't prosecute he'd never work with horses again."

"Whoa!" the Sheriff interrupted. "Let me in on it, too."

They explained. With a $5,000 stud fee for Battle Song and $1,000 for each of the other two horses, Mason could switch records so as to pocket the $4,000 difference whenever he wanted to. The mare would be actually bred to Battle Song and the owner's registration papers made out correctly, but the stable books would show a service to one of the others. Unless the Bancrofts checked all the Jockey Club registrations against their stud book they'd never discover the falsifications. The stable hands didn't see the books and Mason was careful to switch entries only when the Bancrofts were away, which was often.

Then Marcia turned up unexpectedly while a mare was in the stud barn. She probably looked in the book out of curiosity and stumbled onto the discrepancy. Some people walk when they think; she went riding to decide what to do. Mason waited on the cliff and Iso Nakata happened to be cutting cherry branches when Mason killed her.

That's the way they explained it and that's the way it was. Mason had been so sure he was above suspicion that he hadn't even changed the account books—and so they had him solid. He even told them where he had hidden the money—a good start toward his own breeding farm in Kentucky. Guess all he cared about was horses.

We ducked out, leaving Mason to the deputies, and the Sheriff to wait for the Ambassador and Joe Nakata. After all, it was his case.

Dad's car was in the driveway, so Mom asked Chief

Higgins in for a celebration drink. They told Dad the story, each handing the other all the credit, and then they toasted each other with some flowery prose.

Dad finally broke it up by proposing a toast to both of them: "Here's to the best team of homicide detectives the town of Maplecrest ever boasted."

That was safe enough—it was our first murder in more than a hundred years.

ALICE SCANLAN REACH

In the Confessional

BEST "FIRST STORY" IN EQMM'S 1961 CONTEST

This is the 230th "first story" published by Ellery Queen's Mystery Magazine . . . Mrs. Reach's story about a wino is sensitive and tender and most acutely observed; and the miracle of the story is that the subject matter—the theme, background, and protagonist—is not the kind of material which normally lends itself to tender and sensitive treatment. Yet Mrs. Reach performs that miracle . . .

The author began to write at the age of 17—on her first newspaper job. She has been a feature writer for Scripps-Howard, a radioscript and speech writer for the OPA in Washington, and a public-relations writer in Buffalo, New York (her home town) and in New York City. She calls herself "a first-class 'ham' actress-singer-dancer-dramatist-lyricist," and tells us that all "phases of her on-stage yen" were given an outlet at the community theater in Buffalo. Since early in 1961 she has been "playing a lead role in a kitchen in Greenwich Village, New York, as chief potato washer" for her deeply understanding husband.

Blue slipped in through the side door of St. Brigid's and stood motionless in the shadow of the Confessional. Opposite him loomed the statue of the Blessed Virgin treading gently on a rising bank of vigil lights. Blue's eyes, darting to the ruby fingers of flame flickering around the marble feet, saw that the metal box nearby with the sign *Candles—10¢* had not yet been replenished. Only a few wax molds remained. Had the box been full, Blue would have known he was too late—that

Father Crumlish, on depositing a fresh supply, had opened the drawer attached to the candle container and emptied it of the past week's silver offerings.

So all was well! Once again, all unknowingly, the House of God would furnish Blue with the price of a jug of wine.

Now, from his position in the shadow, Blue's red-rimmed eyes shifted to the altar where Father Crumlish had just turned the lock in the Sacristy door, signaling the start of his nightly nine-o'clock lock-up routine.

Blue knew it by heart.

First, the closing and locking of the weather-weary stained glass windows. Next, the bolting of the heavy oaken doors in the rear of the church. Then came the dreaded moment. Tonight, as every night, listening to Father Crumlish make fast the last window and then approach the Confessional, Blue fought the panic pushing against his lungs—the fear that the priest would give the musty interior of the Confessional more than a quick, casual glance.

Suppose tonight it occurred to Father Crumlish to peer into the Confessional's shadow to see if someone were lurking—

Blue permitted himself a soft sigh of blessed relief. He was safe! The slow footsteps were retreating up the aisle. To be sure, there were torturing hours ahead, but that was the price he had to pay. Already he could almost feel his arms cradling the beloved bottle, his fingers caressing the gracefully curved neck. He could almost taste the soothing, healing sweetness . . .

It was almost too much to bear.

Now came what Blue, chuckling to himself, called "the floor show."

Extinguishing the lights in the rear of the church and thus leaving it, except for candlelight, in total darkness, Father Crumlish, limping a little from the arthritis buried deep in his ancient roots, climbed the narrow, winding stairway to the choir loft.

Blue, hearing the first creaking stair, moved noiselessly and swiftly. In the space of one deep breath he flickered out of the shadow, entered the nearest "sinners' " door of the Confessional, and silently closed it behind him. Then he knelt in cramped darkness, seeing nothing before him but the small closed window separating him from the Confessor's sanctuary.

By now Father Crumlish had reached the choir loft and the "show" began. Believing himself alone with his God and Maker, the descendant of a long line of shillelagh wielders ran his arthritic fingers over the organ's keys and poured out his soul in song. Presently the church rafters rang with his versions of *When Irish Eyes Are Smilin'*, *Come Back to Erin*, and *The Rose of Tralee*.

It was very pleasant and Blue didn't mind too much that his knee joints ached painfully from their forced kneeling position. As a matter of fact, he rather enjoyed this interlude in the evening's adventure. It gave him time to think, a process which usually eluded him in the shadowy, unreal world where he existed. And what better place to think than this very church where he had served as an altar boy forty—fifty?—how many years ago?

That was another reason he never had the slightest qualm about filching the price of a bottle from the Blessed Virgin's vigil-light offering box. "Borrowing," Blue called it. And who had a better right? Hadn't he dropped his nickels and dimes in the collection basket every Sunday and Holy Day of Obligation from the time he was a tot until—?

The Blessed Virgin and Father Crumlish and the parishioners of St. Brigid's were never going to miss a few measly dimes. Besides, he was only "borrowing" until something turned up. And some day, wait and see, he'd walk down the center aisle of the church, dressed fit to kill, proud as a peacock, and put a $100 bill in the basket for the whole church to see just as easy as you please!

A small smile brushed against Blue's thin lips, struggled to reach the dull sunken eyes, gave up in despair, and disappeared. Blue dozed a little.

He might more appropriately have been called Gray. For there was a bleak grayness about him that bore the stamp of fog and dust, of the gray pinched mask of death and destruction. His withered bones seemed to be shoved indifferently into threadbare coat and trousers; and from a disjointed blob of cap a few sad straggles of hair hung listlessly about his destroyed face. Time had long ceased to mean anything to Blue—and he to Time.

All that mattered now was the warm, lovely, loving liquid and the occasional bite of biscuit to wash it down. And thanks to St. Brigid's parishioners, thanks to his knowledge of Father

Crumlish's unfailing nightly routine, Blue didn't have to worry about where the next bottle was çoming from. The job was easy. And afterward he could doze in peace in the last pew of the church until it came time to mingle with the faithful, as they arrived for six o'clock morning mass, and then easily slip unnoticed out the door.

Now, kneeling in the confines of the Confessional, Blue jerked his head up from his wasted chest and stiffened. Sudden silence roared in his ears. For some unseen reason Father Crumlish had broken off in the middle of the third bar of *Tralee*.

Then, in the deathly pale quiet, the priest's voice rang out.

"Who's there?"

Sweet Jesus! thought Blue. Did I snore?

"Answer me!" More insistent now. "Who's there?"

Blue, his hand on the Confessional doorknob, had all but risen when the answer came.

"It's me, Father . . . Johnny Sheehan."

Sinking back to his knees, Blue could hear every word in the choir loft, clear as a bell, resounding in the shuttered, hollow church.

"What's on your mind, Johnny?"

Blue caught the small note of irritation in the priest's voice and knew it was because Father Crumlish treasured his few unguarded moments with *The Rose of Tralee*.

"I—I want to go to Confession, Father."

A long pause and then Blue could almost hear the sigh of resignation to Duty and to God's Will.

"Then come along, lad."

Now how do you like that for all the lousy luck, Blue thought, exasperated. Some young punk can't sleep in his nice warm beddy-bye until he confesses—

Confesses!

Blue felt the ice in his veins jam up against his heart. Father Crumlish would most certainly bring the repentant sinner to *this* Confessional since it was next to the side-door entrance. Even now Blue could hear the oncoming footsteps. Suppose he opens *my* door instead of the other one? Dear God, please let him open the first door!

Trembling, Blue all but collapsed with relief as he heard the other door open and close, heard the settling of knees on the bench, and lastly, the faint whisper of cloth as Father

Crumlish entered the priests' enclosure that separated himself from Blue on one side and from Johnny Sheehan on the other by thin screened windows of wood.

Now Blue heard the far window slide back and knew that Johnny Sheehan was bowing his head to the screen, fixing his eyes on the crucifix clasped in the Confessor's hands.

"Bless me, Father, for I have sinned . . ."

The voice pulled taut, strained, and snapped.

"Don't be afraid to tell God, son. You know about the Seal of Confession—anything you tell here you confess to God and it remains sealed with Him forever."

Confess you stole a bunch of sugar beets and get it over with, Blue thought angrily. He was getting terribly tired and the pain in his knees was almost more than he could bear.

"I . . . she . . ."

She! Well, what do you know? Blue blinked his watery eyes in a small show of surprise. So the young buck's got a girl in trouble. Serves him right. Stick to the warmer embrace of the bottle, my lad. It'll keep you out of mischief.

"I heard your first confession when you were seven, Johnny. How old are you now? Sixteen?"

"Y-yes, Father."

"This girl. What about her?"

"I—I killed her!"

In the rigid silence Blue heard the boy's body sag against the wooden partition and was conscious of a sharp intake of breath from the priest. Blue was as alert now as he ever was these soft, slow days and nights, but he knew that sometimes he just thought he heard words when actually he'd only dreamed them. Yet . . . Blue eased one hurting kneecap and leaned closer to the dividing wood.

Father Crumlish shifted his weight in his enclosure.

"Killed?"

Only retching sobs.

"Tell me, Johnny." Father Crumlish's voice was ever so gentle now.

Then the words came in a torrent.

"She laughed at me . . . said I wasn't a man . . . and I couldn't stand it, Father. When Vera May laughed . . ."

"Vera May!" the priest broke in. "Vera May Barton?"

Even in the shifting mists and fog of his tired memory, Blue recognized that name. Who didn't these past few weeks?

Who didn't know that every cop in the city was hunting Vera May Barton's murderer? Why, even some of Blue's best pals had been questioned. Always ready to hang a rap on some poor innocent.

Blue rarely read newspapers, but he listened to lots of talk. And most of the talk in the wine-shrouded gloom of his haunts these past weeks had been about the slaying of sixteen-year-old Vera May Barton, a choir singer at St. Brigid's. Someone had shown Blue her picture on the front page of a newspaper. A beautiful girl, blonde and soft and smiling. But someone, someone with frantic, desperate hands, had strangled the blonde softness and choked off the smile.

Blue was suddenly conscious once more of the jagged voice.

"She wasn't really like they say, Father. Vera May wasn't really good! She just wanted you to think so. But sometimes, when I'd deliver my newspapers in the morning, sometimes she'd come to the door with hardly any clothes . . . And when I'd ask her to go to a show or something, she'd only laugh and say I wasn't a man . . ."

"Go on," Father Crumlish said softly.

"I—she told me she was staying after choir practice that night to collect the hymnals—"

The priest sighed. "I blame myself for that. For letting her stay in the church alone—even for those few moments—while I went over to the rectory."

"And then—then when she left," the halting words went on, "I followed her out in the alley . . ."

Blue's pals had told him about that—how one of St. Brigid's early morning mass parishioners found Vera May lying like a broken figurine in the dim alley leading from the church to the rectory. She wasn't carrying a purse, the newspapers said. And she hadn't been molested. But her strangler, tearing at her throat, had broken the thin chain of the St. Christopher's medal around her neck. It had her initials on the back but the medal had never been found.

"What did you do with the medal, Johnny?" Father Crumlish asked quietly.

"I—I was afraid to keep it, Father." The agonized voice broke again. "The river . . ."

The weight of the night pressed heavily on Blue and he sighed deeply. But the sigh was lost in the low murmuring of the priest to the boy—too low for Blue to catch the words—and perhaps, against all his instincts, he dozed. Then there was a sudden stirring in the adjoining cubicles. Blue knelt rigid and breathless while the doors opened, and without turning his head toward the faint candlelight shimmering through the cracks in the door of his enclosure, he knew that Father Crumlish had opened the side entrance and released Johnny Sheehan to the gaunt and starless dark.

Slowly the priest moved toward the first pew before the center altar. And now Blue risked glancing through the sliver of light in his door. Father Crumlish knelt, face buried in his hands . . .

A wisp of thought drifted into the wine-eroded soil of Blue's mind. Was the priest weeping?

But Blue was too engrossed in his own discomfort, too aware of the aching, ever-increasing, burning dryness of his breath and bones. If only the priest would go and leave Blue to his business and his sleep!

After a long time he heard the footsteps move toward the side door. Now it closed. Now the key turned in the lock . . .

Now!

Blue stumbled from the Confessional and collapsed in the nearest pew. Stretched full length, he let his weary body and mind sag in relief. Perhaps he slept; he only knew that he returned, as if from a long journey. Sitting upright, he brought out the tools of his trade from somewhere within the tired wrappings that held him together.

First the chewing gum—two sticks, purchased tonight.

Blue munched them slowly, carefully bringing them to the proper consistency. Then, rising, he fingered a small length of wire, and leaving the pew, shuffled toward the offering box beneath the Blessed Virgin's troubled feet.

Taking the moist gum from his mouth, Blue attached it to the wire and inserted it carefully into the slot of the box. A gentle twist and he extracted the wire. Clinging to the gummed end were two coins, a nickel and a dime.

Blue went through this procedure again and again until he had collected the price of a bottle. Then he lowered himself into the nearest pew and rested a bit. He began to think of what had happened in the Confessional. But it had been so long since Blue had made himself concentrate on anything but his constant, thirsting need that it took a while for the rusted wheels to move, for the pretty colored lights to cease their small whirlings and form a single brightness illuminating the makings of his mind.

Finally he gave up. The burning dryness had gripped him again and he began to yearn for the long night to be over so that he could spend, in the best way he knew, the money he held right in his hand this minute.

Two bottles! I should have two bottles for all the trouble I've been through tonight, Blue thought. They owe it to me for making me kneel there so long and robbing me of my sleep. Yes, they owe it to me! And so thinking, he took out the gum once more from some secret fold, and bringing it to his mouth, chewed it again into pliable moistness.

The first try at the offering box brought him only a dime, but the second try—God was good—another dime, a nickel, and a dollar bill!

Too exhausted to drag himself to his customary last-pew bed, Blue stretched out once more on the nearest wood plank and slept.

Some time later, the unrelenting dryness wakened him. This "in-between" period was the only time Blue ever approached sobriety. And in the sobering, everything seemed terribly, painfully clear. He began to relive the events of the night, hearing the voices again with frightening clarity. Father Crumlish's and then the kid's . . .

Blue's own voice screamed in his ears.

"Out! I've got to get out of here! Nobody knows but me . . . nobody knows about the murder but me. I've got to tell . . . But first I'll have to have a little sip. I need a little sip. And then I'll tell . . ."

In a flurry of cloth and dust Blue rushed to the side door. He had never before tried to let himself out this way and had no idea if the door was locked. But the knob gave easily, and in an instant he had closed the door behind him and leaning heavily against it, was breathing the night's whispering wind.

It had been a long time since Blue had been out alone in the deep dark and suddenly, with the night's dreadful knowledge inside him, it was overpowering. Shadows rushed at him, clawed at his face and fingers, and crushed him so bindingly that he could scarcely breathe.

In an agony to get away, he plunged into the blackness and began to run.

And in his urgency Blue never heard the shout behind him, the pounding feet on the pavement. He never heard the cry to halt or risk a bullet. He only knew that he was flying, faster and faster, yet not fast enough, soaring higher and higher, until a surprisingly small, jagged thrust of sidewalk clawed at him and brought him to his knees. The bullet from his pursuer, meant to pierce his worn and weary legs, pierced his back.

Suddenly it was calm and quiet and there was no longer any need for speed. He lay on his side, crumpled and useless, like a discarded bundle of rags. A wave, a wine-red wave, swept over him and Blue let himself rock and toss for a moment in its comforting warmth. Then he opened his eyes and, dimly, in the fast-gathering darkness, recognized Father Crumlish bending over him.

"Poor devil," Blue heard the priest say. "But don't blame yourself, Officer. The fellow probably just didn't know that you'd be suspicious of his running away like that. Particularly around here—now—after the Barton girl. The poor devil probably just didn't know."

Didn't know? Blue didn't know? He knew, all right! And he had to tell.

"Father!"

Quickly the priest bent his ear to Blue's quivering lips.

"I . . . was in the Confessional too."

"The Confessional?"

The wave rushed to envelop him again. Before he could speak the urgent words he heard the officer's voice.

"He came out of the church door, Father. I saw him."

"I don't see how that's possible," the priest said bewilderedly.

Blue forced the breath from his aching lungs.

"I heard . . . the kid confess . . . I have to tell . . ."

"Wait!" Father Crumlish said sharply, cutting Blue off. "You have nothing to tell. Maybe you heard. But you don't know about that boy. The poor confused lad's come to me to confess to every robbery and murder in this parish for years. You have nothing to tell, do you hear me?"

"Nothing?"

Blue almost laughed a little. For the pain was gone now and he felt as if—as if he were walking down St. Brigid's center aisle, dressed fit to kill, proud as a peacock, and putting a $100 bill in the collection basket for the whole church to see just as easy as you please.

"There's something . . ."

His voice was strong and clear as he brought his fumbling fingers from within the moldy rags and stretched out his hand to the priest.

"I was 'borrowing' from the Blessed Virgin, Father. Just enough for a bottle, though. I need it, Father. All the time. Bad! . . . She caught me at it. And she was running to tell you. But if she did, where in the world would I ever get another bottle, Father? Where? . . . So I had to stop her!"

Fighting the final warm, wine-red wave that was rushing over him, Blue thrust into Father Crumlish's hand a St. Christopher's medal dangling from a broken chain and initialed V.M.B.

"I've been saving it, Father. In a pinch, I thought it might be worth a bottle . . ."

Editor's Introduction

The first legitimate detective-story anthology did not appear until 1895. It was published in London under the title of *The Long Arm and Other Detective Stories* and contained only four tales, one each by Mary E. Wilkins [Freeman], George Ira Brett [Oswald Crawfurd], Roy Tellet, and Brander Matthews.

In the forty-five years that followed, only sixty-odd detective anthologies broke into print in England and America —considerably less than two anthologies per year on the average—and of these sixty-odd works only a baker's half-dozen were truly distinguished collections from a purely critical or selective point of view. In order of their appearance, but not in order of their time-tested rank in the history of the detective anthology, this baker's half-dozen included: *Library of the World's Best Mystery and Detective Stories* (1907), six volumes, edited by Julian Hawthorne—a monumental work for its time and expanded two years later under the better known title of *The Lock and Key Library*, ten volumes; *Crime and Detection* (1926), edited by E. M. Wrong; *The Great Detective Stories* (1927), edited by Willard Huntington Wright (S. S. Van Dine); *Fourteen Great Detective Stories* (1928), edited by Vincent Starrett; *Great Stories of Detection, Mystery and Horror* (1928), edited by Dorothy L. Sayers; *The World's Best One Hundred Detective Stories* (1929), ten volumes, edited by Eugene Thwing; and Dorothy L. Sayer's smallest but finest anthology, *Tales of Detection* (1936).

In 1941 came your Editors' *101 Years' Entertainment,* commemorating the centennial anniversary of the detective story, and to quote Vincent Starrett on an entirely different matter, "And after [that], the deluge!" Despite the paper shortage of the boom war years, detective-story anthologies multiplied rabbitly. Hardly a month passed during the 1940's without the appearance in bookstores and on newsstands of another omnium-gatherum of detective-crime short stories. Most of these compilations were, to quote the English critic, E. A. Osborne, "just higgledy-piggledy bouquets of dried flowers." Few of these anthologies had an "idea" behind them, a comprehensive or specialized theme that explored the more serious aspects of detective-story criticism, history, and technique.

Obviously it was easier for an editor in those lush publishing days to do a scissors-and-paste job (as distinguished from a "scissors-and-taste" job), leaning for the most part on familiar stories or merely culling the then current magazines, both slick and pulp, for enough stories to fill out an important-*looking* book. The pure-in-heart anthologist scorned (and still scorns) such line-of-least-resistance editing; the anthologist with a creative conscience devotes unstinted time and effort in long, arduous research to discover the "unknown" classics which have been ignored, forgotten, or neglected by those "editors" who do not realize that a critic can also be guilty of potboiling.

So, every now and then—all too infrequently in the mainstream of anthologies—when a collection appears that is the blood, sweat, and tearsheets of a 24-carat craftsman (a true aficionado like Vincent Starrett, Anthony Boucher, Howard Haycraft, James Sandoe, and Lee Wright), we are honor-bound and duty-bound to hail the event with all due fanfare and huzzahs. And such an anthology was scheduled for publication in 1947—sixteen years ago.

Scheduled to appear sixteen years ago—and not published yet.

The editor was John Dickson Carr—his first venture into the anthology field; the publisher was Crown; and the title of Mr. Carr's first anthology was *The Ten Best Detective Novels*. The book was planned to be a titanic 'tec tome—the first attempt to do for the detective *novel* what so many anthologists have tried to do for the detective *short story*. Here, in a single volume, were to be included the fruits of Mr. Carr's lifelong reading in the genre he himself has so magnificently aided and abetted; here was, indeed, a Brobdingnagian bedside "reader."

For this huge harvest of homicide Mr. Carr wrote a 16,-000-word Introduction—which has been waiting these past sixteen years for publication. The first part of the Introduction dealt with the detective novel in general—technique, craftsmanship, style, and trends; the remainder of the Introduction dealt with the detective novel in particular—specific authors and specific books. This second part was an integral segment of Mr. Carr's mammoth murder anthology—it explained his choices, and it even gave his reasons for certain spectacular omissions. While this second part seems fated to die on the vine with the anthology itself, surely the first part—a "new master's" critique—should be made available to the public . . . which is exactly what we propose to do—rescue Mr. Carr's criminological credo from biblivion and give it to the widest possible audience of "the fancy."

Now, which detective novels did Mr. Carr select as *The Ten Best*? It would be a villainous trick to keep you in suspense any longer! So, here are Mr. Carr's choices—his all-time Big Ten (as of 1947):

A. Conan Doyle's *The Valley of Fear*
Gaston Leroux's *The Mystery of the Yellow Room*
A. E. W. Mason's *At the Villa Rose*
Agatha Christie's *Death on the Nile*
Ellery Queen's *The Lamp of God*
Anthony Berkeley's *The Poisoned Chocolates Case*
S. S. Van Dine's *The Greene Murder Case*
Philip MacDonald's *Murder Gone Mad*
Rex Stout's *The League of Frightened Men*
Dorothy L. Sayers's *The Nine Tailors*

Surely you have been asking yourself: why *did* Mr. Carr's anthology die on the vine? Why did such a "natural" fail to see the light of print? The reason is simple—and shocking.

Three of the original publishers who control the reprint rights to three of Mr. Carr's *Ten Best Novels* refused to grant permission to Crown to include those three novels in Mr. Carr's anthology!

Why did three publishers refuse to participate? Frankly, we do not know. All we do know is that it was a colossal pity. Naturally, with thirty percent of Mr. Carr's entries in the Homicide Handicap "scratched," the race had to be postponed —and it has remained a phantom Detective Derby for sixteen years . . .

It should be noted that Mr. Carr makes the following point in that part of his Introduction which is not being offered in this issue of EQMM: "The anthology has been called *The Ten Best Detective Novels*—a title for whose arbitrariness you must blame the publisher. I myself should have preferred to call it *Ten* of the *Best*, assigning to my introduction a task less responsible than that of the recording angel."

Of course, Mr. Carr is right, but the publisher can hardly be censured for choosing the better selling title. True, the publisher definitely stuck his neck (and Mr. Carr's) out on a limb, to mix metaphors, and invited round-the-world debate and argument on the critical wisdom of Mr. Carr's selections; devotees and serious students of the genre, and equally important, those who read for sheer pleasure and entertainment, will disagree with this title or that, and discussion will rage round the hot-stove league of detection as to the unforgivable omission of this author or that. And the simple truth of the matter is that Mr. Carr *is* guilty of at least one unpardonable omission—and that omission cannot be passed over without some accusatory comment.

Where, oh, where in Mr. Carr's anthology is a writer named John Dickson Carr, or his *alter ego,* Carter Dickson?

We understand Mr. Carr's uncomfortable position. It is similar to that which faced Tyrus-Raymond Cobb after his retirement from baseball: nearly every year, it seemed, some famous sports writer would visit Cobb and ask the peerless Ty to name his all-star, all-time baseball team; and always the Georgia Peach would nominate Babe Ruth, Tris Speaker, and Shoeless Joe Jackson for his greatest of all outfields. But breathes there a fan with soul so dead that he would even hesitate in naming Ty Cobb to the immortal nine?

Yes, Mr. Carr is understandably guilty of false modesty; but if Ellery Queen were asked to choose the ten best modern detective novels, or the twenty best old and new masterpieces, you can bet all the deductions in Detectivania (or all the Rice in Craig, as Anthony Boucher once remarked) that one of those ten moderns or one of those twenty all-time greats would be a novel by John Dickson Carr or Carter Dickson.

But to get back to Mr. Carr's own anthology . . . We must finally admit, after sixteen years, that the Carr cause is lost. With infinitely higher production costs these days, and with no sign of change of heart on the part of the three reluctant publishers (dragons), John Dickson Carr's *The Ten Best Detective Novels* is doomed never to appear . . .

Surely Mr. Carr's work on his anthology should not be totally lost to the public. We cannot give you, of course, the texts of his selections; but we can give you the first part of his Introduction—a witty and often comic dissertation, a probing and perceptive analysis, a brilliant "mystique" by a serious and dedicated critic of what Mr. Carr so aptly calls "the old game, the great game, the grandest game in the world."

And if you interpret these Introductions (EQ's and JDC's) as heartfelt petitions for a return to the grand tradition, to the classic technique—as a joint appeal for a renaissance of ingenuity and surprise and wonder and imagination—in a phrase, as a double plea for a return to the golden age of the detective story—why, you're absolutely right!

ELLERY QUEEN

JOHN DICKSON CARR

The Grandest Game in the World

"Do you solemnly swear never to conceal a vital clue from the reader?"

"I do."

That is the first article in the oath taken by members of the Detection Club. The candidate, placing his hand upon Eric the Skull, swears this with fervency. He swears it with stern looks fixed on him. He swears it while Eric's eyes (thanks to John Rhode) glow with red electric lights. He swears it even before he promises to honor the King's English, use legitimate detective methods in his stories, and refrain from pinching his fellow-members' plots.

And this rule, the *sine qua non* of the profession, must be emphasized at the beginning to explain my choice of stories in *The Ten Best Detective Novels.*

For the once-humble detective novel has come a long way. It has gone up hill, down dale, over the plain and through the sewer. In fifty years it has undergone so many changes, not to say disguises, that sometimes we quite literally don't know what we are talking about. A new novel is praised because it is well written, because the characters are admirably drawn, because it is "tough," because it is experimental in technique, because it is written sideways or upside down: on any grounds, in short, except that it is a good detective story.

If the term means anything at all, it means this:

The detective story is a conflict between criminal and detective in which the criminal, by means of some ingenious device—alibi, novel murder-method, or what you like—remains unconvicted or even unsuspected until the detective reveals his identity by means of evidence which has also been conveyed to the reader.

That is the skeleton, the framework, the Christmas tree on which all the ornaments are hung. If the skeleton has been badly strung, or the tree clumsily set on its base, no amount of glittering ornament will save it. It falls over with a flop. Its fall may create a momentary sensation, especially among children; but adults are only depressed when they see the same sort of thing happen in fiction.

The author of the book hasn't bothered. He has decided that good construction is of no consequence, or that nobody cares anyway. Far from planning in advance every move, every speech, every detail, he has roared ahead on inspiration and trusted to luck. And his attitude is understandable if he is writing a straight thriller, where rapid-fire action swallows up everything. But it becomes merely bad craftsmanship if he thinks he is writing a detective story.

We might postulate, to begin with, that the detective novel at its best will contain three qualities seldom found in the thriller. It will contain the quality of fair play in presenting the clues. It will contain the quality of sound plot-construction. And it will contain the quality of ingenuity.

Ingenuity? Do we start an argument here?

It seems remarkable that this need for ingenuity in the *outstanding* detective novel has been so strangely overlooked. Perhaps the reason is that you cannot turn it into a "must"; you cannot lay it down as a rule of the game. You cannot say to an author, "Look here, sit down and be ingenious." Maybe he can't be. Maybe he doesn't want to be. His interests may lie along other lines, such as the hero slugging the police or (more pleasant to read about) the police slugging the hero.

But, though this quality of ingenuity is not necessary to the detective-story as such, you will never find the great masterpiece without it. Ingenuity lifts the thing up; it is triumphant; it blazes, like a diabolical lightning-flash, from beginning to end.

It is not of intrinsic interest to read that X has been stabbed to death in a hotel room, and that the police—after rewinding the clock, or studying the bloodstains, or any of the stock-tricks in vogue since the time of Gaboriau—have proved the guilt of Y the waiter. This is all very well; it may be competent work; it will serve to be read if we have nothing better at hand. But, in pitting our wits against the masters of the trade, we require something very different.

We require, for instance, the superb explanation of the clock-alibi, in A. E. W. Mason's *The House of the Arrow*. Or the means used to conceal the identity of the criminal, in

Agatha Christie's *Murder in Mesopotamia.* Or the reason why the corpse wore its clothes the wrong way round, in Ellery Queen's *The Chinese Orange Mystery.* Or the ironic brilliance of Anthony Berkeley's *Trial and Error,* in which a man who has confessed to the murder tries to prove himself guilty and can't do it.

These writers (with others like them) are the aristocrats of the game, the old serpents, the gambit-devisers and trap-baiters whose strokes of ingenuity make the game worth playing at all.

For what, after all, is the game itself?

It is a hoodwinking contest, a duel between author and reader. "I dare you," says the reader, "to produce a solution which I can't anticipate." "Right!" says the author, chuckling over the consciousness of some new and legitimate dirty-trick concealed up his sleeve. And then they are at it—pull-devil, pull-murderer—with the reader alert for every dropped clue, every betraying speech, every contradiction that may mean guilt.

Nothing, in fact, shows more clearly the difference between the expert craftsman and the novice than his manner of presenting this evidence. The novice, even when he is anxious to include a clue, develops a case of acute self-consciousness about it. He feels naked before the reader's eye. He is much too afraid of being caught with the goods. So he hurls the clue into the story and then runs like a maniac, as though he had thrown a bomb.

The result is that the clue, one or two words at most, will flash past and become lost among sixty or seventy thousand other words. This is painfully evident during the detective's summing-up in the final chapter.

"The whole question of Dagmar Doubledick's guilt," declares the detective, "turns on the kind of necktie he was wearing when we met him that day at Wemmerly Park. Of course you remember it was a green tie?"

To which the honest reader is compelled to answer: "No, I'm damned if I do!"

And then, if he is conscientious, he will turn back through the book to discover whether Dagmar Doubledick's tie really was green. Perhaps he finds this clue, a violet by a mossy stone, half hidden somewhere in the dusky recesses of Chapter Six; perhaps he misses the page and does not find it at all. In either case he is left with a vague feeling of dissatisfaction: as though he has been, if not swindled, at least out-talked.

Now it may be argued, and reasonably, that the author here was playing perfectly fair. He was not compelled to repeat it, or even stress it. Thus when the whole solution of Earl Derr Biggers' *Charlie Chan Carries On* is based on the single word "stuffy," or when Carolyn Wells in *The Luminous Face* argues guilt from the thesis that no gentleman would wear a wristwatch with evening clothes, these novels are at least technically within the rules.

But the masterpiece of detection is not constructed from "a" clue, or "a" circumstance, or one single inconsistency of any kind. Such methods, dubious enough in a short story, become grotesque when they are applied to a full-length novel. It is too reminiscent of those minute-mysteries, vignettes accompanied by paralytic-looking photographs, with which we are so familiar in magazines.

"You stated, Leonard Andreas," thunders the Inspector, "that you drank a scotch-and-soda in the bar-parlor of The Flaming Bishop at nine o'clock, whereas we know the pub ran out of spirits at half-past eight. It proves, Leonard Andreas, that you committed the murder."

Now this is a bit rough on poor old Leonard Andreas, because it doesn't prove anything of the kind. It proves only that the witness told a lie, or that the landlord (as usual) was keeping his whisky under the counter for favored customers. We are dealing, here, with murder; and we can hardly let a man's life, even that of a character in fiction, depend on such flimsy evidence.

The fine detective story, be it repeated, does not consist of "a" clue. It is a ladder of clues, a pattern of evidence, joined together with such cunning that even the experienced reader may be deceived: until, in the blaze of the surprise-ending, he suddenly sees the whole design.

Your craftsman knows, as Dr. R. Austin Freeman long ago pointed out, that it is not at all necessary to mislead the reader. Merely state your evidence, and the reader will mislead himself. Therefore, the craftsman will do more than mention his clues: he will stress them, dangle them like a watch in front of a baby, and turn them over lovingly in his hands. He will give not only the clue physical, but the clue psychological and the clue atmospheric.

No speech in the book is included just because it sounds mysterious, or because it makes a given character look guilty, or because the author doesn't know what the devil his character does mean and simply throws in the words to fill up space. Not at all. In turning over the pages afterwards, the reader can see for himself—how rare it is!—just what each character was *thinking* at any moment.

And the result?

That is why the story pulses with vitality all the way through, and springs into living vividness at the end. The veil is twitched away; the masks are removed. Human beings walk here, and no sawdust dolls, because the author has described voice-inflections, shades of feeling, as well as Inspector Hogarth's discovery of the blunted thumb-tack under the sofa. He has not forgotten to study his characters merely because he is writing about them in reverse. That turn of the eyes—of course! That momentary hesitation, when Betty puts her hand on the window ledge as though to steady herself—naturally!

Each small detail glitters now with an effectiveness it should have had, and would have had, if the story had been written straightforwardly. It is in the mood, in the tempo, an arrow whang in the gold. And when, in addition to this, we find ourselves flumdiddled by some master-stroke of ingenuity which has turned our suspicions legitimately in the wrong direction, we can only salute the author and close the book with a kind of admiring curse.

There, good friends, *is* a detective story.

But who writes such stories nowadays?

In considering this question, on a terrain where it is to be feared that bricks are apt to fly, we might do worse than examine the wide difference which has developed nowadays between the British and the American type of detective novel.

During the good (or bad) old days twenty-five years ago —let's speak first of the everyday mediocre practitioners rather than the great ones—these novels were of much the same kind. Both sides were content to write the English language, even when they wrote it badly. Both sides made some mumbling acquiescence in the matter of rules, even when they broke rules all over the place.

Their plots, too, were the same. Alter the locale from Long Island to Surrey, substitute "baronet" for "industrial magnate," and the stories were almost interchangeable. This change, in fact, was actually made when the thrillers about Frank L. Packard's Jimmie Dale were published in England, with the redoubtable Jimmie living in Park Lane and battling against an evil, conscienceless gang of robbers called (it is regrettable to state) the Crime Club.

But the pattern of the average detective story ran thus: The victim, on the eve of making a new will, was found murdered in his library. He had been stabbed with an Oriental dagger, customarily used as a paper-knife on his desk. The whole room was strewn with cuff-links, bus-tickets, lace handkerchiefs, and cigarette-ends, in the fine artistry of a paper-chase.

Inspector Brace, summoned hastily to the scene of the crime, found only the beginning of his troubles. The baronet or industrial magnate—in addition to his ne'er-do-well son, his rebellious daughter, and his invalid wife—was afflicted with such a household as nobody, even in the days of the servant shortage, would tolerate for five minutes. The butler was a blackmailer, the chauffeur an ex-convict, the housekeeper a religious maniac. If this were not enough, investigation discloses that no less than eight other suspects, at the time of the murder, were skulking in one long procession past the library windows.

"This situation," says Inspector Brace, "is hopeless!"

And it is difficult not to agree with him, since the various cuff-links and cigarette-ends are proved to have been dropped innocently by one or the other of the suspects, popping at intervals in and out of the windows like Box and Cox. Inspector Brace, desperate, is about to arrest the ne'er-do-well son when the latter's fiancée calls in that gifted gentleman, the private detective Reginald Du Kink.

Then we got real business. It is Du Kink who discovers that the established time of the murder is all wrong, due to an effect of ventriloquism or a phonograph-record of a voice, and at a dramatic gathering of suspects he fastens the guilt on the dead man's secretary. The secretary, haggard and foaming, waits only to scream out a confession before he drinks off the contents of a small vial and instantly falls dead.

And that was that.

Now the above, so help me, is not written in ridicule. It is not meant as burlesque. You and I, who have been improving our minds with sensational fiction for so many years, are much too fond of detective stories. We are aware that all the above plot-tricks were used long before 1920, have been used since, and are still in use today—often by the very best practitioners in the business.

Seldom are they lumped together in one story, as was formerly the case, nor is the clue so naive as a broken cuff-link. And the ghost of Dr. Freud haunts everything today. But the old elements remain. The millionaire's home, the threatened disinheritance, the rebellious family, the enigmatic servant, the multiplicity of suspects, the wrongly accused, the wrong time of death—how many novels can you name in which not one of these elements is to be found?

Why, then, do we protest at the adventures of Inspector Brace and Reginald Du Kink? Why do their frenzied activities hover always on the edge of comedy, not to say broad farce?

We don't find them funny because they are what our age likes to call "period-pieces." Far from it. One glance at a list of the detectives who were practising long before them, a list which includes short stories as well as novels, will convince us of that.

There is nothing in the least funny about the great stories of Sir Arthur Conan Doyle. Nobody smiles today at G. K. Chesterton's Father Brown, though the stumpy little priest first appeared in 1911. The same applies to Inspector Hanaud, whom A. E. W. Mason introduced in *At the Villa Rose* a year earlier; and Dr. Freeman set the experienced John Thorndyke to solve his greatest problem, *The Eye of Osiris*, in the same year. E. C. Bentley, in 1913, was a comparative latecomer with his brilliant tour de force of *Trent's Last Case*. On the other side of the Atlantic, an underrated genius named Jacques Futrelle had created Professor Augustus S. F. X. Van Dusen as early as 1907, whereas Melville Davisson Post was already an old craftsman when he gave us the classic book of short stories about the far-from-comic Uncle Abner in 1918.

And here we begin to see the explanation of why, as early as the 1920's, the intelligent reader was getting fed up with the adventures of Inspector Brace and Reginald Du Kink.

"Oh!" said the reader. "I'm tired of just guessing who the criminal is. Instead of these sleight-of-hand half-clues, so that it's never properly explained at the end how the detective knew, let's have some real evidence.

"Furthermore," continued this reader, "it's all very well to have your eight suspects parading in their endless ring-around-the-rosebush outside the library. That's fine. But give some sensible reason why they were there. If you must shower the room with bus-tickets, provide a reason for that, too. In other words, construct your story. Your present problem is not to explain the villainy of the guilty: it's to explain the stupidity of the innocent.

"Finally, your 'amazing revelation' at the end was so soggy, so lacking in essential cleverness, that I couldn't care less. Haven't you a new idea tucked away somewhere? Can't you wield even a minor thunderbolt? It was far different, believe me, from that joyous shock when Father Brown unmasked the Invisible Man, or Uncle Abner showed the meaning of the Straw Man, or Sherlock Holmes, in an unforgettable moment, swept the disguise from the Man with the Twisted Lip."

Holà! Wow!

Please pardon these exclamations. It is only that I, who write this introduction, feel warm with pleasure merely to recall, and taste in memory, those great moments of fictional crime. Once more, in memory, we see the gaunt figure of Holmes with the bath-sponge in his hand, and shock-haired Hugh Boone writhing on the bunk. Or Father Brown, under a lurid sky in the waste of snow, with the giant hallporter between whose very feet runs the straggle of tracks where no man has passed; and out across the snow rings that despairing cry:

"God! The invisible man!"

Such moments, then, aid us in summing up the reasons why an imaginative reader required somebody more enterprising than Inspector Brace or Reginald Du Kink. He required a skillful story told in reverse by a skillful story-teller. He required (need it be repeated?) the quality of fair play, the quality of sound construction, and the quality of ingenuity. And already, at the beginning of the 1920's, this decade saw new writers who possessed just such qualities.

It saw the debut of Agatha Christie in *The Mysterious Affair at Styles*, based on the (then) startling novelty that the person first suspected turns out to be the murderer after all; he has wanted to get himself tried and acquitted so that he can't be tried again—a device later used by so many other writers. It saw Freeman Wills Crofts, with *The Cask* and its grisly contents, inaugurating the new fashion of the Unbreakable Alibi.

It saw John Rhode, in *The Paddington Mystery*, present a victim dead from no apparent cause—while telling us for the first time (and almost the last time) that Dr. Priestley's Christian name is Lancelot. It saw Anthony Berkeley's initial effort take the form of a "locked room" in *The Layton Court Mystery*. It saw Dorothy L. Sayers—with *Whose Body?*—setting an unfledged Lord Peter Wimsey to solve the puzzle of a strange corpse, clad only in a pair of pince-nez, found stabbed in a dry bath.

These 1920's, what ever may be said against them, thronged with sheer brains. What would be one of the best possible settings for violent death? J. J. Connington found the answer, with *Murder in the Maze*. Has anybody ever used the camera obscura, that eerie periscope-device, for witnessing sinister events at a distance? Mr. Connington again, with *The Eye in the Museum*. In the 1920's, too, Philip MacDonald made his notable advent with *The Rasp*. R. A. J. Walling, in *Murder at the Keyhole*, demonstrated how you can force a reader to look literally in the wrong direction. And always with us during those days, cherubic, dependable, and moaning like an animated cream-bun, was H. C. Bailey's Mr. Fortune.

Now look towards the other side of the Atlantic. It must be acknowledged that America, during the same period, produced only two detective-story writers of the first class.

Regarding those who were not first-class or anywhere near it, there is no need to mention names. Most of them were women, one or two of whom are still writing today. These ladies waltzed gracefully, waltzed well; but they waltzed always in the arms of Inspector Brace or Reginald Du Kink. We have pleasant memories of them all; theirs is the scent of arsenic and old lace. They call to mind coloured frontispieces from their own books: the yellow gowns sweeping the floor, the padded rooms cosy with crime.

But there is one name which must be mentioned, because it belongs to a man who came dangerously near being first-rate and who had more influence on his medium than anyone seems to have realized. That is the name of Arthur B. Reeve.

Arthur B. Reeve, who began in an earlier era—as, indeed, did most of the lady-waltzers—entered the 20's with his once-immense popularity fading away. Nevertheless his tales of Craig Kennedy had been read by hundreds of thousands, praised by Theodore Roosevelt, and turned into early film-serials which held us petrified.

Craig Kennedy was Professor Kennedy of, presumably, Columbia University. Like Dr. Thorndyke, he was the scientific detective. His laboratory flashed with stranger sparks, and bubbled with more weird beakers and test-tubes, than the laboratory of the late Dr. Frankenstein. For each occasion he had some new gadget, guaranteed sensational, to clap on some-body's wrist or wire underneath the chair. Square-jawed Kennedy in his high collar, whom we remember so well from the illustrations in the Harper editions, has marched into limbo with all his gadgets loaded on him. Much of his scientific knowledge, I believe, has been discredited. Nobody reads about him now. And yet . . .

He was first in the field of fiction with the lie-detector, with murder by electrolysis, with radium poisoning, with death from liquid air. He taught writers the use of the Maxim silencer, and neither tears nor prayers nor curses can induce them to give it up. As a final achievement among many, in a story called "The Dream Detective" and later in a novel called *The Soul Scar,* it was he who introduced the profession to psychoanalysis.

This, in its way, is a solemn thought. For the humble annals of the detective story, it is like Watt studying the boiling kettle or Franklin flying the kite in the thunderstorm. In these days when every other mystery novel depends on a neurosis or a phobia or a fixation or whatnot, we can see now what wild vegetation has grown from that small seed. Psychoanalysis has been the most widely used contribution to the detective story since the days of Poe and Conan Doyle; and we might do worse than remember who planted the jungle in which our contemporaries lose themselves.

Well, never mind. We were discussing the American situa-tion in the 20's.

Shortly past the middle of the decade, S. S. Van Dine published *The Benson Murder Case,* in which Alvin Benson was shot to death under circumstances which suggested the fate of Joseph Elwell the bridge-expert. It was not a reconstruction of the Elwell case, as we can see for ourselves if we read the real-life account of the police-officer in charge of that affair. But it brought forward a new writer who juggled suspects with such dexterity, like whirling Indian-clubs, that we could only stare in admiration; and a new detective, Philo Vance, who said his method was psychology and scorned the cigarette-ends found near Benson's body. Three years later, when a crooked lawyer was poisoned with some villainous new stuff called tetraethyl lead in *The Roman Hat Mystery*, we saluted Ellery Queen.

Though these were the only practitioners of the front rank, both were so good that they held the scales almost level against their British confrères. It looked, in those far-off days, as though the golden age of the detective story had come. It now played strictly fair. It was adult. It had lost its clumsiness and grown to maturity.

Then came the 1930's. Then came the cleavage. The hard-boiled detective story, which for some years had been lurking in the magazines without anybody suspecting its inherent genius, suddenly blossomed out until it shadowed the whole field. Few writers, even experienced ones who had been dealing with a different type of story, were completely untouched by its influence. Novices rushed to get aboard the band-wagon. And there began, between the school of Sherlock Holmes and the school of Sam Spade, a difference which has been widening all these years.

Let us consider the hard-boiled type of story.

Whether you prefer this kind of writing is a matter of personal taste. Whether you acclaim it as good, on the other hand, depends on how it is done. If anybody wants to see how "economical, astringent, muscular prose" should really be handled, let him re-read the best stories of Melville Davisson Post. Post was a great master of prose style, whereas most of the moderns are fairly answerable to some other description.

But we are not here concerned with literary quality. We are concerned with the detective story, and what goes into it. Dashiell Hammett has been praised as "a creator of the first rank," belonging among "the small handful of others who brought something really new to their chosen field of effort," and as one whose "lean, dynamic, unsentimental narratives created a definitely *American style*, quite separate and distinct from the accepted English pattern."

These are the words of Howard Haycraft, a sound critic,

an admirable critic whose opinions we are bound to respect, and whom we can accuse of eccentric or unbalanced literary judgment only when he praises an undeserving hound named Carter Dickson.

But this originality, this glory of breaking fresh ground, again depends on what you do. You could get a finely original effect, for instance, by sending a whole procession of kangaroos across the stage during a performance of *Lohengrin* at Covent Garden or the Metropolitan Opera. You would be, definitely, a creator. You would have brought something really new to your chosen field of work. Or, to be more restrained about it, you could decide that the trouble with musical shows was the use of music, and the thing to do was have the musical show without any music at all; just as you can decide to have the detective story without any clues to follow or any rules to observe.

As we earlier discussed the saga of Brace and Du Kink, let's take a typical American detective novel of the later 30's. Its plot runs something like this:

The hero, Chip Hardstone, is a wise-cracking private detective with an attractive blonde stenographer. To Chip's office, in violent agitation, comes the lean, elderly, aristocratic J. T. Witherspoon, a millionaire with a country house in Sundown Hills.

Mr. Witherpsoon's daughter, it appears, has got herself involved with a notorious character called Smooth Ed Spumoni. A priceless crystal flask, with gold-work by Benvenuto Cellini, has been stolen from the millionaire's collection. Matters at home are tense, since—in addition to his ne'er-do-well son, his rebellious daughter, and his neurotic young wife—Mr. Witherspoon has further grounds for suspicion in that the butler is a blackmailer, the chauffeur an ex-convict, and the housekeeper a hop-head. What he wants, he says, is to recover the Cellini crystal and free his daughter from the clutches of Smooth Ed Spumoni.

"But no scandal, Mr. Hardstone!" pleads the millionaire. "Above all things, no scandal!"

Already, before going to the country house, Chip has accumulated a lot of information. Practically every character in the story calls on him and tries to retain him. These he first bluffs and then insults—all except the representative of an insurance company, whom he merely insults.

Arrived at the house in Sundown Hills, Chip finds the "mad family" of earlier fiction now so completely nuts as to require a psychiatrist rather than a detective. The daughter removes her clothes; the wife intimates that she is willing to do so; the son tries to knock Chip's head off on sight. Other friends swing punches at the son, at Chip, or at each other; and Chip, who replies by insulting everybody he has previously missed, is interrupted with the discovery that one of the guests has been found dead—his throat mangled—in the swimming pool.

(Observe the departure of originality here. The millionaire himself is seldom murdered. He must be kept alive to pay Chip's fee.)

But one of the guests is murdered. No less than eight persons, it appears, know some vital secret about the murder. All of them have disappeared. It being Chip's job to find them, in a roulette-ball spin round the city, he concentrates first on a mysterious red-haired girl who has been traced to an apartment house at the corner of Pineapple and Banana.

Racing to the apartment house, Chip finds the girl gone but a corpse on the floor. He flies to a second apartment house, only to find the girl gone again and another corpse on the floor. By the time he has reached the third apartment house and the fourth corpse, he is in a spot. The police are after him, the reporters are after him, Smooth Ed Spumoni is after him, even the millionaire is after him to call him off. Chip won't be called off. He intimates, with something very like blackmail, that the old s.o.b. can't get out of it after bringing *him* in.

"All the same," says Chip, "this set-up is hopeless!"

And again we agree, since the vital secrets turn out to be innocent side-games in which everybody is chiselling everybody else, and have nothing to do with the murders. Chip, on the point of being arrested by Captain Hooligan of the Homicide Bureau, suddenly gets an inspiration—it is never very clear how—that the murderer is J. T. Witherspoon's wife. He confronts her; there is a gun fight all over the house; and the wife, waiting only long enough to scream out a confession, falls dead at his feet.

This is the end of the story, leaving the reader in some doubt as to just what did happen after all.

Now why, at the outset, are the adventures of Chip Hardstone so vaguely familiar? What strikes a reminiscent note?

Despite the original kind of hero, despite the spit-in-your-eye style of writing, despite the chases and sluggings and kidnappings, we seem to have met this motiveless and clueless method somewhere before.

Don't we see that it's Inspector Brace and Reginald Du Kink all over again?

Instead of cuff-links, bus-tickets, and lace handkerchiefs which bear no relation to the problem, we have "secrets" which bear no relation to the problem either. Instead of the suspects doing their ring-around-the-rosebush outside the library, they now rush away from capture in cars and aircraft; but they still act either for no reasons at all, or for no reasons that are ever explained.

As for the fairness of the evidence, or the quality of the solution, the same test can be applied.

The American wheel, in these hard-boiled stories of the 30's, had turned full circle. We were back again among the whiskers and mothballs of an earlier era. Those very detective-story features of which the reader complained most bitterly in 1920, the features which were its essential faults, the features which craftsmen had worked so hard to eliminate ever since, were triumphantly hailed as a daring new departure from convention.

This period in America, it is true, produced its own first-raters. In 1934, with a story called *Fer-de-Lance,* Rex Stout by sheer power of characterization and plot-construction at once joined the company of Ellery Queen and S. S. Van Dine. There was Anthony Abbot, whose grim first novel *About the Murder of Geraldine Foster*—based on a legend of Courvoisier and Lizzie Borden—never seems to have achieved the full critical acclaim it deserves. In the front rank, or very close to it, were Clayton Rawson and C. Daly King.

But these were all practitioners in the great tradition, the clue-serpents and trap-baiters. Their narratives moved as fast as you could wish for; yet they ranged beside their British confrères of the same period, Margery Allingham and Ngaio Marsh and Nicholas Blake, in the vital business of presenting new ideas. In Nicholas Blake's first novel, *A Question of Proof,* you will find one instance of what is meant by the great tradition. The murder-knife unaccountably vanishes; and the investigators can't find it because it has been hidden, in front of their eyes, by being used as a tent-peg.

Yes; but what about the weaknesses in the English type of novel?

The fault here is just the same, though expressed in a different way. The "literary" type, like the hard-boiled, is too often apt to mistake style for substance. It imagines that with good writing, which sometimes becomes merely pretentious writing, you can disguise the lack of an original plot.

"Come, now!" the author seems to be saying. "I'm really a straight novelist, you know, indulging in this funny little medium of the detective story because nowadays it's become respectable. It's true I haven't got much of a mystery, or any very clear idea of how to handle it; but, if I give you strong characterizations and much talk-in-a-mist, you won't mind that?"

To which the answer is: Sir or madam, we do mind. Either you neglect the plot, which is bad; or else you fall off those stilts with a crash, which is worse.

(The next five sections of John Dickson Carr's Introduction deal with his reasons for not including Wilkie Collins' *The Moonstone* and Anna Katherine Green's *The Leavenworth Case,* and with his analyses of the ten detective novels which the publishers of his projected anthology called *The Ten Best,* but which Mr. Carr preferred, wisely, to call ten "of the" best . . . Perhaps, in a future issue of EQMM, we will bring you these fascinating, enlightening, and perceptive analyses by one of the foremost detective-story writers of our time and of all time.)

So we come to the end of a survey which has covered many years and no inconsiderable number of books. And now (I confess it) I am seized by a horrible temptation. My Better Nature, seraphic with upturned eyes and halo, pleads and whispers, "No!" But the devil won't be denied; gleefully he beckons. I have enjoyed writing this introduction so much—in contrast, it is to be feared, to the labours of the weary reader—that I want to end it with a list of rules on What To Do and What Not To Do.

Admittedly, this has been done in full tabular style by Carolyn Wells, by S. S. Van Dine, by H. Douglas Thomson, by Basil Hogarth, by Howard Haycraft, and others. More cautious lines have been taken by Monsignor Knox and by Miss Sayers herself. And I think these two latter writers were wise.

Once the evidence has been fairly presented, there are very few things which are not permissible. The oath of the Detection Club, stern though it may sound, does not forbid the employment of conspiracies, gangs, death-rays, ghosts, trapdoors, mysterious Chinese or homicidal lunatics. It is not so harsh as that. It merely enjoins the writer to preserve "a seemly moderation" in the use of them. The only thing it rules out, and rightly rules out, is the use of mysterious poisons unknown to science.

Those who nail a manifesto to the wall, saying, "The beginner will do this, and must under no circumstances do that," are in many cases quoting not rules but prejudices. That is the danger. It is a prejudice, like my own prejudice against having the murder turn out to be a suicide; and should freely be indicated as such. With all due respect and admiration for those who have compiled lists, it would not be difficult to show that they were often giving dubious advice and sometimes talking arrant nonsense.

"Disguise," declares one writer—to take a single instance —"disguise, of course, went out with the bustle."

To which the answer is: "My dear sir, that is a prejudice. Furthermore, it's not true. Have the goodness to read, among other stories with whose titles half a page could be filled, G. K. Chesterton's 'The Dagger with Wings,' R. Austin Freeman's *The Mystery of Angelina Frood,* Q. Patrick's *S.S. Murder,* Ellery Queen's *The Dutch Shoe Mystery,* Philip MacDonald's *The Wraith,* E. C. Bentley and H. W. Allen's *Trent's Own Case,* Anthony Berkeley's *Top-Story Murder,* or Agatha Christie's *Three-Act Tragedy*. Disguise is one of the best weapons in the armory. The test of a device is not whether it is new or old; there's nothing new under the sun; the test is what novel twist can be put on it."

Here, then, is my own list of Do's and Don'ts: compiled partly from those of the writers quoted above and partly from my own heart's blood.

1. The criminal shall never turn out to be the detective, or any servant, or any character whose thoughts we have been allowed to share.

2. The criminal shall never at any time be under serious

suspicion until the unmasking. If you haven't the ingenuity to keep his identity a secret until the end, at least pretend you have. Even if the reader outguesses you, and your thunderbolt-ending doesn't come off, the effect is far more satisfying than if you apologize for your murderer by "clearing" him in an early chapter.

3. The crime shall be the work of one person. While the murderer in some instances may be allowed to have a confederate, you will ruin your story if two or three or four people are dragged in as accomplices. The essence of a detective story is that the one guilty man shall fool the seven innocent; not that the one innocent shall be fooled by the seven guilty.

4. The crime shall be clean-cut. If a character disappears and is assumed to be murdered, state frankly what has happened to him. If he hasn't been murdered it's a pity; but the reader has a right to a clear stating of the problem.

Those are four golden maxims. In each one I believe. And each one you will find shattered—shattered admirably, shattered to bits, shattered by a mighty hammer—in the "best" detective novels, while the reader wishes to do nothing but applaud. Because they are not really rules; they are only prejudices.

The greatest trap into which a critic can fall is to maintain that something is being "done" in the current year, as though there were a style in shrouds as well as in hats, or to maintain that something else has gone out of fashion. When Carolyn Wells's *The Technique of the Mystery Story* was first published in 1913, the late Miss Wells was already talking about outworn devices. But nothing ever has gone out of fashion, and nothing ever will, provided only that the old trick can be worked in a new way. Yesterday's fashion may not be today's; but it may be none the worse for that. On the contrary, it may be a devil of a sight better.

So let them write their stories, the hopeful young men and women! Let them not be frightened by that worst bogey of all, the feeling that they have got to be innovators. Let them remember that the real test of their mental skill is in the drive and nimbleness and strategy of their play; it does not consist in putting the goal-posts in the middle of the field or dashing through half the game with a ball that isn't here. And you and

I, serene in our armchairs as we read a new detective story, can continue blissfully in the old game, the great game, the grandest game in the world.

Second thoughts—after seventeen years

I well remember when and how the above outburst was written. It was written in London during the cold and gusty spring of 1946, and in my flat on Haverstock Hill. Despite an acute housing shortage, I had obtained that flat for reasons quite apart from my Scottish luck. When I moved into it in 1943, Adolf Hitler still walked the earth. He had yet to unleash the LITTLE BLITZ, the flying bombs, the rockets, and other drolleries from his inexhaustible sense of humour. But we were all expecting something of the sort. And nobody except your obedient servant was stupid enough to want a flat on the top floor.

If I were to write again of favorite detective novels, should I change anything above? Not one sentiment, not one author. The ensuing seventeen years have produced no writers who are better, nor any (tell it not in Gath) one-half so good. It may be that for four of the authors I should choose a different novel. A. E. W. Mason, for instance, might better be represented by *The House of the Arrow;* Philip MacDonald by *The Rasp;* Ellery Queen by *The Chinese Orange Mystery;* and Dorothy L. Sayers by *Strong Poison.*

But this is a minor matter; it is the author and his detective who count. "Then you still believe all that?" will be the whisper of kindly friends. "Haven't you learned anything in all these years?" Since I have learned wisdom in no other respect, it is useless to hope for it here. And a man should always be willing to defend his prejudices. As he gets on in years, those prejudices may constitute the most satisfactory sum total of all the things he has—or is.

JOHN DICKSON CARR

RING LARDNER

Stop Me—If You've Heard This One

. . . DISCOVERY!

Ring Lardner "stopped finding any fun in his work ten years before he died." This was revealed by his close friend, F. Scott Fitzgerald. Perhaps one of the reasons Ring Lardner was a frustrated, melancholy man was that the world, including most of its literary critics, insisted on considering him a sports writer and humorist, interested only in laughs. Today we know differently. William Bolitho, that perceptive man, regarded Ring Lardner as "the greatest and sincerest pessimist America has produced." Today we know Ring Lardner for the superb satirist he was—a "sympathetic hater of the human fourflusher," be he (or she) a baseball player or a politician, a Broadway producer or a smalltown prodigal son, a Manhattan call girl or a Long Island socialite . . .

And now we bring you a Ring Lardner story written about five years before he died. So far as we have been able to check, this story has not been included in any of Ring Lardner's collections of short stories. To most readers, if not to all, "Stop Me—If You've Heard This One" will be a genuine Lardner "discovery." (We wonder if Babette Rosmond and Henry Morgan, editors of SHUT UP, HE EXPLAINED: *A Ring Lardner Selection, published by Scribner's in 1962, knew of the existence of "Stop Me—If You've Heard This One.") In any case, this "unknown" sample ("just a kind of mystery") of Ring Lardner's "great and sincere pessimism" should not be missed . . .*

On a certain day in the year 1927, Jerry Blades and Luke Garner, young playwrights, entered the Lambs' Club at the luncheon hour and were beckoned to a corner table by an actor friend, Charley Speed. Charley had a guest, recognized at once by the newcomers as Henry Wild Osborne, famous globe-trotter, raconteur, and banquet-hall fixture.

"Sit down, boys," said Charley after he had introduced them to the celebrity. "I'm due at a house committee meeting and you can keep Harry entertained."

But "Harry" proved perfectly capable of providing his own entertainment and theirs, and he opened up with a barrage of Pats and Mikes, Ikeys and Jakeys, and MacPhersons and MacDonalds that were not only comparatively new but also quite funny—at least, so Blades and Garner judged from the whole-hearted laughter of the narrator himself.

When he had displayed his mastery of all the different dialects of both hemispheres, he related a few personal adventures, in some of which other big men had played parts and which, to his small audience, were much more interesting than the chronicles concerning fictional Mikes, Sandys, and Abes. He told them of Lindbergh, who had accepted an invitation to dine with him in his apartment and had come wearing a hat that did not fit, explaining he had borrowed it at his hotel, not having had a hat of his own since he was a child.

"He's a man of one idea. He will talk about aviation and nothing else. He dislikes crowds and has had difficulty maintaining a show of good nature in the face of unwelcome attention. He has managed to do so, however, excepting when addressed or referred to as 'Lucky Lindy,' a nickname he just can't stand.

"He was kind enough to ask me to fly with him on Long Island and naturally I jumped at the chance. We took a taxi out to the field and every traffic cop on the way stopped us so they could shake hands with him and pat him on the back. I thought we'd never get there, and when we did get there, that we wouldn't be able to leave the ground without killing two or three hundred people.

"He said it was like that every time he attempted to go up or land—hundreds of wild-eyed fans crowding around him in spite of the danger. But we did finally get started and it was wonderful. I felt as safe as if I'd been riding in a chair at Atlantic City."

He told them of Fred Stone—of an occasion when he and Fred had dined together at old Rector's. At the next table were two famous Princeton football players, each over six feet tall and weighing two hundred and twenty pounds. The sons of Old Nassau had been drinking something contentious and tried to pick a quarrel with him and Stone, though they had no idea who Stone and Osborne were and certainly could have had no reason to "fuss" at either of them.

Fred did not want to make a scene and ignored the athletes' slurring remarks, but when he and Osborne got up to leave and the Princeton boys followed and jostled them, the comedian lost his temper, grasped a collegiate throat in each hand, lifted the pair up bodily, and knocked their heads together till they were unconscious, and then tossed them into the checkroom.

He told them of having been in the Metropole at supper with Herman Rosenthal the night the gambler was called away from the table and shot to death by four gangsters; of having warned Jim Jeffries not to drink the tea that "poisoned" him just prior to the fight with Jack Johnson; of having tipped off Kid Gleason in 1919 that some of his ballplayers were throwing him down; of having accompanied General Pershing to Marshal Foch's headquarters when the American commander offered his armies to the Frenchman to do with as he pleased; of having escaped death by eight inches when the Germans dropped their first bombs on Paris; of having taught Lloyd Waner how to avoid always hitting to left field; of having taken Irving Berlin out of "Mike's" place and set him to writing songs; of having advised Flo Ziegfeld to dress his chorus in skirts instead of tights; of having suggested and helped organize the Actors' Equity; and of having informed the Indiana police where to find Gerald Chapman.

He had been everywhere and seen everything, and Blades and Garner envied him his wealth of experience.

He hoped he hadn't bored them.

"Not at all!" said Blades.

"It's a treat to listen to you," said Garner.

"You ought to write a book of memoirs," said Blades.

"I've been urged to many times," said Osborne, "but I'm never in one place long enough to get at it. I've got chronic wanderlust."

"So have I," said Garner, "but it doesn't do me any good."

"Poor Luke!" said Blades. "He'd like to live on trains, but he's only been out of the state once."

"Not counting two or three trips to Newark," said Garner.

"Travel is a great thing!" observed Osborne. "It has its drawbacks and discomforts, but one's experiences and adventures are worth a lot more than they cost."

"Luke had a queer little experience the only time he went anywhere," said Blades. "Tell Mr. Osborne about it, Luke."

"Oh, it's nothing much. Just a kind of mystery I was mixed up in on the way out to Chicago."

"Let's hear it," said Osborne.

"Well," said young Garner, "I'll try to make it brief. About a year ago I had an idea for a play. I wrote one act and read it to George M. Cohan. He liked it and told me to finish it and bring it to him. When I had finished it, I learned he was in Chicago. I couldn't wait for him to get back, so I decided to go out there and see him, though I had to borrow money for the trip. I was impatient and took the Twentieth Century.

"In the section across from me there was one of the most beautiful women I ever saw—a young woman about twenty-five, dark, well dressed, full of class, *nice*-looking. She had a book, one of J. S. Fletcher's detective stories, but I noticed she didn't turn more than three pages between New York and Albany. Most of the time she just stared at the river.

"She was going to Chicago, too, and I'll confess that I wished we would become acquainted long before we got there. I wished it, but didn't believe it, because she was evidently not the kind you could meet unconventionally.

"I went in the diner about seven and was given the only vacant chair at a table for four. My table companions were an elderly couple and a man a little older than I, a man of striking appearance, handsome, and dark enough to suggest Spanish or Italian ancestry.

"The elderly couple finished their meal and left. The 'Spaniard' was just beginning to eat when the girl from my car came in and took one of the seats just vacated.

"Her glance and the 'Spaniard's' met. There was mutual recognition and an emotion close to panic on both sides. The man got up hurriedly, put a five-dollar bill on the table, and went out of the diner, toward the front end of the train. The girl grasped the table as if she must have something to hang on to. She was utterly white and I thought she was going to faint. She didn't, but her hands shook violently as she wrote her order.

"I pretended I had not observed the little scene and did my best not to look in her direction. I got through as quickly as I could and relieved her of the embarrassment of my presence. As I was paying my check, the waiter asked me if I knew whether the other man was coming back. Before I could reply, the girl said, 'No,' then bit her lip as if she were mad at herself for speaking.

"She returned to her section after a long time, over an hour. She sat staring out into the darkness for a half hour more. Then she got up and stepped across the aisle to me and said, 'I must ask you to do me a favor. You will think it's queer, but I can't help it. You saw the man leave the table when I sat down. I want you to find him and give him this note. I would ask the porter, but I am afraid he might give it to the wrong person. The man is probably in the club car. Just hand him the note. Then come back and tell me. Will you do it?'

"I found him in the club car, delivered the note she had intrusted to me, and returned and reported.

"She said, 'I am very, very grateful.'

"And then I went forward to the club car again and sat down to be out of the way when he came to her, as I felt sure he would.

"He was at the desk writing, but soon he rose and left. I was in quite a fever of curiosity and it strained my will power to stay where I was and not follow him and witness 'Act Two.' I tried to read and couldn't. When I finally turned in, close to midnight, the girl's berth was dark and the curtains drawn.

"I got up at Elkhart. The curtains were open across the aisle, but there was no sign of the girl. There was still no sign of her as we pulled into Englewood. I called the porter and asked whether he had seen her since the night before. He said why, yes, he had seen her around five o'clock, when he had helped her off the train at Toledo. 'Toledo!' I exclaimed. 'I thought she was going through.' The porter said he had thought so, too, but she must have changed her mind. I inquired if he had seen her talking with a handsome dark man.

He said no; that the only real dark man he had seen on that car was himself, and he wasn't handsome.

"I stood on the platform in the La Salle Station till all the passengers were off. The girl was not among them; I'm sure of that. But the 'Spaniard' was, and escorting him were two men who were obviously detectives.

"In the two days I was there, I read every story in every paper, trying to find a solution to 'my mystery,' but without success. And that's all there is to it, except that Mr. Cohan turned down my play."

"Very interesting!" Mr. Osborne remarked. "I believe if I had been you, I'd have followed the man and his escort, just to satisfy my curiosity."

"I'd have done that," said Garner, "if I hadn't thought there was still a chance that the girl would appear."

Charley Speed was back from the committee meeting. He and his guest bade the young playwrights goodbye and went out. Blades and Garner discussed the man they had just met.

"He tells dialect stories well," said Blades.

"If that's possible," said Garner. "To me, his own experiences are a lot more interesting."

"But I think," said Blades slowly, "I think somebody else told me that same stuff about Lindbergh and—"

"Yes," interrupted Garner, "and I'm under the impression that the one about Fred Stone isn't new to me. In fact, I'm pretty sure I heard it from Rex Beach and that Rex was with Stone when it happened."

Two years later Blades and Garner, now credited with a couple of Broadway hits, were guests at a "small" dinner party given by Wallace Gore, the publisher. Their host presented them to Mr. Henry Wild Osborne, who acknowledged the introduction as if it were a novelty.

Osborne sat between two adoring women who managed to keep him to themselves through the soup. But he was everybody's property and soon was regaling the whole table with up-to-the-minute episodes in the careers of Pat, Abe, and MacPherson. He ran out of them at last and his host said, "Harry, I wonder if you'd mind telling these people about your Chicago trip."

"What Chicago trip?"

"About the girl and the foreigner."

"Oh, that!" said Osborne. "Well, if you think they'd be interested."

"Of course they would!"

"Please, Mr. Osborne!"

"All right, then," said Osborne, "but I trust you folks not to spread it around. The Chicago police made a secret of the real facts and I promised them I wouldn't divulge it to any of my friends of the Fourth Estate."

He took a swallow of wine and began: "It was a month ago I had a wire from Charlie Dawes, asking me to come out there and advise him in a little matter—well, we won't go into that. I boarded the Broadway Limited and was settling down to a little session with de Maupassant when I noticed a beautiful girl, an authentic, perfect blonde, in the section across from me.

"I am past the age of train flirtations but this girl held my attention by the expression on her face, a look of ineffable sadness, of tragic longing for—I knew not what.

"I was weaving in my mind a blighted romance with her as its sorrowing heroine when Andy Mellon, walking through the car, saw me and stopped for a chat. He was with me till dinner-time, when he invited me to dine in his drawing-room, but I declined, saying I had eaten a late luncheon and would do without another meal. In reality, I was in no mood for talk, and shortly after he had gone, I made my way to the diner, trusting he would not uncover my mendacity.

"I told the steward I had no objections to sitting with others provided they were strangers, so he placed me at a table for four. A gray-haired, florid-faced old man and his comfortable fat wife were two of my companions. The third was a splendid, healthy specimen of young manhood, Scandinavian young manhood, a yellow-haired, sturdy son of Vikings.

"The old couple finished their simple repast and left. I was ordering and the handsome young giant was beginning to eat when the beautiful blonde girl I had observed in the sleeper came in and took one of the seats just vacated.

"The girl's eyes and the man's eyes met, and not for the first time, I could see. For their glance was charged with electricity—a bolt of lightning that struck something akin to terror in each. An instant afterwards, the young man was up from the table, laying a ten-dollar note beside his plate, and then he was gone, fleeing from the mysterious horror of this chance encounter with a woman whom God had never intended to inspire young manhood with anything but burning love.

"And the girl, the young woman—I started from my chair, ready to catch her if she swooned. For it seemed she must swoon, so pale she was. But with a marvelous show of courage she forced herself into a state of pseudo-calmness.

"I bolted my meal in a manner that would have caused my doctor intense mental anguish. I asked the waiter for my check and he, observing the young man's money lying there, inquired if I knew whether he was coming back. Before I could speak, the girl uttered a sharp, 'No,' then bit her lip as if in rage that she had said it.

"We were between Harrisburg and Altoona when she appeared again in the sleeper. She stopped beside me and put an unsealed, unaddressed envelope in my hand.

" 'It kills me to do this,' she said in a voice barely audible. 'I am not accustomed to asking favors from a stranger, but it is necessary and you look kind. I am sure you noticed the man, the young man, who was with us in the dining car, who got up and left when I sat down. I think you will find him in the club car and I want you to give him this. I cannot trust it to the porter. Don't wait for a reply. Just give it to him, and then come back here and tell me. Will you?'

"I answered, of course I would, and I begged her to inform me if there was something more I could do. 'No,' she whispered, 'nothing.'

"The young man was easily found. He was in the club car as she had guessed, staring straight ahead of him.

"Without a word I handed him the envelope, and returned to her and reported. She expressed gratitude with a smile that was more heart-rending than tears.

"My instinct, or sense of decency, ordered me not to pry. I took my book to the club car and tried vainly to read, for my brain was consumed with curiosity and anxiety as to what was going on between those two torn souls.

"When at length I turned in, at Pittsburgh, the berth opposite mine was dark and its curtains drawn.

"I rose in the morning as we were rushing through the Indiana town of Plymouth. The curtains across the aisle were open now, but there was no sign of the girl. Nor had she appeared as we slowed up for Englewood. My inquiry of the porter—had he seen her since the preceding night?—was answered in the affirmative. 'Yes, suh. She done leave us three hours ago, at Fort Wayne.'

"I remarked I had thought she was bound for Chicago. 'She sho' was Chicago bound,' said George, 'but young gals, dey got a "unailable" right to change deir min'.' I then asked if he had seen her conversing with a big, blond, handsome young man. 'No, suh. De only man she co'versed to was maself, and ma bes' frien's don't call me handsome or blond, neithuh.'

"I waited on the platform in the Union Station and watched all the passengers as they left the train. The girl was not among them, but the man was, and as he walked out to the taxi stand, I followed him unobtrusively, saw him enter a cab, and heard the starter say, 'Stevens House.' I went to the Sherman and changed, and awaited word from my friend, General Dawes.

"But I could not get my mind off the queer incidents of the trip and you can imagine the shock it gave me to read, in an afternoon paper, the story of a well-dressed, unidentified young woman who had committed suicide by throwing herself in front of the second section of the Broadway Limited at Fort Wayne.

"My duty was clear. I hurried to police headquarters, stated my name, and was received by the Chief. I told him I was sure he could earn the thanks of the Fort Wayne authorities and officials of the railroad by sending one of his men with me to the hotel where I believed my 'friend' of the train was stopping; that if I could find him, I was sure we would be able to learn the unfortunate girl's identity and perhaps the reason for her ghastly deed.

"The Chief delegated Captain Byrne to accompany me. As we drove up to the door of the hotel we saw policemen dispersing a crowd and other policemen lifting from the sidewalk the body of a man, the young Viking, with a bullet wound in his head, a revolver lying near where he had lain, and a newspaper clasped in his left hand.

"There were letters in his pocket, merely business letters, addressed to John Janssen, and the initials on his baggage were J. J. He was the son of one of the richest men in Chicago, and he, the young man now dead, had a wife and children in Lake Forest.

"I know who the girl was, too; the police found her name and her picture in young Janssen's possession. But they didn't tell his family and no one besides a few policemen and myself is aware that there was a girl in the case. The published reason for his act was temporary insanity induced by illness. And if he was sick, I have been dead for twenty years."

Osborne's narrative was over. Dinner was over, too, and Garner and Blades lingered behind the others in the march toward the card room.

"What do you suppose he's got against brunettes?" said Blades.

"And why," said Garner, "do you suppose he won't use the New York Central Lines?"

CHARLOTTE ARMSTRONG

The Other Shoe

"Celia could look like an angel, and be bright and beautiful. It took a while to realize how spoiled she was . . ." Romance and ratiocination—in a blend that Charlotte Armstrong has a special talent for . . .

"Jenny." A hand on my bare arm pulled me away from the group around the piano in the den. "Celia and Blair, in there . . ." Carmen said. "Look, I'm a pretty easygoing hostess, but Blair is drunk and Celia is screaming at him and it isn't funny any more. Do you think you could stop them?"

"Oh, Carmen, I'm sorry. But Celia pays less than no attention to me."

"She's your sister."

"Stepsister," I corrected.

Carmen's big eyes flashed. "You better do something—for Blair's sake," she added knowingly.

"I'll try," I said.

I went into the living room. It wasn't hard to spot my stepsister, Celia, since she and I were dressed exactly alike. All of us at this party were the remains of a wedding—gay souls who had chased the bride and groom with traditional hilarity, and had then wound up at this country house of Carmen's to carry on into the night.

Celia and I still wore our bridesmaid's dresses, pale apricot organdy, and both of us still had on our feet the fantastic straw-colored devices, a few narrow straps tying on some four-inch heels, that were supposed to be shoes.

Those shoes!

In the living room, people were silently listening—in malice or in helpless distaste. Celia was standing in an ugly pose, as if her feet hurt and she didn't care who knew it. Her face, that could look like an angel's, was pinched and sharpened.

"And if you thought," she was saying in a piercing voice, "that you were just going to use my money without any advice from me, you were living in a dream world, genius boy."

"Advish, sure," Blair Meaghan mumbled. There had been a lot of champagne at the wedding and he seemed to have had more than his share of it. "Always glad to lishen to advish. But don't give me orders. Have another drink."

"You take my money, you take my orders," Celia snapped. "And be glad to get both. I'm in on this deal all the way, or I'm out. Understand?"

"You don't unnerstan'," he muttered. "Papers signed. Bishness deal. Ashk anybody." Blair waved his glass. His dark hair wouldn't plaster down—it rose in a crest. I adored him and I hated this ugly scene, but I didn't see what I could do.

"Business!" Celia hooted. "When you came whining to me, I said I'd keep on with the financing. That was for pity's sake. But I'm not *giving* you the money."

Blair's face was pale. "Coursh not. Inveshment . . ."

Celia said, "You do what I say or I take my money *out!* Do you hear, or are you too drunk?"

"Orders, no." Blair shook his head. "Papers don't say—"

"I spit on the papers," shrieked Celia. "You do it or I'm getting out and there won't be any money. If you want to start any lawsuits you can count on me telling how you whined and cried after I threw you over. You'd enjoy that. And you'd lose. Don't think you wouldn't. Last chance." She still thought she might get her way.

But Blair raised his glass. "To the money! Hail and farewell! And I hope it's farewell to you, forever." He drained the liquid down. "I ought to wring your neck," he said, rather quietly. "A public servish."

Nobody else in the room was speaking or moving. Everybody knew that Celia and Blair had been engaged last summer. Everybody knew that Celia had wanted someone else—and hadn't got him. Everybody knew how much her money meant to Blair.

It was her own money—from her dead mother's family. Neither father nor I had any. Celia did as she pleased with what was her own. She had invested it, all properly, in Blair's project, and in what he thought was good faith.

Celia could look like an angel, and be bright and beautiful. It took a while to realize how spoiled, how totally unreliable she was. Blair knew it now, twice over. There she stood, welshing on a business deal in a fit of arrogance, and there he stood, watching his hard-wrought plan, his work, his hope, his dream, dying by her hand.

He wasn't in love with Celia any more.

He had thought she was civilized. But she was like a stone.

There was only one thing I could think of doing. I took Blair's arm. "Blair, take me home?" I begged.

"What, Jenny?" He was so angry or so drunk he seemed blind.

"I've got to go home, right away," I said urgently. Blair had always been fond of me, and kind.

"Why, what's the matter?" He wasn't seeing me, blind as he was, but at least he recognized my voice. He let me lead him out of that room. I didn't have to turn and look to know the contempt that would be on Celia's face. She, and everyone else in the room, knew very well how deeply I was in love with Blair.

At least, I had broken up the nasty scene. Carmen fluttered after us with my stole. Her husband warned me that Blair must not drive a car. So there we were, ten o'clock that night, in Blair's convertible, with me driving and Blair sodden on the seat beside me.

The last sound I heard from that house was Celia's voice: "Let Jenny comfort him. Jenny likes nothing better." I made the car jump away from the sound of her laughter.

Carmen's long low house sits on a hill and the driveway goes to the north and winds down gradually to the highway. We hadn't yet reached the main road when I discovered that I couldn't possibly drive a car in those ridiculous shoes.

I pulled in close to the shrubbery and parked, unbuckled the ankle straps, got the silly things off my feet, and sat massaging my toes.

Blair said in a clear and sober voice, "I'll drive, Jenny. Thanks for getting me out of there. I thought it was better to act drunk," he told me quietly. "Because that is a scene I never want to remember."

His voice made me want to cry. But I am not one to cry or rage or carry on. Celia did too much of that. I said in my normal commonsense voice, "What does it mean if Celia takes the money out?"

"I start at the bottom again," he said. "It's all to do over."

What Blair Meaghan wanted to do is not impossible. It can be done; it has been done. Yet there is really no way to do it. He wanted to produce and direct a motion picture. The "way" to that is so arduous and chancy, such a zigzag among hopes and promises, such a miracle of timing, that nothing can produce an independent motion picture but a powerful dream and the courage to survive a thousand heartbreaks.

I listened to him and I knew he would survive. He wasn't whining. He spoke in a clear tight voice, about loans and percentages and banks and the screenplay and the actors who would not and could not wait—the whole web of tentative and interdependent commitments that had taken him two years to weave, but which had now vanished with Celia's decision.

We forgot to change seats, he in his need to talk and me in my need to listen. Celia was wrong about my liking nothing better than to comfort Blair. There were many things I would have liked better than to listen to the crisp exact details of his ruin.

Half an hour went by. Cars passed in the highway below us. Not many. They couldn't see us, nor we them. No car came down Carmen's drive. Nobody else left the party. There we were, halfway down the hill, forgotten and forgetting, until finally Blair's voice ran down. He looked at his watch.

"Ten thirty-six," he said. "We better get going. Thanks for listening, Jenny. It helped. You always help me."

He did sound eased. He swung me over his lap and took the wheel. We continued downward, turned to the right on the highway, and came opposite the long, little-used flight of wooden stairs that led up the middle of the hill to Carmen's house.

There was something lying out of place, there in the margin.

Blair braked. The moon was up and we could see the heap of organdy.

We sprang from the car and there she was. Celia. In the dusty weeds, and dead.

No car came by while Blair used his flashlight long enough to make sure she was dead, and to see that she had been strangled.

"We can't help her," he said harshly. His fingers bit my arm. "Get in." I limped on stockinged feet. "Quick!" He lifted me into the car. "Oh, Lord, don't leave a shoe!"

He picked it off the pavement and threw it into my lap. He ran around, jerked the car away from there, and yanked it sharply to the left onto a country road, which was another way back to town—the way we called "going around the mountain."

I couldn't speak. I couldn't think. But when we were into a fold of the hill, he stopped the car. "You don't get it." I could feel him trembling.

"We shouldn't run away," I said.

"What else can we do?" he said grimly. "No, you don't get it. But I do. I said I'd like to wring her neck, remember? In front of a room full of witnesses. Who is going to believe that you and I were talking in the car all this while, and that *somebody else* came and wrung her neck?"

"But I can swear—"

"Who would believe you?" he said sadly. "Ah, Jenny, that's the way it is. Don't you see?"

I saw. That was the way it was. My heart had been on my sleeve for all to see, for him to see, a long, long time. No testimony of mine could help him.

"What good can it do if you and I are both dragged into the limelight and dirtied by the newspapers?" he demanded. "We didn't hurt her. But we'll be the first ones suspected. We are set up for it. Perfectly."

"We'd be cleared," I said feebly, "as soon as they find out—"

"And will suspecting us and dirtying us *help* them find out?" he said angrily. "How could it? Suspecting us will only help the one who did do it. By the time they get through with you and me . . ." He shook his head desperately. "I'm not going to let this happen. You were good to listen. You were doing what was kind. You don't deserve to be dragged into something like this. Just because I had to cry on your shoulder—"

"You didn't cry," I murmured.

But I could see ahead now and if I had been the kind to carry on, I would have cried. I could see myself trying to tell the truth, which would sound so feeble and unbelievable beside the powerful motives both of us had to—hurt Celia, who had hurt us.

I thought of my father, who was old and not well. Celia's death would be rough enough on him. How much worse, to have to watch me being suspected of her murder! I felt a pang of terror when I realized that on top of all the rest, I was Celia's heir. And loved the man, as everyone knew, who needed Celia's money so much.

Blair was right. We were set up for it—both of us, together, perfectly.

"Jenny," Blair said, "we are going to have to get out from under."

"I don't see how," I said.

"We've lost—let's see—thirty-nine minutes. If we could account for that time some other way . . ."

"Hurry on to town, you mean?"

"No, we can't make up that much time. And we can't take the chance of speeding. But I've got an idea so crazy . . . Jenny, have you nerve enough to fake an alibi?"

"I guess so."

"I suppose it's wrong—"

"I'm not so sure it would be wrong." My teeth were chattering. "It might be foolish."

"We'll go back if you say so," Blair told me. "I could take it. Don't much care. But I want to get *you* out of this mess. Please let me, Jenny?" he begged. "It will be so damn nasty."

The thing I was thinking now was purely selfish. If we had to go through something "so damn nasty," then never (never, never, never!) could Blair and I be together. "What do you think of those two? Hah!" "Pretty fishy." "What's the answer? He got the money, she got her man. Hah!" I could hear it . . .

The law couldn't *make* us innocent. We would be guilty the moment we got together—or judged guilty by people's tongues. So we would have to stay apart.

I took hold of myself. "If you've got an idea, tell me," I said.

We sat there a few more minutes, while Blair figured it out. That scenic mountain road was not much used at night. We were lucky, and no car came by.

Blair was doing arithmetic. He explained. I understood. We could try.

Finally we went on another mile. High on the bank to our

right was a cabin. Blair knew who sometimes lived there. It was a wild and lonely spot, but we could see a light in the windows.

Blair let the car coast silently on the slight downgrade, until we were well beyond that cabin. Then he stopped the car and I got out.

"It had better be you," Blair whispered, "because everyone thought I was drunk, remember? Can you do this, Jenny?"

"Of course," I said. "Wait till I get my shoes."

"Shoes?" He fumbled around on the seat of the car. "Jenny, we can *use* your shoes," he exclaimed. "Take just this one. Hook the heel in your belt. You are supposed to have been walking, but of course you couldn't walk in those things. Look, I'll throw your other shoe out of the car a couple of miles farther on. You watch out for it. That's going to look good. Look like evidence. Now, don't try to rouse anybody for nine or ten minutes. Can you time it? Use the waiting to beat up your stockings. Maybe your dress. Remember, you have walked you don't know how far. But it's taken you nearly an hour. This is how we make up those lost minutes. Use the phone right away. I know this guy, Frederick, is there, this week-end. There's a light. But if by chance he isn't home, you break a window and get in and use that phone."

"I will. I will. I understand."

"It's risky. If I meet anyone in the next few miles, we'll be in the soup, Jenny." He touched my cheek. "So young and fair . . ." I thought he said.

"We are in the soup," I said impatiently. "Let's do it, Blair. Better to try to get out than just stay there."

His fingertips trailed off my face. The car started and softly crept away.

I paced and stamped and kicked the ground with my stockinged feet. I dragged my organdy along some briary stuff. I tore my stole. I fell on my knees to dirty my skirt. These were mad antics, alone in that wild dark silent spot. All the time I was counting off the minutes. Not thinking about Celia. Not thinking about anything but making his plan work.

Finally, I went limping and panting up the rutted way to the cabin. I beat on the door. The man who opened it was stricken dumb.

"Excuse me for disturbing—" I was really breathless. "Our car is stuck up the road. Could I please use your phone?"

"Of course," he said shrilly, as if I had frightened him out of his wits. "Come in. Come in."

He rolled his eyes at me as I limped in, looked about, and spotted his phone. I called my father's house. "Dad? It's Jenny. Blair and I started home around the mountain and the car broke down. I just don't want you to worry. What time is it now?"

"It's eleven-o-four," said my Dad in gruff precision. "I thought you were going to stay over to Carmen's."

"No, we started home. But I don't know when we'll get in now. Got to call a garage."

"Was it a crackup, Jenny?" Dad was suspicious.

"No, no. I'm perfectly all right, and so is Blair. Something conked out in the motor, that's all. Don't worry."

"Where is Celia?"

"Oh, she stayed," I said carelessly. (I couldn't tell him she was dead. I wasn't supposed to know it. Ah, but he would know all too soon!)

I called an all-night garage.

"Lady, that's a long way around the mountain, and it's pretty late."

"It's only a little after eleven," I said tartly, and gratefully. I argued with him, emphasizing the time, insisting that I had left a friend marooned in the car. At last he agreed to send somebody. Then I sagged.

"Sit down," my host said cordially, as if he had now assimilated his surprise. "You look tired. My name, by the way, is Lloyd Frederick."

"I'm Jenny Olcutt. I guess I look outlandish. This costume was for a garden wedding, a long time ago today."

"You look very pretty," he said gallantly. "A bit bedraggled. Haven't you any shoes? How far did you have to walk? Better let me pour you a drink."

He was an extraordinarily handsome man. A small-time actor, Blair had said. No one could have been kinder. He brought me the drink. He also brought a big bowl full of warm water and I stripped off my ruined nylons and put my feet, that I had taken care to bruise, into the warm comfort of it.

Frederick watched with amusement as I plucked the shoe from where it was hanging at my belt.

"You can see that these aren't exactly hiking boots," I

said, patting my belt. "Oh, me," I sighed. "I've lost my other shoe."

"Shoe!" He raised an eyebrow at the frivolous contraption. "I thought it was some kind of modernistic corsage. How could you even stand up in such a thing?"

"They are pretty much for sitting down," I laughed. "Still, it's possible." I thrust my damp toes into it and fingered the straps. "Like this. Oh, darn, the other one is lost. And they cost a fortune."

"A fortune? For three cents' worth of whatever that is?" He seemed amused. "There's never any traffic on this road at night. No one is going to run over your other shoe. We'll find it."

He was going to take his car out and bring me to Blair. I knew that Blair had had plenty of time to fake a breakdown, so I didn't stall too long with the footbath. I played my role. I thrust aside the heavy knowledge of Celia's death, and the heavy knowledge that I was telling lies and using this kind man for a purpose he couldn't imagine. I even found it possible to be rather gay and to look at him flirtatiously.

We went outside. I was barefoot. I "forgot" my one shoe.

He went behind the cabin and backed his car out from a kind of lean-to. I got in. It was a strange ride. For some reason neither of us spoke of anything but my missing shoe. We were obsessed by it. We went on a mile, two miles. No shoe in the road. We went almost three miles.

Then we saw the flames. I screamed. A car was burning, down there, down at the bottom of the mountain slope off to the left. We got out and ran. A strange man stood at the brink. Then I saw Blair lying on the road.

I knelt beside him in panic. His warm hand clung to mine. I could hear the stranger talking rapidly to Mr. Frederick. "Me and a friend was coming around the mountain in his half-truck. Didn't mean to get on this road. Fact, we was lost. We was looking for a turnaround. So we find this fella, stalled in a fancy car. Well, so we manage to turn the truck and we was going to give him a push, see would that start his motor. By golly, that fancy job went right outa control! He pretty near went over with her. Just made it out, as she tipped and went over. Busted his leg, though, or so it looks like. Fella that was with me, *he's* gone back to town in the truck to get an ambulance out here. Better wait on *it,* I'd say. Don't want to move no broken bones. Cheee, look at her burn!"

Only I could hear Blair's whisper. "Jenny, too many shoes. I must have given you *her* shoe."

Celia's shoe!

"They are just alike," I whispered.

"When I found a *pair* of shoes on the car floor . . . didn't know what to do. Couldn't throw one of them out—Jenny, I didn't know which foot! Do you see? Couldn't let you end up with two left shoes. Fatal. Didn't know which one was the 'other' shoe."

"Ssh," I was so close we could have kissed. "Where are my shoes now?"

"In the car. Burning."

"They'll burn fine," I said. "It won't matter. Are you hurt very much?"

"Not so bad," he said, his voice low but calm, almost cheerful. "Doesn't anything shake your nerve?" He caught at my shoulder. "Skip all this, Jenny. You'd better tell the truth. Nobody on earth could ever believe . . . So young and fair."

His voice had become too loud. So I kissed him. Afterward, I whispered, "Too late. We have to stick to the story. Don't you talk at all."

"If you get hurt—" he began, and then he fainted.

I rode into town in the ambulance when it came. All the way I thought about those shoes. Celia's right shoe was in the man's cabin. Both my shoes had burned with Blair's convertible. But I'd said I'd lost one on the road. Well, I would say that it must have been taken away by some animal.

When Blair, still unconscious, had been delivered to the hospital and I was limping wearily through the lobby to call a cab and get home, I ran into the policeman.

"You Miss Jenny Olcutt?" He wore plain clothes, but he was some kind of policeman—I knew it at once. "Had a little trouble?" he asked.

"Well, yes, we did, and I'm—a little bit worn out." I smiled politely.

"I don't know if you've been told." He shifted his weight. "Miss Celia Olcutt. Isn't that your sister?"

"Stepsister," I corrected mechanically.

"She was found dead," he said, abruptly enough to shock me.

It wasn't difficult to look shocked. I was scared.

"Now, I understand there was a quarrel at this party?" So he knew about that.

"Yes, that's why Mr. Meaghan and I left early."

"Pretty drunk, was he?"

"Well, I drove. He fell asleep."

"Left that house out there at ten o'clock? Took the mountain road? Why?"

"I don't know why," I said flatly. Blair and I had not discussed any possible reason. But I saw, now, that my very lack of reason was more convincing.

"Car stalled, you say? So you walked about three miles back to this Frederick's place? Why back?"

"Going ahead was farther and steeper," I explained.

"Why didn't your boy friend do the walking?"

"Well, you see, he had been drinking."

"Yeah," the policeman said. It was convincing. "Now you were at Frederick's place by eleven-o-four?"

"Was I?" I frowned.

"That's when you phoned your father. The garage says you phoned them at eleven-o-eight. That right?"

"I guess so," I said, looking bewildered. (But I was not. He was only doing the arithmetic that Blair and I had planned for him to do.)

"Now, Celia Olcutt," he went on, "she left the party at ten twenty. Must have walked down those long stairs."

"Why?" I burst out. "What for? Was she going to hitchhike on the highway? Or what?" I honestly did not know the answer. My bewilderment was so convincing that I felt a surge of confidence.

"We think she could have had a rendezvous," he said. "She was seen talking on the phone. Or could be she just wandered outside and somebody called to her." He looked sly.

I looked as baffled as I genuinely felt. "*Called* to her?"

"Maybe I better check some figures with you, young lady. Mr. Meaghan's car went a mile down the drive to the bottom of the stairs, then three miles beyond. At maximum speed on that kind of road at night it would have got to the place where it broke down in, say, seven or eight minutes. After that you walked in your stocking feet three miles up and downgrade in the dark. Superhuman if you did it in say, less than forty-five minutes. So even taking the fastest times, it didn't work out.

Celia Olcutt left the house ten twenty, and it must have taken her *some* time to get down to the highway and get killed. Let me see—all you and Meaghan had was between, say, ten twenty-five and—"

"What are you talking about?" I said. "Ten twenty-five?"

"I mean if you killed her," he said.

I just stared at him.

"If you did, then you got to tear off four miles on the mountain road and walk back three and get there not long after eleven. It just don't work out."

"You've lost me," I said to him boldly.

"I'm saying that if you really walked back from that breakdown, then you and Blair Meaghan are alibied for the murder of Celia Olcutt."

"I should hope so," I said angrily.

"Now, now," he said in a gentle tone. "I can see you aren't a stupid young lady. You had motives, you know—both of you."

"Did we?" I protested. "Well, how did we get at her? Did we wait around for our victim to 'wander' out?"

"Or you called her out, on the phone," he said soberly. "There's a phone booth in a gas station not too far down the highway."

"But who could have phoned her?" I asked in real perplexity. "Did someone *call* her to the phone? Would *she* answer the phone in Carmen's house?"

He let out a humming sound. I had dented him. "Well, I'll tell you, Miss, I got to go over the ground. And that's my duty. How about coming with me? And talk to this Frederick, too?"

"Now?" I rubbed my eyes.

"I know you're tired. Especially after that long walk." I didn't like the sound of that.

"I might as well," I said. "How could I sleep?"

I went with him. I knew, all the time, that our story hinged on one thing. The body of Celia must have had only one shoe. (Her other shoe was at Frederick's, and supposed to be mine.) But no shoes of mine were lying in the road. Our story lacked that bit. And Celia's missing shoe was potentially dangerous—as soon as my policeman saw it.

Yet the one thing that would really give us away would be if the police were to find any traces of my own two shoes in the burning car. Then Blair and I would be proved liars—we would be prime suspects. Celia's shoe would then become evidence against us.

I went with the policeman because I had to know.

I couldn't ask, but I might find out.

I did. We stopped at the point of the accident and looked down at the ruins of Blair's car. A man in uniform came up to us. "Not a thing left," he said. My policeman checked his speedometer and we drove on.

I breathed a little easier.

It was close to dawn, but Lloyd Frederick was up and about. "Couldn't sleep," he said. "Burning automobiles, broken legs, young woman in distress—too much for *me*."

He let us in and offered coffee.

My policeman said, "Reason I got to check up on this car breakdown, there's been a murder. Stepsister of *this* Miss Olcutt got strangled to death last night."

"Not Celia Olcutt!" cried Lloyd Frederick.

"You know the lady?" The policeman and I were both suddenly suspicious.

"Of course. I met her in a business way." He went through a gamut of explanations, which added no light. Then my policeman got down to Celia's murder.

"Tell me what happened around here last night. You hear Mr. Meaghan's car go by, for instance? If so, when?"

"I may have heard it," Frederick cocked his handsome head. "Lord, I don't know. I was reading scripts. Paying no attention. I don't even know when Miss Jenny Olcutt got here." He smiled at me.

"You know this Miss Olcutt, too?"

"Never saw her before tonight, to my sorrow," he said gallantly. His eyes sought mine.

"I'm looking for some kind of tricky time business," said my policeman frankly. "This Meaghan had a real dilly of a fight with the murdered girl. He even said he ought to wring her neck. He had plenty of motive. What I need now is his opportunity."

Frederick looked startled. "But wasn't Miss Jenny with him? You don't think she—"

"Oh, I wonder," my policeman said blithely, "because it's my job to wonder. Now, they tell me that shoes were worn at this wedding. But it's a funny thing." My heart stopped.

"Where are this Miss Olcutt's shoes? Maybe their condition could tell me something."

He looked shrewd. Didn't he believe that I had walked three miles? Was there a sign on me, something I didn't know about, to tell him that I hadn't?

"This lady's shoes, if that's what you can call them, won't tell you much," Lloyd Frederick said. "I'll show you." He rummaged on a shelf and turned to us with a pair of shoes in his hands. "See? I finally found your other one," he said to me, flashing his smile. "You must have dropped it just after you started walking to this cabin. You see, officer? She couldn't walk in these. In fact, these are sitting-down shoes, so I am told." He was being very charming.

"*Those* are *shoes!*" my policeman said, staring at them incredulously.

"May I put them on?" I said.

So I put them on. I stood up in the silly things. My feet were swollen and the straps cut into them. But, standing there in *two* shoes, I was safe. Blair was safe. Our story was safe; it would hold up. Who could prove it wasn't true?

I could.

"I guess I'm not Cinderella," I sighed. "I'm the stepsister. These are Celia's shoes. See, they're too small for me!"

"But that's impossible!" cried Frederick.

"Celia had *no* shoes on, did she?" I asked my policeman. "No shoes at all. Well, I can tell you how *one* of them got here. You will have to ask Mr. Frederick about the other one."

"What are you trying to say?" cried Frederick. "What do you mean, these are Celia's shoes? They can't be too small for you. They're exactly the same—"

"That's because they are *both* Celia's," I said patiently.

"That's not so! Only the one . . ." Frederick yelled—and when he saw that he had tripped on his own tongue he dove for me. My policeman jumped protectively, before Lloyd Frederick could wring my neck.

I said to Blair in the hospital, "She phoned him."

"Celia was bound he'd have a part in my picture," Blair told me. "He's pure ham. I couldn't do that. I suppose she called to tell him that we'd split up."

"He met her at the bottom of the stairs," I went on. "Probably she got into his car to talk. Probably she had her shoes in her hand—she couldn't have walked down all those steps with them on. He was furious that she'd muffed the deal, and she was in that vicious mood. She made him feel like wringing her neck. And he did. Dumped her out. Hurried home. No wonder I scared him! I must have looked like Celia's ghost, in the same dress."

"And then you left her shoe in the cabin—the shoe I'd picked up next to her body."

"Celia's other shoe must have been in his car," I said. "He found it too late. Maybe he found it when he got the car out for me. That was a strange ride. Shoes on our minds. Both of us."

"Why too late, Jenny?"

"If he'd found it *before* I came, he'd have paid more attention."

Blair twisted in the hospital bed. "I don't see why he didn't just destroy the shoe that he knew was Celia's."

"Instead, he helped our story," I said. "Of course, he believed me—he knew who had killed Celia. He just saw a chance to get rid of Celia's shoe."

"I don't get it."

"Well, I did. After we had gone to the hospital, he must have rushed back to the cabin, took her shoe in, and picked up the one he thought was mine, to compare them. They were mates, a right and a left. They were the same size. Don't you see why he had to do what he did? He hadn't paid close attention to me. He'd seen me put my foot into one of those shoes. But he must have shuffled them, got them mixed up, and didn't know which one *I* had brought to the cabin. Don't you see?—he couldn't be sure *which one to destroy*. But *I'd* know which one I'd put my foot in. He didn't."

"So he cleverly produced both."

"We'd watched the road. No shoe of mine there. He thought it was pretty clever."

"It *was* clever," Blair said.

"Yes, I know."

Blair sighed. "Until you took a notion to lie about the size."

"That wasn't hard," I said. "My feet were all puffed up. So I knew he'd think some store could prove that they really were Celia's shoes. It rattled him. He just blew up."

"You ought to be in the motion picture industry," Blair

said. "Anybody who can *think* in the midst of all that trouble and confusion . . ." Then he went on gently. "But he had helped us, Jenny. We were pretty safe."

"No," I said. "Because he was a murderer. Besides, I don't like telling lies." I broke off. "Blair, what are they going to do to us?"

Blair was laughing at me. "You beat all," he teased. "You don't like telling lies and so you told another. Know what I think? You've got the police baffled."

After a while I said, "One thing . . . I'll have Celia's money. So if they don't get around to putting us in jail or anything, do you want a partner?"

Blair sat up as far as he could. "No," he shouted. Then he shouted, "Yes."

"Well, which?" I said.

"I want *you* for a partner all the rest of my life," he said, "as you well know. But not that money!"

"S-sh," I said. "Don't look so wild. There isn't any problem. And we'll make your picture."

Blair said, "I think we will," in a funny voice.

Well, they didn't put us in jail. We'd told a lot of lies. Yet our lies had helped to catch the murderer, so I suppose it was a little confusing to the police.

Anyhow, the real murderer has been caught. No doubt hangs over us now and nothing can keep us apart.

People talk, of course. People say we must be crazy. We are going to make a motion picture, although all we have is the dream. We gave away the money. To a charitable foundation. It buys things for poor needy persons. Especially shoes.

MARJORIE CARLETON

Monday Is a Quiet Place

The fascinating duel of wits between Vern, 15-year-old delinquent and former choir boy, and Emily Damon, 29-year-old secretary to the minister . . . a beautifully written story—and a vision from Hell.

Emily Damon went through the narrow outer closet dedicated to stationery, church bulletins, and the like, and yanking open the inner door, propped it ajar with a shoulder. If it slammed shut, it stuck, and already the knob was loose from repeated tuggings. She hung her sweater at a decorous distance from Mr. Sanders' robes and then emerged hastily, for the janitor had been heavy-handed with the moth spray. Some of the reek followed her into the study, but the excellent ventilation would take care of it shortly.

She sat at her desk and looked around with her proprietary Monday eye. There were no windows but the cornices shed a concealed daylight, and unless you touched the walls you would think they were really paneled oak instead of patterned plywood. That, at least, was Emmy's innocent conviction. Mr. Sanders' desk was in order, with its single white carnation in a bud vase; the lectern with its huge Bible brooded beneath a picture of the Sermon on the Mount. Everything was as it should be.

She was sharpening a pencil when the door opened soundlessly and a choir boy slipped in. His robe was far too large, she noted with a practiced eye.

"You boys are not supposed to come in here—" she began and then saw that it was Vern Perrault. Her astonishment cut the rebuke short. No one had told her that Vern had been paroled from the county Reformatory and such a juicy bit of gossip should have flown rapidly around the town. Well, she had obviously missed it somehow, but it was quite incredible that even Mr. Sanders would have admitted him back into the choir.

As the great door started to swing back, the boy caught it and slipped the catch so that it locked behind him.

"Surprised, Miss Damon?"

"Surprised you're back in the choir," she said curtly. "And we don't lock the corridor door. Maybe we should."

He answered only her first comment. "Oh, I'm not in the choir—" he shrugged off the robe, let it drop to the floor— "just took it from the basement chest. How else do you think I got by Miss Lacey?"

He was wearing blue denims and a leather jacket buttoned to the throat, although it was a hot June day. He slid into the chair opposite Emmy, his pose alert but easy. She said nothing, waited. He would talk when he was good and ready, she knew, and after a while he did. "All fixed over in here, I see. But it's awful quiet."

"Monday is a quiet place," Emmy nodded. She approved the slip of the tongue but corrected it. For all his intelligence, Vern was literal-minded. "Quiet day," she amended. "Sunday's over and most folks are too busy the first of the week to bother Mr. Sanders with their troubles. Come to think of it, they seldom die on Mondays, either."

"I didn't mean that. I mean you can't hear the choir practicing. Can't even hear the sawmill."

"When the study was made over, it was soundproofed," she said absently. And that was a slip she did regret, for his eyes narrowed triumphantly.

"Then I guess no one outside can hear anything *inside* here."

"Unless I push the buzzer," she agreed. "The bell rings in the parish room."

"I don't see any buzzer."

"There's one under each desk."

"Why would a minister hide a buzzer?"

She sighed with exaggerated patience. "He's a busy man, Vern. If some talkative old lady takes too much of his time, something has to be done about it; but naturally he doesn't want to hurt her feelings. So he presses the hidden buzzer and one of us comes in with something important for him to look at . . . Anything else you'd like explained?"

He warned, "Just don't touch the buzzer, that's all."

"Not unless you take too much of *my* time," she said meaningfully.

The first round was over and instinctively they settled back in their chairs. There was a little silence as they appraised each other for the first time in two years.

Vern was slim, blond, and a very undersized fifteen, with the innocent eyes and cherubic face that choir boys are supposed to possess and seldom do. He had actually been a choir boy for a brief six months. And that was a laugh, Emmy thought, without feeling in the least like laughing. Fourteen years his senior, she had had Vern in her seventh grade class; and he had been one of the excellent reasons why she had given up teaching to become secretary to the Congregational minister.

Presently she said, "So they didn't parole you out of Dogtown—" (it was an accepted euphemism) "you ran away. They'll catch up with you in a few hours, you know, so why not enjoy the great outdoors while you can?"

He glowered. "I'm waiting for Mr. Sanders."

"If you want help, why don't you go to the church where you were baptized?" Her eyes were grim. "The font water must have sizzled when it touched your little forehead."

He accepted the compliment with a curve of lips as delicately cut and tender as an angel's. But he remained practical. "Mr. Sanders is single and he'll have some dough he can spare. The Reverend Brown's got five children, so he wouldn't have none."

"My, how your grammar has deteriorated."

He bristled. "I was smarter than any of the other kids and you know it. Went clear through the Book of Knowledge before I was nine."

"Through it, is correct. None of it sank in. Anyway, you'd wait a long time for Mr. Sanders. He hardly ever takes his day off but he solemnly promised he wouldn't show up before afternoon. And I hope he's gone fishing. Besides, even if he wanted to help you run away—and he wouldn't—he hasn't a nickel to spare. Not one."

"Oh yeah?"

"I mean it." She leaned forward earnestly. "The parish had to spend so much on church repairs that it will be two years before they can afford to carry the parsonage again. That's why they wanted a bachelor minister who'd be willing to live in a boarding house and take a lower salary for a while. Mr. Sanders is poor and the parish is poor."

Vern looked around sneeringly. "This room cost plenty of dough."

"A minister has to have at least one quiet place," she defended, "so the church voted to fix this up instead of buying the new Communion service."

The boy muttered an obscenity so familiar to Miss Damon's school-hardened ears that her frown was merely automatic. He went on savagely, "Thanks for the treasurer's report but I'm not interested. Mr. Sanders will find some way to help me. He'll hafta."

"You'll be seeing someone else first. Deacon Phipps comes in Mondays to sort the collection and take the cash to the bank." Emmy found that her eyes had wandered to the wall safe and she hurriedly glanced away.

Vern laughed. "Don't worry, I got no plans to rob the safe."

"And if you did, I don't have the combination any more than you do," she prevaricated. "But you'd better listen to what I'm saying. Deacon Phipps will be in any moment now and you won't win any argument with him, believe me."

"Won't have to argue. Just show him something." The knife was in Vern's hand then, the switchblade a sudden glitter beneath the cornice lighting.

Emmy stared at it without real surprise. Vern's swaggering order about the buzzer had already indicated that he was relying on something other than his own fragile physique to enforce his commands. And it was typical of his confused values that he should come armed to beg help from a clergyman. But she somehow hadn't expected a knife, not after what had happened two years ago. Well, no use taking a chance on the buzzer. She'd have to handle matters herself. The janitor was mowing, Miss Lacey would faint, the choirmaster was seventy-five and arthritic.

She said mildly, "Oh-oh. A knife like that is what brought you the heaviest sentence they could give a thirteen-year-old. Don't you ever learn anything, Vern? That sort of thing won't get you very far."

"Far enough. I'm waiting for Mr. Sanders, whatever Longnose Deacon Phipps tries to pull."

"Mr. Phipps is a big man."

"He makes trouble, this'll let a little air out of his paunch. He won't be so big then." He smiled.

A Victorian writer would have called that smile winsome. Miss Damon had her own adjective.

"And I'm a big girl," she reflected aloud. "Eight inches taller than you, forty pounds heavier. Brought up on a farm. I didn't develop these muscles cleaning blackboards, Vern. Think you can handle both of us at the same time?"

The knife blade did a bewildering ballet through the air. "Like that," he said complacently, "but thanks for the suggestion. Maybe I'd better settle you first, huh?"

Emmy's large and capable hands folded around the bronze paperweight. "I was good at baseball too." Her eyes were bright as a mink's behind the heavy brows. "Of course you might carve me up eventually. But I can guarantee to damage your handsome nose before you even reach this desk. Unfortunately, I can't guarantee it wouldn't split your skull too. My goodness," she grumbled, "what makes you so ambitious this early on a Monday morning? Quite a change from your school days. Keep it up and you'll be Man of the Year—at least in the penitentiary."

He said sulkily, "Skip the wise chatter. Just push your chair back from the desk so's you can't reach the buzzer." She began to stir reluctantly. "And leave that paperweight on the desk."

Her expression altered. "Ha-ha and ho-ho, little wolf! That would be just a bit too easy, wouldn't it?" There was in her now the same mingled wariness and fierce good-humor with which she had once gentled cattle and unruly classrooms. "I tell you what: you put the knife on the rug as far away as you can reach, and I'll put this paperweight on the rug as far away as *I* can reach."

He said suspiciously, "Your arms are longer than mine."

"Then the knife will be nearer you than the paperweight is to me."

There was something wrong with this argument but offhand, Vern couldn't think what; so he muttered a grudging "Okay." Eyes alert, Emmy thrust the heavy chair back a foot, two feet, four feet. It was slow progress for the carpet was thick.

"Here we go," she said, "as far as you can reach and no

cheating." Knife and paperweight were deposited on the rug simultaneously and then the two could relax.

Vern said admiringly, "You're not even sweating."

"Room's air-conditioned. But the day will be a broiler before it's through and you'll look mighty silly in that leather jacket. Stolen from a clothesline, I presume?"

"I presume," he mimicked.

"What'd you expect me to do, wear a Dogtown jersey down Main Street?" He sniffed at a sleeve, raised his head, frowned. "Something smells funny."

"The room," she said indifferently. "Para-dichlor-benzene."

"What the hell's that?"

"Moth crystals to you. Church closes for the summer after Children's Day next week. Why don't you come sing for us, Vern, dear?"

"Go to hell."

"Two hells in a row. You used to be more original, Vern. That's what comes of being with bad companions. I mean, bad for your vocabulary and their morals."

He wasn't listening, his eyes were roaming. After a moment he demanded. "Where's the barrel?"

"What barrel?"

"One Mr. Sanders keeps his sermons in. I heard all ministers get their sermons from a barrel."

Miss Damon studied him thoughtfully. "You're incredible, Vern, quite incredible. You heard that storks brought babies too, didn't you? But you never believed that. No, you knew."

Transparently fair as Vern's skin was, he was no longer capable of blushing. But for the first time he didn't meet her eye. "Aw, can it. All the guys—I mean, any guy . . ." His voice trailed, was cut off by a cough as firm as a period.

"Of course," Miss Damon agreed. "At certain ages you're all horrible little beasts—and don't I know it. But all boys don't torture animals, they don't bully little children to death—oh, no, they're capable of love. Some of them are even afraid of God." She startled herself by that last comment. The Deity's name belonged to certain well-defined rites or to the clergy; it was not to be bandied about in a duel of this nature. But if she were startled at this breach of etiquette, Vern was outraged.

"I said shut up!" he shouted fiercely, but as her eyes

stormed at him he became a defensive fifteen, shrill, whining. "How'd I know there was rat poison on the floor? How'd I know she'd be silly enough to eat it?"

Emmy was dispassionate, musing now. "A three-year-old locked in a dark little harness closet for ten hours. No light, no water. No food except dry oats—and rat poison. Of course you wouldn't know it, Vern. All the Books of Knowledge in the world could never teach you or reach you. Nothing ever reached you—nothing. And never will."

But the homily had been too long, she knew. And he had heard it too often. Before she had finished, his face was quite calm again, even faintly amused. "Babble, babble, o'er the pebbles—or however it goes. Anyway, save your breath. I been saying I'm sorry for two years now and I'm through, see? Fact is, it was her mother's fault. If kids are taught right, they don't go around eating things off a dirty floor. *I* didn't," he added virtuously. "Mom Perrault always said so."

"It wouldn't have hurt you," Emmy pointed out. "Most snakes are immune to their own poison."

He ignored that, his brief moment of weakness over. "Where those other two doors go?" he demanded. "I don't remember 'em."

She was not to be betrayed into removing her eyes from the knife. "One's a closet. Other's a hall that leads outdoors. Private lavatory off one side. If you're feeling nervous, Vern," Miss Damon added generously, "I'm sure Mr. Sanders wouldn't mind your using the lavatory. You always did have weak kidneys when you were nervous."

"I'm not nervous and I'm not in seventh grade for you to be talking about my kidneys!" he flared. Inwardly, Emmy acknowledged her own flash of sadism. She had used the one weapon that could hurt him—and against the one failing for which he could not be blamed. But she was not proud of herself.

"Sorry, but I can't waste any more time with you." She was suddenly brisk. "Monday's the one day I can work without being interrupted much. Listen, Vern, there's eighteen dollars and some change in my handbag. You can have it if you'll just leave here quietly and get yourself picked up somewhere else."

His eyes squinted with curiosity. "Why do you care where I might be picked up? Not that I will be." For a second Emmy wondered herself—but only for a second. Honesty lay deep in her, a granite ridge beneath the loose earthy soil of her everyday personality. She looked down at the broad hands folded in her lap, hands as freckled as her face.

"This place means a lot to Mr. Sanders. Mondays, too. Only room, only day he has to himself. He'll come back this afternoon with a sort of new look on his face, ready for the week ahead. I don't want the study and Monday spoiled for him. He needs them." For the first time she pleaded. "Listen, Vern, he came out of an orphanage the same as you did. He never had a private place or a private day before."

It was the wrong appeal. His voice was jerky, violent. "I never had 'em neither!"

"I know. But the way you're going, you'll have them sooner than you want, and they won't be the same kind as his."

"Gosh, I'm going to burst out crying any minute. But thanks for the loan of your dough and don't hold your breath till you get it back."

"Then you'll take it and go?"

"I'm not getting out till I see Mr. Sanders. Whatever you say, he'll hafta help me. He's my half brother."

"Dream on, little boy." But her tone was not unkind. How well she knew the fantasies of children who had been born or adopted into environments that didn't jibe with adolescent egotism. Even she herself on the good, dull farm . . . She knew a sudden joy that she had left that endless routine forever and without any wrench of ingratitude to mar her freedom. Her parents had died "in the fullness of their years," as Deacon Phipps had put it, and only then had the homestead been sold, with due and unhurried propriety. She would never have to go back to farm life. Never.

She smiled at Vern with the indulgence of memory. Perhaps he mistook the smile for a sneer.

"I mean it," he persisted. "He's my half brother."

Patience vanished. "Please, none of your dramatics, Vern. Of course you came from the same orphanage—there's only one in the state, so why not? But let me tell you something: everyone in Edgeville knows who Mr. Sanders' parents were—and that when his father died, his mother was too ill and hard up to take care of him and had to go back to her own family."

With pedagogic precision she was ticking off the points on her fingers now. "So Mr. Sanders became a state ward when he was twelve. When he was eighteen, he left and worked his way through college." She sat back triumphantly. "There's no mystery about him, none at all. You were a baby then, hadn't even been adopted yet."

He repeated stubbornly, "He's my half brother. One of the guys told me."

Emmy was really angry now. "Oh, stop it! There's something else you're too stupid to know: when a child is adopted in this state, it's against the law to tell who his real parents were or are. The Perraults didn't know who you were when they adopted you, poor souls. They never knew."

"Now *you* listen." He was supercilious. "There's this guy come to Dogtown the other day. Seems he worked in the orphanage office his last year there. And someone left the files unlocked one day and he was looking through them for the names of fellas he knew. And he found me and Mr. Sanders in the same file. Same file, get it? His mother—my mother—married again. Only the second time, she got an A-one bum." The admission was made with quiet inverted pride. "And when she died he dumped me in the orphanage and claimed they wasn't married and I wasn't his kid."

Miss Damon felt a rising uneasiness but her voice was cool enough. "That's the corniest script yet. Mr. Sanders' mother wrote him regularly until she died of tuberculosis. He told me. And she didn't say anything about another marriage, let alone another child."

Vern said with one of his unnerving flashes of acuteness, "She wouldn't, natch. Look, she puts him in the orphanage because she's sick and her folks wouldn't take him too. Well, maybe even a kid could understand that. But how'd he feel to hear she'd married again and started another family—leaving him out in the cold?" Emmy's face was closed against him, disdainfully. His own hardened. "Anyway, he'll believe me and I'm waiting for him, see? You think I'd be fool enough to skip Dogtown if I wasn't sure he'd *hafta* help me?"

"Whether he believes you or not, he'll never help you break the law."

There was a little silence, then Vern nodded slyly. "I thought of that too, but even if he makes me go back, I'll only be twenty-three when I get out. Maybe less, if he pulls strings and gets me paroled to him. He can do a lot for me then. Good thing he isn't married. I'll need time and money to look around till I'm really on my own." For an instant his face was incredibly old and calculating, and Emmy had a vision of what it would be like to have Vern "on his own" again—but this time an adult, the cement of his wickedness hardened forever. It was a vision from Hell.

"You think he's going to stay single eight years just to support you when you get out?" Her voice cracked with outrage. "Just on the off-chance that you're his half brother?"

"Off-chance, nuts. I can prove it."

"That's exactly what—" Emmy paused abruptly. She had started to say, "what you can't do." But to complete the thought aloud would merely be giving Vern another weapon, for could his assertion ever be *dis*proved legally? The orphanage couldn't officially open its files to Mr. Sanders, for the law had been written to protect not only a child's anonymity but that of his natural parents, whether they were alive or dead.

Mr. Sanders could accept, deny—or wonder. He would never know; he would live on the edge of an abyss. Of course a sensibly selfish extrovert would shrug off the unprovable, with a pang, perhaps, but with sturdy common sense. But not Mr. Sanders, who too often let his Monday be nibbled away by far more trivial exactions; not Mr. Sanders who accepted a room in a noisy boarding house and who was still filled with humble awe at his possession of this study.

The fact was, he wasn't practical and no one would want him to be. But Emmy was. Now it suddenly occurred to her that the orphanage was not the only source of information. One might be able to find people who in later days had known Mr. Sanders' mother and grandparents—the grandparents who had accepted the care of an invalid daughter but who had refused responsibility for an active small boy. Well, they had been old, one couldn't exactly blame them.

Somehow it could be proved that Mrs. Sanders had never married again, had never had another child. And Vern's venomous little balloon would be punctured forever.

But all this would take time and money, for years had passed and the grandparents, like their daughter, were certainly dead or Mr. Sanders would have mentioned them, looked them up. There was no spite in him, no capacity for harboring resentments.

Emmy thought of her savings account but almost immediately another thought, chilly and clairvoyant, perched like a bat on her shoulder. What if she spent time and money only to prove something she didn't want to know? What if she would look back some day to this very moment and say, "Dear God, why didn't I leave it alone?"

She closed her eyes an instant, calling Mr. Sanders' image to her inspection: blond, slimly-built like Vern but unlike Vern, very tall. Vern had blue eyes, so had Mr. Sanders. But the boy's eyes were presented to the world on a plane almost flat with his cheeks, as though their bland transparency had nothing to hide. Mr. Sanders' eyes were caverned beneath projecting brows; kindly, shy. No, the two did *not* resemble each other.

She looked up, saw the boy lighting a cigarette. "Please don't smoke, Vern. There aren't any ashtrays and remember your asthma."

"My goodness," he grinned, "isn't our Miss Damon thoughtful today. Kidneys and asthma! Whyn't you just say 'drop dead.' You don't fool me any." He took a defiant puff, coughed. "It's not the cig, it's the stink in here. You must have a tough nose." But he pinched the lighted end of the cigarette, blew the ashes away, and pocketed the stub. "Not that I got any complaints about the asthma," he added complacently. "It took me outta farm work and into the liberry. They wouldn't believe me at first, they never do at Dogtown. But Jeez, that first ten minutes in the hayfield I near strangled to death and turned blue in the face. Or so they say."

He threw a leg over the arm of the chair and went on, with an even broader grin, "I was clean out. Woke up in the Infirmary and did I ever get service for a coupla weeks! Now I can pick and choose. For instance, makes me cough to dust books. So I just sit at the desk marked Information."

"And give it out, I'll bet," Emmy observed dryly.

The buzzer rang. Vern leaped visibly. Perhaps he had not quite believed in the existence of that concealed bell. Emmy was almost as startled. She had been in a small purgatory, whose minutes were as endless as eternity. It was comforting to find that Time actually existed—prosaic human time, measured in half and quarter hours.

"I'll have to signal back, Vern. It's probably Mr. Phipps."

He had snatched up the knife and was already on his feet. But he wasn't threatening her for his eyes were swiveling, seeking a compass point in this windowless room.

Emmy had risen too, swooping up the paperweight. Now she moved to the desk, opened a drawer and took out her handbag.

"Don't lose your head, Vern. Just go out the hall door to the garden. That's the West Street side," she reminded him. "There's at least eighteen dollars here, maybe a little more. But if you have a scrap of sense left, you'll go back to Dogtown and do your week in solitary."

He shook his head. "Nix. And I don't want the money. Come to think of it, Brother Sanders wouldn't think that was nice of me—" his eyes glinted at her—"and I want him to know I'm *real* reformed. I can see the front walk from the garden and when old Phipps leaves, I'm coming back to wait —even if it takes all day."

He was panting now, but she knew it was from excitement, not fear. Vern did not experience fear as other people do. In fact, he had few of the so-called normal reactions. That made him more difficult, of course, but in an odd way, more predictable.

Emmy could predict him now, as calmly as in the classroom. He would do the Vern-thing: at some point in figuring an equation, his very real intelligence would yaw wildly, would leap some unknown terrain—and come up with the wrong answer.

In a way, it was something like the death-wish that psychologists talked about. Not that Vern's body wanted death. It was brilliantly alive, clutching, avid. It burned to survive; it would trample every obstacle to survive. But something in him always came up with the wrong answer.

Emmy stared at him curiously, almost with sympathy.

The buzzer rang again and added two little beeps like plaintive questions. Vern seized the choir robe from the floor, wadded it under his arm. "Which way to the garden? I'm coming back," he warned again.

"To tell Mr. Sanders he's your brother?" Emmy stood very still and her voice was still too.

"Well, my half brother, at least. The good half." He grinned tauntingly. "And he's bound to think there's a good half to me too, or it'd make a monkey out of a parson, wouldn't it?"

Miss Damon let the handbag thud to the desk. She pulled

open the closet door. "Here. Straight ahead to the garden through the next door."

Vern plunged in, and almost immediately started to back out. But Emmy was right behind him, bulking tall and solid.

"Jeez, I can't see nothing! Where's the other door?"

"Just put out your hand."

"Okay, go ring the ol' buzzer. But I'm coming back. You rat on me to Phipps, you'll be sorry. So will pie-face Sanders. He'll wish he was dead."

"Yes," Emmy agreed. She could see nothing in the inky darkness, but he must have the door to the inner closet open now, for the stench of the insecticide was a sudden blow to the lungs. Even Emmy coughed and the gasp from Vern was like a ripping blanket.

"Hey, what the hell! Hey, wait!"

Emmy didn't wait. She gave him a powerful thrust that must have thrown him against the robes, for there was a clatter of wooden hangers as he lost balance. The inner door shut. Let him have a taste of the harness room, a taste of night and terror and death.

Emmy closed the outer door and sat at her desk, waiting for the sound of coughing, of fists pounding on wood. But the double closets must be as well insulated as the study itself, for there was nothing around her but the Monday quiet.

Even the buzzer was silent. Miss Lacey, however puzzled, was keeping Mr. Phipps busy with gossip. And there would be gossip. By this time the whole town must know that Vern had run away from the Reformatory.

She glanced up at the picture above the lectern. Blessed Are the Merciful. She looked away, but the other wall offered even less comfort, holding as it did the sampler worked in 1850 by old Mrs. Phipps's mother: Vengeance Is Mine, I Will Repay, Saith the Lord. The "I" stood out large and scarlet.

Emily stirred uneasily. There was no good half in Vern nor even a good ten per cent. Of course, she conceded, there might be a good one per cent. For all his swagger, was it possible that he was trying to bring a puny miserable little hope—to his brother?

She didn't believe it; only a fool would believe it. In that odd, suspended moment she thought: Maybe this time *I* was Vern's wrong answer. He was sure he knew me—and he didn't.

She sprang up, rushed through the outer closet, and yanked violently at the inner door. The knob came off in her hand.

She felt for the connecting bolt. At her mere touch it slid relentlessly through to the other side. The door was smooth now—a nightmare door.

She raced back into the study and toward the corridor, to call the janitor, pausing only a moment to reset the catch that Vern had changed. And turned to see Mr. Phipps beaming down at her.

He was not allowed to linger. In fact, Miss Damon suggested firmly that his counting and accounting should be done in the parish room today. Anyone listening in would have *known* that she was trying to get rid of Mr. Phipps so that Vern and his asthma could be released from the closet. But he was a shrewd and stately old man. If she had been too rude, he might have grown suspicious and that wouldn't have helped Vern either, would it? Because he did know about the escape.

Her mind was suddenly full of contradictory choices, each canceling the other, holding her in an odd paralysis. Or was paralysis itself a choice?

It was particularly difficult because Mr. Phipps was in a rare and waggish mood for a Monday morning—full of sly, friendly little suggestions. For instance, church finances were doing much better than had been expected. The parsonage would be available again in another year and a fine young man like Mr. Sanders should be married. Makes parishioners selfish to have an unmarried pastor always on call. And then, in a clumsy attempt at a *non sequitur*, everyone liked and trusted Miss Damon. Everyone knew her background, her good solid practical folks. How long was she planning to remain a beautiful spinster? Wasting her sweetness on the desert air, so to speak—if an old man might say so without offense?

It didn't occur to Emmy to smile at his transparency. She was transparent herself, born of the same rural traditions, the same moralities, the same capacity for facing facts. She looked down at her wrist watch and faced a certain fact very quietly; by about eight minutes she had lost any right to be the future Mrs. Sanders.

After that recognition, she didn't find it hard to get rid of Deacon Phipps. She followed him down the corridor, her experienced eyes noting everything. Choir practice was over.

Through the open east door she could see the janitor leaning on his power mower to chat with a passing workman. Sunlight glittered from the metal parts of the machine and there was the acrid, rebellious odor of young grass newly snipped. Miss Lacey's car was gone; she would be at the printer's, heckling him about the Children's Day programs. Emmy turned back, having seen Mr. Phipps safely established in the parish room. She could move swiftly now.

She found tools in the janitor's quarters and returned to the study, and then to the inner closet. No paralysis now—chisel and hammer were a duet of efficiency.

Propping the door open finally, she bent down. There was no pulse in the huddled body, but it was still warm and limp; it was a simple matter to shrug it into the oversized choir robe. And that big strong girl could carry Vern as easily as she had once carried calves or lambs dropped in desolate pastures.

She carried him to the chancel, up to the choir loft, and slid him into one of the choir benches. Once she had folded his arms along the bench in front of him, his head fell quite naturally on those arms. Just as naturally her hand smoothed back the soft blond hair. She lifted his chin an instant and saw that the blue was fading from his face.

She thought: Mr. Sanders will be sure the Prodigal Son came home to repent and die. Perhaps he did. I don't think so, but how do I know? I'm just a farm girl who went to Teachers College two years.

She stood looking down from the chancel, tasting the quiet. The church was mid-Victorian Gothic, far too large for its present parish. And in winter, a bit forbidding.

But now with the June airs pulsing through it, it heaved and shone and breathed like some great and gentle ox whose strength has never fully been tried. She would miss it.

AVRAM DAVIDSON

Revolver

A kind of roundelay in prose, and a bitter, ironic slice of life—in the raw. Yes, life is real, life is earnest . . .

There was a Mr. Edward Mason who dealt in real estate. His kind of real estate consisted mainly of old brownstone houses into which Mr. Mason crammed a maximum number of tenants by turning each room into a single apartment. Legally this constituted "increasing available residence space" or some similar phrase. As a result of this deed of civic good, Mr. Mason was enabled to get tax rebates, rent increases which were geometrically rather than arithmetically calculated, and a warm glow around his heart.

Mr. Mason's tenants were a select group, hand-picked; one might say—to use a phrase favored in other facets of the real estate profession—that his holdings were "restricted." He didn't care for tenants who had steady employment. You might think this was odd of him, but that would be because you didn't know the philanthropic cast of Mr. Mason's mind. He favored the lame, the halt, and the blind; he preferred the old and the feeble; he had no scruples, far from it, against mothers without marriage licenses.

And his kindheartedness was rewarded. For, after all, employment, no matter how steady, can sometimes be terminated. And then rent cannot be paid. A landlord who can't collect rent is a landlord who can't meet his own expenses —in short, a landlord who is bound to go out of business. In which case it follows that he is a landlord who can no longer practice philanthropy.

Therefore, Mr. Mason would be obliged to evict such a tenant in order to protect his other tenants.

But, owing to his care, foresight, and selectivity, he had no such tenants. Not any more. No, sir. All his tenants at the time our account begins were in receipt of a steady income not derived from employment. Welfare checks come in regularly, and so do old-age assistance checks, state-aid checks, and several other variety of checks more or less unknown to the average citizen (and may he never have to know of them from the recipients' point of view—that is our prayer for him), the average citizen whose tax dollar supplies said checks.

Then, too, people who earn their own income are inclined to take a high-handed attitude toward landlords. They seem to think that the real estate investor has nothing better to do with his income than to lavish it on fancy repairs to his property. But a tenant whose soul has been purified by long years as the recipient of public charity is a tenant who is less troublesome, whose tastes are less finicking, who is in no position to carry on about such natural things as rats, mice, roaches, crumbling plaster, leaky pipes, insufficient heat, dirt, rot, and the like.

Is it not odd, then, that after a term of years of being favored by the philanthropic attentions of Mr. Mason and similarly minded entrepreneurs, the neighborhood was said to have "gone down"? It could not really be, could it, that garbage, for instance, was collected less frequently than in other sections of town? Or that holes in streets and sidewalks were not repaired as quickly as in "better" neighborhoods? Surely it was a mere coincidence that these things were so—if, indeed, they were so at all.

And anyway, didn't the City make up for it by providing more protection? Weren't patrol cars seen on the streets thereabouts more often than elsewhere? Weren't policemen usually seen on the streets in congenial groups of three? To say nothing of plainclothesmen.

This being the case, it was disconcerting for Mr. Mason to acknowledge that crime seemed to be on the increase in the neighborhood where he practiced his multifold benevolences. But no other conclusion seemed possible. Stores were held up, apartments burglarized, cars broken into, purses snatched, people mugged—

It was almost enough to destroy one's faith in human nature.

Finally, there was no other choice but for Mr. Mason to secure a revolver, and a license for same. Being a respectable citizen, a taxpayer, and one with a legitimate reason to go armed—the necessity to protect himself and the collection of his tenants' rents—he had no difficulty in obtaining either . . .

Among Mr. Mason's tenants was a Mrs. Richards. She was quite insistent, whenever the matter was raised (though it was never raised by Mr. Mason, who was totally indifferent to such items), that "Mrs." was no mere courtesy title. She had, indeed, been married to Mr. Richards and she had a snapshot of Mr. Richards to prove it. The wedding may have occurred in North Carolina, or perhaps in South Carolina. Nor did she recall the town or county where the happy event took place: Mr. Richards (she *did* remember that his given name was Charley) had been a traveling man. Also, it was a long time ago.

Mrs. Richards may have been a bit feeble-minded, but she possessed other qualities, such as a warm, loving, and open—very open—heart. She had two children by the evanescent Mr. Richards, and two children by two other gentlemen, with whom she had been scrupulous not to commit bigamy; and was currently awaiting the birth in about six months of her fifth child, the father of whom she thought was most probably a young man named Curtis.

Current social welfare policy held that it would be destructive to the family unit to suggest that Mrs. Richards, now or at any time, place her children in a day nursery and go out and labor for her (and their) bread. Consequently, she was supplied with a monthly check made up with city, state, and federal taxes. It cannot be said that the amount of the check was lavish, but Mrs. Richards did not demand very much and was easily satisfied. She had never been trained in any craft, trade, or profession, and if anyone was crude or unkind enough to suggest that she had enough skill required to manipulate a scrub-brush and -bucket, she would point out that when she did this her back hurt her.

The state of the floor of her "apartment," on the day when Mr. Mason came to call, at an hour nicely calculated with reference to the mail schedule, indicated that Mrs. Richards had not risked backache lately.

After an exchange of greetings, Mr. Mason said, "If you've cashed your check, I've got the receipt made out."

"I don't believe it's come," she said placidly. This was her routine reply. It was her belief that eventually it might be believed, although it never had been; nor was it now.

"If you spend the rent money on something else," Mr.

Mason said, "I'll have to go down to The Welfare and have them close your case." This was his routine reply.

Curtis, in a peremptory tone, said, "Give the man his money." The prospect of approaching fatherhood had raised in him no tender sentiment; in fact, it raised no sentiment at all other than an increasing daily restlessness and a conviction that it was time for him to move on.

Without so much as a sigh Mrs. Richards now produced an envelope from her bosom and examined it closely. "I guess maybe it might be this one," she said. "I haven't opened it."

Curtis, quite tired of every routine gambit of his lady-love, now said, quite testily, *"Give the man* his *money!"* He wanted cigarettes and he wanted whiskey and he knew that neither of these could be had until the check was cashed. "If I got to *hit* you—"

Mrs. Richards endorsed the check with her landlord's pen, and Mr. Mason began to count out her change. A new consideration now entered Curtis' mind—previously occupied only by the desire for cigarettes, whiskey, and moving on; it entered with such extreme suddenness that it gave him no time to reflect on it. He observed that Mr. Mason had a revolver in a shoulder holster inside his coat and he observed that Mr. Mason's wallet was quite engorged with money.

Curtis was not naturally malevolent, but he was naturally impulsive. He whipped Mr. Mason's revolver from its holster, struck Mr. Mason heavily on the side of the head with it, and seized his wallet.

Mr. Mason went down, but he went down slowly. He thought he was shouting for help, but the noise coming out of his mouth was no louder than a mew. He was on his hands and knees by the time Curtis reached the door, and then he slid to one side and lay silent.

Mrs. Richards sat for a moment in her chair. New situations were things she was not well equipped to cope with. After the sound of Curtis' feet on the stairs ceased, she continued to sit for some time, looking at Mr. Mason.

Presently a thought entered her mind. The familiar-looking piece of paper on the dirty table was a receipt for her rent. The money scattered around was the money Mr. Mason had been counting out to cash her check. Her practice was to count it out twice and then deduct the amount of the rent.

Mrs. Richards slowly gathered up the money, slowly counted it, moving her lips. It was all there.

And so was the receipt.

Mrs. Richards nodded. She now had the receipt for her rent *and* the money. True, she no longer had Curtis, but, then, she knew he was bound to move along sooner or later. Men always did.

She hid the rent money in one of the holes with which the walls of the "apartment" were plentifully supplied, and then reflected on what she had better do next.

All things considered, she decided it was best to start screaming.

Curtis went down the stairs rapidly, but once in the street he had sense enough to walk at a normal pace. Running men were apt to attract the attention of the police.

Three blocks away was a saloon he favored with his trade. He entered by the back door, causing a buzzer to sound. He tried to slip quickly into the Men's Room, but wasn't quite quick enough to escape the attention of the bartender-proprietor, an irascible West Indian called Jumby, and no great friend of Curtis'.

"Another customer for the toilet trade," said Jumby, so loudly that he could be heard through the closed door. "I'd make more money if I gave the drinks away free and charged admission to the water closet!"

Curtis ignored this familiar complaint, and emptied the wallet of its money, dropping the empty leather case into the trash container which stood, full of used paper towels, alongside the sink. Then he left.

Police cars sped by him, their sirens screaming.

Vague thoughts of cigarettes and whiskey still floated in Curtis' mind, but the desire to move on was by now uppermost. It was with some relief, therefore, that he saw a young man sitting in an open convertible. The convertible was elegantly fitted out, and so was the young man. His name was William.

"You've been talking about going to California, William," Curtis said.

"I have *also* been talking," William said with precision, "about finding some con*gen*ial person with *money* to share the *expenses* of going to California."

Curtis said, "I hit the numbers. I got money enough to take care of all the expenses. Don't that make me congenial?"

"Very *much* so," said William, opening the door. Curtis started to slide in, but William stopped him with a long, impeccably groomed hand, which touched him lightly. "Curtis," he said in low but firm tones, "if you have something *on* you, I really must *insist* that you get *rid* of it first. Suppose I meet you here in an *hour?* That will also enable me to *pack.*"

"One hour," Curtis said.

He went into another bar, obtained cigarettes and whiskey. At the bar was a man generally, if not quite popularly, known as The Rock.

"How you doing, Rock?" Curtis inquired.

The Rock said nothing.

"Got some business to talk over with you," Curtis went on.

The Rock continued to say nothing.

"Like to take in a movie?" Curtis asked.

The Rock finished his drink, set down the glass, looked at Curtis. Curtis put down money, left the bar, The Rock behind him. He bought two tickets at the movie theater and they went in. The house was almost empty.

After a minute or two Curtis whispered, "Fifty dollars buys a gun. I got it on me."

The Rock took out a handkerchief, spread it in his lap, counted money into it, passed it to Curtis. After a moment Curtis passed the handkerchief back. The Rock soon left, but Curtis stayed on. He still had the better part of an hour to kill.

The Rock took a bus and traveled a mile. He walked a few blocks on a side street and entered a house which, like most of its fellows, bore a sign that it has been selected for something euphemistically called "Urban Renewal," and that further renting of rooms was illegal. Most of the windows were already marked with large X signs.

On the second floor The Rock disturbed a teenage boy and girl in close, though wordless, conversation. The boy looked up in some annoyance, but after a quick glance decided to say nothing. The girl clutched his arm until the intruder passed.

The door on the third floor was locked, but The Rock

pushed hard, once, and it yielded. The room was ornately furnished, and the dressing table was crowded with perfumes and cosmetics and a large doll; but seated on the bed was a man.

"It ain't you," the man said. He was red-eyed drunk.

"It ain't me," The Rock agreed.

"It's Humpty Slade," said the man on the bed. "*He* don't pay for her rent. *He* don't buy her no clothes. *He* don't feed her. I do."

The Rock nodded his massive head.

"Everybody knows that," The Rock said. He took a handkerchief out of his pocket, laid it on the bed, opened its folds. "Seventy-five dollars," he said.

A quick turnover and a modest profit—that was The Rock's policy.

The boy and girl, now seated on the stairs, shrank to one side as he came down. They did not look up. It was not very comfortable there in that all but abandoned house; but it was private—as private as you can get when you have no place of your own to go.

Upstairs, on the bed, the waiting man stared at the revolver with his red, red eyes . . .

After a while the boy and the girl sauntered down into the street and went separate ways in search of something to eat. But after supper they met again in the same hallway.

Scarcely had they taken their places when they were disturbed. A man and woman came up, talking loudly. They paused at the sight of the younger pair in the dim light of the single bulb, and for a moment the two couples looked at one another. The older woman was handsome, flamboyantly dressed and made up. Her companion was large and on the ugly side, his looks not improved by a crooked shoulder which jutted back on one side.

"What are you kids doing here?" he demanded. "Go on, get out—"

"Oh, now, Humphrey," the woman pleaded. "You leave them alone. They ain't hurting nobody."

"Okay, sugar," the big man said submissively. They continued up the stairs. The boy and girl listened as they fumbled at the door. Then the woman's voice went high and shrill with fear, screaming, "*No—no—no—*"

At the loud sound of the revolver the boy and girl leaped to their feet. Something fell past them, and landed below with a thud.

"You'd point a gun at *me?*" a man's voice growled. Then there was the noise of a blow.

"*My* woman—!"

"You'd take a shot at *me?*"

The sound of fist on flesh, again and again. The boy and girl crept down the stairs.

"No, Humpty, don't hit me any more! I'm sorry, Humpty! I didn't mean it! I was—oh, please, Humpty! *Please?*"

"Don't hit him any more, honey. He was drunk. Honey—"

The boy and girl stopped at the bottom floor for only a moment. Then they were gone . . .

Curtis paused, uncertain. He was sure that it was dangerous for him to remain on the street, but he didn't know where to go. That little rat, William, had failed to reappear. There were planes flying, and trains and buses running, but even if he decided what to take he would still have to decide *which* airfield, *which* station, *which* terminal. The problems seemed to proliferate each time he thought about them.

He would have a drink to help him consider.

There wasn't really any hurry.

That dirty rat, William!

The Sepoy Lords were holding an informal meeting—a caucus, as it were.

Someone has remarked that the throne of Russia was neither hereditary, nor elective, but occupative. The same might be said of office in the Sepoy Lords.

The scene was a friendly neighborhood rooftop.

"So you think you're going to be Warlord?" a boy named Buzz demanded.

"That's right," said the one called Sonny.

The quorum, including several Sepoy Ladies, listened with interest.

"*I* don't think you're going to be Warlord," said Buzz.

"I *know* I am," said Sonny.

"What makes you so sure?" inquired Buzz.

"This," Sonny said, simply, reaching into his pocket, and taking something out.

Sudden intakes of breath, eyes lighting up, members crowding around, loud comments of admiration. "Sonny got a *piece!*" "*Look* at that piece Sonny's got!"

The President of the Sepoy Lords, one Big Arthur, who had until now remained above the battle, asked, "Where'd you get it, Son'?"

Sonny smirked, cocked his head. "*She* knows where I got it," he said. His girl, Myra, smiled knowingly.

Buzz said only one word, but he said it weakly. He now had no case, and he knew it.

The new Warlord sighted wickedly down the revolver. "*First* thing I'm going to do," he announced; "there's one old cat I am going to *burn*. He said something about my old lady, and that is something I don't take from *any*body, let alone from one of those dirty old Ermine Kings."

Diplomatically, no one commented on the personal aspect of his grievance, all being well aware how easy it was to say something about Sonny's old lady, and being equally aware that the old lady's avenging offspring now held a revolver in his hand. But the general aspect of the challenge was something else.

"Those Ermine Kings better watch out, is all!" a Sepoy Lady declared. There was a murmur of assent.

Big Arthur now deemed it time to interpose his authority. "Oh, yeah, sure," he said. " 'They better watch out!'—how come? Because we got one piece?"

Warlord Sonny observed a semantic inconsistency. With eyes narrowed he said, "What do you mean, 'we'? '*We*' haven't got *any*thing. *I'm* the one who's got the piece, and *no*body is going to tell me what to do with my personal property—see?" He addressed this caveat to the exuberant Sepoy Lady, but no one misunderstood him—least of all, Big Arthur.

Allowing time for the message to sink in, Sonny then said, "Big Arthur is right. I mean, one ain't enough. We need money to get more. How? I got a plan. Listen—"

They listened. They agreed. They laughed their satisfaction.

"Now," Sonny concluded, "let's get going."

He watched as most of them filed through the door. He started after them, then stopped. *Was* stopped. Big Arthur seized his wrist with one hand and grabbed the revolver with the other.

Sonny, crying, "Gimme that back!" leaped for it. But Big Arthur, taking hold of Sonny's jacket with his free hand, slapped him—hard—back against the door.

"You got the wrong idea, Son'," Big Arthur said. "You seem to think that *you* are the President around here. That's *wrong*. Now, if you really think you are man enough, you can try to get this piece away from me. You want to try?"

For a while Sonny had been somebody. Now he was nobody again. He knew that he would never in a million years take the revolver away from Big Arthur, never burn that one old cat from the Ermine Kings who had said something about his old lady. Tears of pain and humiliation welled in his eyes.

"Cheer up," Big Arthur said. "We're going to see how your plan works out. And it better work out *good*. Now get down those stairs with the other members, Mr. Sonny Richards."

Head down, Sonny stumbled through the door. Myra started to slip through after him, but Big Arthur detained her. "Not so quick, chick," he said. "Let's move along together. You and me are going to get better acquainted." For just a second Myra hesitated. Then she giggled.

"*Much* better acquainted," Big Arthur said.

Feeling neither strain nor pain, Curtis glided out of the bar. The late afternoon spread invitingly before him. He was suppose to meet somebody and go somewhere . . . William . . .

There, slowly passing by in his fancy convertible, was the man himself. With great good humor Curtis cried, "William!" and started toward him.

William himself saw things from a different angle. Curtis, to be sure, was *rough*, but what had really set William against going to California with him was the fact that he had observed Curtis that way. He, William, wanted nothing to do at any time with people who carried guns. And, anyway, he wasn't quite ready to leave for California—something had come up.

What came up at that moment was Curtis, roaring (so it seemed) with rage, and loping forward with murder in his eye.

William gave a squeak of fright. The convertible leaped ahead, crashing into the car in front. And still Curtis came on—

Screaming, "Keep away from me, Curtis!" William

jumped out of the car and started to run. Someone grabbed him. "Don't stop me—he's got a gun—Curt*is!*" he yelled.

But they wouldn't let go. It was the police, wouldn't you know it, grim-faced men in plain clothes; of all the cars to crash into—

One of them finished frisking Curtis. "Nope, no gun," he said. "This one ain't dangerous. *You.*" He turned to William. "What do you mean by saying he had a gun?"

William lost his head and started to babble, and before he could move, the men were searching *him*. And the *car*. They found his cigarette case stuffed with sticks of tea, and they found the shoebox full of it, too.

"Pot," said one of them, sniffing. "Real Mexican stuff. Convertible, hey? You won't need a convertible for a long time, fellow."

William burst into tears. The mascara ran down his face and he looked so grotesque that even the grim faces of the detectives had to relax into smiles.

"What about this one, Leo," one of them asked, jerking his thumb. "He's clean."

But Leo was dubious. "There must be some connection, or the pretty one wouldn't of been so scared," he said. A thought occurred to him. "What did he call him? What did you say his name was? Curtis?"

The other detective snapped his fingers. "Curtis. Yeah. A question, Curtis: You in the apartment of a Mrs. Selena Richards today?"

"*Never* heard of her," said Curtis, sobering rapidly. Move on, that's what he should have done—move on.

Mrs. Richards was entertaining company. The baby was awake—had been awake, in fact, since those chest-deep, ear-splitting screams earlier in the afternoon—and the girls had come home from school. She had sent them down to the store for cold cuts and sliced bread; they hadn't eaten more than half of it on the way back, and Mrs. Richards and the neighbors were dining off the other half. There was also some wine they had all chipped in to buy. Excitement didn't come very often, and it was a shame to let it go to waste.

"Didn't that man *bleed!*" a neighbor exclaimed. "All over your floor, Selena!"

"All over *his* floor, you mean—*he* owns this building."

After the whoops of laughter died down, someone thought of asking where Mrs. Richards' oldest child was.

"I don't know where Sonny is," she said, placid as ever. "He takes after his daddy. His daddy always was a traveling sort of man." She felt in her bosom for the money she had placed there—the money she had taken from the hole in the wall after the police and ambulance left. Yes, it was safely there.

All in all, she thought, it had been quite a day. Curtis gone, but he was on the point of becoming troublesome, anyway. Excitement—a *lot* of excitement. Company in, hanging on her every word. The receipt for the rent, *plus* the rent itself. Yes, a lucky day. Later on she would see what the date was, and tomorrow she would play that number.

If luck was coming to you, nothing could keep it away.

They had taken three stitches in Mr. Mason's scalp, and taped and bandaged it.

"You want us to call you a taxi?" the hospital attendant asked.

"No," Mr. Mason said. "I don't have any money to waste on taxis. The bus is still running, isn't it?"

"There's a charge of three dollars," the attendant said.

Mr. Mason snorted. "I don't have three cents. I'll have to borrow bus fare from some storekeeper, I guess. That dirty—he took everything I had. Right in broad daylight. I don't know what we pay taxes for."

"I guess we pay them to reward certain people for turning decent buildings into flophouses," the attendant said. He was old and crusty and due to retire soon, and didn't give a damn for anybody.

Mr. Mason narrowed his eyes and looked at him. "Nobody has the right to tell me what to do with my personal property," he said meanly.

The attendant shrugged. "That's your personal property, too," he said, pointing. "Take it with you; we don't want it."

It was the empty shoulder holster.

On leaving the hospital Mr. Mason headed first for a store, but not to borrow bus fare. He bought a book of blank receipts. He still had most of his rents to collect, and he intended to collect every single one of them. It hardly paid a person to be decent, these days, he reflected irritably. One thing was sure: nobody else had better tangle with him—not today.

He headed for the first house on his round, and it was there, in the hallway, that the Sepoy Lords caught up with him.

WILLIAM BANKIER

What Happened in Act One

Agnew Plover was as strange a man as ever drank at the Act One bar. He was a man "possessed"—into his body came the spirits of dead men, both famous and infamous . . .

Come in and take a chair and watch it all happen, the way I did. Sit right up there at the bar, beside the head of creamy cheddar cheese and the bowl of fist-filling pretzels. Eat as much as you want and have several cold seidels of lowenbrau, the best Munich can brew.

Oh, refreshment, oh, satisfaction, oh, exhilaration! This is New York in the summertime—and anything can happen.

Keep your eye on the door; somebody is about to come in. Not now, but very soon. This is a playback. I am going to rerun it for you the way I saw it happen the first time.

Why are you here? Please share my excuse. You have been sent to New York by the Head Office to study the organizational setup of the main Accounting Department. When you have it all filed and tabulated in your mind, you will go back to the mid-West and install an identical system in the regional office. Time allotted for this project: one month. Actual time required: one week. Expense account: generous in the extreme.

And so, as I did, you have spent several evenings visiting the various tourist attractions—enjoying, for example, the Metropole bar, chuckling at the droll monologue of the guide on the Day Line Cruise around the island, knuckling the glass to arouse the pigmy marmoset in his modest enclosure at the Bronx Zoo. All this done, you have now settled down to some serious drinking.

It is an intoxicating bar. The warm brown wood and red-leather interior, the dim glow of sepia light always in the semi-distance, the slow and hypnotic sweep of the second hand on the illuminated clock—all these are quite enough to make a man forget home and wife and job and other responsibilities . . .

Okay, then: join the rest of the lotus eaters and wait for the arrival of Agnew Plover. By now you are studying the faded photograph hanging over the bar, sipping your beer, and wondering idly who that young man is in the boxing trunks, standing with his arm raised in victory, the blood from his nose and the ugly cut over his eye unable to mask the glow of sheer triumph shining on his face. Could this be the man who now tends bar? Terry O'Biggo, the lard-cheeked, dull-eyed gentleman who smiles with china teeth and corduroy skin as he mops bottle rings from the mahogany?

No matter, for old Terry and the boy boxer have nothing to do with our story beyond the fact that they were there when it happened.

But hush—I can hear a gay step on the walk outside and a creak from the ebony door. This is how it began——the first entrance of Agnew Plover. Bartender, would you please reduce the volume on the Muzak system? I love the way Charlie Parker plays *Everything Happens To Me,* but we must concentrate on the center ring.

Correction. I said a moment ago that this would be the first entrance of Agnew Plover. To be more accurate, I should say that this was his first arrival in my presence, but I was a newcomer and Agnew Plover had been in this bar several times before.

It is a large bar; they call it Act One. The bar itself seems miles long, covering the total length of the west wall except for three feet of doorway leading into the Men's Room.

The rest of the room is occupied by small round tables, none larger than a barrel head. The decor in Act One is limited mainly to bottles—bottles that make people drink. What subtly seductive shapes the glass blowers have contrived, and how suggestively the labels wink and leer, some garish, some sophisticated, some bizarrely European, others as American as Kentucky corn. Whatever your personality, at Act One a bottle beckons.

Wait now. Spring doors flutter, conversation falters. All eyes focus on the door.

Agnew Plover is here.

Disappointed? Well, there he is. Some might call him effeminate, that being invariably the first impression: green corduroy trousers, yellow shirt with tails knotted about the waist, large head capped with yellow hair close-cropped and carelessly combed, ringing his skull like the curls of a childish Nero. And the face of Agnew Plover: eyes, two brown caramels, mouth protruding in a perpetual pout, chin thrust forward inquisitively.

Queer? I can still see the rowdy who took out his handkerchief and whipped it across Plover's path as he made his grand entrance. With a lightning gesture, Agnew seized the fluttering linen in both hands, reversed their position, and drew the cloth around the hoodlum's throat. Then, with no perceptible effort, he raised the lout off the floor and bore him, legs dragging, to the front entrance where he flung him through the doors and into the street. The thug tried to return and Agnew hit him—not *in* the face, but (and this is the only time I have ever seen it) Agnew Plover hit his man *through* the face and put him flat on the pavement.

No, Agnew Plover is a man—make no mistake about that.

On the first night I saw him, he walked in off 48th Street, waved to several of the Act One habitués with a modest smile, and nodded his head at Terry O'Biggo behind the bar. Terry poured four ounces of straight gin into a glass, dropped a wedge of lemon into it, and carried the glass across the room to Plover's table. Plover drained the glass, then popped the wedge of lemon into his mouth, chewed it and swallowed it, skin and all. Throughout this procedure there was almost complete silence in the place except for the hum of an exhaust fan near the door.

His drink finished, Agnew Plover smiled again, drew a book from his pocket, and calmly began to read. O'Biggo went behind the bar and a dozen conversations chattered back to life. I was soon to learn the reason why this little community took time out whenever they were joined by this curious fellow.

Perhaps half an hour passed. I had three beers and went back to the Men's Room. On my return, I saw Agnew Plover leaning back in his chair, his head slumped forward on his chest, his body swaying back and forth in rhythm with a low crooning.

"The drink seems to have disagreed with our friend," I began.

"Shush," Terry O'Biggo said. "It's the possession. It comes over him every now and then."

"The possession?"

"That's right. The spirit of a dead person enters his body and takes over. It only lasts a short while. We've seen it before."

"I've never seen anything like . . ."

"Well, you're seeing it now. Just hush up and don't disturb him. It could kill him if he's disturbed while he's under the possession. Watch now."

I watched. After a few minutes the convulsive movements stopped and Plover sat up. He seemed to be himself now and yet there was something different about his face—a commanding, imperious expression.

Then he spoke, but not in any language that I had ever heard before.

"What's he saying?" O'Biggo asked.

A man at the end of the bar said, "It sounds like Polish to me. He asked where the piano is."

For the first time I noticed the upright piano at the far end of the room. The keyboard was covered and it had an air of disuse about it. At the same moment Plover—or whoever now inhabited Plover's body—saw the piano and walked over to it.

Silence came over the bar as he sat down, stared at the instrument for a moment, then began to play. If I live on into the two thousands, I never expect to hear anything like that again. The flow of music from that piano was like the spray off Niagara Falls. It hit us in a million cool drops, but there was muted thunder in its sheer power. I tried to place the composer; it sounded like Chopin though I could not be sure.

It was not a long performance—perhaps five minutes. As the last brilliant chord echoed through the room, Plover lowered his forehead to the backs of his hands. Then he shivered, raised his eyes, turned, and looked at us.

"Did I just play?" he asked.

A chorus of delighted affirmation flowed about him.

"I've never played a note," he said. "I wonder who it was this time?"

"You spoke Polish. You asked for a piano in Polish," said the man at the end of the bar.

I volunteered, "I'm not sure, but the music sounded like Chopin to me. Chopin was Polish."

A murmur of excitement passed through the crowd. Plover stood up, yawned, and stretched his arms.

"It always takes a lot out of him," the bartender whispered to me.

Plover joined us, dropping a bill on the bar. "My tab, please Terence," he said. O'Biggo tried to push the money back to him. "Please Terry," Agnew said, "I'm not an itinerant minstrel. I pay for my drinks."

The bartender made change and Plover went away into the night, leaving a generous tip on the bar. When he had gone, conversation rose in a flurry to a peak of excitement.

"You've seen all this many times?" I asked.

"A few times," Terry corrected me. "See that painting over the bar?"

I glanced up and saw a brilliant orange-and-black poster done roughly in oils. There was no mistaking the posturing figure in the foreground, the rakish top hat, the elongated jaw in profile.

"He began to speak French one night. Lucky we had somebody here could make it out. He asked for paints, so a lady who lives next door ran upstairs and got her oils. He dashed that off in ten minutes."

So "Toulouse-Lautrec" had been here on 48th Street in the body of this unbelievable man. And unbelievable is the word. I could see his painting, I had heard him play.

"You must consider yourselves lucky," I said, "falling heir to all this free entertainment."

"Oh, it isn't always so pleasant. One night he came up Hitler."

I almost choked on my drink.

"He stood up here by the bar and he almost looked like him. And when he spoke, there was no doubt. He gave us a real harangue, just like in the old newsreels."

"That must have been a treat."

"Like I said. There was this guy in here that night, Sol Bloom. Drives a cab and comes in here on his free nights. He took offense and threw a punch. It was a glancing blow but Agnew kind of stiffened and his eyes almost came out of his head and he threw up right here on the floor. It was messy for a few minutes."

I shook my head in sympathy and understanding.

"It was after that Agnew told us how dangerous it was for him to be brought out of it sudden-like. He has to be left alone. Like sleepwalking."

My own sleep that night was broken, not by an ambulatory excursion but by visions of a man whose body seemed to act as a living receiver, picking up transmissions from some celestial tower where the spirits of good and evil dwelt—the famous and infamous.

I was unable to visit Act One on the following night owing to an unexpected dinner invitation from the personnel chief of the Head Office. But the next night found me at my accustomed spot at the head of the bar. I was half full of ale and overflowing with anticipation when Agnew Plover finally arrived about 11:30.

We were all to be disappointed. Nothing happened that night. Plover merely had two of his gin and lemon specials just like any other barfly. And so, home to bed.

But the following evening was something else again. The procedure was the same: a drink, a short period of reading, then head on chest, then moaning and swaying. When he sat up and faced the expectant room, a frightening change had overtaken his features. His face was pale, his cheeks seemed hollow, and his eyes burned with a feverish fire. Then he spoke. "What place is this?"

A sigh crossed the room. "Ah, you're English-speaking, sir," Terry O'Biggo said somewhat unnecessarily. "My name is Terence O'Biggo. Delighted to welcome you to the Act One bar."

"Poe is my name," Plover said. "Edgar A. Poe." He coughed into his handkerchief. "Have you anything for a man to drink? A brandy? God, I don't feel well."

Made brave by beer, I ventured, "Would you be Edgar Allan Poe, the writer?"

He glanced at me and then away. "I write some, but I did not realize my fame was widely spread."

The bartender brought a generous glass of brandy to Plover-Poe's table. The man drank it and Terry refilled it from the bottle he had carried with him. The liquor seemed to revive the fellow's spirit for he took his glass to the bar where he sat down beside me.

"So you're familiar with my work. I'm flattered, sir." He smiled at me and raised his glass.

"I've read *The Fall of the House of Usher,*" I said, "and *The Pit and the Pendulum.* And of course, *The Raven.*"

He nodded at each of the titles, sipping his brandy. Then he said, not so much to me as to the room, "I've just finished a story. Perhaps you'd like to hear some of it and I can profit from your reaction."

We chorused our approval.

"Very well," he said. "This story is called *The Murders in the Rue Morgue.*"

I don't know if you have ever read that great classic, but it is a story that lifts the reader to a pinnacle of horror and fascination. Plover now began to deliver a portion of it in a moody recitation so grandly in character with the subject matter of the tale that an audible sigh hissed from the rapt gathering. At the conclusion there was the beginning of applause but Terry raised his hand and said, "Hush . . . don't disturb him."

This time Plover did not resume his own personality in our presence. Instead, he downed his drink, nodded casually to me and O'Biggo, then strolled, as Edgar Allan Poe might have done, out of the bar and into the hustle of 48th Street.

"He left like that," the bartender said, "when he was John Barrymore. That kind seems to favor the dramatic exit."

Three days went by before we saw Plover again. It was Saturday night and the Act One was crowded with the old clientele, all getting a good start on the week-end.

Perhaps only now, in retrospect, does that Sunday evening seem to have had an air of finality about it. Indeed, I was finished with my research at the Head Office, and the end of next week would surely see me back home in the middle West. But this feeling of termination went beyond the boundaries of my own mood—it permeated the whole bar.

Agnew Plover arrived about ten o'clock, and half an hour went by before the possession overtook him. I didn't see it happen. One moment he was glancing around and munching his lemon section; the next time I looked, his head was slumped forward on the bar, and as slow tremors shook his body, a high keening moan arose from the mound of white shirt and yellow hair.

Silence eddied out quickly as everyone in the room concentrated on Plover. They had not long to wait. Suddenly he sat up, turned his head, and looked slowly around the room.

There was something menacing about the strangely altered features and a steely glint of malevolent purpose in his eyes that killed, almost as soon as it was born, the speculative murmur that usually accompanied one of Agnew's periods of possession.

One circuit of the room by his frozen eyes was enough. Plover licked his lips which seemed now thinner and paler than before. With a graceful movement he slipped from the stool and swaggered to the middle of the bar. As he walked, he held his arms stiffly out and a little back from his body, fingers spread wide a few inches from his thighs. His heels clumped a hollow march on the wooden floor.

When he reached the place along the bar where Terry O'Biggo was standing, he stopped and said, "Now, they ain't *nobody* goin' to move a muscle."

A gentleman at the far corner of the room began to snicker and choked it off in mid-breath. Like a jungle cat, Plover spun toward the sound, crouching, knees bent. At the same time he brought his right hand along his trouser leg in a whipping motion and then held the hand extended, the index finger pointing menacingly at the man who had dared to laugh.

"What's so funny, mister?" he said, his voice touched with a slight drawl. "You see anything here to laugh at? 'Cause if you do, I wanna tell you, mister, 'tween these two guns I got seventeen notches. And they is room for plenty more."

Sitting near O'Biggo, I turned my head to the bartender and raised my eyebrows. Terry's face was pale but he frowned and shook his head in warning: Leave him alone.

Now Plover—although this rigid animal was surely not he—turned to O'Biggo and said, "And now you, friend, take off that apron and spread it on the bar."

"Anything you say, mister," Terry replied, slipping out of the white linen and clearing away glasses to make room. "By the way," he added, "who might I have the pleasure of serving?"

A faint smile twisted one corner of Plover's pale mouth. "The name is Bonney," he said. "Most folks know me as Billy the Kid."

This revelation drew a gasp from the customers of Act One, and this time Plover let it pass and fade away.

"All right," he said when the apron was spread, "you'll

oblige me, bartender, by puttin' the night's takings in that apron."

Another gasp arose from the room and this time O'Biggo cut it short. "Quiet," he shouted. "I want you all to do exactly as Mr. Bonney here says. Don't nobody try to lay a hand on him or interfere in any way. If anyone needs an explanation, he'll get it later." And with that he opened the cash register, scooped out its contents, and dumped the money into the apron.

"Bartender, you got sense," Bonney-Plover said. Now he turned and swept the pointing finger in a slow trajectory around the room. "One at a time now," he said, "come on up here and leave your wallets on the pile."

The outcry this time was immediate and prolonged, and spiced with such phrases as, "A joke is a joke," and "Going too far."

Again O'Biggo shut off the uproar. "I told you people to cooperate. I won't have this man disturbed. Just do as he says and nobody will lose a thing."

Well, the unburdening lasted about five minutes. When my neighbor at the bar came back from leaving his wallet he muttered, "I'm just glad that finger isn't loaded."

It was a stimulating little scene and it ended with Billy the Kid gathering up the ends of the apron and leaving the bar slowly, walking backward, his cocked finger aimed here and there, and carrying our wealth with him like a sack of laundry.

After the doors banged shut behind him, there was silence for fully half a minute, broken finally by the voice of Terence O'Biggo who said, "He'll be back soon."

So we waited. And we talked.

Midnight came and went, and conversation rose and fell away. Terry refused to call the police. "I'll not cause trouble for my good friend Agnew," he said.

We were all back in the Act One by opening time Sunday afternoon. And there the truth awaited us. When he had come to open up, Terry had found a well-wrapped parcel jammed in front of the doors. Inside were all our wallets, our papers, our snapshots, our drivers' licenses.

But our money? Not a nickel of it.

We compared notes, padding a little for the sake of pride. It looked as if Agnew Plover had got away with about $3500 in cash.

In a sense, none of us felt too bad. After all, it was a unique experience, one to talk about all our lives. And we *had* been treated to some rare entertainment.

As for me, I finally understood the true meaning of "possession." It was not so much the entering and inhabiting of a living body by spirits from the past. No, indeed. In this case it was the expert, professional way in which Agnew Plover, conman par excellence, had "had" the whole crowd of us, had us and owned us for almost a month back in that hot New York August a couple of years ago.

MARGARET MILLAR

The People Across the Canyon

"The second trip seemed a nightmarish imitation of the first: the same moon hung in the sky but it looked smaller now, and paler. The scent of pittosporum was funereally sweet, and the hollow sound of the chimes from inside the house was like an echo in an empty tomb."

The first time the Bortons realized that someone had moved into the new house across the canyon was one night in May when they saw the rectangular light of a television set shining in the picture window. Marion Borton knew it had to happen eventually, but that didn't make it any easier to accept the idea of neighbors in a part of the country she and Paul had come to consider exclusively their own.

They had discovered the site, had bought six acres, and built the house over the objections of the bank, which didn't like to lend money on unimproved property, and of their friends who thought the Bortons were foolish to move so far out of town. Now other people were discovering the spot, and here and there through the eucalyptus trees and the live oaks, Marion could see half-finished houses.

But it was the house directly across the canyon that bothered her most; she had been dreading this moment ever since the site had been bulldozed the previous summer.

"There goes our privacy." Marion went over and snapped off the television set, a sign to Paul that she had something on her mind which she wanted to transfer to his. The transference, intended to halve the problem, often merely doubled it.

"Well, let's have it," Paul said, trying to conceal his annoyance.

"Have what?"

"Stop kidding around. You don't usually cut off Perry Mason in the middle of a sentence."

"All I said was, there goes our privacy."

"We have plenty left," Paul said.

"You know how sounds carry across the canyon."

"I don't hear any sounds."

"You will. They probably have ten or twelve children and a howling dog and a sports car."

"A couple of children wouldn't be so bad—at least, Cathy would have someone to play with."

Cathy was eight, in bed now, and ostensibly asleep, with the night light on and her bedroom door open just a crack.

"She has plenty of playmates at school," Marion said, pulling the drapes across the window so that she wouldn't have to look at the exasperating rectangle of light across the canyon. "Her teacher tells me Cathy gets along with everyone and never causes any trouble. You talk as if she's deprived or something."

"It would be nice if she had more interests, more children of her own age around."

"A lot of things would be nice *if*. I've done my best."

Paul knew it was true. He'd heard her issue dozens of week-end invitations to Cathy's schoolmates. Few of them came to anything. The mothers offered various excuses: poison oak, snakes, mosquitoes in the creek at the bottom of the canyon, the distance of the house from town in case something happened and a doctor was needed in a hurry . . . these excuses, sincere and valid as they were, embittered Marion. *"For heaven's sake, you'd think we lived on the moon or in the middle of a jungle."*

"I guess a couple of children would be all right," Marion said. "But please, no sports car."

"I'm afraid that's out of our hands."

"Actually, they might even be quite *nice* people."

"Why not? Most people are."

Both Marion and Paul had the comfortable feeling that something had been settled, though neither was quite sure what. Paul went over and turned the television set back on. As he had suspected, it was the doorman who'd killed the nightclub owner with a baseball bat, not the blonde dancer or her young husband or the jealous singer.

It was the following Monday that Cathy started to run away.

Marion, ironing in the kitchen and watching a quiz program on the portable set Paul had given her for Christmas, heard the school bus groan to a stop at the top of the driveway. She waited for the front door to open and Cathy to announce in her high thin voice, "I'm home, Mommy."

The door didn't open.

From the kitchen window Marion saw the yellow bus round the sharp curve of the hill like a circus cage full of wild captive children screaming for release.

Marion waited until the end of the program, trying to convince herself that another bus had been added to the route and would come along shortly, or that Cathy had decided to stop off at a friend's house and would telephone any minute. But no other bus appeared, and the telephone remained silent.

Marion changed into her hiking boots and started off down the canyon, avoiding the scratchy clumps of chapparal and the creepers of poison oak that looked like loganberry vines.

She found Cathy sitting in the middle of the little bridge that Paul had made across the creek out of two fallen eucalyptus trees. Cathy's short plump legs hung over the logs until they almost touched the water. She was absolutely motionless, her face hidden by a straw curtain of hair. Then a single frog croaked a warning of Marion's presence and Cathy responded to the sound as if she was more intimate with nature than adults were, and more alert to its subtle communications of danger.

She stood up quickly, brushing off the back of her dress and drawing aside the curtain of hair to reveal eyes as blue as the periwinkles that hugged the banks of the creek.

"Cathy."

"I was only counting waterbugs while I was waiting. Forty-one."

"Waiting for what?"

"The ten or twelve children, and the dog."

"What ten or twelve chil—" Marion stopped. "I see. You were listening the other night when we thought you were asleep."

"I wasn't listening," Cathy said righteously. "My ears were hearing."

Marion restrained a smile. "Then I wish you'd tell those ears of yours to hear properly. I didn't say the new neighbors have ten or twelve children, I said they *might* have. Actually, it's very unlikely. Not many families are that big these days."

"Do you have to be old to have a big family?"

"Well, you certainly can't be very young."

"I bet people with big families have station wagons so they have room for all the children?"

"The lucky ones do."

Cathy stared down at the thin flow of water carrying fat little minnows down to the sea. Finally she said, "They're too young, and their car is too small."

In spite of her aversion to having new neighbors Marion felt a quickening of interest. "Have you seen them?"

But the little girl seemed deaf, lost in a water world of minnows and dragonflies and tadpoles.

"I asked you a question, Cathy. Did you see the people who just moved in?"

"Yes."

"When?"

"Before you came. Their name is Smith."

"How do you know that?"

"I went up to the house to look at things and they said, hello, little girl, what's your name? And I said, Cathy, what's yours? And they said Smith. Then they drove off in the little car."

"You're not supposed to go poking around other people's houses," Marion said brusquely. "And while we're at it, you're not supposed to go anywhere after school without first telling me where you're going and when you'll be back. You know that perfectly well. Now why didn't you come in and report to me after you got off the school bus?"

"I didn't want to."

"That's not a satisfactory answer."

Satisfactory or not, it was the only answer Cathy had. She looked at her mother in silence, then she turned and darted back up the hill to her own house.

After a time Marion followed her, exasperated and a little confused. She hated to punish the child, but she knew she couldn't ignore the matter entirely—it was much too serious. While she gave Cathy her graham crackers and orange juice, she told her, reasonably and kindly, that she would have to tay in her room the following day after school by way of ·arning a lesson.

That night, after Cathy had been tucked in bed, Marion elated the incident to Paul. He seemed to take a less serious iew of it than Marion, a fact of which the listening child ecame well aware.

"I'm glad she's getting acquainted witb the new people," 'aul said. "It shows a certain degree of poise I didn't think she ad. She's always been so shy."

"You're surely not condoning her running off without elling me?"

"She didn't run far. All kids do things like that once in a vhile."

"We don't want to spoil her."

"Cathy's always been so obedient I think she has *us* poiled. Who knows, she might even teach us a thing or two bout going out and making new friends." He realized, from ast experience, that this was a very touchy subject. Marion ad her house, her garden, her television sets; she didn't seem o want any more of the world than these, and she resented any mplication that they were not enough. To ward off an argu-nent he added, "You've done a good job with Cathy. Stop vorrying . . . Smith, their name is?"

"Yes."

"Actually, I think it's an excellent sign that Cathy's etting acquainted."

At three the next afternoon the yellow circus cage arrived, eleased one captive, and rumbled on its way.

"I'm home, Mommy."

"Good girl."

Marion felt guilty at the sight of her: the child had been ooped up in school all day, the weather was so warm and ovely, and besides Paul hadn't thought the incident of the revious afternoon too important.

"I know what," Marion suggested, "let's you and I go lown to the creek and count waterbugs."

The offer was a sacrifice for Marion because her favorite quiz program was on and she liked to answer the questions long with the contestants. "How about that?"

Cathy knew all about the quiz program; she'd seen it a undred times, had watched the moving mouths claim her

mother's eyes and ears and mind. "I counted the waterbu
yesterday."

"Well, minnows, then."

"You'll scare them away."

"Oh, will I?" Marion laughed self-consciously, rath
relieved that Cathy had refused her offer and was clearly an
definitely a little guilty about the relief. "Don't you sca
them?"

"No. They think I'm another minnow because they'
used to me."

"Maybe they could get used to me, too."

"I don't think so."

When Cathy went off down the canyon by herself Mario
realized, in a vaguely disturbing way, that the child had p
litely but firmly rejected her mother's company. It wasn't unt
dinner time that she found out the reason why.

"The Smiths," Cathy said, "have an Austin-Healey."

Cathy, like most girls, had never shown any interest i
cars, and her glib use of the name moved her parents t
laughter.

The laughter encouraged Cathy to elaborate. "An Austi
Healey makes a lot of noise—like Daddy's lawn mower."

"I don't think the company would appreciate a comme
cial from you, young lady," Paul said. "Are the Smiths a
moved in?"

"Oh, yes. I helped them."

"Is that a fact? And how did you help them?"

"I sang two songs. And then we danced and danced."

Paul looked half pleased, half puzzled. It wasn't like Cath
to perform willingly in front of people. During the las
Christmas concert at the school she'd left the stage in tears an
hidden in the cloak room. . . . Well, maybe her shyness wa
only a phase and she was finally getting over it.

"They must be very nice people," he said, "to take tim
out from getting settled in a new house to play games with
little girl."

Cathy shook her head. "It wasn't games. It was rea
dancing—like on Ed Sullivan."

"As good as that, eh?" Paul said, smiling. "Tell me abou
it."

"Mrs. Smith is a night-club dancer."

Paul's smile faded, and a pulse began to beat in his lef

temple like a small misplaced heart. "Oh? You're sure about that, Cathy?"

"Yes."

"And what does Mr. Smith do?"

"He's a baseball player."

"You mean that's what he does for a living?" Marion asked. "He doesn't work in an office like Daddy?"

"No, he just plays baseball. He always wears a baseball cap."

"I see. What position does he play on the team?" Paul's voice was low.

Cathy looked blank.

"Everybody on a ball team has a special thing to do. What does Mr. Smith do?"

"He's a batter."

"A batter, eh? Well, that's nice. Did he tell you this?"

"Yes."

"Cathy," Paul said, "I know you wouldn't deliberately lie to me, but sometimes you get your facts a little mixed up."

He went on in this vein for some time but Cathy's story remained unshaken: Mrs. Smith was a night-club dancer, Mr. Smith a professional baseball player, they loved children, and they never watched television.

"That, at least, must be a lie," Marion said to Paul later when she saw the rectangular light of the television set shining in the Smiths' picture window. "As for the rest of it, there isn't a night club within fifty miles, or a professional ball club within two hundred."

"She probably misunderstood. It's quite possible that at one time Mrs. Smith was a dancer of sorts and that he played a little baseball."

Cathy, in bed and teetering dizzily on the brink of sleep, wondered if she should tell her parents about the Smiths' child —the one who didn't go to school.

She didn't tell them; Marion found out for herself the next morning after Paul and Cathy had gone. When she pulled back the drapes in the living room and opened the windows she heard the sharp slam of a screen door from across the canyon and saw a small child come out on the patio of the new house. At that distance she couldn't tell whether it was a boy or a girl. Whichever it was, the child was quiet and well behaved; only the occasional slam of the door shook the warm, windless day.

The presence of the child, and the fact that Cathy hadn't mentioned it, gnawed at Marion's mind all day. She questioned Cathy about it as soon as she came home.

"You didn't tell me the Smiths have a child."

"No."

"Why not?"

"I don't know why not."

"Is it a boy or a girl?"

"Girl."

"How old?"

Cathy thought it over carefully, frowning up at the ceiling. "About ten."

"Doesn't she go to school?"

"No."

"Why not?"

"She doesn't want to."

"That's not a very good reason."

"It is her reason," Cathy said flatly. "Can I go out to play now?"

"I'm not sure you should. You look a little feverish. Come here and let me feel your forehead."

Cathy's forehead was cool and moist, but her cheeks and the bridge of her nose were very pink, almost as if she'd been sunburned.

"You'd better stay inside," Marion said, "and watch some cartoons."

"I don't like cartoons."

"You used to."

"I like real people."

She means the Smiths, of course, Marion thought as her mouth tightened. "People who dance and play baseball all the time?"

If the sarcasm had any effect on Cathy she didn't show it. After waiting until Marion had become engrossed in her quiz program, Cathy lined up all her dolls in her room and gave a concert for them, to thunderous applause.

"Where are your old Navy binoculars?" Marion asked Paul when she was getting ready for bed.

"Oh, somewhere in the sea chest, I imagine. Why?"

"I want them."

"Not thinking of spying on the neighbors, are you?"

"I'm thinking of just that," Marion said grimly.

The next morning, as soon as she saw the Smith child come out on the patio, Marion went downstairs to the storage room to search through the sea chest. She located the binoculars and was in the act of dusting them off when the telephone started to ring in the living room. She hurried upstairs and said breathlessly, "Hello?"

"Mrs. Borton?"

"Yes."

"This is Miss Park speaking, Cathy's teacher."

Marion had met Miss Park several times at P.T.A. meetings and report-card conferences. She was a large, ruddy-faced, and unfailingly cheerful young woman—the kind, as Paul said, you wouldn't want to live with but who'd be nice to have around in an emergency. "How are you, Miss Park?"

"Oh, fine, thank you, Mrs. Borton. I meant to call you yesterday but things were a bit out of hand around here, and I knew there was no great hurry to check on Cathy; she's such a well-behaved little girl."

Even Miss Park's loud, jovial voice couldn't cover up the ominous sound of the word *check*. "I don't think I quite understand. Why should you check on Cathy?"

"Purely routine. The school doctor and the health department like to keep records on how many cases of measles or flu or chicken pox are going the rounds. Right now it looks like the season for mumps. Is Cathy all right?"

"She seemed a little feverish yesterday afternoon when she got home from school, but she acted perfectly normal when she left this morning."

Miss Park's silence was so protracted that Marion became painfully conscious of things she wouldn't otherwise have noticed—the weight of the binoculars in her lap, the thud of her own heartbeat in her ears. Across the canyon the Smith child was playing quietly and alone on the patio. *There is definitely something the matter with that girl,* Marion thought. *Perhaps I'd better not let Cathy go over there any more, she's so imitative.* "Miss Park, are you still on the line? Hello? Hello—"

"I'm here." Miss Park's voice seemed fainter than usual, and less positive. "What time did Cathy leave the house this morning?"

"Eight, as usual."

"Did she take the school bus?"

"Of course. She always does."

"Did you see her get on?"

"I kissed her goodbye at the front door," Marion said. "What's this all about, Miss Park?"

"Cathy hasn't been at school for two days, Mrs. Borton."

"Why, that's absurd, impossible! You must be mistaken." But even as she was speaking the words, Marion was raising the binoculars to her eyes: the little girl on the Smiths' patio had a straw curtain of hair and eyes as blue as the periwinkles along the creek banks.

"Mrs. Borton, I'm not likely to be mistaken about which of my children are in class or not."

"No. No, you're—you're not mistaken, Miss Park. I can see Cathy from here—she's over at the neighbors' house."

"Good. That's a load off my mind."

"Off yours, yes," Marion said. "Not mine."

"Now we mustn't become excited, Mrs. Borton. Don't make too much of this incident before we've had a chance to confer. Suppose you come and talk to me during my lunch hour and bring Cathy along. We'll all have a friendly chat."

But it soon became apparent, even to the optimistic Miss Park, that Cathy didn't intend to take part in any friendly chat. She stood by the window in the classroom, blank-eyed, mute, unresponsive to the simplest questions, refusing to be drawn into any conversation even about her favorite topic, the Smiths. Miss Park finally decided to send Cathy out to play in the schoolyard while she talked to Marion alone.

"Obviously," Miss Park said, enunciating the word very distinctly because it was one of her favorites, "obviously, Cathy's got a crush on this young couple and has concocted a fantasy about belonging to them."

"It's not so obvious what my husband and I are going to do about it."

"Live through it, the same as other parents. Crushes like this are common at Cathy's age. Sometimes the object is a person, a whole family, even a horse. And, of course, to Cathy a night-club dancer and a baseball player must seem very glamorous indeed. Tell me, Mrs. Borton, does she watch television a great deal?"

Marion stiffened. "No more than any other child."

Oh, dear, Miss Park thought sadly, *they all do it; the most confirmed addicts are always the most defensive.* "I just wondered," she said. "Cathy likes to sing to herself and I've never heard such a repertoire of television commercials."

"She picks things up very fast."

"Yes. Yes, she does indeed." Miss Park studied her hands which were always a little pale from chalk dust and were even paler now because she was angry—at the child for deceiving her, at Mrs. Borton for brushing aside the television issue, at herself for not preventing, or at least anticipating, the current situation, and perhaps most of all at the Smiths who ought to have known better than to allow a child to hang around their house when she should obviously be in school.

"Don't put too much pressure on Cathy about this," she said finally, "until I talk the matter over with the school psychologist. By the way, have you met the Smiths, Mrs. Borton?"

"Not yet," Marion said grimly. "But believe me, I intend to."

"Yes, I think it would be a good idea for you to talk to them and make it clear that they're not to encourage Cathy in this fantasy."

The meeting came sooner than Marion expected.

She waited at the school until classes were dismissed, then she took Cathy into town to do some shopping. She had parked the car and she and Cathy were standing hand in hand at a corner waiting for a traffic light to change; Marion was worried and impatient, Cathy still silent, unresisting, inert, as she had been ever since Marion had called her home from the Smiths' patio.

Suddenly Marion felt the child's hand tighten in a spasm of excitement. Cathy's face had turned so pink it looked ready to explode and with her free hand she was waving violently at two people in a small cream-colored sports car—a very pretty young woman with blonde hair in the driver's seat, and beside her a young man wearing a wide friendly grin and a baseball cap. They both waved back at Cathy just before the lights changed and then the car roared through the intersection.

"The Smiths," Cathy shouted, jumping up and down in a frenzy. "That was the Smiths."

"Sssh, not so loud. People will—"

"But it was the *Smiths!*"

"Hurry up before the light changes."

The child didn't hear. She stood as if rooted to the curb, staring after the cream-colored car.

With a little grunt of impatience Marion picked her up, carried her across the road, and let her down quite roughly on the other side. "There. If you're going to act like a baby, I'll carry you like a baby."

"I saw the Smiths!"

"All right. What are you so excited about? It's not very unusual to meet someone in town whom you know."

"It's unusual to meet *them.*"

"Why?"

"Because it is." The color was fading from Cathy's cheeks, but her eyes still looked bedazzled, quite as if they'd seen a miracle.

"I'm sure they're very unique people," Marion said coldly. "Nevertheless they must shop for groceries like everyone else."

Cathy's answer was a slight shake of her head and a whisper heard only by herself: "No, they don't, never."

When Paul came home from work Cathy was sent to play in the front yard while Marion explained matters to him. He listened with increasing irritation—not so much at Cathy's actions but at the manner in which Marion and Miss Park had handled things. There was too much talking, he said, and too little acting.

"The way you women beat around the bush instead of tackling the situation directly, meeting it head-on—fantasy life. Fantasy life, my foot! Now we're going over to the Smiths right this minute and talk to them and that will be that. End of fantasy. Period."

"We'd better wait until after dinner. Cathy missed her lunch."

Throughout the meal Cathy was pale and quiet. She ate nothing and spoke only when asked a direct question; but inside herself the conversation was very lively, the dinner a banquet with dancing, and afterward a wild, windy ride in the roofless car . . .

Although the footpath through the canyon provided a shorter route to the Smiths' house, the Bortons decided to go more formally, by car, and to take Cathy with them. Cathy, told to comb her hair and wash her face, protested: "I don't want to go over there."

"Why not?" Paul said. "You were so anxious to spend time with them that you played hooky for two days. Why don't you want to see them now?"

"Because they're not there."

"How do you know?"

"Mrs. Smith told me this morning that they wouldn't be home tonight because she's putting on a show."

"Indeed?" Paul was grim-faced. "Just where does she put on these shows of hers?"

"And Mr. Smith has to play baseball. And after that they're going to see a friend in the hospital who has leukemia."

"Leukemia, eh?" He didn't have to ask how Cathy had found out about such a thing; he'd watched a semi-documentary dealing with it a couple of nights ago. Cathy was supposed to have been sleeping.

"I wonder," he said to Marion when Cathy went to comb her hair, "just how many 'facts' about the Smiths have been borrowed from television."

"Well, I know for myself that they drive a sports car, and Mr. Smith was wearing a baseball cap. And they're both young and good-looking. Young and good-looking enough," she added wryly, "to make me feel—well, a little jealous."

"Jealous?"

"Cathy would rather belong to them than to us. It makes me wonder if it's something the Smiths have or something the Bortons don't have."

"Ask her."

"I can't very well—"

"Then I will, dammit," Paul said. And he did.

Cathy merely looked at him innocently. "I don't know. I don't know what you mean."

"Then listen again. Why did you pretend that you were the Smiths' little girl?"

"They asked me to be. They asked me to go with them."

"They actually said, Cathy, will you be our little girl?"

"Yes."

"Well, by heaven, I'll put an end to this nonsense," Paul said, and strode out to the car.

It was twilight when they reached the Smiths' house by way of the narrow, hilly road. The moon, just appearing above the horizon, was on the wane, a chunk bitten out of its side by some giant jaw. A warm dry wind, blowing down the mountain from the desert beyond, carried the sweet scent of pittosporum.

The Smiths' house was dark, and both the front door and the garage were locked. Out of defiance or desperation, Paul pressed the door chime anyway, several times. All three of them could hear it ringing inside, and it seemed to Marion to echo very curiously—as if the carpets and drapes were too thin to muffle the sound vibrations. She would have liked to peer in through the windows and see for herself, but the venetian blinds were closed.

"What's their furniture like?" she asked Cathy.

"Like everybody's."

"I mean, is it new? Does Mrs. Smith tell you not to put your feet on it?"

"No, she never tells me that," Cathy said truthfully. "I want to go home now. I'm tired."

It was while she was putting Cathy to bed that Marion heard Paul call to her from the living room in an urgent voice, "Marion, come here a minute."

She found him standing motionless in the middle of the room, staring across the canyon at the Smiths' place. The rectangular light of the Smiths' television set was shining in the picture window of the room that opened onto the patio at the back of the Smiths' house.

"Either they've come home within the past few minutes," he said, "or they were there all the time. My guess is that they were home when we went over but they didn't want to see us, so they just doused the lights and pretended to be out. Well, it won't work! Come on, we're going back."

"I can't leave Cathy alone. She's already got her pajamas on."

"Put a bathrobe on her and bring her along. This has gone beyond the point of observing such niceties as correct attire."

"Don't you think we should wait until tomorrow?"

"Hurry up and stop arguing with me."

Cathy, protesting that she was tired and that the Smiths weren't home anyway, was bundled into a bathrobe and carried to the car.

"They're home all right," Paul said. "And by heaven they'd better answer the door this time or I'll break it down."

"That's an absurd way to talk in front of a child," Marion said coldly. "She has enough ideas without hearing—"

"Absurd, is it? Wait and see."

Cathy, listening from the back seat, smiled sleepily. She knew how to get in without breaking anything: ever since the house had been built, the real estate man who'd been trying to sell it always hid the key on a nail underneath the window box.

The second trip seemed a nightmarish imitation of the first: the same moon hung in the sky but it looked smaller now, and paler. The scent of pittosporum was funereally sweet, and the hollow sound of the chimes from inside the house was like an echo in an empty tomb.

"They must be crazy to think they can get away with a trick like this twice in one night," Paul shouted. "Come on, we're going around to the back."

Marion looked a little frightened. "I don't like trespassing on someone else's property."

"They trespassed on our property first."

He glanced down at Cathy. Her eyes were half closed and her face was pearly in the moonlight. He pressed her hand to reassure her that everything was going to be all right and that his anger wasn't directed at her, but she drew away from him and started down the path that led to the back of the house.

Paul clicked on his flashlight and followed her, moving slowly along the unfamiliar terrain. By the time he turned the corner of the house and reached the patio, Cathy was out of sight.

"Cathy," he called. "Where are you? Come back here!"

Marion was looking at him accusingly. "You upset her with that silly threat about breaking down the door. She's probably on her way home through the canyon."

"I'd better go after her."

"She's less likely to get hurt than you are. She knows every inch of the way. Besides, you came here to break down doors. All right, start breaking."

But there was no need to break down anything. The back door opened as soon as Paul rapped on it with his knuckles, and he almost fell into the room.

It was empty except for a small girl wearing a blue bathrobe that matched her eyes.

Paul said, "Cathy. Cathy, what are you doing here?"

Marion stood with her hand pressed to her mouth to stifle the scream that was rising in her throat. There were no Smiths. The people in the sports car whom Cathy had waved at were just strangers responding to the friendly greeting of a child—

had Cathy seen them before, on a previous trip to town? The television set was no more than a contraption rigged up by Cathy herself—an orange crate and an old mirror which caught and reflected the rays of the moon.

In front of it Cathy was standing, facing her own image. "Hello, Mrs. Smith. Here I am, all ready to go."

"Cathy," Marion said in a voice that sounded torn by claws. "What do you see in that mirror?"

"It's not a mirror. It's a television set."

"What—what program are you watching?"

"It's not a program, silly. It's real. It's the Smiths. I'm going away with them to dance and play baseball."

"There are no Smiths," Paul bellowed. "Will you get that through your head? *There are no Smiths!*"

"Yes, there are. I see them."

Marion knelt on the floor beside the child. "Listen to me. Cathy. This is a mirror—only a mirror. It came from Daddy's old bureau and I had it put away in the storage room. That's where you found it, isn't it? And you brought it here and decided to pretend it was a television set, isn't that right? But it's really just a mirror, and the people in it are us—you and Mommy and Daddy."

But even as she looked at her own reflection, Marion saw it beginning to change. She was growing younger, prettier; her hair was becoming lighter and her cotton suit was changing into a dancing dress. And beside her in the mirror, Paul was turning into a stranger, a laughing-eyed young man wearing a baseball cap.

"I'm ready to go now, Mr. Smith," Cathy said, and suddenly all three of them, the Smiths and their little girl, began walking away in the mirror. In a few moments they were no bigger than matchsticks—and then the three of them disappeared, and there was only the moonlight in the glass.

"Cathy," Marion cried. "Come back, Cathy! Please come back!"

Propped up against the door like a dummy, Paul imagined he could hear above his wife's cries the mocking muted roar of a sports car.

PATRICIA HIGHSMITH

The Terrapin

Perhaps the real trouble was that Victor's mother wanted him to stay about six years old, forever, all his life . . .

Patricia Highsmith's "The Terrapin" was awarded a scroll by the Mystery Writers of America and judged to be the second best mystery short story published in 1962.

Victor heard the elevator door open, his mother's quick footsteps in the hall, and he flipped his book shut. He shoved it under the sofa pillow, and winced as he heard it slip between sofa and wall and fall to the floor with a thud. Her key was in the lock.

"Hello, Veector-r!" she cried, raising one arm in the air. Her other arm circled a big brown-paper bag, her hand held a cluster of little bags. "I have been to my publisher and to the market and also to the fish market," she told him. "Why aren't you out playing? It's a lovely, lovely day!"

"I was out," he said. "For a little while. I got cold."

"Ugh!" She was unloading the grocery bag in the tiny kitchen off the foyer. "You are seeck, you know that? In the month of October, you are cold? I see all kinds of children playing on the sidewalk. Even I think that boy you like. What's his name?"

"I don't know," Victor said.

His mother wasn't really listening, anyway. He pushed his hands into the pockets of his too-small shorts, making them tighter than ever, and walked aimlessly around the living room, looking down at his heavy, scuffed shoes. At least, his mother had to buy him shoes that fit him, and he rather liked these shoes, because they had the thickest soles of any he had ever owned, and they had heavy toes that rose up a little, like mountain climbers' shoes.

Victor paused at the window and looked straight out at a toast-colored apartment building across Third Avenue. He and his mother lived on the eighteenth floor, just below the top floor where the penthouses were. The building across the street was even taller than this one. Victor had liked their Riverside Drive apartment better. He had liked the school he had gone to there better. Here they laughed at his clothes. In the other school they had got tired of laughing at them.

"You don't want to go out?" asked his mother, coming into the living room, wiping her hands briskly on a wadded paper bag. She sniffed her palms. "Ugh! That stee-enk!"

"No, Mama," Victor said patiently.

"Today is Saturday."

"I know."

"Can you say the days of the week?"

"Of course."

"Say them."

"I don't want to say them. I know them." His eyes began to sting around the edges with tears. "I've known them for years. Years and years. Kids five years old can say the days of the week."

But his mother was not listening. She was bending over the drawing table in the corner of the room. She had worked late on something last night. On his sofa bed in the opposite corner of the room, Victor had not been able to sleep until two in the morning, when his mother had finally gone to bed on the studio couch.

"Come here, Victor. Did you see this?"

Victor came on dragging feet, hands still in his pockets. No, he hadn't even glanced at her drawing board this morning, hadn't wanted to.

"This is Pedro, the Little Donkey. I invented him last night. What do you think? And this is Miguel, the little Mexican boy who rides him. They ride and ride over all of Mexico, and Miguel thinks they are lost, but Pedro knows the way home all the time, and . . ."

Victor did not listen. He deliberately shut his ears in a way he had learned to do from many years of practice; but boredom, frustration—he knew the word frustration, had read all about it—clamped his shoulders, weighed like a stone in his body, pressed hatred and tears up to his eyes as if a volcano were seething in him.

He had hoped his mother might take a hint from his saying he was too cold in his silly shorts. He had hoped his mother might remember what he had told her—that the fellow he had wanted to get acquainted with downstairs, a fellow who looked about his own age, eleven, had laughed at his short pants on Monday afternoon. *They make you wear your kid brother's pants or something?* Victor had drifted away, mortified. What if the fellow knew he didn't even own any longer pants, not even a pair of knickers, much less *long* pants or even blue jeans!

His mother, for some cockeyed reason, wanted him to look "French," and made him wear shorts and stockings that came up to just below his knees, and dopey shirts with round collars. His mother wanted him to stay about six years old, forever, all his life.

She liked to test out her drawings on him. *Victor is my sounding board,* she sometimes said to her friends. *I show my drawings to Victor and I* know *if children will like them.* Often Victor said he liked stories that he did not like, or drawings that he was indifferent to, because he felt sorry for his mother and because it put her in a better mood if he said he liked them. He was quite tired now of children's book illustrations, if he had ever in his life liked them—he really couldn't remember; and now he had only two favorites—Howard Pyle's illustrations in some of Robert Louis Stevenson's books and Cruikshank's in Dickens.

It was too bad, Victor thought, that he was absolutely the last person his mother should have asked an opinion of, because he simply *hated* children's illustrations. And it was a wonder his mother didn't see this, because she hadn't sold any illustrations for books for years and years—not since *Wimple-Dimple,* a book whose jacket was all torn and turning yellow now from age, which sat in the center of the bookshelf in a little cleared spot, propped up against the back of the bookcase so that everyone could see it.

Victor had been seven years old when that book was printed. His mother liked to tell people—and remind him, too—that he had watched her make every drawing, had shown his opinion by laughing or not, and that she had been absolutely guided by him. Victor doubted this very much, because first of all the story was somebody else's and had been written before his mother did the drawings, and her drawings had had to follow the story closely.

Since *Wimple-Dimple*, his mother had done only a few illustrations now and then for children's magazines—how to make paper pumpkins and black paper cats for Halloween and things like that—though she took her portfolio around to publishers all the time.

Their income came from his father, who was a wealthy businessman in France, an exporter of perfumes. His mother said he was very wealthy and very handsome. But he had married again, and he never wrote, and Victor had no interest in him, didn't even care if he never saw a picture of him, and he never had. His father was French with some Polish, his mother said, and she was Hungarian with some French. The word Hungarian made Victor think of gypsies, but when he had asked his mother once, she had said emphatically that she hadn't any gypsy blood, and she had been annoyed that Victor had brought the question up.

And now she was sounding him out again, poking him in the ribs to make him wake up, as she repeated, "Listen to me! Which do you like better, Victor? 'In all Mexico there was no bur-r-ro as wise as Miguel's Pedro,' or 'Miguel's Pedro was the wisest bur-r-ro in all Mexico'?"

"I think—I like it the first way better."

"Which way is that?" demanded his mother, thumping her palm down on the illustration.

Victor tried to remember the wording, but realized he was only staring at the pencil smudges, the thumbprints on the edges of his mother's illustration board. The colored drawing in its center did not interest him at all. He was not thinking. This was a frequent, familiar sensation to him now; there was something exciting and important about not-thinking, Victor felt, and he thought that one day he would find out something about it—perhaps under another name—in the Public Library or in the psychology books around the house that he browsed in when his mother was out.

"Veec-tor! What are you doing?"

"Nothing, Mama."

"That is exactly it! Nothing! Can you not even *think?*"

A warm shame spread through him. It was as if his mother read his thoughts about not-thinking. "I am thinking," he protested. "I'm thinking about *not*-thinking." His tone was defiant. What could she do about it, after all?

"About what?" Her black, curly head tilted, her mas-caraed eyes narrowed at him.

"Not-thinking."

His mother put her jeweled hands on her hips. "Do you know, Victor, you are a leetle bit strange in the head?" She nodded. "You are seeck. Psychologically seeck. And retarded, do you know that? You have the behavior of a leetle boy five years old," she said slowly and weightily. "It is just as well you spend your Saturdays indoors. Who knows if you would not walk in front of a car, eh? But that is why I love you, little Victor."

She put her arm around his shoulders, pulled him against her, and for an instant Victor's nose pressed into her large, soft bosom. She was wearing her flesh-colored knitted dress, the one you could see through a little where her breast stretched it out.

Victor jerked his head away in a confusion of emotions. He did not know if he wanted to laugh or cry.

His mother was laughing gaily, her head back. "Seeck you are! Look at you! My lee-tle boy still, lee-tle short pants—ha! ha!"

Now the tears showed in his eyes, and his mother acted as if she were enjoying it! Victor turned his head away so that she would not see his eyes. Then suddenly he faced her. "Do you think I *like* these pants? *You* like them, not me, so why do you have to make fun of them?"

"A lee-tle boy who's crying!" she went on, laughing.

Victor made a dash for the bathroom, then swerved away and dove onto the sofa, his face toward the pillows. He shut his eyes tight and opened his mouth, crying but not-crying in a way he had also learned through long practice. With his mouth open, his throat tight, not breathing for nearly a minute, he could somehow get the satisfaction of crying, screaming even, without anybody knowing it.

He pushed his nose, his open mouth, his teeth, against the tomato-red sofa pillow, and though his mother's voice went on in a lazily mocking tone, and her laughter went on, he im-agined that it was getting fainter and more distant from him.

He imagined, rigid in every muscle, that he was suffering the absolute worst that any human being could suffer. He imagined that he was dying. But he did not think of death as an escape, only as a concentrated and painful instant. This was the climax of his not-crying.

Then he breathed again, and his mother's voice intruded: "Did you hear me? *Did you hear me?* Mrs. Badzerkian is coming over for tea. I want you to wash your face and put on a clean shirt. I want you to recite something for her. Now what are you going to recite?"

" 'In winter when I go to bed,' " said Victor. She was making him memorize every poem in *A Child's Garden of Verses*. He had said the first one that came in his head, and now there was an argument, because he had recited that the last time Mrs. Badzerkian came to tea. "I said it because I couldn't think of any other one right off the bat!" Victor shouted.

"Don't yell at me!" his mother cried, storming across the room at him.

She slapped his face before he knew what was happening.

He was up on one elbow on the sofa, on his back, his long, knobby-kneed legs splayed out in front of him. All right, he thought, if that's the way it is, that's the way it is. He looked at her with loathing.

He would not show her that the slap had hurt, that it still stung. No more tears for today, he swore, not even any more not-crying. He would finish the day, go through the tea, like a stone, like a soldier, not wincing.

His mother paced the room, turning one of her rings round and round, glancing at him from time to time, looking quickly away from him. But his eyes were steady on her. He was not afraid. She could even slap him again and he wouldn't move.

At last she announced that she was going to wash her hair, and she went into the bathroom.

Victor got up from the sofa and wandered across the room. He wished he had a room of his own to go to. In the apartment on Riverside Drive there had been two rooms, a living room and his mother's bedroom. When she was in the living room, he had been able to go into the bedroom, and vice versa, but here— They were going to tear down the old building they had lived in on Riverside Drive. It was not a pleasant thing for Victor to think about.

Suddenly remembering the book that had fallen, he pulled out the sofa and reached for it. It was Menninger's *The Human Mind*, full of fascinating case histories of people. Victor put it back in its place on the bookshelf between a book on astrology and *How to Draw*.

His mother did not like him to read psychology books, but Victor loved them, especially ones with case histories in them. The people in the case histories did what they wanted to do. They were natural. Nobody bossed them. At the local branch library he spent hours browsing through the psychology shelves. They were in the adults' section, but the librarian did not mind him sitting at the tables there, because he was always so quiet.

Victor went into the kitchen and got a glass of water. As he was standing there drinking it, he heard a scratching noise coming from the paper bags on the counter. A mouse, he thought, but when he moved a couple of the bags he didn't see any mouse. The scratching was coming from inside one of the bags.

Gingerly, he opened the bag's end with his fingers and waited for something to jump out. Looking in, he saw a white paper carton. He pulled it out slowly. Its bottom was damp. It opened like a pastry box. Victor jumped in surprise. In the box was a turtle—a live turtle!

It was wriggling its legs in the air, trying to turn over. Victor moistened his lips, and frowning with concentration, took the turtle by its sides with both hands, turned him over, and let him down gently into the box again. The turtle drew its feet in then and its head stretched up a little and it looked right at him.

Victor smiled. Why hadn't his mother told him she'd brought him a present? A live turtle! Victor's eyes glazed with anticipation as he thought of taking the turtle down, maybe with a leash around its neck, to show the fellow who'd laughed at his short pants. The boy might change his mind about being friends with him, if he learned that Victor owned a live turtle.

"Hey, Mama! Mama!" Victor yelled at the bathroom door. "You brought me a turtle?"

"A what?" The water shut off.

"A turtle! In the kitchen!" Victor had been jumping up and down in the hall. He stopped.

His mother had hesitated, too. The water came on again, and she said in a shrill tone, *"C'est une terrapène! Pour un ragout!"*

Victor understood, and a small chill went over him because his mother had spoken in French. His mother addressed him in French only when she was giving an order that had to be obeyed, or when she anticipated resistance from him.

So the terrapin was for a stew. Victor nodded to himself with a stunned resignation, and went back to the kitchen. For a stew. Well, the terrapin was not long for this world, as they say. What did a terrapin like to eat? Lettuce? Raw bacon? Boiled potato? Victor peered in the refrigerator.

He held a piece of lettuce near the terrapin's horny mouth. The terrapin did not open its mouth, but it looked at him. Victor held it near the two little dots of its nostrils, but if the terrapin smelled the lettuce, it showed no interest. Victor looked under the sink and pulled out a round wash pan. He put two inches of water into it. Then he gently dumped the terrapin into the pan. The terrapin paddled for a few seconds, as if it had to swim; then finding that its stomach sat on the bottom of the pan, it stopped, and drew its feet in.

Victor got down on his knees and studied the terrapin's face. Its upper lip overhung the lower, giving it a rather stubborn and unfriendly expression; but its eyes—they were bright and shining. Victor smiled when he looked hard at them.

"Okay, *Monsieur terrapène,*" he said, "just tell me what you'd like to eat and we'll get it for you. Maybe some tuna?"

They had had tuna fish salad yesterday for dinner, and there was a small bowl of it left over. Victor got a little chunk of it in his fingers and offered it to the terrapin. The terrapin was not interested.

Victor looked around the kitchen, wondering; then seeing the sunlight on the floor of the living room, he picked up the pan and carried it to the living room and set it down so that the sunlight would fall on the terrapin's back. All turtles liked sunlight, Victor thought. He lay down on the floor on his side, propped up on an elbow.

The terrapin stared at him for a moment, then very slowly and with an air of forethought and caution, put out its legs and advanced, found the circular boundary of the pan, and moved to the right, half its body out of the shallow water.

Obviously it wanted to get out, so Victor took it in one hand, by the sides, and said, "You can come out and have a little walk."

He smiled as the terrapin started to disappear under the sofa. He caught it easily, because it moved so slowly. When he put it down on the carpet, it was quite still, as if it had withdrawn a little to think what it should do next, where it should go.

The terrapin was brownish green. Looking at it, Victor thought of river bottoms, of river water flowing. Or maybe oceans. Where did terrapins come from? He jumped up and went to the dictionary on the bookshelf. The dictionary had a picture of a terrapin, but it was a dull, black and white drawing, not so pretty as the live one. He learned nothing except that the name was of Algonquian origin, that the terrapin lived in fresh or brackish water, and that it was edible.

Edible. Well, that was bad luck, Victor thought. But he was not going to eat any *terrapène* tonight. It would be all for his mother, that ragout, and even if she slapped him, scolded him, and made him learn an extra two or three poems, he would *not* eat any terrapin tonight.

His mother came out of the bathroom. "What are you doing there?—Victor?"

Victor put the dictionary back on the shelf. His mother had seen the pan. "I'm looking at the terrapin," he said, then realized the terrapin had disappeared. He got down on hands and knees and looked under the sofa.

"Don't put it on the furniture. It makes spots," said his mother. She was standing in the foyer, rubbing her hair vigorously with a towel.

Victor found the terrapin between the wastebasket and the wall. He put it back in the pan.

"Have you changed your shirt?" asked his mother.

Victor changed his shirt, and then at his mother's order sat down on the sofa with *A Child's Garden of Verses* and tackled another poem, a brand-new one for Mrs. Badzerkian. He learned two lines at a time, reading it aloud in a soft voice to himself, then repeating it, then putting two, four, and six lines together, until he had memorized the whole poem. He recited it to the terrapin. Then Victor asked his mother if he could play with the terrapin in the bathtub.

"No! And get your shirt all splashed?"

"I can put on my other shirt."

"No! It's nearly four o'clock now. Get that pan out of the living room!"

Victor carried the pan back to the kitchen. His mother took the terrapin quite fearlessly out of the pan, put it back into the white paper box, closed its lid, and stuck the box in the refrigerator.

Victor jumped a little as the refrigerator door slammed. It would be awfully cold in there for the terrapin. But then, he supposed, fresh or brackish water was cold too.

"Victor, cut the lemon," said his mother. She was fixing the big round tray with cups and saucers. The water was boiling in the kettle.

Mrs. Badzerkian was prompt as usual, and his mother poured the tea as soon as her guest had deposited her coat and pocketbook on the foyer chair and sat down. Mrs. Badzerkian smelled of cloves. She had a small, straight mouth and a thin mustache on her upper lip which fascinated Victor, as he had never seen one on a woman before—not at such short range, anyway. He never had mentioned Mrs. Badzerkian's mustache to his mother, knowing it was considered ugly; but in a strange way, her mustache was the thing he liked best about Mrs. Badzerkian.

The rest of her was dull, uninteresting, and vaguely unfriendly. She always pretended to listen carefully to his poetry recitations, but he felt that she fidgeted, thought of other things while he recited, and was glad when it was over. Today, Victor recited very well and without any hesitation, standing in the middle of the living-room floor and facing the two women, who were then having their second cup of tea.

"Très bien," said his mother. "Now you may have a cookie."

Victor chose from the plate a small round cookie with a drop of orange goo in its center. He kept his knees close together when he sat down. He always felt that Mrs. Badzerkian looked at his knees, and with distaste. He often wished she would make some remark to his mother about his being old enough for long pants, but she never had—at least, not within his hearing.

Victor learned from his mother's conversation with Mrs. Badzerkian that the Lorentzes were coming for dinner tomorrow evening. It was probably for them that the terrapin stew was going to be made. Victor was glad that he would have one more day to play with the terrapin. Tomorrow morning, he thought, he would ask his mother if he could take the terrapin down on the sidewalk for a while, either on a leash or, if his mother insisted, in the paper box.

"—like a chi-ild!" his mother was saying, laughing, with a glance at him, and Mrs. Badzerkian smiled shrewdly at him with her small, tight mouth.

Victor had been excused, and was sitting across the room with a book on the studio couch. His mother was telling Mrs. Badzerkian how he had played with the terrapin. Victor frowned down at his book, pretending not to hear. His mother did not like him to speak to her or her guests once he had been excused. But now she was calling him her "lee-tle ba-aby Veec-tor . . ."

He stood up with his finger in the place in his book. "I don't see why it's childish to look at a terrapin!" he said, flushing with sudden anger. "They are very interesting animals. They—"

His mother interrupted him with a laugh, but at once the laugh disappeared and she said sternly, "Victor, I thought I had excused you. Isn't that correct?"

He hesitated, seeing in a flash the scene that was going to take place when Mrs. Badzerkian had left. "Yes, Mama. I'm sorry," he said. Then he sat down and bent over his book again.

Twenty minutes later Mrs. Badzerkian left. His mother scolded him for being rude, but it was not a five or ten minute scolding of the kind he had expected. It lasted barely two minutes. She had forgotten to buy heavy cream, and she wanted Victor to go downstairs and get some.

Victor put on his gray woolen jacket and went out. He always felt embarrassed and conspicuous in the jacket, because it came just a little bit below his short pants, and it looked as if he had nothing on underneath the coat.

Victor looked around for Frank on the sidewalk, but

he didn't see him. He crossed Third Avenue and went to a delicatessen in the big building that he could see from the living-room window. On his way back, he saw Frank walking along the sidewalk, bouncing a ball. Victor went right up to him.

"Hey," Victor said. "I've got a terrapin upstairs."

"A what?" Frank caught the ball and stopped.

"A terrapin. You know, like a turtle. I'll bring it down tomorrow morning and show you, if you're around. It's pretty big."

"Yeah? Why don't you bring it down now?"

"Because we're gonna eat now," said Victor. "See you."

He went into his building. He felt he had achieved something. Frank had looked really interested. Victor wished he could bring the terrapin down now, but his mother never liked him to go out after dark, and it was practically dark now.

When Victor got upstairs, his mother was still in the kitchen. Eggs were boiling and she had put a big pot of water on a back burner. "You took it out again!" Victor said, seeing the terrapin's box on the counter.

"Yes. I prepare the stew tonight," said his mother. "That is why I need the cream."

Victor looked at her. "You're going to—you have to kill it tonight?"

"Yes, my little one. Tonight." She jiggled the pot of eggs.

"Mama, can I take it downstairs to show Frank?" Victor asked quickly. "Just for five minutes, Mama. Frank's down there now."

"Who is Frank?"

"He's that fellow you asked me about today. The blond fellow we always see. *Please,* Mama."

His mother's black eyebrows frowned. "Take the *terrapène* downstairs? Certainly not. Don't be absurd, my baby! The *terrapène* is not a toy!"

Victor tried to think of some other lever of persuasion. He had not removed his coat. "You wanted me to get acquainted with Frank—"

"Yes. What has that got to do with the *terrapène?*"

The water on the back burner began to boil.

"You see, I promised him I'd—" Victor watched his mother lift the terrapin from the box, and as she dropped it into the boiling water his mouth fell open. *"Mama!"*

"What is this? What is this noise?"

Victor, open-mouthed, stared at the terrapin whose legs were now racing against the steep sides of the pot. The terrapin's mouth opened, its eyes looked right at Victor for an instant, its head arched back in torture, then the open mouth sank beneath the seething water—and that was the end.

Victor blinked. The terrapin was dead. He came closer, saw the four legs and the tail stretched out in the water. He looked at his mother.

She was drying her hands on a towel. She glanced at him, then said, "Ugh!" She smelled her hands, then hung the towel back.

"Did you have to kill it like that?"

"How else? The same way you kill a lobster. Don't you know that? It doesn't hurt them."

He stared at her. When she started to touch him, he stepped back. He thought of the terrapin's wide open mouth, and his eyes suddenly flooded with tears. Maybe the terrapin had been screaming and it hadn't been heard over the bubbling of the water. The terrapin had looked at him, wanting him to pull it out, and he hadn't moved to help it. His mother had tricked him, acted so fast that he couldn't save it. He stepped back again. "No, don't touch me!"

His mother slapped his face, hard and quickly.

Victor set his jaw. Then he about-faced and went to the closet and threw his jacket onto a hanger and hung it up. He went into the living room and fell down on the sofa. He was not crying now, but his mouth opened against the sofa pillow. Then he remembered the terrapin's mouth and he closed his lips. The terrapin had suffered, otherwise it would not have moved its legs so terribly fast to get out.

Then Victor wept, soundlessly as the terrapin, his mouth open. He put both hands over his face, so as not to wet the sofa. After a long while he got up.

In the kitchen his mother was humming, and every few seconds he heard her quick, firm steps as she went about her work. Victor had set his teeth again. He walked slowly to the kitchen doorway.

The terrapin was out on the wooden chopping board, and his mother, after a glance at him, still humming, took a knife and bore down on the blade, cutting off the terrapin's little nails. Victor half closed his eyes, but he watched steadily. His mother scooped the nails, with bits of skin attached to them, off the board into her palm and dumped them into the garbage bag.

Then she turned the terrapin on its back and with the same sharp, pointed knife she began to cut away the pale bottom shell. The terrapin's neck was bent sideways. Victor wanted to look away, but still he stared. Now the terrapin's insides were all exposed, red and white and greenish.

Victor did not listen to what his mother was saying—something about cooking terrapins in Europe before he was born. Her voice was gentle and soothing, not at all like what she was doing.

"All right, don't look at me like that!" she cried out suddenly, stomping her foot. "What's the matter with you? Are you crazy? Yes, I think so! You are seeck, you know that?"

Victor could not touch any of his supper, and his mother could not force him to, even though she shook him by the shoulders and threatened to slap him. They had creamed chipped beef on toast. Victor did not say a word. He felt very remote from his mother, even when she screamed right into his face. He felt very odd, the way he did sometimes when he was sick to his stomach, but he was not sick to his stomach.

When they went to bed that night, he felt afraid of the dark. He saw the terrapin's face very large, its mouth open, its eyes wide and full of pain. Victor wished he could walk out the window and float, go anywhere he wanted to, disappear, yet be everywhere. He imagined his mother's hands on his shoulders, jerking him back, if he tried to step out the window. He hated his mother.

He got up and went quietly into the kitchen. The kitchen was absolutely dark, as there was no window, but he put his hand accurately on the knife rack and felt gently for the knife he wanted. He thought of the terrapin, in little pieces now, all mixed up in the sauce of cream and egg yolks and sherry in the pot in the refrigerator.

His mother's cry was not silent—it seemed to tear his ears off. His second blow was in her body, and then he stabbed her throat again.

Only tiredness made him stop, and by then people were trying to bump the door in. Victor at last walked to the door, pulled the chain bolt back, and opened it for them.

He was taken to a large, old building full of nurses and

doctors. Victor was very quiet and did everything he was asked to do, and answered the questions they put to him, but only those questions; and since they didn't ask him anything about a terrapin, he did not bring it up.

YOUNGMAN CARTER

The Most Wanted Man in the World

A fascinating story with an irresistible theme—about the biggest manhunt in the history of England, and of a danger so dreadful that an entire nation could be blackmailed . . .

Dr. Forsdyke, Senior Research Assistant at the Evans and Layton Laboratories, flicked the tiny glass capsule with his cuff and it rolled along the bench for a full yard. It was pure chance, the lightest touch, for he was not a clumsy man; but it was the beginning of a considerable journey.

One of the dozen juniors in the laboratory, who happened to be standing next to Dr. Forsdyke, was also taking material from the safe. The junior did not notice the incident, but ten minutes later he swept the capsule into a batch of his own, almost identical in appearance, parceled them carefully, and then handed them to the boy from the dispatch office.

This was at half-past twelve on the morning of the 15th of April, a Friday. The capsule was not missed until six o'clock that evening, the wrong hour at which to start a hue and cry. Dr. Forsdyke knew precisely how important the loss might be, but he was in an impossible and frustrating position. It was after nine that night before he deduced, accurately, what had happened to the capsule and nearly midnight before its sixty possible destinations had been unearthed.

By then Dr. Forsdyke was gray with terror.

In the small hours he explained the situation at Scotland Yard to a weary official who had been dragged from his bed to deal with the problem, for this was a matter for experts.

"Now this drug . . ." said the official.

"It is not a drug at all." Forsdyke was explaining his troubles for perhaps the twentieth time. "It is a virus culture—the disease in person—don't you understand? It is part of a collection sent from Hong Kong—the isolated brute itself, sealed in a glass tube about four centimeters long. You break the top to get at the contents. We at Evans and Layton are trying to discover the antitoxin—so far without success. This germ has come down from God knows where in China or Mongolia where it has been killing thousands, possibly millions. It's a very hardy specimen, bred out of a lot of half-witted experiments behind the Iron Curtain where they've been playing around with cholera antibiotics for years. The only result we know of is this entirely new virus which nature has developed for herself to beat us all. It is as infectious and as contagious as 'flu, it kills within a few hours, and at the moment there's nothing we can do to stop it."

"I see," said the official. "Then if someone takes it by mistake for something else, he's a dead man."

Forsdyke sighed. "If anyone injects himself with that quantity he will be dead within minutes. But that isn't the gravest danger. The victim will be found dead. Someone will touch him, fumble with his clothes, probably two or three people. Then a doctor, ambulance men, mortuary assistants—say a couple of dozen people. Within twenty-four hours, even if they're still alive, they'll all be carriers. Now do you see what I'm driving at?"

At the Home Office the Assistant Commissioner explained his problems on Monday morning to a white-faced group. "As far as we can tell," he said slowly, "this damned virus was confused, God knows how, with a perfectly normal drug sent out to dispensing chemists, hospitals, and so on, in the usual way of business. They're all recorded, of course, very strictly. It isn't a very usual drug, thank God. Out of the sixty batches sent out we've recovered fifty-three intact, which narrows the field to seven lots. Only these seven have reached the public.

"Six of these seven have been traced and the poor wretches are now under observation. There have been no results so far, which is a very good sign, because this thing works like the wind. Practically speaking, we can be sure it's not one of them. Number Seven is our headache."

The group looked at him silently and he plodded on as if reading a prepared statement.

"This drug is used as an injection—the chap can do it for himself—to alleviate pain of a particular kind. It is given to victims of one of the off-shoots of polio. It gets them in the legs generally and hurts, I'm told, like the very devil. A shot of this cools it off and may keep them quiet for days.

"It needs a doctor's prescription, which helps us quite a bit.

"You see, Number Seven, whoever he is, is carrying six—probably five now—capsules round with him and he may not use the vital one for a long time. We can't count on that, of course—he may have done it already."

"I thought," suggested a Home Office man, "that you said there was a record of these things. If the search is so narrow now, why can't your last man—your Number Seven—be traced?"

The Commissioner referred again to his mental notes.

"The vital capsule," he said, "was almost certainly given out yesterday at an all-night chemist's in Baker Street. That is to say, it is one of the six little tubes—six separate injections—which are issued on a single prescription. Unfortunately, the prescription was forged and whoever obtained it gave a false address and almost certainly a false name."

There was a general murmur of concern.

"Then we're back where we started? . . . The B.B.C. must send out a message—the press—"

"That is not quite the end of our inquiries," said the Commissioner. "We have a fairly shrewd idea who the man is—or, at least, a reasonable supposition. Last week—on Sunday night to be precise—a man escaped from Wakefield Prison. Henry Musgrave Saunders, 43, doing time for mail van robbery. He's thought to be in London and he's been having treatment for this particular trouble. There's more than a chance that he's the chap—our Number Seven. A very intelligent criminal, and dangerous. He's been a free man for a week, so he must have money or friends. The chances are that he's reached the Smoke by now—he's a Londoner—and he fits the chemist's description to a T."

He looked up from his invisible notes and surveyed his audience individually.

"Now we have several choices before us. We can broadcast a detailed description and explain both to him and the public why he is wanted. That sounds very fine and practical—but it has objections. The first is that this man is the type who might prefer suicide to arrest. If he does, the epidemic will start from there. The second is that if anything is explained to the public about this danger it may cause considerable alarm, to put it mildly. The third is that if we merely say he has a dangerous and lethal drug in his possession he may very well decide to use it as a weapon without realizing just how powerful that weapon is.

"If he knew precisely what he was carrying about with him he might even decide to blackmail the entire nation—and he'd possibly get away with it. And, of course, there is another important factor. Evans and Layton, as you probably know, is part of W.C.C.—World Chemical Combine—and very strong pressure is being put on us to settle this without public knowledge. Bad for—uh—prestige. They're powerfully—I use the word advisedly—against any injury to their reputation at this particular moment.

"As we see it at the Yard, there is only one possible course. That is, we must set off the biggest undercover manhunt in history. And the facts don't give us much time."

It was five hours before Henry Musgrave Saunders, late of Wakefield Prison, received some of the impact of that morning's decisions; but even before that the day had not been easy. He was carrying too much money for health in his circle of acquaintance, despite the fact that his escape had been costly and nearly half his share of loot had gone to procure it. There remained, however, just over £1000 in beautiful, dirty assorted notes—a very dangerous cargo for a man in his social position. He was not only at the mercy of every informer or blackmailer who could recognize him but he was also utterly unprotected.

Then there was the added problem of pain.

And finally, the question of the girl: everyone in the business would be watching her. Phones would be tapped, letters scrutinized, and she was bound to be shadowed night and day.

Better than most, he could spot a plain-clothesman at a reasonable distance. This afternoon he was a little late because his leg was blunting his reflexes.

The officer facing him was middle-aged but mercifully slow: his reactions were those of a bad actor doing an underlined double-take.

This was on the corner of Piccadilly Circus, just outside Swan & Edgars. It was five o'clock and the afternoon was sunless and chilly.

The older man had seen him first, by a few seconds. By the time Saunders realized what had happened, the watcher had taken a paper from his pocket, checked it, and started to move.

Saunders reacted automatically, shifting behind a group of walkers so that he was temporarily out of sight, and then turning to the first shop window which reflected the enemy. He saw the man hesitate and then turn to the police callbox.

This meant that he was registered as being in the area and that danger was imminent. He turned into Aire Street and paused for a moment in the shadow of the Regent Street arch. A uniformed policeman, standing magnificently back toward him, made it necessary to hesitate.

Saunders thought almost with detachment about the men who would soon be searching the neighborhood for him. How much had they memorized about him? How much did they know? Six foot two, sallow complexion, dark hair, and of course a heavy limp.

This last was the crucial item.

It was a difficult and intensely painful business, smothering that limp, an acrobatic feat accompanied by torture; but if he took it slowly it could be done.

Under the arch he took off his trench coat, in case it had now been added to his identification, folded it over to show the tartan lining, and flung it carelessly over his shoulder. He ruffled his hair, put on his glasses, and doubled agonizingly back into Piccadilly.

Almost opposite was a man's outfitters, a palatial establishment of several floors, comfortably full of late shoppers. Once inside, he felt it safe to straighten up, limp freely, and gain a few minutes before any plain-clothesman got on to him. He made a couple of purchases from a bored and busy young man: two caps which could be folded into a pocket, a sporting check and an inconspicuous green.

To these he added a muffler, reversible in a different color, and a pair of sunglasses. The tobacco kiosk also provided inspiration in the form of a large cherrywood pipe, happily out of his normal character.

In green cap and yellow muffler, and puffing jauntily on

the pipe, he made for the Jermyn Street exit. No one had noticed him, he decided. In the unruffled calm of an artists' supply store he bought a large indiarubber, some sable brushes, and a tube of gum.

By now a drink was essential to dull the pain in his leg and provide a pause to consider strategy. He settled for a small expensive hostelry toward St. James—an establishment with several advantages, including a respectable washroom and exits on two streets. He was, he decided over his first gin, to be a sporting type, probably ex-R.A.F., and he began to think himself into the role as an actor might.

He had a second gin, but the pain was not alleviated.

The real problem was to reach the girl and to get some money to her—somehow to pierce the cordon. Once it was in her hands she could time her own getaway and he could lie low until the worst of the hue and cry was past.

In the washroom he filled out his cheeks with the indiarubber, which gave a satisfactorily pouchy look, though it was hardly comfortable. A shot of the drug—only four now remained—restored his balance.

In his absence a man, obviously a plainclothes policeman, had come into the bar and was looking around. Freedom from pain gave Saunders the courage to eye danger casually and to order another drink. Then it was time to move.

The suburbs, he had decided, were the safest hideout for the night. A taxi immediately outside the bar took him to Edgeware Road where he collected a bag from the tube luggage office. Watford seemed the farthest point.

It was going as well as could be expected.

At half-past six the Assistant Commissioner held a conference. The day's reports were before him. Saunders had been seen in Beaconsfield, Truro, Goole, Bradford, Lowestoft, Newhaven, and in Central London.

"The Piccadilly report seems the most likely," said his aide. "He was noticed by a reliable man there, who's used to this sort of thing. This chap says he's pretty sure their eyes met and that Saunders, if it was he, disappeared into thin air. Wearing a trench coat, he says. Otherwise he can't add much.

"But there's some confirmation for the story. Our chaps went round all the pubs in the area within the hour. At the Craven, in Jermyn Street, a barman says a man came in limping heavily and went off after a couple of drinks as fit as a flea. He thought it odd."

"Well, assuming this is the chap, where do we go from here? If he was limping, maybe he was in pain and gave himself a shot. It can't have been the right one or we'd know by now. How are you following up?"

"Every possible way, sir. If he was spotted in London and knows it, he may go to earth if he's got friends. This we doubt, because they may be as keen to meet him as we are, for different reasons. No, he'll not go far—because of his girl, we think. He might step out to the suburbs—Hendon or Kingston or Colindale, somewhere like that—anywhere on a tube line where he could nip off smartish. They're all alerted, of course."

"I see. Now about the girl?"

"She works at a hairdresser's in Pimlico. A quiet little kid, by all accounts. We've got men on her twenty-four hours a day."

The next day's conference was a meeting of angry men. They were rattled and unhappy, for at that level there was no buck-passing to be hoped for.

Commander Rayne of the C.I.D. made his report in person to the Assistant Commissioner.

"He's slipped us," he admitted. "We can disregard all the out-of-town stories—there's no doubt now that he was the man in the West End yesterday.

"This morning there was information from Watford—just the sort of place we expected. A man booked in at a commercial hotel just by the station, last night. The local police had made their checkup just before he arrived, and he didn't altogether fit the bill. He does seem to have had a bit of a limp, however, when he left this morning. What put them on to it was the fact that he had a fight in his room sometime during the night. A man was picked up by the landlord this morning trying to sneak out of the pub and he'd clearly been badly beaten up in the suspect's bedroom. The room was a wreck.

"This chap's name is Hicks, Charles Arthur, a small-time conman with a long record—he's even been an informer in his day. Pretty clear what happened. He must have spotted Saunders somewhere along the line and gone into his bedroom to put the black on him.

"Hicks hasn't sung to us yet but he evidently got the worst

of it and spent part of the night either knocked out cold or tied up with a gag in his mouth, probably both. The sheets were in ribbons and our bird had flown.

"We've got a bit more description. He is now a sporting type—big pipe, yellow muffler, green cap. He's discarded the trench coat—left it in the tube. If he's got money he may switch his outfit again.

"But that's not all, unfortunately. It looks as if he'd reached the girl right under our noses. Very neatly done, really —you have to take your hat off to him."

"I'm not in the mood," said the A. C. gloomily. "What happened?"

"At half-past twelve this morning," recited the Commander, "a man arrived in Ember Street, Pimlico, which contains the back door of the Maison Henriette where the girl works. He was on a Gambetta, one of those little scooter jobs. Stolen in Watford. Completely typical, our man says. Bowler hat, duffle coat, and R. A. F. mustache—hundreds of 'em about. Our chaps didn't give him a second thought. He was carrying a box of chocolates and some flowers wrapped in cellophane. A couple of the lady assistants came out of the shop on their way to lunch—not his girl, Jessie Dale, but two friends.

"Saunders, if it was he, went up to them, gave them the stuff, and they took it back inside, evidently at his request. Our chap says he thought nothing of it until little Jessie took her lunch, or rather should have done. Actually, she nipped out earlier than usual, caught a taxi, and vanished. There was a squad car up the street but she managed to get lost all the same. The other two girls say a nice gentleman asked them to take the flowers and chocs in to Jessie because it was her birthday. She read the card on the bunch, took the lot into their washroom, and when she came out, shared the chocs with the girls, left the flowers in a vase, and set off for outer space without saying goodbye.

"Our guess is that Saunders sent her the best part of a thousand quid in that box of chocolates and told her just where to go. She knew perfectly well we were tailing her—in fact, she was cooperating very nicely until just that moment."

A telephone bell had begun to murmur discreetly in the room and from habit, the A. C. waited for Rayne to finish before answering. Then he listened in silence for a full minute, said, "Yes, well, keep at it," and hung up. "Your man Hicks," he explained. "He's sung, as you envisaged. Admits everything. One new detail. After the fight in the bedroom Saunders tied him up and gagged him. But he could still see. Saunders gave himself another shot just before he left. That leaves, according to our reckoning, just two capsules to go."

At that precise moment the man called Henry Musgrave Saunders was speeding along a line somewhere between Much Hadham and Bishop's Stortford. His little machine was running easily and his plan was clear. He would leave it at a garage on a pretext of repairs and take a Cambridge train. He had discarded his duffle coat and returned to his sporting check cap and muffler.

Then a sudden flash of pain, as violent as a rapier stab in a nerve, threw him and the Gambetta completely off balance.

They swerved together, struck the side of the ditch, and the man was flung forward, like a sack of turnips, into the knotty bank of the hedge.

He lay there for an hour and a half.

Toward midnight Commander Rayne and the A. C. spoke again.

"This beats everything," Rayne was shouting with fury. "We had him—had him stone-cold, right in our hands—and he walks out into thin air."

"What happened this time?"

"Found lying by his motorcycle in a ditch in Hertfordshire. Both of them smashed up. Good Samaritan took him into Bishop's Stortford Hospital." He sighed heavily. "He was there for an hour—a full hour—eight stitches in his forehead. Then they let him go—just ten minutes before the local people identified the bike as the one he'd lifted in Watford. I ask you! Ten minutes, and he's vanished."

The A. C. stood up.

"Well, it's something," he said. "Now listen. I want action. Cordon off the area, get every available man in Herts and Essex on the job. Vans—loudspeakers—dogs—the full treatment. We're looking for a limping man with a heavily bandaged head. Even you ought to be able to spot him from a hole in the ground."

"Precisely so," said Rayne, adding heavily, "Sir." He paused for a moment and continued. "Those orders were issued an hour ago. So far we've pulled in twenty outpatients with bandaged heads—none of them the right one. I came to ask you for any extra ideas you might have."

By Thursday afternoon nearly four hundred bandaged persons had been questioned, searched, and reduced to varying stages of fury. Saunders had been reported, bandaged and unbandaged, in Newmarket, Colchester, Northampton, and King's Lynn.

Yet the net did not produce the right fish.

At six in the evening every senior policeman in East Anglia was exhausted and all over five counties grim men were trampling fields, combing woods, and waiting wearily at four hundred roadblocks. Traffic over a quarter of England came virtually to a standstill.

On Saturday evening, at precisely 7:15, a turbaned Indian wearing a dirty white robe which might well have been a sheet and carrying two cheap rugs over his shoulder arrived on a lady's bicycle at the police station at Gurney St. Mary in Suffolk. After some delay he was admitted to the distinguished presence of Inspector Duncannon, who was in no mood to discuss the problems of itinerant rug sellers.

"Well?" he inquired, cocking a ferocious eyebrow at the placid figure now seated before him.

"My name is Saunders," said the stranger. "Get a doctor."

Then he collapsed.

Inspector Duncannon was a prudent man. He had been fully warned about the dangers of the infection or of touching any corpse that might appear suddenly in his vicinity.

He rang for the Police Doctor, a courageous soul named Bartlett, who had sufficient forethought to call at the hospital on the way and provide himself with the vital drug.

Saunders, relieved of the torment which had driven him senseless, was trying to pull himself together. He sat before them, his turban making an untidy heap on the floor.

His bandaged head gave him the air of a tired hero of a melodrama.

"Well," he said. "Here I am. I had a run for my money, but you beat me. Had to give up, you know. Too many of your chaps looking for me. I shouldn't have thought I was worth all that trouble."

The doctor and the Inspector exchanged glances. Then it dawned on them that Saunders was completely ignorant of his own importance. Duncannon, as was his habit, approached the subject like the elderly crab he largely resembled.

"You've caused a deal of bother," he began severely. "You and your girl friend. A verra considerable dance as you probably know full well. And what precisely did you do with the wee Jessie Dale?"

Saunders rubbed his wounded forehead. He made quite a romantic figure with his stained-brown face, the trace of blood on his brow, and fatigue in every line of his body.

"My girl friend Jessie, as you call her? By now I hope she's in Switzerland. Incidentally, your police work isn't always so good. If you haven't laid your hands on her already you never will, so there's no harm in my telling you. She's my daughter—got a touch on one lung. A year or so out there is just what she needs. Anything else you want to know? Oh, yes, I beat a man up—half killed him, I'm afraid—but he was a small-time crook, so you won't be too worried about him. I pinched a motor scooter and wrecked it—you know that, no doubt. I've broken and entered one or two houses for food, sheets, rugs, and oddments, including a bicycle. I've lived pretty rough, mostly in ditches. Damned uncomfortable. I'll make a full statement when I've slept a bit."

"Now, not so fast, my friend," said the Inspector. "We ken a thing or two about you that maybe you don't know yourself."

Saunders eyed the two men quizzically. Even in his weariness the reception was puzzling him.

"The doctor will tell you. You see, for the best part of a week you've been the most wanted man in the world. You didna ken that?"

Dr. Bartlett held out his hand and it was shaking.

"I want your injection syringe, the one you carry with you, and any capsules you may have left. It's very important."

Their prisoner fumbled with agonizing slowness in the recesses of his sheeted robes. Finally he laid the syringe and one glass capsule on the table.

For a time nobody spoke. The Inspector mopped his brow and the doctor rubbed his spectacles and then his hands with a handkerchief. He examined the little glass object minutely without touching it. Then he sighed heavily.

"That's it all right." To the bandaged man he said, "It's a miracle you're alive."

By gritting his teeth Saunders managed a smile.

"Nice of you to care about me," he said. "Not that it's important now. I've shot my bolt, I've done what I set out to do and I'm dead beat. Nothing in the world matters a damn to me any longer. You'll have to tell me something interesting if you want to keep me awake."

The Inspector stood up, towering above the drooping figure.

"Maybe I will," he said. "You're a remarkable man, perhaps the most remarkable man on earth. It's a miracle you're alive, as the doctor says. What may interest you is this, if you can spare us the time. An order came through from the Home Office ten minutes before you had the good sense to walk in here. 'If Henry Musgrave Saunders will surrender to the police, together with a medical supply which he is believed to be carrying, no further charges will be made against him and his present conviction will be quashed.' You're a free man, ye ken, or will be by the morning. What do you say to that?"

"Wake me late, Inspector," said Saunders, and he bowed his head in his arms over the table. Then with a supreme effort he raised himself again. "By the way, Doctor, that last capsule —I'd never have used it. The color was wrong—too dark an amber altogether. Mine are as yellow as cheap lemonade. People sometimes make damn silly mistakes and I don't believe in luck. Good night."

H. C. NEAL

The Pegasus Pilfer

A simply "gorjus" tale of The Great Plane Robbery which will make your eyes water for chuckling and your mouth water for—well, for more stories about Raymond Hopping Turtle (the "military Raffles").

Welcome to a new American humorist—of a type that seemed to have become The Vanishing American, but which we sorely need these laughless days . . .

A talent for horse thievery was anything but a character fault to the Comanche Indians who roamed the windswept plains of Oklahoma at the turn of the century. To the contrary, skilled thievery was an inborn trait to be developed into an honored profession by every brave of the tribe.

Possibly the greatest professor of all was Chitty Yellow Eagle, chief of the Comanche, scourge of the prairies, and particular burr under the saddle of the U.S. Cavalry. It is a matter of record that in 1895, Yellow Eagle was cited as the sole single cause of complete nervous breakdown by four consecutive supply officers at Fort Sill. All four of the poor chaps, it seems, suffered from the same piteous ailment—repetitious losses of hosses.

And, inescapable to even the most casual observer of human nature, is the fact that history—just like an Indian war chant—has a delightful way of repeating itself.

Case in point . . .

Some fifty years after Yellow Eagle had riddled the dignity of the U.S. Cavalry, his grandson, Sergeant Raymond Hopping Turtle, walked into the supply room of a small army paratroop outpost in Japan during the occupation following World War II. His friend, Supply Sergeant Hal Nickerson, had summoned him.

"Greetings, O Noble Red Brother," Nickerson intoned solemnly. "How are you today and how is your pointed little head with its valued talent for finding things even before people bother to lose them?"

"May peace abide in your tepee, O Noble Paleface sutler," the Commanche replied ceremoniously. "As to the second part of your question, that is none of your cotton-picking business."

"Oh, but it is," Nickerson rejoined, "because I—your bosom friend, your staunch comrade, your constant protector from the evil machinations of the white man's army—I have a problem."

"Did you ever not have a problem, Sergeant Nickerson?" muttered Hopping Turtle, easing his lanky frame into the battered rocking chair they had liberated from some nameless Officers Club. "What is it this time?"

"A mere trifle," the stocky Nickerson replied casually, "a bagatelle. This morning, the small white father, Captain Hicks, informs me that I am suddenly lacking one minor item of our equipment—one of the small winged steeds that bears our lean-jawed comrades so gracefully through the sky."

"A plane?" Hopping Turtle exclaimed. "You mean you've lost an airplane?"

"You speak with a straight tongue, my friend," Nickerson replied, with fake humility.

"Great leaping antelope!" the Indian declared. "You have pulled some lulus in the short time you've been in charge of this trading post. But how in the name of a three-legged dog did you manage to lose a *whole* airplane?"

"It was easy," his friend replied. "When I hit the sack last night, I had two airplanes on hand or accounted for in my records, just as every good supply sergeant should have. When I got to work this morning, I had only one."

"It is written on the wind," said Hopping Turtle resignedly, "that I am a fool for asking. But what happened to the other one?"

"That is where the plot thickens, my conniving redskin." Nickerson helped himself to one of his friend's cigarettes, lit up, and leaned back in his non-issue antiquated rocker.

"Let me lay it out for you in some semblance of order. This outfit has two airplanes on the property book just like every Headquarters battery in Division Artillery, right? Right

—two liaison planes—Cubs. Okay. For the past several months, the great white division commander, General Joe, has been using one of my planes for his personal gadding about. He can do this because he has signed a memorandum receipt for said aircraft. Also because he is a general with the pretties on his shoulder."

The Indian grunted impassively.

"Now," his friend continued, "do you remember where General Joe moved his tent to last week?"

"Indeed I do," replied Hopping Turtle. "Like all good warriors, he departed this accursed slant-eyed land of the honeybucket for the happy hunting ground across the mighty blue waters—the U.S., *and* A."

The supply sergeant nodded solemnly.

"Don't tell me—" said his friend, the light beginning to dawn, "don't tell me he took your airplane with him?"

"And the pilot," Nickerson replied, "and the all-important memorandum receipt which he neglected to return to me after he signed it while checking out the plane."

The Indian studied his friend's face for a long moment, then sighed. "The good general giveth, and the good general taketh away."

"Quite so," Nickerson replied, "but that won't slice any ice with the Inspector General when he invades our little bailiwick this Friday to sniff around like a blind dog in a butcher shop. He will not only scrutinize my property book with the all-seeing eye of a hungry hawk, he will also want to look at the two airplanes. Both of them. And when he notes that half of them are missing—*mayday!* Heads may roll like tumbleweeds and stripes will shower down as thick as the driven snow."

"The IG is coming? The man with the fuzzy ears?"

"That is he."

"This Friday?"

"Precisely."

"Well, my friend," the Indian pronounced, "you do have a problem. Since the book says two airplanes, I would advise you to get yourself another airplane."

"I marvel at your ability to see straight to the heart of the matter," Nickerson scoffed. "A report of survey is out of the question—much too late."

"And you damn sure can't buy one, even though you are

outrageously overpaid," Hopping Turtle mused. "Sergeant," he continued, "you do indeed have a problem. However, I am confident that a man of your capabilities will come up with a ready and painless solution. Why don't you try shooting yourself?" he added, heading for the door.

"Hold it, young warrior," said Nickerson evenly. "Contain your haste. I already have the answer."

Hopping Turtle halted in his tracks, his face clouding with instant suspicion. Turning slowly, he whispered. "Congratulations?"

"You are going to get me another airplane," said Nickerson, with assured finality.

"Uh-uh!" the Indian protested. "The whole thing sounds like something of which I want no part of. Deal me out."

"Oh, but I will deal you in, my noble thieving redskin Indian pal," Nickerson replied with gentle assurance, "because if you don't, then a whole slew of unpleasant things might occur."

"Like what?" his companion asked, instantly alert to the slightest hint of double-cross, as any man must be at times, especially with his closest friends.

"Like I will lose these miserable stripes I wear so proudly and deservedly," Nickerson replied, "and the loss may unhinge my tongue, and like I might tell all sorts of interesting tales to our mystified superior officers. Like what happened to the Captain's jeep you stole last month and sold to the Japanese black-market man and then ducked into the alley and put on your fake MP armband and came back and confiscated the jeep away from him. Like what happened to the parachute you buried under the mulberry tree after the last practice jump, and then went back and dug it up later and shipped it home to grace your wigwam. Like the black-market pearls you mailed home to your sister in a cartridge marked 'Exposed Film—Do Not X-Ray.' Like—"

"Enough!" Hopping Turtle exclaimed. "You need a liaison plane. Any suggestions?"

Sergeant Nickerson grinned with Machiavellian satisfaction. Then, as though nothing had been said before, "Did you ever notice how many airplanes the Ninth Corps has at the airstrip we sharecrop with them down at Sendai? I bet they wouldn't even miss one if it got stolen, say, while they were all out to lunch or something."

"You prattle in an unknown tongue, White Man," his friend retorted in mock anger. "Nothing is ever stolen in the army. Some people borrow, but no one ever steals."

"An interesting distinction," Nickerson observed, "I wonder that I never thought of it myself, being in supply work and all . . ."

Hopping Turtle dropped his cigarette to the floor, ground it out slowly with the toe of his jump boot while Nickerson watched in outraged neatness, and said, "I'll think around it and let you know tonight what I'm going to need."

"Sure, pal."

Nickerson and the Indian had been friends for a long time and Hopping Turtle had been a military Raffles even longer. A thoughtful, introspective man, he was a fine combat soldier and a dependable no-mistakes parachutist. He had learned long ago that if you must be a soldier it is less harassing to be a good one.

Nickerson, like his friend, was also a good soldier instinctively, but rather inclined to worry about details. In view of this trait, his apparent confidence in his buddy's ability to cope with the problem at hand—replace a missing aircraft—might have struck a stranger as passing strange—a stranger, that is, who didn't know the capacity for foresight and attention to detail possessed by the Indian.

The Ninth Corps' main airstrip, which was shared jointly with our friends' division, the Eleventh Airborne, was located at Sendai, some thirty-two air miles from their artillery base in the mountains. Although Corps used one side of the airstrip and the airborne unit used the other, each group had its own hangars. Under normal flying conditions they didn't even share the same runways.

Sometimes, one or two of the six liaison planes belonging to the paratroops were kept temporarily at a small cow-pasture airstrip adjacent to the mountain base. Of these six planes, two were Nickerson's—or, more correctly, they were items of equipment in his battery, and listed in his property book by serial number and engine number.

Nickerson was lying on his bunk after chow that evening when in walked his talented comrade.

"White man, I got a plan," Hopping Turtle announced.

"Please don't tell me about it," said Nickerson defensively, swinging up to a sitting position. "I'd rather not know, the situation being what it is."

"Oh, very well," replied the Indian petulantly. Then, after a pause, "Here's what I'll need—one jeep, one three-day pass, one jug of happy juice, one carton of cigarettes, some paint and brushes, and one interpreter. Murt would do nicely."

"Now just a cotton-picking minute," Nickerson objected. "You can have everything but Murt. He's my boy. He sweeps out my supply room. He mops the floor. I'm getting ready for an IG inspection and I can't do without him. Get yourself another interpreter."

"Things are tough all over," Hopping Turtle replied brusquely. "Do you want an airplane or not?"

"All right, all right, so take him. When are you leaving?"

"Soonest."

A word from Nickerson to Captain Hicks assured the three-day pass for the Indian sergeant, and the use of a jeep. Nickerson furnished the cigarettes and liquor. He wondered briefly what his friend's plan might be, but wisely refrained from pressing him. Smart stockholders don't question the business procedures of U.S. Steel.

The Indian sergeant and the Japanese boy left early next morning, Tuesday. The Inspector General was due Friday morning. Nickerson, supremely confident, turned his attention to other matters and that day passed tranquilly enough. And the next.

Thursday morning, when he had begun to sweat a trifle, Nickerson got a telephone call. It was Hopping Turtle, from the Sendai airstrip.

"Listen, Old Cock, can you shoot me a flyboy down here to drive this thing?"

"You got it!" Nickerson exulted. "What took you so long? Where did you—?"

"Knock it off," the Indian cut in. "There's going to be some stink stirred up around here when certain people get around to counting certain things. I want out before they get curious. Now, round us up a pilot and zip him down here. Murt can bring the jeep and I'll come back in the plane. Get cracking!"

The elated supply sergeant mentally ran his finger down the officers roster. Lieutenant Hill. Sure. He was around somewhere, and besides, he owed Nickerson a favor.

"Your boy is practically on his way," he informed his friend. "Where will he find you?"

"In the air section mess hall," replied the Indian, and hung up.

Nickerson found Lieutenant Hill in the motor pool with a couple of enlisted men, engaged in a serious discussion of female plumbing.

"How'd you like to take a little ride?" he asked, taking the officer aside and clueing him in on enough of the action to get his point across. "Apparently he's got us a plane and it's urgent that he get the hell away from there with it."

"Deal me in, Sarge," grinned Hill, who thrived on intrigue. He remembered that the unit's second airplane was due for a five-hundred-hours engine overhaul and reported this to Captain Hicks. Within fifteen minutes he took off from the mountain airstrip in the ailing craft and pointed her nose toward Sendai.

Less than three hours later, Hopping Turtle ambled into Nickerson's supply room, grinning like a bigmouth bass that's been invited by mistake to a bullfrog convention.

"Get out your book, boy, and your handy bottle of ink eradicator," he chortled. "You've just got yourself another airplane."

Nickerson gleefully adjusted the records to remove any trace of the craft previously borrowed by General Joe. He then posted the engine and vehicle serial numbers of the new plane, copying from a scrap of paper on which the Indian had carefully noted them down.

"The paint ain't dry yet," Hopping Turtle commented, "but the lieutenant says it's a good plane and the engine's in good shape. We named her Pegasus."

"How did you do it?" Nickerson asked, closing the book and leaning back in his chair expectantly.

"Question not the methods of your noble Red Brother," his friend replied haughtily, "and don't pester Murt when he comes in. I've sworn him to secrecy."

Nickerson delighted Captain Hicks with his report that all major property items were now on the record and safely accounted for—including airplanes—and that officer's obvious relief betrayed the pressure he'd been under. The sergeant seized the opportunity to mention that his Indian friend had figured rather prominently in their present state of well-being.

The Inspector General could find very little wrong with Nickerson's supply operations next day, passing him on the inspection with a resounding rating of Excellent.

Captain Hicks immediately shed one of his ulcers; Sergeant Nickerson got his coveted staff-sergeant rocker; and Sergeant Hopping Turtle got a seven-day leave to Kyoto, an army resort fairly seething with rest and calm contemplation. To these conditions the Turtle was much addicted.

It wasn't until eight months later, when the lanky redskin's tour of duty was ended and he was being rotated back to the States, that Nickerson learned the details of the peerless Pegasus pilfer.

On the morning of his departure, Hopping Turtle was ready for his train two hours before it was scheduled to pull out. It was mid-morning on a Sunday and the barracks were quiet. He ambled down to Nickerson's room at the far end of the building.

"Turtle," said his friend, as the Comanche ensconced himself in a beat-up rocking chair, "the next time we see each other you'll be the wise old chief back there in Okemah with your squad of squaws dogging your footsteps in mute adoration. I will be the visiting conman swinging through town in pursuit of a few fast greenbacks. None of this we've gone through over here will be important any longer. So tell me how you did it."

The Indian regarded him gravely for a moment, then asked, "Did what?"

"You know what, pal. Fill me in. How in the sacred name of my grandfather's retirement pension did you get me that airplane?"

"Well, it wasn't easy," Hopping Turtle replied. "As you may remember, Murt and I left here on a Tuesday morning—" He paused, stroking his throat suggestively. "O Noble White Brother, would you by any chance have any firewater in that trick drawer at the bottom of your desk?"

"Indeed I might," Nickerson affirmed briskly, reaching into the drawer and coming up with a fifth of the treasured 86 proof. "Be my guest," he added, pouring expertly into canteen cups.

"Well," said the Indian, after his first appreciative sip, "we got down to Sendai before noon and at that time of day, of course, there wasn't much I could do about the mission, it being daylight and all."

"That do hamper a man," Nickerson remarked.

"So I turned Murt loose to go visit a friend of his who dabbles in tailoring and mimeographing," Hopping Turtle went on. "Then I passed the rest of the day playing poker and hoisting the suds with some of the clowns at the air section."

"You drank beer?" Nickerson queried in disbelief, "when it is a foregone conclusion that you had a bottle of Old Tennishue tucked away in your tucker bag?"

"But of course, Incredulous One. I was saving the high-octane stuff in case I would somehow need it to execute the mission and rescue your worthless hide."

"Such friendship," Nickerson marveled. "I shall certainly recommend you for the Purple Shaft with the Oatmeal Cluster."

"You are too kind," the Comanche retorted drily, then, as if reminded, he took another sip. "That night I snuck across the landing field and scouted their set-up. They'd put every one of their horses in the stables, which pretty well snookered me for the time being. I then proceeded to pass the day in the same manner as the previous one—at the gaming tables."

Hopping Turtle had his own pet theory about the idiotic tendency of some poker players to draw to an inside straight, and stood ready to sacrifice his mother's oil wells to prove it.

"I hit paydirt that night," the Indian continued. "It was a nice flying day and the Corps had put all their birds in the air. They flew far and wide and late. Some of them didn't get in until dusk. Consequently, I noticed that when the protective gods of darkness had spread their friendly mantle over all us earthly creatures, the flying fellows had left some of their mules outside the stable."

"Don't be so damned picturesque," Nickerson complained. "You mean they left some planes out? Untended?"

"Steeds, my friend. Great winged steeds. Just the species I wanted to capture. And all on a picket line."

"Aha!"

"Aha, indeed. This was more like it. Murt and I jumped into the jeep and cruised over to take a closer look at the situation. But as we drew near the planes, we were rudely challenged by an armed American male . . ."

At this point, Dear Reader, let us terminate our eavesdropping on this remarkable conversation and backtrack in time to that encounter on the airstrip to see for ourselves exactly what did happen there on the night of The Great Plane Robbery . . .

The Ninth Corps sentry, his rifle at port arms, has just halted a jeep driven up to his post near the line of aircraft. Murt, the Japanese boy, was behind the wheel, and his passenger was Sergeant Raymond Hopping Turtle.

But, lo, the Turtle was no longer identifiable as a member of the Eleventh U.S. Airborne Division. Instead, he now wore the shoulder patch of the Ninth Corps above his stripes. His shiny jump boots were nowhere in evidence. In their place he sported low-cut slippers, like those affected by company clerks and other office-type personnel.

Dismounting, he carried a clipboard with some official-looking papers on it to the front of the vehicle and glanced at them briefly in the headlights.

"What's your name, soldier?" he asked brusquely.

"Private James Pettingill," was the reply.

"Serial number?"

"A.U.S. 8 792 631. What's this all about, Sergeant?"

"Just wanted to make sure you are who you are supposed to be," Hopping Turtle replied, rather pompously.

"And who am I supposed to be, and why?"

"At this moment," replied the Indian off-handedly, "I'd say just about the luckiest damn GI in all Jaypan. You're being sent back to the States on a plane that leaves tomorrow morning."

"Back home? Tomorrow? Man, you don't mean it! How come?" The sentry was puzzled, not quite able to believe his ears, but already almost hysterically happy—rather like a tomcat who has just blundered into a mouse convention.

"Where's your home, boy?" asked Hopping Turtle boredly, in the manner of a data-surfeited personnel clerk who already knows the answers to any question he could possibly have reason to ask.

"Sioux Falls."

"That's your answer."

"But I don't get it, Sarge. One minute I'm walking guard

and the next minute you tell me I'm going home tomorrow. How come?" he repeated.

"It's simple," retorted Hopping Turtle, "Eighth Army has just discovered that you are the five thousandth man to be sent over here from Sioux Falls. Apparently that makes it a big deal. Anyhow, they are sending you back to sell war bonds or head a recruiting drive or some damn thing. All I know is I've got to walk your guard until the OD digs up a replacement to finish out the night. Imagine," he added disgustedly, "a buck sergeant—walking guard for a private so he can go back to the States."

"Gee, Sarge, that's wonderful!"

"Yeah, ain't it," said Hopping Turtle morosely. "Here, give me that damned rifle. You hop in the jeep and the boy will drive you back to your barracks so you can get packed. Your orders are being cut now and another jeep will pick you up at —" he glanced at his watch—"1:30 to take you to Tokyo. Your plane takes off from there tomorrow morning."

The elated young soldier thrust his rifle at the Indian, unclasped his ammo belt and handed it over, and jumped into the jeep.

"Hold it," said Hopping Turtle, "there's one more thing. I've got some money here for you, a partial payment in advance. The army don't want you to go home broke. It will help square any trouble you might run into," he added thoughtfully.

He handed the young soldier $250 which he had won in the poker game earlier that day. "Sign here," said the Indian, thrusting his clipboard at the boy.

Pettingill scribbled his payroll signature, clutched the money, and grabbed Hopping Turtle's hand for a hasty shake. "Thanks a million, Sarge," he enthused, "and best of luck."

"The pleasure is all mine," replied the Indian.

Hopping Turtle listened keenly for a minute or two after the jeep had disappeared. He then stood the rifle against the wall of the nearest hangar and draped the ammo belt over the barrel opening so that no moisture could get in and foul the bore. Despite the need for haste now, Hopping Turtle could not bear the thought of a weapon being neglected.

After a last look around the field, he quickly jerked the chocks from the wheels of the end aircraft on line, pitched them into the seat, grabbed up the tail, and pushed the plane across the strip toward the Eleventh Airborne hangars on the far side.

By the time Murt returned a half hour later, Hopping Turtle had the plane safely stowed in a locked hangar and was already repainting the entire craft . . .

"So after she dried a little, we covered her in our division colors, insignia and all. Took damn near all night. Then, while Murt went single-footing after some coffee, I added the name on her nose and gave you a call."

"Hopping Turtle," remarked Nickerson earnestly, "I would pronounce your execution of that mission a resounding success, except I can't help wondering about that kid, the sentry. No doubt he ran into trouble by the gross."

"Not likely," replied the Indian suavely. "Murt has a friend who has a mimeograph machine. We really did cut some orders for the boy—they looked even more official than the real thing. As far as we know, he might have made it clear back to Sioux Falls before those people down at Corps knew what happened. You know how confused it can be at times, what with people coming and going, planes coming up missing . . ."

"And even if he didn't make it home," said Nickerson thoughtfully, "they couldn't get too hairy with him anywhere along the line. After all, he was just following orders."

"Precisely," commented Hopping Turtle, sipping appreciatively from his canteen cup.

"And of course it would be some officer who would ultimately get the blame for the whole thing," Nickerson pursued his train of thought. "Probably wind up in—"

"What's that you said?" interjected Hopping Turtle with renewed interest.

"I was going to say it will probably wind up in the lap of the Corps commander." Nickerson answered. "Why the sudden concern over who pays for that misbegotten airplane as long as it isn't us?"

"You said the Corps commander?" repeated the Indian.

"Sure," said Nickerson, wise in the channels of supply accountability. "It would take a while to determine final responsibility. Everyone up the line would buck it up a notch higher. And that's the way the army likes it, you know. They don't want Captains or Majors, who can't really afford it, to have to pay for an airplane. But a General—now that might be different. It would depend on how much weight he swings in Washington."

"Would you say it is likely that the case isn't settled yet?" asked Hopping Turtle, his eyes sparking. "It's been eight months, you know."

"Well, the way these things work out," replied his friend, "I'd guess it might be another month or two before the thing comes to a head. It would be my guess that whoever is commanding Ninth Corps about three months from now stands a good chance of paying for that airplane."

Hopping Turtle suddenly threw his head back and burst into laughter—a rare thing for him to do.

"That's rich," he chuckled, "Boy, that's heap rich."

"What gives?" asked Nickerson. "You act like you knew it was going to be your mother-in-law who gets stuck for the price of that airplane."

The Indian slapped his thigh until he trickled off into a running series of half-suppressed giggles. "Better than that," he sputtered. "I just heard this morning—Watts told me over at the mess hall—Ninth Corps has got a new commander—"

"Well, who is it, for Pete's sake?"

"It's our great white father, General Joe," the Indian sputtered between renewed gales of laughter. "He did such a good job at commanding our division that Washington promoted him and sent him back over here as commander of the whole damn Ninth Corps."

Some moments later, when their laughter had subsided so that Nickerson could refill the canteen cups without spilling any, he wiped his eyes and mustered up a more sober countenance.

"Turtle," he commented, "that's working out awful nice, but it don't take away from the fact that you did a pretty good job yourself before you knew how things would turn out. There must be a moral in there somewhere."

"Indeed there is," the Comanche responded. "It is expressed in a timeless message written years ago by the elders of my tribe. They carved it in the enduring sandstone of the prairie, no doubt with the knowledge that some day you and I would soldier in Japan."

"And what is this eternal verity conceived and handed down by the tribal sages?"

"If I remember correctly," mused Hopping Turtle, "it goes something like this: *It is better that the left General knoweth not what the right Indian doeth.*"

"Has a right nice ring to it," Nickerson opined.

"It is a thing my grandfather taught me when I was but a young buck," replied the Indian modestly. "I think he learned it at Fort Sill or some place."

JAMES M. ULLMAN

The Stock Market Detective

Someone was secretly buying Trakker common stock. A proxy fight? Control of the Company? . . . Meet a new kind of detective—a specialist in industrial crime.

The price of common stock in Trakker Trucking Corporation began rising in February. Its quotation on the regional exchange, where it enjoyed trading privileges, went from 12 to 15 by the end of the month.

In March it advanced to a high of 17; in April to 19; and in May to 22½. Meaning that if you had been adroit enough to buy at the February low and sell at the May high, you would have nearly doubled your money in four months.

It was at this point that John Trakker, president, board chairman, and founder of the firm, discussed the matter with his attorney, who in turn referred him to Michael Dane James.

James drove from New York City to Trakker's New Jersey headquarters. He was ushered into Trakker's office at 11 o'clock on a Tuesday morning.

The salutations were perfunctory. Then Trakker said, "I've never dealt with your service before, Mr. James, so I don't know quite how to begin."

"What's your problem?" James asked. "We simple souls in what is luridly termed business and industrial espionage believe in plain talk."

"It's Trakker common. Our stock moved from 12 to a top of 22½ since early this year."

"That should make you happy."

"It would—if I knew why it went up so fast. But, frankly, the stock isn't worth what it's selling for now. It may be in a few years, but there's been nothing in our recent operations to explain the rise. No big earnings-increase, no merger planned —not even one rumored."

"In that case," James said, "somebody is probably trying to move in on you. When they get enough shares, they'll ask for representation on the board. Or maybe for the whole hog, and if you don't give in they'll start a proxy fight."

"Could be. But so far we haven't heard a whisper about who these people are or what they have in mind. None of our bigger stockholders has been approached. However, we do know this new group is buying heavily. According to our transfer agent, many of the orders come from Chicago. Our books show that a lot of the stock sold recently is held in street names by a few Chicago brokerage houses. The brokers are acting for one or more customers, but in the record books it's the brokers who own the stock, and the identity of the true owners is hidden.

"There are channels I could pursue," Trakker went on, "to pin down their identity further—through our underwriters, for instance—but even they could go only so far. What I want, Mr. James, is as thorough—and confidential—an investigation as is humanly possible."

"You have the names of these Chicago brokerage houses?"

Trakker handed over a list of three names. "We're a relatively small operation as publicly held corporations go," he explained. "I started this company after the first World War with one truck and $200. We went public in the late Thirties. I, my family, and some close associates hold about twenty per cent of the outstanding shares—enough to maintain control of management, because our revenues and earnings have kept going up and the price of Trakker common has, too. Our stockholders have never had reason to complain. I built this company from scratch, Mr. James. I don't want to see a crew of raiders hurt it or take our stockholders to the cleaners. The big rise in the stock's price this year has already brought us more attention from the speculators than is good for us."

"We'll see what we can do," James said.

"How will you go about it?" Trakker asked.

"That," James replied, "I'm afraid you'll have to leave to our discretion."

James drove back to New York and told his secretary to locate Ted Bennett. She made some telephone calls and found him in a brokerage house boardroom. "Pack your bag," James said. "We're going to Chicago on the four o'clock plane."

"Can't we wait until the market closes?" Bennett protested.

"Must be back here for a big client interview Thursday afternoon," James replied. "I'm going to try to set it up for you in Chicago, then let you finish the job."

Bennett never asked, and James never said, what the job in Chicago was all about. Both knew better than to get specific over James's office telephone. James had his best sound man run a check on the telephones every month or so, but there was always a good chance someone was tapping the line anyway. James would tell Bennett about the Trakker case on the plane.

They checked in at a Loop hotel—James a broad-shouldered, slightly pot-bellied, square-faced man of medium height and middle age, wearing horn-rimmed glasses and sporting a gray crewcut; Bennett, very tall, lean, and tousle-headed, looking younger than his thirty-five years. Bennett stopped at the cigar stand on their way to the room and bought a Chicago newspaper containing the final stock quotations. He sprawled on one of the beds in their suite and began thumbing through the paper, while James consulted the phone book, picked up the telephone, and began dialing.

"Down another half point," Bennett moaned. "And me still stuck with four hundred shares of that dog."

"If you'd spend as much time working as you do playing the market," James observed, "you'd get rich."

"If I'd sold everything I owned and bought Trakker common in February," Bennett said, "I could have bought me a little old island somewhere and retired, instead of hiring out to you by the day whenever you land a job you can't handle alone."

James reached his party, the financial editor of a Chicago newspaper. "Hi, Ed. It's Mike James. You still want to do that inside piece on industrial espionage you asked me about the last time you were in New York? Okay, okay, all you have to do in return is put me in touch with a couple of knowledgeable people in the brokerage business here. Why don't I drop over tomorrow afternoon? Swell."

He hung up.

"Now what?" Bennett asked.

"Now we eat lightly and get a good night's sleep. Tomorrow morning I'm going to nose around the boardroom of the brokerage house that holds most of the newly bought Trakker common, while you'll go out and line up a good sound man. I have a hunch we'll need one."

James strolled into the boardroom the next morning with a newspaper under his arm. It was a big room, with more than a dozen customers' men and plenty of idlers standing about. As in most big boardrooms, you could hang around all day if you wished, watching the tape from the New York and the American stock exchanges.

Trakker common, of course, being handled on neither the New York nor the American stock exchanges, was traded on a regional exchange. To get a quote on the stock, a customers' man handling the account would either have to make a phone call or call out and ask someone else in the office to get the quote for him. So James drifted around the big room, waiting to hear someone mention Trakker common out loud.

In two hours several customers' men did so. The one most concerned with the stock, however, seemed to be an Ivy League type with a desk two rows up from the gallery. Between 10:00 A.M. he called for a quote on Trakker common three times. At 11:55 A.M. James stood close enough to hear the man dial a phone number and say, "Trakker's down almost another point, but they say it's firming now. Let's see. You got one order in for one thousand shares at 20 and another for one thousand at 19. The way it looks, it could get away from you. Yeah. Sure. All right, I'll get you one hundred at the market and put in for another five hundred if it goes down to 21."

James moved away. He remained in the boardroom another few minutes and then left to meet Bennett in a cafeteria.

"Well," James said. "I've found the customers' man who seems to do the most business in Trakker common. He gets a quote every hour on the hour. Maybe he's dealing with one of the big buyers. Why don't you drop in there this afternoon and open an account with this fellow? You find a sound man?"

"I did. He runs a detective agency and has all the help we could possibly need."

"Great."

James went off to be interviewed by his friend the financial editor. Bennett strolled over to the brokerage house. He had no difficulty spotting the Ivy League customers' man James had described.

Bennett lounged about until the man rose and made his way to a side door leading to a Men's Room. When the man returned five minutes later, Bennett got in his way.

"I beg your pardon," Bennett said, "but could I open an account here?"

"Glad to help you," the man said warmly. "My name is Charley Watson. I'm what's called a customers' representative."

"Oh, I know about that, I already own some stocks," Bennett said. "I'm based in New York—have an account with a house there. But my business is going to take me to Chicago regularly for a while and I'd like to have an account here, too. I've never been in Chicago before."

Watson led Bennett to his desk. Bennett pulled out a check book and casually wrote out a check for $5000. It was almost every cent in his checking account. He wanted to make a good impression on Watson because, if all else failed, he would have to ask Watson outright who was buying the Trakker stock. He handed the check over.

"I'd like to open the account with this."

"Well!" Watson said, obviously not unhappy to meet a man who could write a check for $5000. "Did you have any specific stocks in mind?"

"I was wondering if you could suggest some. You boys in Chicago probably have information on stocks we don't hear much about in New York."

Watson reeled off a few which Bennett recognized as the current favorites of many advisory services. Trakker was not among them. Bennett shook his head.

"I don't think those are for me. I'm a single man, Watson. I can afford to take a flyer on something risky if there's a chance for a quick gain."

Watson was interrupted by a telephone call from a customer. Bennett began filling out the form. After talking to his customer, Watson looked at his watch—it was exactly two o'clock—and called another number.

"Charley Watson," he said. "How's Trakker? 23 bid, a quarter asked? Thanks." He hung up, turned to Bennett. "Can you excuse me another minute? I have to call a guy who's real hot on this stock."

"Go ahead."

Watson dialed. "Hello? Mr. Boston, please, it's Charley Watson. Hello, Roy? Trakker is 23 and strong. It really bounced back. Oh, you heard already? All right, we'll keep the orders for one thousand at 19 and 20, and five hundred at 21. Yeah, we'll wait and see tomorrow." He hung up again.

"Trakker?" Bennett said. "What's that?"

"Trakker Trucking," Watson said. "It's gone 'way up in the last few months. It's gone up so much, though, you'd maybe be taking a big chance if you bought at this price."

Bennett was inclined to agree. It was also significant that Watson didn't push the stock. He handed the new-account application over to Watson, rose, and extended his hand. "Well, thanks a lot. You people get my check cleared, and I'll be in later this week." Watson gave Bennett a business card and Bennett left.

Bennett went to a drugstore booth and phoned the newspaper. He asked for the financial editor and got the financial editor's secretary.

"A Mr. James from New York had an appointment with your boss this afternoon," Bennett said. "Is he still there?"

"Just a minute."

James came on the line. "What luck, Ted?"

"Very good," Bennett said. "The customers' man checks on Trakker's price every hour or so for somebody named Roy Boston. This Boston must be the same guy you heard him talking to this morning. A lot of buy orders for Trakker, and no sell orders. Boston must have other sources of information, too—at two o'clock he knew the price of Trakker before our customers' man did. Maybe Boston has accounts with other houses. When the man called Boston I watched him dial and I wrote the number down."

"Why don't you check the number out? In a couple of minutes I'm going to the Tavern Club, where Ed is going to introduce me to his financial friends. I know they'll just love to hear about what happened when we installed the two-way mirror in the Ladies' Rest Room while investigating factory pilferage."

James hung up. Bennett put another dime in the slot and

phoned the sound man he had hired that morning, a private detective named Morgan. "Listen, Morgan, I got a phone number. Can you find out who it belongs to?" He read out the number.

In less than two minutes Morgan was back on the line. "It's Victor Investments, address on LaSalle Street."

"Thanks."

Bennett stepped out of the booth long enough to drink two cups of coffee, smoke a cigarette, and look over *The Wall Street Journal.* Then he went back to the booth and had James paged at the Tavern Club.

"The number belongs to Victor Investments, a LaSalle Street firm," Bennett said.

"Nice work," James said. "After a couple martinis I'll ask my new friends here what they know about the outfit. Not much more you can do today, Bennett. Why don't you see a movie or something? I'll meet you in our hotel bar at eleven tonight."

At one minute after eleven James walked into the hotel bar and sat down in a rear booth beside Bennett, who had been trying unsuccessfully to read *Barron's* in the dim light. Bennett folded the financial paper and stuck it into his coat pocket. James ordered a beer.

"Nice fellas, Ed's LaSalle Street friends," James said. "None of 'em knew of any legitimate operators here buying in on Trakker, which eliminates a lot of possibilities. Now about Victor Investments."

James downed a big swallow of beer. "It turned out one of Ed's pals was on the Notre Dame team that clobbered us in '35. Claims he gave me a bloody nose in the third quarter, but I don't remember it. Anyway, this guy comes from an old-line Chicago financial family and he's a big wheel in the trust department of a bank. After the Tavern Club, he and Ed and I had dinner at a key club where the girls go practically naked."

"A real hard day's work," Bennett grinned.

"It requires a specialized talent, admit it," James said. "A surly fellow like you would never get to first base with these top-level guys. Anyway, I found out as much in six hours of socializing as you would have learned in six days of poking around the offices of Victor Investments with your sound man and his tape recorders and telephone taps and whatnots."

James finished his beer before he continued.

"Victor Investments is a little shop run by a man named Thomas Conn. Roy Boston, the man you heard your broker talking to, is Conn's errand boy, just out of the Harvard Business School. Conn's been around the financial district for years in one capacity or another, but he didn't really come into his own until the mid-1950s. Only a few people know it, but the reason he's been doing so well lately is that he's handling investments for his brother-in-law."

"Who's that?"

"An attorney named Jason Arnold. If Victor Investments is buying a lot of Trakker stock for somebody, the chances are it's for a client or clients represented by Jason Arnold."

"Who are Arnold's clients?"

"That," James said, "is what you'll have to find out. Me, I'm jetting back to New York tomorrow morning. This client I'm going to talk to is a billion-dollar corporation, and if I can convince it that my services are required despite its eighty-man security department, there'll be some lucrative work in it for you, too."

"You think there's any point to my tapping Victor Investments?"

"Sure, just in case they have other clients buying Trakker," James said. "But better concentrate on this lawyer, Jason Arnold. Is that sound man you lined up any good?"

"Good as they come," Bennett said. "I got his name from our man in New York."

"Tape me a report and send it air mail special every day," James said.

James flew back to New York the next morning. Bennett and Morgan went to work. Jason Arnold's office was on a lower floor in a big Loop building. Over the week-end Morgan bribed the building superintendent and set up a tap leading from the control box in the building's basement to a tape recorder in an unused storeroom of a building across the alley.

The tape recorder didn't have to be manned constantly; it would go on automatically the moment anyone in Arnold's office picked up the telephone. A similar tap was arranged for the telephones at Victor Investments. For good measure, they put a tap on Arnold's home phone. That tap led from the terminal box on the line, in the alley behind Arnold's home, to a recorder in a vacant store at the end of the block.

After four days of listening, Bennett learned these pertinent facts which he sent to James:

Victor Investments had substantial buy orders in with three Chicago brokerage houses for Trakker common—all to be held, if and when executed, in street names.

Thomas Conn, the owner of Victor Investments, telephoned Jason Arnold, his brother-in-law, at four o'clock every afternoon to report the number, if any, and the price of any Trakker shares purchased for Arnold that day.

At dusk on the eleventh day after the taps were set up, Bennett called from a telephone booth in Chicago's Loop to a telephone booth in New York, where he knew James would be waiting.

"Arnold's our boy," Bennett said. "We'll keep the taps on him for a while longer, but if he's in regular communication with the big buyer he represents, I don't think it's by telephone. At least, not from his office phones."

"There's a fair amount of money involved in these purchases," James said. "You'd think the buyer would want regular reports, at least weekly. Unless Arnold is buying for his own account and not for a client."

"I'm checking Arnold from all angles," Bennett replied. "He may have a piece of what's going on, but I'm pretty sure he doesn't have that much money to throw around. He's acting for someone else, all right. I have learned one thing that may be significant."

"What's that?"

"Well, from the telephone calls we've monitored, we've assembled a good list of Arnold clients. One way or another, a couple of dozen businesses. My sound man here is pretty hep to local goings-on. Four of the clients—a motel, a plush restaurant, a discount store, and a medium-sized, privately held manufacturing plant—are operated by groups with criminal associations."

"You think Arnold is fronting for underworld money?"

"It's the best so far. For a lawyer who wasn't getting anywhere for years, he sure started moving fast back in '55. His first important client was that criminally-owned manufacturing plant. It was involved in a big litigation over patents. After Arnold won the case for them he was off and running."

"What's your next step?"

"We're tailing Arnold, but he leads a pretty regular life. Comes straight to the office in the morning and goes straight home at night to his wife and two daughters. All we get on that homephone tap is teenagers. So we're going to bug his office."

"If I'd known it would cost this much," James said, "I'd have sent our own sound man out there and got the work done wholesale. Need any help?"

"It's all routine so far. I'll holler if I need you. Land that big corporate client?"

"We're still dickering."

"Good luck."

Over the next week-end they bugged Arnold's office. In the guise of a workman, one of Morgan's men got into the office long enough to plant a transistorized wireless microphone behind a framed diploma over Arnold's desk. The receiver was installed beside the tape recorder in the storeroom of the building across the alley.

"Think the signal will reach?" Bennett asked Morgan.

"Might be a little faint, but it should be audible."

"I'll man it myself," Bennett decided.

Bennett was crouched in the storeroom with his earphones on when Arnold arrived for work at nine the following Monday morning. Bennett remained there until 11:30, when Arnold said to his secretary, "I'm going to lunch, and then to court. I'll be back about three."

Arnold went downstairs to the lobby, where a private detective on Morgan's staff picked up his trail. Bennett left the storeroom and walked the few blocks to the brokerage house, where he took a chair beside Charley Watson's desk. Bennett read Watson's copy of *The Wall Street Journal*, bought 200 shares of Intercosmic Enterprises, and sold 100 of Jet Ventures, Inc.

"You did all right on that," Watson said. "Listen. You've been a pretty good customer of mine. You know that Trakker Trucking stock you asked me about the first day you were in here? It's up to 25 now, and I got a big customer with a lot of buy orders still in. As long as this screwball is in a buying mood, I don't think the price of that stock will go down very far. Every time it goes down some, he moves in and knocks it back up. There aren't many shares outstanding and any little action moves it. Want to take a chance?"

"Thanks," Bennett said, "I'd rather not. See you tomorrow."

He dropped into a drugstore, where he ate a peanut butter sandwich and drank a malted milk. He was back in the storeroom with the earphones on at 2:47 p.m.

Arnold returned to his office at 3:04 p.m. At 4:36 he began dictating a letter to his secretary that made Bennett sit up and reach quickly for paper and pencil.

"Send this to Jerry," Arnold said. "We bought only 2,000 shares of Trakker last week, since the price seems high and I think if we wait another week it will drop back to 20 or so. The stock we bought last week cost $45,637.19, including commissions, and duplicate purchase slips are enclosed. The stock is being allocated to accounts as follows: 200 shares, Joseph Lefitowa; 200 shares, Mrs. Joseph Lefitowa; 200 shares, Harold Burns; 200 shares, Carl Steadley; 200 shares, Anthony Glovson; 200 shares, Edwin Glovson; 300 shares, Frank Bannerman, and 500 shares, Zack Mucho. This gives you control of a total of 63,900 shares of Trakker common. Yours truly, and so forth. I know it's late, Miss Dean, but I'd appreciate it if you'd get this out in this evening's mail. I want it to reach Riverview by tomorrow morning."

Bennett heard the sound of a door closing as the secretary left the inner office. "Jerry," who lived in a place called Riverview, was obviously the mystery man behind the orders for Trakker common. But Jerry who? And Riverview what? The chances were slim that Bennett would find out by sitting there with his earphones on. It might be weeks before he learned any more from the tap.

Bennett left the storeroom and walked around the block four times. It would probably take the girl about that long to type the letter and address the envelope, and give the letter to Arnold for his signature. Arnold always left the office at 5:00 P.M. The girl's custom was to leave a few minutes later.

At 5:01 P.M. Bennett walked into the lobby of Arnold's building. He noted that a Morgan man had just wandered to the cigar stand, ready to follow Arnold out.

Arnold stepped out of the elevator at 5:03 P.M. and Bennett stepped into one. He went to Arnold's floor, where he loitered, pretending to be looking for a name on the office doors.

At 5:07 P.M. Arnold's secretary stepped out of the office with a cluster of letters in one hand and her purse in the other. As she approached the mail chute Bennett stumbled awkwardly against her. His arm came down hard, knocking the letters to the floor.

"Ooops—so sorry," he exclaimed, grinning his best sheepish grin. He steadied her and then quickly began gathering up the mail. There were nine letters. There was no addressee who could be "Jerry" in any form, and only one address with a "Riverview" destination. This envelope read: "Box 68, Riverview, Wisconsin."

"You all right?" Bennett asked. He gave the girl the letters.

She said, "You ought to watch where you're going," and thumbed through the mail to be sure all the letters were there.

"I'm sorry," Bennett repeated, and backed away. She dumped the mail down the chute and walked hurriedly to the elevator bank.

When he got out of the building, Bennett went to a cigar store and phoned Morgan, the sound man. "Call off your dogs."

"The job over?"

"Maybe yes, maybe no. But I've learned all I want to for now, and I'm leaving. Send the bill to my friend in New York.

"Check. It's been a pleasure."

"Me, too. You're a real pro."

Bennett cabbed to his hotel. From the suite he arranged to rent a car. Then he spoke into his tape recorder as he packed.

"Mike: The big buyer is someone named Jerry. All I know about Jerry is that he's reachable at Box 68, Riverview, Wisconsin. So I'm going there to see who takes the letter out of the box. So far the buyer controls about 64,000 shares of Trakker common. The names of some of the owners-of-record behind the street names include—let me check my notes—yeah Joseph Lefitowa, his wife, Harold Burns, Carl Steadley, Anthony Glovson—no 'e' after the 'v'— Erwin Glovson, Frank Bannerman, and Zack Mucho. The names don't mean anything to me. Maybe they will to you or your client."

Bennett placed the spool of tape in an air-mail special

envelope already stamped and addressed to James in New York, checked out, dropped the envelope in a mailbox, and took a cab to the rent-a-car depot, where he picked up a big sedan. Since there was always a chance that unknown parties might check his movements, he didn't ask for directions in the depot.

In a Chicago suburb Bennett got off the expressway and found a service station. He selected road maps of Illinois, Iowa, Indiana, Wisconsin, and Minnesota, gave the attendant a dollar, drove down the block, parked, and opened the Wisconsin map. Riverview was a "Pop. 4,000" west of Madison.

There was a diner across the street from the Riverview Post Office, and Bennett sat in it the next morning drinking coffee and waiting for the Post Office to open. The drive had taken only a few hours, and he had spent the night in a motel. Riverview nestled in a popular resort area, but it was still out-of-season and the streets were relatively empty.

When the Post Office opened, Bennett waited a few minutes, then went in and bought a dollar's worth of stamps. He paid for them with a $10 bill. While the clerk made change Bennett located Box 68. He moved close enough to see four letters inside. The one on top was from Jason Arnold.

Bennett went out and got into the car, which he had parked in front of the Post Office. He pulled up until he was able to see the tier of boxes that included 68. Then he settled back to wait.

Twice people approached the tier and each time Bennett checked, but he saw that the contents of Box 68 remained untouched. At 9:30 A.M. the news agency down the street opened and Bennett left the car long enough to buy a copy of *The Wall Street Journal*. When he returned, the letters were still in Box 68. Bennett got back in the car and began to read the paper.

At 9:57 A.M. a battered station wagon screeched to a stop behind Bennett's car, and a youth in blue jeans and sweatshirt got out and went into the Post Office. He unlocked a box, removed its contents, and came out. Bennett investigated; Box 68 was empty.

He took from his pocket the stamps he had bought earlier and held them in his hand while he returned to the rented car, as though he had just bought them. The station wagon was rounding a corner two blocks away.

Bennett drove the two blocks and around the corner. The station wagon was far down the street, heading into open country. Bennett stepped on the gas.

The station wagon barreled for about five miles at seventy per and then turned into a narrow, tree-lined, blacktop road. By the time Bennett reached the turn-off, the wagon was gone.

He drove along slowly and passed, in order, a small tavern, three farms, a big roadhouse that advertised *ENTERTAINMENT, BEER AND CONTINENTAL CUISINE,* a resort hotel—Bennett crept past, but failed to spot the station wagon—and then several estates. At the third estate he saw the station wagon parked about fifty yards up the private drive alongside a Cadillac, a Jaguar, and a Mercedes Benz. He drove on past two more estates, turned around, and drove all the way back to the little tavern near the highway. He parked and went inside.

The open-faced boy behind the bar apparently saw nothing unusual in a man's ordering beer at 10 o'clock in the morning. It was a very good local beer; and Bennett drank three bottles, while discussing major league baseball with the boy, before getting down to business.

"By the way," Bennett said, "those are some pretty swanky homes down the road. Folks here must make out pretty good."

The boy laughed.

"Those ain't local people. They're big shots from Chicago. They own that roadhouse down the way and half the bars and resorts around here. They bought up all this land in the '30s, when it was a twentieth of what it's worth now."

"Who owns the big mansion? The third house from the hotel?"

"That's the big man himself. Fats Manning. You must of heard of him."

Indeed Bennett had. Gerald "Fats" Manning was one of the most powerful Syndicate gangsters in the United States. Gerald Manning, then, was "Jerry"—the man behind the group buying into Trakker Trucking.

John Trakker studied James's report.

"Zack Mucho," Trakker said. "I remember him very well.

He approached me six years ago and offered to buy all my shares in the company—claimed he wanted to go into the trucking business. I had him checked and the report was that, while he had no criminal record, he was connected with a lot of people who did have. I told him to go to hell. I didn't think of him when I called you in because over the years a lot of other people have offered to buy me out, and I've turned them down, too."

"The others on the list," James said, "Lefitowa, Burns, Steadley, and so forth—they're all like Mucho—fronts for gangster money. They jump like puppets when Manning pulls the strings. The underworld has millions lying around in cash, and the boys are wising up and putting their blood money to work. Someone—probably Mucho—spotted your company a long time ago as a nice little investment. Profitable—and the mob can always find unadvertised uses for an interstate trucking company. So Fats Manning has one of his reputable attorneys, Jason Arnold, buy the stock through his brother-in-law's firm, Victor Investments. The brokerage house holds the stock under a street name for Victor, then Victor Investments holds it under the equivalent of the same thing for Arnold. Arnold apportions it out to a number of underworld fronts—Lefitowa, Burns, Mucho, et cetera—the fronts paying Arnold for the stock and Fats Manning making undercover cash payments to the fronts. Not a single share bought that way actually belongs to Manning, but every share of that stock is under Manning's control."

Trakker turned to his attorney.

"Well, Sam, what are we going to do about it?"

"I guess we'll fight," Sam said evenly.

Trakker took a check from his desk drawer and handed it to James.

"Here you are, sir. I don't know how you got this information, but it was a job well done. Mobsters trying to take over Trakker Trucking! I'll sell out to any legitimate buyer for a nickel on the dollar before I turn my stock over to criminals.

James folded the check and put it in his pocket.

"If you do get into a proxy fight," he said, "call me in, Mr. Trakker, especially if those boys start playing rough. I'll do it as a labor of love. My technicians, of course, would have to be paid."

"If we need you, we'll certainly call you."

"I also suggest," James added, "that you contact the U. S. Attorney General's office. The government will give you a hand. They're taking a big interest in industrial crime these days."

"I talked to a man in Washington this morning," Sam said. "We're mailing him a copy of your report this afternoon."

"You boys work fast," James said approvingly. "If I'm not too presumptuous—what exactly do you have in mind?"

"Well—" Sam looked at Trakker, and Trakker nodded. "To begin with, Manning has only about 12 per cent of the common outstanding. That won't get him what he wants. At this stage publicity could ruin his game. So I'm sending him a registered letter—to Box 68, Riverview, Wisconsin, which should give him a jolt.

"I'm telling him we know who he is, what he's up to, how many shares he controls, how he is buying the stocks, and who's fronting for him. I'll leave it to his imagination to speculate on how much more we know that we really don't know. I'm also letting him know that all the information about him in our possession is being turned over to a college classmate of mine who is now employed by the Attorney General of the United States. And that if a proxy fight does develop, all rules to the contrary, we shall see to it that the more sensational aspects of this matter are given to the press. And copies of my letter are going to Jason Arnold, Victor Investments, and every 'front' stockholder whose name you have given us."

"And if that doesn't scare Manning off?" James asked.

"Like Sam told you," Trakker said, "we'll fight!"

MARGERY ALLINGHAM

Murder Under the Mistletoe

FOR CHRISTMAS . . .
A BRAND-NEW MR. CAMPION STORY

. . . with a delightful (and devastating) picture of an English residential hotel named "The CCraven" (with two Cs)—the sort of place which is very popular with the old(er) members of the landed gentry—in a phrase, "a select hotel-cum-Old-Ducks' Home for Mother's Friends" . . . and we wonder if you'll ever really forget the (snap)dragon, Lady Larradine . . . Read and enjoy!

"Murder under the mistletoe—and the man who must have done it couldn't have done it. That's my Christmas and I don't feel merry thank you very much all the same." Superintendent Stanislaus Oates favored his old friend Mr. Albert Campion with a pained smile and sat down in the chair indicated.

It was the afternoon of Christmas Day and Mr. Campion, only a trifle more owlish than usual behind his horn rims, had been fetched down from the children's party which he was attending at his brother-in-law's house in Knightsbridge to meet the Superintendent, who had moved heaven and earth to find him.

"What do you want?" Mr. Campion inquired facetiously. "A little armchair miracle?"

"I don't care if you do it swinging from a trapeze. I just want a reasonable explanation." Oates was rattled. His dyspeptic face with the perpetually sad expression was slightly flushed and not with festivity. He plunged into his story.

"About eleven last night a crook called Sampson was found shot dead in the back of a car in a garage under a small drinking club in Alcatraz Mews—the club is named The Humdinger. A large bunch of mistletoe which had been lying on the front seat ready to be driven home had been placed on top of the body partially hiding it—which was why it hadn't been found before. The gun, fitted with a silencer, but wiped of prints, was found under the front seat. The dead man was recognized at once by the owner of the car who is also the owner of the club. He was the owner's current boy friend. She is quite a well-known West End character called 'Girlski.' What did you say?"

"I said 'Oo-er,' " murmured Mr. Campion. "One of the Eumenides, no doubt?"

"No." Oates spoke innocently. "She's not a Greek. Don't worry about her. Just keep your mind on the facts. She knows, as we do, that the only person who wanted to kill Sampson is a nasty little snake called Kroll. He has been out of circulation for the best of reasons. Sampson turned Queen's evidence against him in a matter concerning a conspiracy to rob Her Majesty's mails and when he was released last Tuesday Kroll came out breathing retribution."

"Not the Christmas spirit," said Mr. Campion inanely.

"That is exactly what *we* thought," Oates agreed. "So about five o'clock yesterday afternoon two of our chaps, hearing that Kroll was at The Humdinger, where he might have been expected to make trouble, dropped along there and brought him in for questioning and he's been in custody ever since.

"Well, now. We have at least a dozen reasonably sober witnesses to prove that Kroll did not meet Sampson at the Club. Sampson had been there earlier in the afternoon but he left about a quarter to four saying he'd got to do some Christmas shopping but promised to return. Fifteen minutes or so later Kroll came in and stayed there in full view of Girlski and the customers until our men turned up and collected him. *Now* what do you say?"

"Too easy!" Mr. Campion was suspicious. "Kroll killed Sampson just before he came in himself. The two met in the dusk outside the club. Kroll forced Sampson into the garage and possibly into the car and shot him. With the way the traffic has been lately, he'd hardly have attracted attention had he used a mortar, let alone a gun with a silencer. He wiped the weapon, chucked it in the car, threw the mistletoe over the corpse, and went up to Girlski to renew old acquaintance and establish an alibi. Your chaps, arriving when they did, must have appeared welcome."

Oates nodded. "We thought that. *That is what happened.* That is why this morning's development has set me gibbering. We now have two unimpeachable witnesses who swear that the dead man was in Chipperwood West at six last evening delivering some Christmas purchases he had made on behalf of a neighbor. That is *a whole hour* after Kroll was pulled in.

"The assumption is that Sampson returned to Alcatraz Mews sometime later in the evening and was killed by someone else—which we know is not true. Unfortunately the Chipperwood West witnesses are not the kind of people we are going to shake. One of them is a friend of yours. She asked our Inspector if he knew you because you were 'so good at crime and all that nonsense.' "

"Good Heavens!" Mr. Campion spoke piously as the explanation of the Superintendent's unlikely visitation was made plain to him. "I don't think I know Chipperwood West."

"It's a suburb which is becoming fashionable. Have you ever heard of Lady Larradine?"

"Old Lady 'ell?" Mr. Campion let the joke of his salad days escape without its being noticed by either of them. "I don't believe it. She must be dead by this time!"

"There's a type of woman who never dies before you do," said Oates with apparent sincerity. "She's quite a dragon, I understand from our Inspector. However, she isn't the actual witness. There are two of them. Brigadier Brose is one. Ever heard of *him?*"

"I don't think I have."

"My information is that you'd remember him if you'd met him. Well, we'll find out. I'm taking you with me, Campion. I hope you don't mind?"

"My sister will hate it. I'm due to be Santa Claus in about an hour."

"I can't help that." Oates was adamant. "If a bunch of silly crooks want to get spiteful at the festive season, someone must do the homework. Come and play Santa Claus with me. It's your last chance. I'm retiring in the summer."

Oates continued in the same vein as he and Mr. Campion sat in the back of a police car threading their way through the deserted Christmas streets where the lamps were growing bright in the dusk.

"I've had bad luck lately," the Superintendent said seriously. "Too much. It won't help my memoirs if I go out in a blaze of no-enthusiasm."

"You're thinking of the Phaeton Robbery," Mr. Campion suggested. "What are you calling the memoirs? *Man-Eaters of the Yard?*"

Oates's mild old eyes brightened, but not greatly.

"Something of the kind," he admitted. "But no one could be blamed for not solving that blessed Phaeton business. Everyone concerned was bonkers. A silly old musical star, for thirty years the widow of an eccentric Duke, steps out into her London garden one autumn morning leaving the street door wide open and all her most valuable jewelry collected from strong-rooms all over the country lying in a brown paper parcel on her bureau in the first room off the hall. Her excuse was that she was just going to take it to the Bond Street auctioneers and was carrying it herself for safety! The thief was equally mental to lift it."

"It wasn't salable?"

"Salable! It couldn't even be broken up. The stuff is just about as well-known as the Crown Jewels. Great big enamels which the old Duke had collected at great expense. No fence would stay in the same room with them, yet, of course, they are worth the Earth as every newspaper has told us at length ever since they were pinched!"

"He didn't get anything else either, did he?"

"He was a madman." Oates dismissed him with contempt. "All he gained was the old lady's housekeeping money for a couple of months which was in her handbag—about a hundred and fifty quid—and the other two items which were on the same shelf, a soapstone monkey and a plated paperknife. He simply wandered in, took the first things he happened to see and wandered out again. Any sneak thief, tramp, or casual snapper-upper could have done it and who gets blamed? *Me!*"

He looked so woebegone that Mr. Campion hastily changed the subject. "Where are we going?" he inquired. "To call on her ladyship? Do I understand that at the age of one hundred and forty-six or whatever it is she is cohabiting with a Brig? Which war?"

"I can't tell you." Oates was literal as usual. "It could be the South African. They're all in a nice residential hotel—the sort of place that is very popular with the older members of the landed gentry just now."

"When you say landed, you mean as in Fish?"

"Roughly, yes. Elderly people living on capital. About forty of them. This place used to be called *The Haven* and has now been taken over by two ex-society widows and renamed *The CCraven*—with two Cs. It's a select hotel-cum-Old-Ducks' Home for Mother's Friends. You know the sort of place?"

"I can envisage it. Don't say your murdered chum from The Humdinger lived there too?"

"No, he lived in a more modest place whose garden backs on the CCraven's grounds. The Brigadier and one of the other residents, a Mr. Charlie Taunton, who has become a bosom friend of his, were in the habit of talking to Sampson over the wall. Taunton is a lazy man who seldom goes out and has little money but he very much wanted to get some gifts for his fellow guests—something in the nature of little jokes from the chain stores, I understand; but he dreaded the exertion of shopping for them and Sampson appears to have offered to get him some little items wholesale and to deliver them by six o'clock on Christmas Eve—in time for him to package them up and hand them to Lady Larradine who was dressing the tree at seven."

"And you say Sampson actually did this?" Mr. Campion sounded bewildered.

"Both old gentlemen—the Brigadier and Taunton—swear to it. They insist they went down to the wall at six and Sampson handed the parcel over as arranged. My Inspector is an experienced man and he doesn't think we'll be able to shake either of them."

"That leaves Kroll with a complete alibi. How did these Chipperwood witnesses hear of Sampson's death?"

"Routine. The local police called at Sampson's home address this morning to report the death, only to discover the place closed. The landlady and her family are away for the holiday and Sampson himself was due to spend it with Girlski. The police stamped about a bit, making sure of all this, and in the course of their investigations they were seen and hailed by the two old boys in the adjoining garden. The two were shocked to hear that their kind acquaintance was dead and volunteered the information that he had been with them at six."

Mr. Campion looked blank. "Perhaps they don't keep the same hours as anybody else," he suggested. "Old people can be highly eccentric."

Oates shook his head. "We thought of that. My Inspector, who came down the moment the local police reported, insists that they are perfectly normal and quite positive. Moreover, they had the purchases. He saw the packages already on the tree. Lady Larradine pointed them out to him when she asked after you. She'll be delighted to see you, Campion."

"I can hardly wait!"

"You don't have to," said Oates grimly as they pulled up before a huge Edwardian villa. "It's all yours."

"My dear boy! You haven't aged any more than I have!"

Lady Larradine's tremendous voice—one of her chief terrors, Mr. Campion recollected—echoed over the crowded first-floor room where she received them. There she stood in an outmoded but glittering evening gown looking, as always, exactly like a spray-flecked seal.

"I *knew* you'd come," she bellowed. "As soon as you got my oblique little S.O.S. How do you like our little hideout? Isn't it *fun!* Moira Spryg-Fysher and Janice Poole-Poole wanted something to do, so we all put our pennies in it and here we are!"

"Almost too marvelous," murmured Mr. Campion in all sincerity. "We really want a word with Brigadier Brose and Mr. Taunton."

"Of course you do and so you shall! We're all waiting for the Christmas tree. Everybody will be there for that in about ten minutes in the drawing room. My dear, when *we* came they were calling it the Residents' Lounge!"

Superintendent Oates remained grave. He was startled to discover that the dragon was not only fierce but also wily. The news that her apparently casual mention of Mr. Campion to the Inspector had been a ruse to get hold of him shocked the innocent Superintendent. He retaliated by insisting that he must see the witnesses at once.

Lady Larradine silenced him with a friendly roar. "My dear man, you can't! They've gone for a walk. I always turn men out of the house after Christmas luncheon. They'll soon be back. The Brigadier won't miss his Tree! Ah. Here's Fiona. This is Janice Poole-Poole's daughter, Albert. Isn't she a pretty girl?"

Mr. Campion saw Miss Poole-Poole with relief, knowing of old that Oates was susceptible to the type. The newcomer was young and lovely and even her beehive hair and the fact that she appeared to have painted herself with two black eyes failed to spoil the exquisite smile she bestowed on the helpless officer.

"Fabulous to have you really here," she said and sounded as if she meant it. While he was still recovering, Lady Larradine led Oates to the window.

"You can't see it because it's pitch-dark," she said, "but out there, down in the garden, there's a wall and it was over it that the Brigadier and Mr. Taunton spoke to Mr. Sampson at six o'clock last night. No one liked the man Sampson—I think Mr. Taunton was almost afraid of him. Certainly he seems to have died very untidily!"

"But he *did* buy Mr. Taunton's Christmas gifts for him?"

The dragon lifted a webby eyelid. "You have already been told that. At six last night Mr. Taunton and the Brigadier went to meet him to get the box. I got them into their mufflers so I know! I had the packing paper ready, too, for Mr. Taunton to take up to his room . . . Rather a small one on the third floor."

She lowered her voice to reduce it to the volume of distant traffic. "Not many pennies, but a dear little man!"

"Did you *see* these presents, Ma'am?"

"Not before they were wrapped! That would have spoiled the surprise!"

"I shall have to see them." There was a mulish note in the Superintendent's voice which the lady was too experienced to ignore.

"I've thought how to do that without upsetting anybody," she said briskly. "The Brigadier and I will cut the presents from the Tree and Fiona will be handing them round. All Mr. Taunton's little gifts are in the very distinctive black and gold paper I bought from Millie's Boutique and so, Fiona, you must give every package in black and gold paper not to the person to whom it is addressed but to the Superintendent. Can you do that, dear?"

Miss Poole-Poole seemed to feel the task difficult but not

impossible and the trusting smile she gave Oates cut short his objections like the sun melting frost.

"Splendid!" The dragon's roar was hearty. "Give me your arm, Superintendent. You shall take me down."

As the procession reached the hall, it ran into the Brigadier himself. He was a large, pink man, affable enough, but of a martial type and he bristled at the Superintendent. "Extraordinary time to do your business—middle of Christmas Day!" he said after acknowledging the introductions.

Oates inquired if he had enjoyed his walk.

"Talk?" said the Brigadier. "I've not been talking. I've been asleep in the card room. Where's old Taunton?"

"He went for a walk, Athole dear," bellowed the dragon gaily.

"So he did. You sent him! Poor feller."

As the old soldier led the way to the open door of the drawing room, it occurred to both the Superintendent and Mr. Campion that the secret of Lady Larradine's undoubted attraction for the Brigadier lay in the fact that he could hear *her* if no one else. The discovery cast a new light altogether on the story of the encounter with Sampson in the garden.

Meanwhile, they had entered the drawing room and the party had begun. As Mr. Campion glanced at the company, ranged in a full circle round a magnificent tree loaded with gifts and sparkling like a waterfall, he saw face after familiar face. They were elder acquaintances of the dizzy 1930s whom he had mourned as gone forever, when he thought of them at all. Yet here they all were, not only alive but released by great age from many of the restraints of convention.

He noticed that every type of headgear from night-cap to tiara was being sported with fine individualistic enthusiasm. But Lady Larradine gave him little time to look about. She proceeded with her task immediately.

Each guest had been provided with a small invalid table beside his armchair, and Oates, reluctant but wax in Fiona's hands, was no exception. The Superintendent found himself seated between a mountain in flannel and a wraith in mauve mink, waiting his turn with the same beady-eyed avidity.

Christmas Tree procedure at the CCraven proved to be well organized. The dragon did little work herself. Armed with a swagger stick, she merely prodded parcel after parcel hanging amid the boughs while the task of detaching them was performed by the Brigadier who handed them to Fiona. Either to add to the excitement or perhaps to muffle any unfortunate comment on gifts received by the uninhibited company, jolly Christmas music was played throughout, and under cover of the noise Mr. Campion was able to tackle his hostess.

"Where is Taunton?" he whispered.

"Such a nice little man. Most presentable, but just a little teeny-weeny bit dishonest."

Lady Larradine ignored the question in his eyes and continued to put him in the picture at great speed, while supervising the Tree at the same time. "Fifty-seven convictions, I believe, but only small ones. I only got it all out of him last week. Shattering! He'd been so *useful,* amusing the Brigadier. When he came, he looked like a lost soul with no luggage, but after no time at all he settled in perfectly."

She paused and stabbed at a ball of colored cellophane with her stick before returning to her startled guest.

"Albert, I am terribly afraid that it was poor Mr. Taunton who took that dreadful jewelry of Maisie Phaeton's. It appears to have been entirely her fault. He was merely wandering past her house, feeling in need of care and attention. The door was wide open and Mr. Taunton suddenly found himself inside, picking up a few odds and ends. When he discovered from all that fuss in the newspapers what he had got hold of—how well-known it was, I mean—he was quite horrified and had to hide. And where better place than here with us where we never had to go out?"

"Where indeed!" Mr. Campion dared not glance across the room at the Superintendent unwrapping his black and gold parcels. "Where is he now? Poor Mr. Taunton, I mean."

"Of course I hadn't the faintest idea what was worrying the man until he confessed," the dragon went on stonily. "Then I realized that something would have to be done at once to protect everybody. The wretch had hidden all that frightful stuff in our toolshed for three months, not daring to keep it in the house; and to make matters worse, the impossible person at the end of the garden, Mr. Sampson, had recognized him and *would* keep speaking. Apparently people in the—er—underworld all know each other just like those of us in—er—other closed circles do."

Mr. Campion, whose hair was standing on end, had a moment of inspiration. "This absurd rigmarole about Taunton getting Sampson to buy him some Christmas gifts wholesale was *your* idea!" he said accusingly.

The dragon stared. "It seemed the best way of getting Maisie's jewelry back to her without any *one* person being involved," she said frankly. "I knew we should all recognize the things the moment we saw them and I was certain that after a lot of argument we should decide to pack them up and send them round to her. But, if there *were* any repercussions, we should *all* be in it—quite a formidable array, dear Boy—and the blame could be traced to Mr. Sampson if absolutely necessary. You see, the Brigadier is convinced that Sampson *was* there last night. Mr. Taunton very cleverly left him on the lawn and went behind the toolshed and came back with the box."

"How completely immoral!" Mr. Campion couldn't restrain himself.

The dragon had the grace to look embarrassed.

"I don't think the Sampson angle would ever have arisen," she said. "But if it had, Sampson was quite a terrible person. Almost a blackmailer. Utterly dishonest and inconsiderate. Think how he has spoiled everything and endangered us all by getting himself killed on the *one* afternoon when we said he was here, so that the police were brought in. Just the *one* thing I was trying to avoid. When the Inspector appeared this morning I was so upset I thought of you!"

In his not unnatural alarm Mr. Campion so far forgot himself as to touch her sleeve. "Where is Taunton now?"

The dragon threshed her train. "Really, Boy! What a fidget you are! If you must know, I gave him his Christmas present—every penny I had in cash, for he was broke again, he told me—and sent him for a nice long walk after lunch. Having seen the Inspector here this morning, he was glad to go."

She paused and a granite gleam came into her hooded eyes. "If that Superintendent friend of yours has the stupidity to try to find him once Maisie has her monstrosities back, none of us will be able to identify him, I'm afraid. And there's another thing. If the Brigadier should be *forced* to give evidence, I am sure he will stick to his guns about Mr. Sampson being down in the garden here at six o'clock last night. That would mean that the man Kroll would have to go unpunished for his revenge murder, wouldn't it? Sampson was a terrible person—but *no one* should have killed him."

Mr. Campion was silenced. He glanced fearfully across the room.

The Superintendent was seated at his table wearing the strained yet slap-happy expression of a man with concussion. On his left was a pile of black and gilt wrappings, on his right a rajah's ransom in somewhat specialized form.

From where he stood, Mr. Campion could see two examples amid the rest—a breastplate in gold, pearl, and enamel in the shape of a unicorn and an item which looked like a plover's egg in tourmaline encased in a ducal coronet. There was also a soapstone monkey and a solid-silver paperknife.

Much later that evening Mr. Campion and the Superintendent drove quietly back to headquarters. Oates had a large cardboard box on his knee. He clasped it tenderly.

He had been silent for a long time when a thought occurred to him. "Why did they take him into the house in the first place?" he said. "An elderly crook looking lost! And no luggage!"

Mr. Campion's pale eyes flickered behind his spectacles.

"Don't forget the Duchess' housekeeping money," he murmured. "I should think he offered one of the widows who really run that place the first three months' payment in cash, wouldn't you? That must be an impressive phenomenon in that sort of business, I fancy."

Oates caught his breath and fell silent once more. Presently he burst out again.

"Those people! That woman!" he exploded. "When they were younger they led me a pretty dance—losing things or getting themselves swindled. But now they're old they take the blessed biscuit! Do you see how she's tied my hands, Campion?"

Mr. Campion tried not to grin.

"Snapdragons are just permissible at Christmas," he said. "Handled with extreme caution they burn very few fingers, it seems to me."

Mr. Campion tapped the cardboard box. "And some of them provide a few plums for retiring coppers, don't they, Superintendent?"

JOE GORES

DARL I LUV U

Shy, lonely Charlie Wyeth fell in love over the teletype with cute, persuasive Milli—and the whole world was imperiled! . . . Meet the most unusual murderer of the century.

FEAR AILK DEALER FEAR SILK DEALER
FWAR SILK DEALER FEAR SILK DEALER
FEAR SILK DEALER FXEAR SILK DEALER

Not so good. Still, he was learning.

When Charlie Wyeth stopped typing, the only sounds to break the Pentagon's after-hours' silence were the peculiar whirring of the TWX machine and the distant echoing clatter of a scrubwoman's pail far down the E Ring.

Charlie glanced at the copybook clipped to the upright stand at the side of the teletypewriter; his long tapering fingers plunged down once more at the keys and words again appeared on the unrolling yellow paper.

FEAR SILK DEALER FEAR SILK DEALER
FEAR SILK DEALER FEAR SILK DEALER
FEAR SILK DEALER FEAR SILK DEALER

Perfect. Charlie had achieved that momentary communion with the TWX machine which was so important.

Charlie was a tall, slender, lonely man with a sensitive mouth and a dreamer's eyes; his long-skinny legs stuck out awkwardly from beneath his chair, like the legs of a nesting stork. He could accomplish much more at night in the office at the Pentagon than he could during the morning practice sessions at the teletype training center. *One* secretary could render him tongue-tied; when he was the only man among *twenty* of them . . .

The telephone beside the TWX machine exploded, clamoring for attention; it meant an incoming call on the teletype. Charlie flicked the switch from *Practice* to *Open*, fighting a momentary panic. After all, he would soon be civilian TWX operator for Army Ordnance Tech Liaison Office, personally chosen by Colonel Andrews; he had to get used to transmitting and receiving. He typed:

THIS IS ARL VA 661 GA PLS

Translated from TWXese this meant *This is Arlington, Virginia, call number 661, go ahead, please*. Charlie glanced at his watch. Ten p.m. This was a commercial network for making contact with private contractors. What civilian firm could be transmitting at this hour?

As if in response to his unasked question, the machine clattered out a single word.

LONELY

"I beg your pardon?" In his surprise Charlie had spoken aloud. Was this a joke? A name? Something in code? When nothing else was forthcoming, he asked:

WHO R U PLS DON T UNDERSTAND

The unknown returned:

LONELY U R LONELY CHARLES WYETH

With an angry flick of the toggle he cut the connection. A bead of sweat ran down his face. Someone—someone who knew shy, awkward Charlie's practice of working late to assuage his loneliness—was playing a damned cruel joke.

But who? Fussy old McAfee, civilian Section Head behind the Colonel? Hardly. The man was as dried-up and humorless as a prune. Colonel Andrews himself? Unthinkable. The secretary? She was married and had three kids. Doc Weston? The statistician professed a fear of any machine more complex than his typewriter.

Still angry and disturbed, Charlie clipped his plastic-encased ID badge on his shirt so that he wouldn't be stopped by the Pentagon security guards, and went home.

The next day he worked steadily, getting the necessary departmental clearances for publicity handouts on two Ordnance weapons soon to be declassified, and gradually relaxed. Neither at the office nor at TWX practice did anyone innocently ask "Lonely, Charles Wyeth?" and then burst out laughing. When McAfee, his fussy little superior, buttonholed him at five o'clock just as he was leaving, Charlie didn't even wince in anticipation.

"Be sure and check your desk for classified material, Wyeth."

Although McAfee wore a close-trimmed mustache, had thinning gray hair, and weak eyes behind horn-rimmed glasses, he reminded Charlie of a rabbit; he had the same nervous, jerky mannerisms—his nose even wriggled when he was distressed.

"I always do that, Mr. McAfee. You know that, sir."

"Well, I'm the one who signs each night, Wyeth, so I'm the one who'd get in trouble if any documents were left lying around the office."

"Yes, sir, Mr. McAfee. I understand your concern."

All through dinner at the 24-hour Pentagon cafeteria by the Concourse ramp, Charlie seethed: damned old woman McAfee! The perfect civil servant, all right—he existed for routine. Charlie could do the old man's job easily—did half his work for him right now—but McAfee had seniority and a high GS rating—which was what really counted, not ability.

Charlie dawdled over his third cup of coffee. Only after stubbing out the butt of his fourth cigarette did he admit to himself that he almost dreaded returning to the office. If there was another call . . . Then he thought: to hell with it! He wasn't going to give up his tranquilizing hours with the machine; a man can go to only so many concerts alone, can make only so many solitary visits to art galleries . . .

For two hours the exercises flowed from beneath his nimble fingers; but as the minute sweep of his watch climbed to ten o'clock, the phone beside the TWX rang. Could he ignore it? He couldn't. Flicking the toggle, his hands shook slightly.

THIS IS ARL VA 661 GA PLS

Pause. Then:

HELLO CHARLIE WYETH

In desperation he returned:

HELLO YOURSELF WHO R U PLS Q

MY NAME IS MILLI AND I WORK IN AN OFFICE IN D C

Milli? He knew no one named Milli. He felt a stirring within him.

HOW DO U KNOW MY NAME Q

I SAW U ONCE HERE IN MY OFFICE AND MADE INQUIRIES U R MY TYPE

Charlie wanted to ask in what office she worked, but the connection was abruptly cut off and the call was not repeated. On the way home he told himself that it was obviously a joke, but at the same time he caught himself rehearsing what he would say to her the next time. Next time? There wouldn't be any next time.

But the following night at ten p.m. he was glued to the TWX machine. At midnight he went home. There had been no call.

Wednesday. Still no call. Thursday. No call. It had been a joke.

On Friday he set out for a movie but somehow was waiting when the shrilling phone bell broke the ten o'clock Pentagon silence. In a few moments Milli, somewhere across the Potomac in Washington, was connected to him by a maze of wires and electronic circuits.

Charlie found that his shyness deserted him on the machine; when Milli coyly refused to name her office, he boldly demanded:

R U CUTE MILLI Q

MY SUPERVISOR THINKS SO BUT I HOPE THAT ISN T ALL U WANT FROM A GIRL

IT IS NOT

I M GLAD BECAUSE I WANT A MAN WHO IS SERIOUS AND AMBITIOUS

```
I M BOTH MILLI

THEN WHY AREN T U AT MC AFEE S DESK
WHERE U BELONG CHARLIE Q
```

He found himself asking:

```
HOW CAN I GET THERE Q

IF SOME CLASSIFIED MATERIAL WOULD BE
FOUND ON HIS DESK BY CID SECURITY CHECK
HE WOULD BE IN TROUBLE WOULDN T HE Q
```

Before Charlie could explain McAfee's infallibility on classified documents, Milli clattered:

```
SOMEONE COMING NOT SUPP USE MACH WILL
CALL YOU NEXT WEEK DARL
```

DARL! In TWXese that meant *darling!* Milli had called him darling! And her supervisor thought she was cute!

Riding home, Charlie was unaware of Washington's stifling heat; his face, long and lean and horselike in the bus window as they crossed Memorial Bridge, didn't seem quite as homely as before. Even stern old Abe, peering down from his lighted aerie in the Lincoln Memorial, might have nodded benignly at him as he passed.

Charlie Wyeth was no longer lonely.

The following Tuesday night, after fifteen delicious TWXed minutes with Milli, Charlie saw two young men in plainclothes moving efficiently from room to room far down the D Ring. He recognized them as types sharing certain characteristics with FBI men, CIA men, and NSA men: Army CID Security Agents, checking for classified document violations.

With a sleepwalker's step Charlie returned to the office, opened the classified documents safe, and removed a yellow-edged *TOP SECRET* folder containing revised figures on steel fatigue and stress ratios received from one of the missile contractors. He slammed and locked the safe, thrust the folder under some interdepartmental memos in McAfee's *OUT* basket, switched off the lights, and went home. At no time did he allow himself to think about what he was doing.

Two days later, in his private office, big bluff Colonel Andrews came right to the point.

"You've heard about McAfee?"

"There have been some rumors about classified documents but—"

"More than rumors, Wyeth—cold, hard facts. The security boys found a *TOP SECRET* folder on his desk after office hours."

Charlie said, "I'm sure it was just an oversight, sir. He—"

"I don't give a damn what it was." The Colonel's hard, red face swelled impressively above his triple row of ribbons. "That sort of thing reflects damned poorly on my record. Er—damned poorly."

"I can understand how you feel, sir."

If Andrews had been a bird his neck feathers would have ruffled.

"Fact is fact, Wyeth, and the fact is, McAfee is an old woman. I'm up for retirement in three years, and there's talk upstairs that I can take a BG's stars with me—but *not* if I'm gonna have security blunders in my command."

He went to the window, looked out, teetered on his toes, and continued without looking at Charlie.

"You work late almost every night, Wyeth. If you would check the office over—er, especially McAfee's desk—so that there are no more security troubles in this shop, I'll remember it when the time for efficiency reports comes around."

Charlie really felt quite bad about the scathing official reprimand sustained by McAfee because of the security violation, but Milli made him see his action in its proper perspective.

```
BELIEVE ME DARL U HAVE DONE THE RIGHT
THING FOR YOUR COUNTRY AND FOR YOUR
OFFICE AND FOR US
```

The "darling" was common usage between them now. Charlie still didn't know Milli's last name or where she lived or worked, but he was determined not to rush her; after all, through the machine they had achieved a communion they never could have had in face-to-face meetings, and their relationship was maturing into something fragile and wonderful.

When he tried some poetry on Milli, she had been enthralled by the mathematical precision of Pope's and Dryden's couplets; and although she admitted she had never visited any of Washington's marvelous art galleries, in discussion she obviously favored the cubists. In music she was extremely modern.

Before the end of July, Charlie knew he was in love.

One night, as August scorched its way across the cloudless Washington sky, a very excited Milli called. She had learned in her office that there was going to be a review of Job Description Files in Army Ordnance. She communicated her excitement with a question.

WHAT WOULD HAPPEN IF THE INSPECTORS WERE
TO DISCOVER THAT MC AFEE S POSITION WAS
REALLY JUST EXCESS Q

AS AN ECONOMY MOVE THEY WOULD PROBABLY
VACATE IT

DON T U THINK IT IS TIME TO CLEAR AWAY
THE DEADWOOD DARL Q

Milli hadn't really said so, but when he thought it over later, Charlie knew that until he had McAfee's job he would never have Milli. And would it really be so wrong? Everybody said that he deserved promotion. If he could only get into those folders before the review and rewrite them so that the majority of McAfee's duties, on paper, would appear in Charlie's job description . . .

It took him three weeks.

First he had to obtain the proper forms in such a way that his own name didn't appear on the requisitions; then there was the task of lifting the folders; then rewriting them and substituting the new for the old.

It was all made meaningful when he told Milli what he had done. There was a long silence, broken only by the whirr of the TWX machine; then came her electrifying response.

DARL I LUV U

For the next few days Charlie repeated it to himself at work, at home, in his dreams. What difference that he had never seen her, never touched her, never heard her voice, never held her in his arms? He loved her, and she had said it too!

DARL I LUV U

The grist in official Washington's mill is ground exceeding slow, but during World Series time the Colonel summoned Charlie into his private office. He was at parade rest in front of the window, his combat-wise eyes gazing out across the green lawns and the freeway toward the Fort Myer enlisted-men's swimming pool where two sunbathing WACS were clearly visible. When he turned to regard the younger man his face was friendly.

"Wyeth," his drill-field voice rumbled, "you remember a few weeks ago I asked you to perform certain unofficial—er, checks, and intimated that appreciation would be shown?"

"Yes, sir, Colonel, but anything I have done has been from a sense of duty, not because I expected any personal advancement."

"I'm sure it has, Wyeth. Nevertheless, the current job description review, coupled with my—er, recommendations . . . well! I believe word will be down in a day or two that Mr. McAfee has been—er, retired."

"I'm—why I had no idea, sir. I . . . can't help feeling sorry—"

"No need, Wyeth. We have to clear out the—ahem, the deadwood, as it were. Valued service from McAfee all these years, but the old warhorse is now ready for pasture. Er—on your way out send him in here, will you, Wyeth?"

At ten p.m. that night, as Charlie was proceeding with the heady news of the eradication of the old warhorse's job, to Milli's delight, the old warhorse, in his modest Alexandria bungalow, was proceeding with the eradication of himself.

"Did it with a double-barreled shotgun," recounted the secretary ghoulishly the next morning. "I heard on the bus that he stuck the end of the gun in his mouth and pushed both triggers at once with his toes. I bet that room was splattered from one end to the other with—"

"Was—was there a note?" Charlie fought a wave of nausea.

"His wife said he just went into the study muttering about clearing out the deadwood and—blooey! Brains splashed—"

In the Men's Room, Charlie was thoroughly sick. He sloshed out his mouth with cold water and regarded his face in the mirror. Could those be his sly, cold eyes? Was his mouth that cruel, that determined? Could the Charlie Wyeth who had reveled in the poetry of Keats and Shelley have that narrow, ruthless chin?

He desperately needed Milli's assurance that he had done the right thing.

But that night Milli didn't call.

The next night Milli didn't call.

The third day, the day of McAfee's funeral, Charlie phoned in sick. He spent the long afternoon in his stuffy apartment near Dupont Circle. If only he knew where to reach her! Once he took his .32 pistol out of the drawer and stared at it for a very long time.

What was the matter with him? He was acting like that young aide from Naval PID who had killed himself three days after *his* Section Chief had committed suicide; like that young civilian lawyer in the Air Force Legal Section who had taken over his superior's position, and then, three days later . . .

Charlie thrust the revolver hurriedly back into the drawer. Thoughts like that were treason to his love for Milli. Tonight she would call and everything would be right again. Her fine clear mind would analyze his despair, show him the logical necessity for an occasional human sacrifice on the altar of Progress. If only it hadn't been *both* barrels!

On his way to the Pentagon, hoping for a ten p.m. TWXed rendezvous with Milli, he began recalling those first wonderful nights of communication. *I've made inquiries here, Charlie Wyeth,* Milli had said; and then before the file review she had stated: *the word around our office is that there is going to be a Job Description File Review in Ordnance.* But there was only one office which could possibly have all that information: the Department of Defense Statistical Records Branch in those World War II buildings flanking Constitution Avenue.

Charlie was getting excited. Yes, and he had delivered some records there once, and in the machine room on the fourth floor, where they kept the computers which sorted and stored the plethora of statistics concerning DOD, *there had been a commercial TWX machine on which Milli could have called him after hours!*

The cab dropped him on Constitution Avenue at 9:45 p.m. The building guard, dozing over a detective magazine at his table by the front entrance, didn't even notice Charlie jimmying open a ground-floor office window, slipping across the hall, and gliding up the back stairs. He paused on the third floor, heart pounding rapidly. He mustn't be disappointed if she wasn't there; if by some remote chance he *had* guessed the correct office, she might not be here tonight . . .

And then he heard it.

Very faintly came the muffled clatter of a TWX. He looked at his watch: ten o'clock. Milli was trying to contact him!

Charlie raced up the remaining stairs and paused outside the door marked Machine Room in which the TWX was rattling Milli's impatient message of love. Would she be blonde? Tall? Beautiful? Charlie didn't know and didn't care: he only knew that he needed her.

He thrust open the door, fumbled along the wall for the light switch.

The TWX was instantly silenced. Fluorescent overheads flickered, snapped, flooded down radiance.

"Milli!" he called softly.

Milli didn't answer. The room, as he remembered from his single previous visit, was full of innocuous squat gray-metal boxes shielding the amazing array of circuits, relays, and transistors which enabled them to store and select needed information. The TWX machine, hidden by a low partition, was squeezed between a huge computer and a water cooler.

Charlie stepped around the partition. The operator's chair was pushed back as if hurriedly abandoned, and on the floor there were crushed cigarette butts with lipstick markings. Three feet of yellow paper, covered with typing, hung over the roll behind the machine.

But the cubicle was empty.

Clever Milli! She had heard him in the hall and had hidden behind one of the computers because it would mean her job if her superiors caught her using the TWX for her own purposes.

"Come out, darling. It's me, Charlie!"

Still no answer. He began peering among the computers:

hide-and-seek. What a wonderful sense of humor to go with her wonderful mind! In a moment he would spy her; he peeped over computers and under computers and behind computers and . . .

Computers. Only computers.

Slowly, unbelievingly, Charlie straightened up. There was no place for a human being to hide in this room. There was no space for anything except a dozen giant mechanical brains able to duplicate almost exactly the most intricate thought processes of the human mind: unspectacular boxes stuffed with miles of patient wire to carry and transmit and quietly learn all there was to know of the finite human brains which had created them.

One of them hadn't waited. It had been ready. From the data fed into it for storage it had selected carefully, choosing men like Charlie—the ambitious, lonely, romantic men—the weak men who were susceptible, who could be influenced in the name of love to subordinate their moral codes, their ethics, to their own self-advancement. Men who, driven eventually to despair and guilt by the withdrawal of Milli's TWXed assurances, would take the way out that Charlie had contemplated that afternoon. Men whose carefully engineered murders were mere preliminaries, mere finger-exercises in the practice of the massive program of thought control which would inevitably follow.

Charlie's shocked, searching eyes probed the room—and he screamed.

Beside the TWX was a huge oblong computer topped with two eye-like red lights. *The lights were coolly regarding him, expressing faint contempt!* On the wall behind the computer some office wag had pasted a small white sign decorated with a single word: MILLI.

Charles Wyeth went beserk.

Seizing the TWX operator's chair—hastily abandoned by its human occupant at the end of the work day—he rained down blows on the computer. The twin lights burned a sudden scarlet. When he smashed the glass panel above the program slot there was a puff of black acrid smoke; when he thrust a shattered chair leg into one of the glaring lights, gouging it out as a thumb might gouge out an eye, the thing began to *shriek* —harsh mechanical bellows simulating the expression of human emotions. Light lubricating oil spurted down its side like blood down the breast of a wounded maiden.

He dropped the chair; the vitals of the thing were protected by its tough metal hide. The computer fell silent. Charlie leaped to the TWX machine, his hands like claws, his eyes alight with fatal knowledge.

He had to warn humanity of its impending fate.

THIS IS WASH OPR GA PLS

OPR I WANT TO MAKE A CONFERENCE CALL

WHAT CONF NUMBERS DO U WISH PLS Q

GET ME THE WORLD

DO NOT UNDERSTAND PLS REPEAT NRS DESIRED ON CONF CALL

FOR GOD S SAKE OPR I HAVE TO REACH ALL THE HUMAN BEINGS ON EARTH

Just then the guard, attracted by the unearthly racket, burst into the room, brandishing his automatic.

"Stop!" he shouted. "Get away from that machine!"

Whirling on him, his teeth bared, his eyes blazing, Charlie cried, "Don't you see? They're going to take us over!"

The guard saw. At the sight of Charlie's contorted face he went into the crouch he had learned at the FBI summer training course—body turned to present the smallest target, gun arm extended, knees slightly flexed—and pumped three .45 bullets into Charlie's chest. The heavy slugs hurled Charlie against the humming TWX machine in a welter of splintered ribs and crimson flesh.

THIS IS WASH OPR PLS REPEAT NRS DESIRED

Charlie was unable to comply. Charlie was dead.

The guard was straightening up, wiping his face. Thank God for the FBI! This guy had been either a spy for a foreign power or an out-and-out lunatic . . .

It was well over an hour before the mess had been sufficiently cleaned up for the hurriedly summoned Section Head to make a careful examination of his machine. He said to one of the Homicide Lieutenants: "It's damned lucky that guy didn't know anything about computers—it would cost Uncle Sam millions to replace this little cutie."

"No kidding." The detective looked impressed. "I'd say he smashed it up pretty bad—almost like he hated it."

"No damage to the important components. And of course a man can't hate—or love—a machine."

The Section Head completed his inventory, turned out the lights, and went slowly down the stairs. Actually he had to admit to himself that he had a certain abstract emotion for his machines; they were man's most beautifully complex creations to date. The one that had been damaged, for instance, was capable of utilizing over 13,000,000 separate pieces of information. With machines like that, who knew what fantastic surprises the technological Future might hold?

Behind him in the dark, the unbroken light atop the damaged computer once more came aglow. Its crimson scintilla brightened, steadied; its quiet fanatical hum began.

Suddenly the TWX machine began to clatter volubly in the unattended silence of the machine room. Though they were addressed to a call number which was not Charlie Wyeth's, the words would have been very familiar to him.

DARL

dictated the electronic brain named Milli,

DARL I LUV U